Ring Around *the* Sun

A Novel

Nelson Martin

SUNSTONE
PRESS

SANTA FE

4 —
1/22

Sunstone books may be purchased for educational, business, or sales promotional use.
For information please write: Special Markets Department, Sunstone Press,
P.O. Box 2321, Santa Fe, New Mexico 87504-2321.

Cover painting by Sandra Martin
Book and Cover design › Vicki Ahl
Body typeface › Laurentian Std
Printed on acid-free paper

Library of Congress Cataloging-in-Publication Data

Martin, Nelson, 1938-
Ring Around the Sun : A Novel / by Nelson Martin.
pages cm
ISBN 978-0-86534-961-2 (Softcover : alk. paper)
1. Villa, Pancho, 1878-1923--Mexico--Fiction. 2. Illegal arms transfers--Fiction.
3. Mexico--Fiction. I. Title.
PS3613.A7836R56 2013
813'.6--dc23
                        2013023612

WWW.SUNSTONEPRESS.COM
SUNSTONE PRESS / POST OFFICE BOX 2321 / SANTA FE, NM 87504-2321 /USA
(505) 988-4418 / ORDERS ONLY (800) 243-5644 / FAX (505) 988-1025

Dedicated to my wife, Sandra, who not so long ago, strolled up to me, thumped me on the chest, and said, "There's a story in there and you're going to tell it."

Special thanks to Susan Mary Malone with Malone Editorial Services for her patience and guidance.

Prologue

Dusty Old Border Town—El Paso, June 1945

"Zara, have you ever tried to climb a goose egg?" I asked.

She peered over her wire-rimmed spectacles, a teasing smile on her lips, a bit of a tulip in their shape. "I dare say I haven't, my dear husband of fifty-two years—have you?"

"Matter of fact, I have—several times over the years, at least it seems so on your way up Sacred Mountain."

"Narlow, for months all you've talked about is that mountain. You call it Sacred Mountain. What can be so sacred about a pile of rocks in the very heart of the largest wasteland in America?"

"Well, I'll tell you why. By the time a man on horseback gets halfway up, he'll swear there's no top to that pile of barren rocks. The curve he sees above continues to recede, just out of sight, he cranes his neck ahead for a better look, but it's always just out of reach. He encourages his horse, spurring him on, but all that greets his sun-ruined eyes is that ever-present crescent shape, thrust up like a horned toad on its back with the bloat."

"Well dear, if it's so difficult, why would you insist on climbing it at your age?"

"It's not that I particularly want to *climb* Sacred Mountain again, it's what I want to *see* while I'm up there. I'm not certain that you can see eternity from the top of that no-top pile of rocks, but on a windless night from that great height, I swear eternity's waft swirl in the still."

She came over, hugged my neck. "Oh, Narlow, you're such an adorable romantic. But if you are so dead-set on going up there, why don't you get Big George to drive you up there? Do anything, darling, but quit badgering me about it."

"I may be eighty-six years old, but I can dern sure drive myself. Besides, I want my old Apache friends to go with me, Sly Fox and Broken Chain, just like in my vision. But I can't get those damned old buzzards to answer my letters." I sighed. "I suppose it's asking too much of them. That long trip'd probably do them in. They'd have to make the trip from the Arizona reservation on horseback or a buckboard."

I paused, frowned. "Where the hell is Coot Boldt when I really need the old bastard? Damn, I miss that man. Everything about the old cuss. Even miss eating blood tacos for a mere *centavo* from a street vendor on Juarez Avenue, swished down with a shot of mezcal. We had some times, me and Coot."

"*You two*," Zara said, shaking her kinky-grey head, with that certain smile that sparkled when we talked about Coot and the old days. "You were quite a pair."

I gathered her in my arms, squeezed her hard. She was soft, warm, white as tallow.

"Narlow, what is it, dear?" she asked. "What is it in your past that you cannot share with me?"

I held her tight for a long time, not breathing, trying to find the words to explain what all white folks think of as voodoo. "No, it's really not that. It's—it's—it's, well, it's just hard to talk about all that stuff to a woman like you, and—"

"A woman like me?" She pushed back, her periwinkle-blue eyes narrowing. "Perhaps you'd best explain yourself, my dear."

"Think nothing of it, my dear, but always remember this. Since you were just a very young woman, you've always given me the crazies, make me want to drink the rheum from your eyes and nose."

◉◉◉

Looking back is a good way to find yourself nose deep in a cow pie. But when a man's creeping on up there, he begins to edge into the stark realization that "past" has plenty more years than the scant remaining "future." My reminiscences probably brought on this infernal vision that made a dread of sleep. I'm on the crest of Sacred Mountain with two old Apache *amigos* I've known since my sixteenth year.

Now, they're two old, scrawny, dilapidated, bowlegged men, Sly Fox and Broken Chain. One, the son of an old Apache scout, Many Fast Feet Two Sticks, the other, the nephew of a sainted medicineman, Na-Tu-Che-Puy.

My vision beckoned me without mercy, teasing me like a brazen hussy, enticing me to her boudoir at the summit of Sacred Mountain. I wrote my old friends every week in care of the White Mountain Apache Reservation. I wrote, calling them every unmanly name I could conjure up in three languages—little girls, *jovencitas, ch'ikii lik'aa*. I called them squaws—old squaws with tits hanging to the ground who couldn't walk for fear of stepping on their drooping dried-up milk sacks. Threatened to expose them as lifemate lovers, *le'sheteezh*, who wished to be buried in a solitary, pink satin-lined pine box, solemnly wrapped in the arms of the other, buckass necked.

My dirty-dealings paid dividends. On the 11th of July, I drove my lifelong friend, Coot Boldt's six-wheel-drive truck to Cutter, New Mexico. A toast-dry ghost town, north of El Paso, "The Pass," to the locals, ninety-three-harsh-desolate-miles. Sly Fox and Broken Chain rode horseback the 250-miles from their reservation to this remote spot, trailing along four spare ponies.

Dilapidation and neglect greeted my tired eyes, as I drove into what was once the thriving and prize-of-the desert community of Cutter. The hotel's façade was the only remnant left of the town, dry-rotted gray boards clinging to one another by rusty nails and oxidized wire.

Evidences of other kinds dilapidation and neglect greeted me—the human kind. Seated on the sway-board steps of the hotel sat Sly Fox and Broken Chain, grinning, brown as pecan hulls in a rain barrel, their "friendly" finger served as their greeting, stuck in their bulbous noses. Two old men, craggy as a high-desert mountain ridge, but their sharp rat-eyes flickered like moonlit flint.

We mounted up and headed for Sacred Mountain, thirty-six-dry-miles to the northeast. Late that evening, we camped near a spring at the base of the 9,000-foot peak, passing my jug, reminiscing. I recounted my recurring vision, the three of us sitting atop Sacred Mountain, wooden goggles covering our eyes. The goggles were a mystery, but my vision required them, and I convinced them to help me carve three sets of goggles from a scraggily cedar limb, tied around our heads with twine.

The next morning, Broken Chain edged his pony ahead, and soon found the remnant of the ancient trail to the top of the mountain. It was used by the old ones so long ago, and the three of us when we were boys, tagging along searching for sacred white clay with the medicineman, Na-Tu-Che-Puy. The trail's footing was a treacherous mix of fist-size red lava rocks and green-slick slate. The sun, hot, hollow as a barrel, the air, a sheet of copper. We terrapined long, resting the horses often.

I'd not heard my Apache name in more than a half-century, but on the way up the rough trail, Sly Fox asked, "Kicking Bear, why do you want to go to the top of Sacred Mountain?"

"I don't rightly know. I thought you could answer that one for me, you being the nephew of a medicineman and all. For many months, a vision has taunted me, huge, pulsating, red mushroom that will soon be seen from the top of Sacred Mountain. The mushroom goes far up in the sky—it's *big*—bigger than this mountain. It lingers, then slowly fades to heavy gray. A voice in my vision warns me, then, I am no longer. I don't know if that means I'll no longer have Power, or maybe it means the one with the mushroom will die. What do you think, Sly Fox?"

"I will think on it. Do you remember Na-Tu-Che-Puy saying that he had a vision that the mushroom became many mushrooms, that Mother Earth was killed by the mushrooms?"

"Yes, I do. When I first went to your reservation, he told me of his vision, asked me what I thought it meant. Of course, I could not answer his question."

Broken Chain turned in his saddle, letting his mount pick his way up the narrow switchback trail. "When does your vision say the mushroom will come?"

"Soon. At night. Three figures sitting on the very top of Sacred Mountain, looking north in the dark, wearing wooden, slitted shields over their eyes like the ones we whittled last evening. No mistake. The three of them are us.

"My wife's been after me to have a doctor take a look at a mushroom-shaped birthmark on my hip. When I lived with Na-Tu-Che-Puy, he became convinced that the mushroom was the source of Power that he thought I possessed. I've had it all my life, but now, it's turned ugly-red, inflamed, hot to the touch. In my vision, it disappears, and joins the big mushroom before it fades from view."

We topped out an hour before sundown. The spring that was there in our youth still flowed sweet, cold. There was no moon, thin clouds hiding the stars that peeked through, the night a virgin of vastitude, quiet as a sphinx. Low-growing cedars offered a place to hang our tarp. In its shade, a stiff westerly breeze and high altitude combined for comfort, even under the blister of the July sun.

I glanced again at the ring around the sun that had formed earlier in the day.

Broken Chain asked, "Kicking Bear, you've watched that ring all day. I often see that, maybe for an hour, but this one has been with us all day. What does it mean?"

"I don't know, my friend, but I'm like you—I've never seen it last an entire day. Today's Pale Eye says the ring is nothing more than the sun reflecting off ice crystals like a rainbow, many miles above Mother Earth. My papa's mother was a Louisiana swamp-witch-doctor, and she claimed it foretold danger, ill-goings-on. I've always had the notion that it warns of bad weather. Nothing to concern yourself over, my friend."

I pointed to the far edge of the top of the mountain. "Those tall rocks over there—those overlooking the valley to the north are in my vision, as is everything you see. That's where we'll be spending the next several nights."

Our days were all basackards. With the rising of the sun, we sat round our campsite smoking Bull Durham rolled in corn husks that Broken Chain always carried. We laughed when he swore the smoke kept him potent even at his age. We had a couple of pulls on my jug, ate supper around mid-morning, talked about the ever-present ring around the sun, dozed under the tarp until sundown, donned our cedar eye-goggles, then sat in the rocks looking over the low plain far below, flat as a drum head.

With the rising of the sun, Broken Chain sat peering at the horizon, the ever-present ring around the sun already showing itself. He turned to me, shrugged.

The fourth night came with a tremendous moan, yet ripe with quiet. I squatted to push a boulder aside, and as I stood, Sly Fox asked, "Kicking Bear. What is that on your neck? It is hairy, red, like fire."

I felt my lower neck. No doubt about it—that damn old hairy mushroom was creeping up my neck. I unbuttoned my shirt and asked him to describe precisely what he saw. He adjusted his thick glasses. "Just like your wife says it is so, it is the shape of the mushroom, red, vermillion, purple edge. Hairy. Ugly as hell."

By morning, burning fever had me choking for breath, forcing me to make several trips to the cold spring for relief. My fever turned to chills. Broken Chain stayed after me to let them take me home. I told my friend that I was all right, and even if I died that very night, no way could I be convinced to leave that mountain top.

His gaze shot up to the crystal ring far above my pallet, then dropped to me. He shook his head and strolled off.

Our ordeal was beginning to tell a sorry tale on three old men. An hour before first light, we nudged each other out of the nighttime sleep we craved. We built a small fire, hidden behind the rock line, as our blankets could not hold off the cold.

In the firelight, Broken Chain said, "Kicking Bear."

"Yes?"

"Your mushroom. It has left you."

Sly Fox asked, "Kicking Bear—your vision—what does that mean?"

I did not know the meaning, but pleasured to be shut of that birthmark.

Broken Chain's gaze went up. "*Look there*! This place is evil, Kicking Bear. Have you ever seen that ring with no sun?" Indeed, I had not, but there it was, faint in the starlight, floating high in the sky, centered above the plain we were overlooking.

We fed the small fire with finger-size sticks. Just before the rosy finger of dawn, I reached to untie my goggles as I stood. "Gents, my damn old bones feel like I've been beaten with a tire-iron. I'd give up my share of what's left in that jug if . . . ."

The valley floor lit up like a thousand suns. A huge section of the terrain lifted itself. A column of green and orange, red, purple, and a sinister gray shot up from the middle of the uplifted earth. Formed a sphere, gray warts, pockmarked. It leaped up. Higher than our perch, a mile above the valley floor. In seconds. Higher. Lightning bolts. Columns of burning white smoke shot out in every direction. The top of the column took the shape of a hideous, pulsating mushroom. Distant mountains lit up ten times brighter than noon. A soft warm breeze came from the mushroom. Light shimmering in concentric waves flittered across the flat plane toward us.

The head of the monster grew stronger, ferocious, boiling out a furnace-hot wind, heat waves approaching like that of a locomotive firebox. Then a roar, as the blast from a thousand fireboxes. A scream like the cataclysmic crumbling of ten-thousand earthquakes standing upright, end-to-end, shouting its unfathomable presence. Then, just as suddenly, the bright orange ball faded. The desert fell silent. The dead-gray mushroom stood pulsating began to lean like a spent phallus, as if forever. We stood, smacking our lips, clacking our tacky mouths, tasting vitriol copper and lead.

Sly Fox spit, wiped the stringy saliva from his chin. "What do you mean, Kicking Bear?"

"Huh? About what?"

"Just now, when it grew quiet, you said you were becoming death—that you are the shatterer of worlds."

"Yes, Kicking Bear, that is your words," Broken Chain said as he turned to me. "What does it mean?"

"I do not know, my old friends—I just don't know."

White clouds appeared from the mist and dust, raced skyward, then away to the east faster than they appeared.

Broken Chain's gaze swept around us. The ring in the sky disappeared. "I fear this place. White clouds go from this place—we die here."

The tacky taste swirled our tongues, mixed with the inescapable sense that we had witnessed death. Had we survived? Tomorrow. Would there be? The question plastered the faces of my friends. *Would all our people ever be the same with that demon stalking us?*

☉☉☉

I pulled the truck around behind our house on Mesa Street. Zara came to the screen door leading to the alley, held the door open, her periwinkle-blue eyes flashing, long dress flowing behind her.

God, what a blessing. Witnessing her there in the alley brought the delight of crisp-ripe strawberries and chocolate syrup to my lips.

"There's my darling," she said. "How was your trip? Did your friends make it all right?"

"Sure. Those old buzzards are in better shape than most men half their ages."

"Come in and I'll draw your bath. You can get comfortable, have some lunch, then take a long nap."

The hot soak combined with my aching tired body, made me sleepy to the point of dizzy. I put on my pajamas, stumbled down the stairs to the kitchen, glanced through the stack of newspapers that Zara had saved for me.

The headlines of the July 17 issue of the El Paso *Times* grabbed my attention:

> *Ammunition Magazine Explodes in Central New Mexico—dateline Albuquerque—A spokesman for the Alamogordo Air Base responded to the Albuquerque* Tribune's *reporter's question regarding an ammunition magazine explosion . . . ."*

I bellered, "Ammunition magazine explosion, my white ass."

"Narlow. Dear, your language is atrocious every single time you return from an outing with any of your old friends. Please refrain from such undignified language."

"You're right, Zara. I am a foul-mouthed old toot. I've developed the habit of the language of the mule skinner, and it's way past time I came clean with you."

She peered over her bifocals. "Come clean with me? What about?"

"Shoot, I don't know where to begin. When I first laid eyes on you, you were a little freckled-face girl in pigtails. You graduated from Sacred Heart School for Girls, went off to finishing school. All that while, Coot and I went off chasing Chief

13

Nana and his last remaining Apache band. You came home, all grown up, pretty as a field of rainbows. We courted, married, and the rest is fifty-two years of history."

I gathered her in my arms. "Zara, what was I supposed to do? Tell an educated young lady that her brand-new husband was nuttier than a sack of goobers? That he was a practicing Apache medicineman? Maybe even studying for his doctorate medicinemanology. Had a mushroom on his hip that foretold danger, danced with a mama grizzly?"

I hemmed and hawed, but there was no escaping Zara. I'd put her off for half-a-century. Time to step up to the licklog.

"Wait right here," I said turning to go upstairs.

I came back down the stairs with several reams of yellow-lined paper, stacked them on the dining room table, took her in my arms, held her tight.

"Honey-sweet-darlin'a-mine, if I'd told you all that stuff back then, you'd have accused me of claiming clairvoyance. When Coot was killed, he gave me his journals, told me to use them to jog my memory, write a book about our lives. All these years, I've been doing just that, and now you're going to read it all. You see, just as I promised Coot, every bit of it is in that stack of paper, my sweet."

1

Hueco Mountains, East of El Paso, July 1910

Coot and I just barely ducked getting ourselves tangled up in the management of a ranch owned by the Vanderwater Family Trust. The Trust had purchased the Circle Bar Ranch in 1905 after six consecutive wet years. The winter after they bought the ranch, drought came as is its custom. What they really wanted was someone to bail them out of a ranch they shouldn't have bought in the first place. According to the folks back in Philadelphia, there's nothing to cattle ranching. "Turn 'em out, gather 'em in, take 'em to market, collect that fat check."

A money machine, that ranching business.

We planned a deer hunt while we looked it over, a task I wanted no part of—the ranch, not the hunt. Coot was hell-bent. Our savior arrived in the form of a run-in with a bunch of drunks from a sleepy little hollow located in the green state of Arkansas. A place called, "Hope." Those no-counts were intent on killing the men while in the process of raping every woman and child in a small band of Mexicans coming to Texas for food and work. There were eight of those turds, knee-walking drunk. Hell, Coot could've handled eight scores of those idiots with me just along for the ride in his Model-T pickup.

We took off chasing the drunks and during the melee, danged if Coot didn't flip that Model-T over on its side. Nothing broke but his pride, and one busted carburetor. We nursed the old hag back to town with Coot sitting on the fender feeding gasoline down its gullet out of a fruit jar, singeing his eyebrows, burning his scant hair when his Stetson caught fire. the Model-T belching fire with every splash of petro. We chugged sixty-eight gritty miles to town without stop or mishap, wind blowing a gravely gale. When we got to within sight of Big George's shop on Texas Street, the truck gasped its last. I got out to crank, kick, and twist it back to life.

Coot's butt was numb so he was content to keep his seat on the unforgiving metal fender, feeding, encouraging it with a little gasoline, muttering, "Come on, baby. Give down your milk. Do it for your daddy!"

A big touring car came up behind us, a young, bright-blue-seersucker-bedecked, bow-tie driver at the helm, blasting away on his bulbhorn to spur us into action, out of his noteworthy way.

A-uga, a-uga, Aarrk-aarrk.

"Damn it, Narlow, go back there and explain our situation."

A-uga, a-uga, Aarrk-aarrk.

I winced, kept twisting that crank like a top. Coot stood, west Texas caliche pasted on his outthrust chin and singed brow. He spit, hawked, sat, stood, turned, double-dog glared back at the man squeezing the horns.

A-uga, a-uga, Aarrk-aarrk.

"Forget it, Coot. Ignore the dumb bastard."

But his rage was on point, not to be denied, begged for release. He spit, dry-spit, stormed back to the touring car, hawked-up a prize, spit it on the silver hood ornament. In mid-*aarrk-aarrk*, he yanked the brightly bedecked driver upright, and dragged him out through the side window. Coot's enlightenment to the lad included much punctuation of bellering in his ear, much waving of his arms, wrapping the bulbhorn's brass base around the brightly bedecked bow-tie man's neck for emphasis.

We left the college graduate standing in the dust of Texas Street, Coot driving the touring car, pushing the Model-T, me, firmly ensconced behind the wheel, arriving in style at Big George's shop.

Tornillo, Texas, October 2, 1910

Long before our planned deer hunt went askew, Rodolfo Bustamante had been badgering us to visit him in Tornillo. Had something of great importance to discuss. We caught the afternoon train to pay our old friend a visit.

Rodolfo had heard about our little skirmish with the eight gentlemen from Hope, and laughed at my description of Coot's man with the bulb-horn necktie.

"What intrigues me about both you gentlemen is your commitment to take the side of the downtrodden. Those helpless Mexicans you saved from those Arkansas toughs is an excellent example, and why I am so persistent about involving you in my plan."

My mind went back to the first time Coot and I laid eyes on Rodolfo and his three-year-old daughter, Sarina in 1875. We were sixteen-year-old, raw-boned boys, floating the Rio, proving our manhood in what Papa referred to as *Hombres de Campo*, Men of the Outdoors, 250-miles, afoot and floating the river while in flood stage.

16

Rodolfo paused, intent on a loose golden thread on his brocaded waistcoat, the only indication of his wealth.

"I would like to tell you what has occupied my every moment since you were here in June, and what is going on in Mexico. More importantly, what I think will happen in the very near future. Before year's end. Already, there's a growing unrest. The entire border region is one of recalcitrance. I believe conditions are ripe for Mexico to be soon embroiled in a civil disturbance that will rock that country to its core."

"A civil disturbance?" Coot asked. "Polite manner of saying revolution?"

"Yes. Revolution. The precise word that describes what I see coming to Mexico."

I said, "That's strange the way you described Mexico's growing unrest, Rodolfo. We were in Juarez just last night. We walked over the Santa Fe Street Bridge to have a nightcap at the Central Bar. Something was different, the people were acting strange, ill at ease. Boys scurrying around, delivering messages to this man, then another, men leaning against adobes, their sombreros covering their eyes, street vendors, aloof, men we've known for years who usually return our greetings. But last night, their eyes avoided ours. Even the usual beggars scurried away. It was like they were all—like they were—not exactly afraid but hesitant, maybe . . ."

"Apprehensive?" Rodolfo asked.

"Yes. Apprehensive."

Coot squirmed in his chair. "Seemed as if every man in Juarez knew there was a keg of dynamite set to go off. Not knowing when to duck. All milling around, looking for a kitchen match."

"A keg of dynamite and a kitchen match," Rodolfo said, smiling. "That analogy describes Mexico quite well. But gentlemen, I believe that fuse is already lit. An explosion will occur soon. *Hundreds of thousands* of men, boys, innocents, will be sacrificed before the conclusion of this revolt. The Diaz regime will strike back with a vengeful lash."

His shoulders shook. "Gentlemen, please remember that Mexico is older than your country—older in the sense that the Spaniards followed Columbus to this hemisphere. Much earlier than the English, the Germans, French, and Dutch arrivals in New England. Until silver was discovered, the Spaniards had no interest in northern Mexico. The Apaches were being pushed west and southward out of Texas by the more numerous and powerful Comanches. Apaches began attacking, pillaging Chihuahuan villages.

"By the late 1700s, northern Mexico was colonized by immigrants from both Spain and central Mexico, granted large tracts of land. They learned to protect themselves, their families, their horses, cattle. Soon these *Chihuahueneses* became a fierce fighting force to be reckoned with, one that could hold their own even with the Apache. After Mexico gained her freedom from Spain, she was on her knees. She had no funds to defend northern Mexico, nothing to halt the raiding Apache. The military colonists fought back, *hard*. Then the Chihuahuan government began the atrocious program of offering bounties for Apache scalps. Scalps of Apache warriors, their women, children, infants strapped to their mother's backs."

I said, "Coot and I know a little about scalpers. Our grandfathers saved an Apache princesses named Little Flower from a bunch of those no-counts in 1830. Grisly business."

Rodolfo smiled. "Why does it not surprise me that your forebears saved that Apache lass? But to go on. The men of Chihuahua became self-reliant, confident, with fierce pride. They were tough, ruthless when required, much stronger than their southern brothers."

He paused, leaned over, and put his fists square on his desk. "That is why I believe the revolution will begin in Chihuahua and Sonora. It will begin just south of the Rio Grande, south of a four-strand barbed-wire fence stretching from El Paso to the Pacific for nearly a thousand miles. It would not surprise me at all if the revolution began in Ciudad Juarez."

Coot frowned. "Why are you so certain that revolution is inevitable?"

Rodolfo explained that he'd studied in Paris, an understudy of an Austrian professor whose life work was the history of revolutions. He concluded there were only four basic root causes of revolutions, but in order for a revolution to breathe life, all four of those causes must be in the mix to compel men to fight, to die along countrymen of different economic and social standings. The rich and poor alike had to band together to wrestle the chains of a despot.

The last of the four ingredients was there must be a clear and present alternative to the present regime. Without that critical ingredient, the people will not act, there will be no call to arms.

Rodolfo paced the floor. "Those prerequisites existed prior to 1789 in France as clearly as yours did prior to 1776. The 1773 Boston Tea Party serves as an excellent case in point. The British-imposed tax was minuscule, on the order of a paltry three pence per hundred weight. Yet the colonists were tired of the British's heavy-handed ways. Their patience was very near the breaking point."

Rodolfo was a learned man, an equal to any man, even Na-Tu-Che-Puy, the Apache medicineman who took me in as a boy. Na-Tu believed I possessed the People's Power. Papa's old Apache scout, Many Fast Feet Two Sticks, had convinced him that the mushroom-shaped birthmark on my hip gave me the Power to see through boulders, could foretell danger, that by just glancing at the ring around the sun, I could tell whether rain would come to their parched land, stuff commonly referred to as voodoo among the Pale Eyes.

Rodolfo leaned across his desk, clinched fists before him, his dark eyes flashing. "There is no question in my mind, *whatsoever*, that Mexico is there. *Today*. And *very soon*, gentlemen, revolution will raise its angry head in northern Mexico. The people—*all people* will vault up. Shake. *Break* the chains of the Diaz regime. An ugly dictatorship of thirty-five long *brutal* years.

"A French nobleman said of France's July Revolution of 1830, 'We are dancing on a volcano.' Perhaps you think that bold statement is farfetched, that it cannot be believed, but my friends, we do not have to believe it. It will be come soon enough in the form of mounted men with rifles, revolvers. Hordes of others on foot. Brandishing knives, rocks, sticks, hoes, and pitchforks. They will storm the garrisons of Juarez, Parral, Chihuahua. They will derail trains, fearlessly charge government troops. They will rob government banks of their ill-gotten gain. Law abiding citizens will be become fearless, completely out of control.

"The first three preconditions of rebellion have been met. All that remains, all that is required is the fourth ingredient. A central figure the people can rally around to provide that fourth ingredient, the alternative. I believe that man is Francisco Madero, the grandson of Evaristo Madero. *Senor* Madero is a wealthy *hacendado* who has called on Porfirio Diaz to fund the feeding of Mexico's starving and destitute millions.

"He reminds me of my own father, who fed the *pobres* as well. I must say, that concerns me greatly. *Most greatly!* My father was not cut out for the harsh life of a *ranchero* in Mexico. The entire enterprise went against his nature. My father sold his ranch for an enormous amount of money. Francisco Madero is a strong man. Strong in his convictions to help his people. But I fear naïve, inexperienced. Far too trusting of those around him. I fear he will hasten to make a bargain with the devil, forgetting that a devil's bargain is *the devil's* bargain. Nothing more. However, Madero will suffice, if he only lasts to light the spark to the revolution."

I asked, "So, Rodolfo, how does that involve us?"

He stepped to the window opening to the street, spread his arms to each side of the window frame. Without turning around, he went on. "The revolution-ary army will need rifles, cartridges, dynamite, cannons, rockets, to wage a success-ful campaign. I have the means to acquire all of those materials. But I need men I can trust implicitly. Two men came instantly to mind." He turned to us, patted his breast. "Two men with *simpatia para los pobres*.

"Henry David Thoreau said in *Walden*, 'There are a thousand hacking at the branches of evil to one who is striking at the root.' I am afraid that perhaps I have been one of the thousand. You men have shown on numerous occasions that you instinctively strike at the root. With your help, we will begin to find sources for guns and ammunition to supply the revolutionaries when they are ready and poised to strike. I assure you that I have the required resources to fund this venture for many years."

He pushed away from the window and faced us. "What say you, my old friends?"

Coot and I looked at each other, then at Rodolfo.

"Damn, Rodolfo," Coot said, "we've never known you to ever overstate yourself. You know we would do anything in the world for you. But what you are proposing demands a long-term commitment. Speaking for myself, I'll just have to think on it."

"And you, Narlow?"

"Coot's right. My son, Will, is working in Berlin, Zara's off on her women's rights crusade. I don't know, Rodolfo, I just don't know. There's something I don't like about getting mixed up in this revolution. This is none of my making, none of my business. If pressed right now, I'd say no. The best I can do is just give Coot and me a little time to mull this over."

2

El Paso, October 30, 1910

We didn't talk about a thing except Rodolfo's certainty of a Mexican revolution. Well, there was one other thing we gnashed on—Coot's insistence to get us involved in his 'scheme,' as I referred to it.

"It's *not* a scheme. We agreed that we would either both be involved in Rodolfo's war, or we'd both stay the hell out of it."

He repeatedly hit me with, "We've worked as a team since early childhood. We stayed together with the Apache for almost two years. An eternity for teenage boys, and by god, we're sticking together on this. Exactly, *exactly* like your papa made us promise him when we left to gather renegade Apaches back in '77. He can still take us both on, in spite of his eighty-eight years, and I for one, don't intend to chance that."

"What, may I ask, does Papa whipping our asses have to do with this decision?"

Coot whirled around, a frown a mile wide across his face. "Do you mean I have to explain that to you as well? Papa's your daddy, not mine. But it appears I have more regard for him than his own son. A fine how-do-you-do, if you ask me."

Coot's tactic was so blatantly obvious it defied logic or conversation. He'd go off on a tangent, circling back, hitting my backside, proving his point with a lot of mumbo-jumbo, "the sky's blue, got it?" logic.

For several days, we beat each other up on the subject. I'd come around to Rodolfo's idea, then Coot would back away from the commitment, an obligation that truly was not our concern. Then he'd go full-bore in the other direction, and I'd want nothing to do with Mexico's damnable revolution.

Big George was a friend of ours who went back to 1880, a man ten years our senior who came out of Tennessee with his family to escape the scourge of the Ku Klux Klan. A good, well-read man, one of our very best friends. We dropped by his blacksmith shop, gloomy, tired of our own war, talking about getting ourselves in Mexico's war that Rodolfo was so certain was coming down the track like a freight train without an engineer.

"Why so glum, my friends?" he asked.

"Aw, hell," Coot said, "Rodolfo Bustamante's certain that Mexico's close

21

to a revolution, wants us to get involved, run guns to the revolutionaries. First, I wanted to jump right in, but Narlow held off, then about the time he'd warm up, I'd cool off."

"Sounds like you two are at a checkmate of your own making," Big George said with a deep-throated chuckle.

"That about sums it up," I said. "Have you heard any rumblings about all that revolution stuff in Mexico."

"Only what our housemaid tells us. She says things are heating up across the Rio, have been since last May when Haley's Comet came back around like it does every seventy-five years. Newspapers all over Mexico reported it, said it foretold the overthrow of *Presidente* Portillo Diaz, that sort of thing. I tell you what I'd do if I was in your shoes. I'd just as soon go back and live in the shadow of the Grand Wizard as get myself involved in that hell hole—unless I owed whoever asked me something like that. But that debt would have to be a major indebtedness."

It hit me. Someone landed a brick upside my head.

Our first encounter with Rodolfo Bustamante was back in 1875. We were floating the Rio, a trip that had started when my papa and Coot's uncle Doyl had put us on our own to prove our worthiness, what Papa scrawled on a scrap of paper stuck in a rusty old line shack. We floated home on a raft we made at the headwaters of Cuchillo Creek. It was in flood stage, but nothing compared to the mile-wide Rio Grande. We were sixteen-year-old-reckless, decided to float on by The Pass another two days.

We thought we must be getting close to Tornillo, but too close to dark to attempt to go further in the rushing water. Besides, all day long we'd caught sight of a man on horseback off to the south across the great flood. At first we didn't think anything of it, just a wandering *vaquero*, but as the day progressed, it became apparent that his wandering seemed to be keeping him just behind us, perhaps attempting to stay out of sight.

We made a dry camp, took turns nodding off, and when it was light enough to see, it was evident that the flooded river had come up several feet during the night. No sign of our *vaquero*. I thought we should wait, that maybe the Rio would go back down, the crashing waves would subside. But Coot was determined to get our raft back in the raging water.

He said, "I'll keep us close to the American side, you keep an eye out for that *vaquero*. If he shows himself again, I'm of a mind to cross to his side. See what he wants."

It wasn't long before we saw a man and a small girl standing on a floating wharf tied to the American side of the river. The man was dressed in what I would describe as a red coat with tails, and shiny, black trousers, sorta like Prince Albert. He hailed us over, and since Coot was near helpless to control our raft, I was more than willing to heed his friendly gesture. When we got close, the man made hand motions for me to throw the raft-rope so he could pull us to shore. He was a small man, but powerful as a sixteen-hand mule.

As the man was tying the rope to his wharf, I said, "Coot, I'm hearing the cry of bull elk, far off, but clear as a bell."

"Relax. Churning water and that *vaquero's* got you spooked."

A rifle shot rang out. Next thing I know, I'm in the water, my left shoulder and arm went numb. I grabbed hold of a partially submerged tree trunk. The rushing water swept me around the base of the tree, and away from the Mexican side of the river. I peered around the tree at the far side of the river, but couldn't see anyone, as the flood had pushed the bank several hundred yards to the south.

I turned back to our raft and the wharf, couldn't see Coot, only the Prince Albert man hacking at something on the raft. At first, I thought Coot was down, that the man was hitting at him. The thought went through my mind that we'd been high jacked by the man and his daughter. They'd been used as a decoy while their accomplice took a shot at my backside. I wiped the water out of my eyes and peered around the tree trunk again. The man on the wharf motioned for me to stay down, stay where I was. He wasn't hitting at Coot, but trying to loosen the raft-rope. He kept pulling at it as if it was stuck on something on the far side.

All the while, he kept pleading with the little girl to hide, to go home, pointing at the far side of the Rio, trying to make her understand that a bad man was over there with a gun. Another rifle shot rang out. The bullet spit up splinters close to the little girl on the wharf. The man ran to her, picked her up, and dove under a wagon.

Dense fog seemed to be taking me away. I tried to keep my grip on the tree trunk, but lacked the strength, began swirling downstream.

I awakened sometime later that day in a strange bed. Even stranger voices came from outside the open door, calling for hot water, more bandages, a call for milk and bread for a poultice.

A shout: "Hold him, Armando, hold him!"

◉◉◉

I rolled over, stood, felt my knees buckle, then fell like a wet sack to the floor.

The sun was bright, reflecting like a mirror off a stark-white wall. I couldn't get my bearings, but I was back in the bed. I turned over, a sharp pain grabbed my bandaged shoulder. I pulled at the bedcovers, but couldn't pull them out from under me, couldn't figure out why I as weak as a kitten.

The white wall went dark. Dreamed I heard the two shotgun blasts at close range.

When I awoke, the sun was on the far wall, filtered, shadowed sunlight. Quiet as a yellowed quarter-moon.

Over the next few days, the Prince Albert man, his daughter, and house-keeper, and the man named Armando spent their time nursing Coot and me back to health, telling us what had happened since we first docked at the wharf.

"Young gentlemen, I am Rodolfo Bustamante." He turned to the beautiful little girl at the side of my bed, all dressed up in shiny black shoes and a pretty blue dress. "And this is my daughter, Sarina. I would also like for you to make the acquaintance of Lucicinda Diaz, the most wonderful housekeeper in the land. And this gentlemen here on my right is Armando Valenzuela."

Senor Bustamante recounted what had happened. He was looking at me when I fell in the water, but didn't know that I'd been shot until he heard the report of the rifle an instant later. Coot dashed across the raft as it came around to go in after me, caught his foot in a rope, fell against the floating dock, and went under. *Senor* Bustamante suddenly had his hands full. He had a man firing at him, Sarina on the wharf in harm's way, and two complete strangers, who were injured and in the water. He tugged at the rope that followed Coot into the water, but could not get him out from under the raft. The *vaquero* turned out to be a *desperado*. He continued firing at all of us. *Senor* Bustamante had to get Sarina to safety. Lucicinda Diaz rushed down to the Rio, took Sarina in her arms, and ran back to the *hacienda*. *Senor* Bustamante jumped back on the wharf, took up Coot's rope again, but determined that pulling on it was useless. He had no choice but to dive into the torrent to search for Coot, finding him under the raft with the rope twisted around the limp boy's leg in a death grip. He disentangled Coot and they both popped to the surface, Coot bleeding at the temple, out cold. *Senor* Bustamante said he appeared blue, lifeless, but when he dragged him to shore, he coughed and puked brown water. Another shot rang out, striking the water at Coot's feet. *Senor*

Bustamante dragged him behind a desert willow grove, then raced downstream looking for me.

Frightened out of his wits, as he knew my clock was about out of clicks, he found me facedown, stuck on a limb.

He recounted his thoughts, "That boy is dead, but I cannot leave him there."

He swam out to me and began pulling me, dogpaddling both of us back to shore. Another rifle shot, this one found its mark. The bullet hit the wrist that was dragging me. He loosened his grip, but dove under water, found me and got me to shore. Now the *desperado* fired rapidly, hitting *Senor* Bustamante in the calf of his leg as he pulled me into a dry *arroyo* at the water's edge.

Armando rushed up with his .44-40 repeater, and began firing at the *desperado* to keep him busy and distracted. He reloaded, began dragging first *Senor* Bustamante then me toward the *hacienda*, steadily shooting his rifle one-handed at the *desperado*.

Senor Bustamante recounted that between the time that I hit the water and he dragged me to dry land couldn't have been more than a couple of minutes. He smiled in the telling.

"But, my new friends, it seemed like an eternity."

Coot's wound was a severe cut across his left temple to the top of his head. He had a concussion, and lost a lot of blood. His unconscious time under the raft breathing brown water didn't improve his disposition either. I only had a flesh wound in my shoulder, but also lost a lot of blood.

Senor Bustamante laughed when he said, "Narlow, you were a much better patient than your friend. Armando had to hold him down while I sewed his wound, forty-three stitches. He didn't enjoy the experience, yelled out that if we didn't let him up that he'd kill us all."

It was not until late that night before there was time to tend to our host's own wounds. Minor bleeding at his wrist and calf of his leg, both requiring several stitches.

He said, "You were both still unconscious, so you probably do not recall hearing two shotgun blasts in the middle of the night. Armando had posted himself as a guard on the roof of my *hacienda* in case your *vaquero amigo* decided to pay us a visit. But, he came. How he escaped Armando's watchful eye is a mystery. I heard someone trying the front door. At first I thought it was Armando, but he did not answer my call. I grabbed up my double-barrel shotgun that was very much loaded with double-OO buckshot. The *desperado* burst through the door, leaving a very messy entrance to my *hacienda*."

This wiry, stout man saved our lives, complete strangers, boys who had no names, while his own daughter was in danger. How do you ever repay such single-minded purpose, such dedication to an uninvited crises dropped into your lap?

I asked, "Huh? What'd you say, Big George?"

Big George smiled. "Are you deaf, Narlow? I said, for me to get involved in Mexico's revolution, the debt I owed whoever was asking would have to be a major indebtedness."

◉◉◉

"Damn, Coot, I know we owe Rodolfo, but there's a limit to what one man can do for another, at least at some point in his life. I've got responsibilities, there's Zara to think of, running guns is not a walk around the park. It's *dangerous*. Mexico's damned old, white mustachioed *presidente* won't take kindly to a couple of middle-aged *gringos* sticking their noses in his business. He'd line us up against the first convenient adobe wall and blow our asses to hell and back. We'd best think this through."

We stood at the bar at the Gem Saloon, Coot all the while pounding on the bar and me about the revolution.

"Well, Coot, I guess that settles it. I don't want anything to do with Mexico's revolution. Too chancy for my blood. Rodolfo says hundreds of thousands of Mexicans will be killed. There's no use of us adding our two fifty-one-year-old *gringo* asses to Mexico's death-pit. So, since *I have decided not to participate* in Rodolfo's war, and *at your insistence* that it will be *both* of us, or *none* of us, well, podnah, it's going to be *none of us*."

He turned his back to the bar, glaring at the saloon patrons. "You think. You think," he said turning, pounding his fist on the bar, "*you actually think* that I'm going to let you vote for both of us? You're going to manacle *us* to your decision. Against the oppression of millions of poor Mexicans? Well, I say I am going to get right in the middle of Rodolfo's war, and, podnah, *you're coming with me!*"

"Don't start that crap. I'm as concerned about Mexico's *pobres* as the next man, but I also have an obligation to Zara and Will. She'd twist your ear for pestering your lifelong friend like this, trying every devious tactic in your well-equipped arsenal of dirty dealings. And, there's another reason I don't want to get involved, a man who I hold in the highest regard, a noteworthy man who I must think of during perilous times such as these."

"Yeah, who?"

"Me!"

☉☉☉

We stopped by Big George's place to drop off a plowshare for a neighboring farmer-friend of Coot's, timing our visit to Big George's at closing time. The cooling jug he always kept outback in a burlap sack had a melodious call.

He was busy at his forge, laughed when we stepped through his wide door, honeysuckle draped to the ground. "You know where it is. Help yourself. But tell me, you gents make your decision? Going south to stomp on *Presidente* Diaz's buttoned shoes, or stay here and mind your own business like good little *gringos*?"

"Hell, Big George, I don't know. Coot's about ready to quit talking and commence to kicking my ass. I even tried to get Papa to tell me what to do, told him that my mind was so screwed up trying to think this revolution through, running guns and all, that I'd put myself in his capable hands, do whatever he said to do—run guns or stay home. But Papa didn't fall for my ploy. 'Son, don't try to trick your old daddy. I quit trying to get you to do anything when I gave up trying to get you and Coot to go off to college back in 1875. You boys'll do the right thing.' I just don't know, Big George. Gun running is dangerous business. We owe Rodolfo our lives, no doubt about it, but this gunrunning business may never end—until *after* we do!"

Big George smiled. "I've been thinking about your predicament. But, I don't rightly know whether you gents can fully understand what I'm going to tell you." He grinned. "You're smart men, but you're as snow white as a set of powdered cupcakes."

He banged his heavy ball peen hammer on his steel table. "When I was a boy, my mama and I lived on a sugarcane plantation in south Louisiana. Then late one night when I was—I don't know, ten years old, maybe even twelve—my daddy came to us. He hadn't lived with us since he was sold off two years before, to a widow lady in the next county.

"Daddy shook me awake. 'Come on, boy. Git'chur briches on. We's gots a cho' ta settle.'

"We walked most of the night back to the widow lady's plantation, stayed off the roads, as slaves were known to sneak off and head north to freedom during that long ol' war between neighbors and kin. Daddy told me that I was to swim a swamp to an island where I'd find a rusty iron cage with a man by the name of Zeke in it, probably more dead than alive. The swamp was deep, couldn't walk it, have to swim the entire way. I was to swim to the island with the rope trailing behind, release the cage's iron gate that was latched by no more than a hickory stick, but out of the reach of the caged man. I was to drag Zeke back to the swamp, tie the rope around his chest, then jerk on the rope so daddy would know we were ready. I'd keep Zeke's head above water while holding onto the rope, and daddy would pull us back to his side of the swamp."

Big George's dark eyes sparked from the light of his forge. "About the time daddy had us pulled halfway, I saw flickers of flares back on the island, men shouting, cursing, using the Lord's name in vain. Then musket shots. *Lots of them*, musket balls splashing all around. *Dark*, darker'n the underside of number-two washtub. With all those musket flashes, Daddy started pulling harder, *faster*."

Big George laughed. "That strong man just about had me and Zeke heading for shore like a skip-rock. When he got us to shore, Daddy threw Zeke over his shoulder like a five-pound sack of spuds, shouted, 'Run, boy! Run faster'n you knows how.' If the men who were shooting at us had dogs, they'd chased us down for certain. Ran all night until we came upon the Mississippi River. Daddy stopped at a shack on a loading dock, talked in whispers to a man in the dark. The only thing I could make out was the man say, 'Shor', Jerome, we'll get this man north of the Mason-Dixon Line inside a week's time. Kind'r strange, but we'll handle if for you.'

"I didn't know what he meant by 'kind'r strange,' but I was getting ready to find out."

Big George drew back his five-pound ball peen hammer, and pounded out the words on his anvil. "My daddy was the strongest man in Louisiana, carried Zeke more miles than I could count. He did all that when Zeke couldn't walk to get water or make it. Daddy's heart took over when his body was spent. I've seen him back up to a cotton bale, reach over his shoulder with a hook, stab that bale, lean forward, set that 500-pound bale on the bed of a mule-drawn cotton trailer. But I learned that night about daddy's other strengths that mocked his physical traits. He was a man who left no debt unpaid. Honest to a fault. Honest even if it cost his life, committed to his core beliefs, even if meant the life of his son. You see, my friends, the man I swam out to the island to retrieve was the same man who refused his mistress' demand that he serve-up 300 lashes from a cat-a-nine-tails on my daddy's back. Zeke threw the whip to the ground, told her it would kill him, refused to do it. The plantation foreman convinced the mistress to split the punishment—hundred-fifty lashes for my daddy, an equal number for the man named Zeke. The lashes were served up, but the mistress was not finished with Zeke. She directed her foreman to tie a rope around Zeke's neck, that he be thrown in the swamp, the other end of the rope tied on the deadeye holes of a skiff. That was done, then four men were put to the oars, dragged that man until he sank in the murky water. They thought he drowned, but he soon sprang to the surface, coughing, sputtering, throwing up slimy, green water. The mistress directed the foreman to lock up Zeke in an iron cage on the island, a cage used to fatten feral hogs for butchering time."

Big George shook his head. "That woman was sure a mean one. As she turned to leave, she shouted for all to hear, 'And tomorrow, you give Zeke another hundred lashes, and another turn in the swamp on the end of the rope. Make him beg to mete out 300 lashes to that black nigra the next time I give him an order.'"

Big George's ball peen hammer blows softened for a spell. The cadence quickened. The sharp clang of strong steel on solid cast-steel became deafening.

"Daddy told me that the very next morning, Zeke was chained to a stump and another hundred were laid to his back, and another tour of the swamp followed on the end of the rope was served up. Zeke was caged again, no food, no water. Daddy knew that Zeke'd had saved him, he owed him, that he'd surely die if he didn't do something. But all Daddy could find was a rope. He knew he couldn't swim to the island, then swim back to shore with a beaten man to tend to, leaving no reserve to carry him from harm's way. He needed someone he trusted—his boy."

Big George's hammer slowed to an occasional sharp rap of a ping on the anvil.

"It was dark as a tub of tar when Daddy was talking to the man on the loading dock by the river, and he agreed to take Zeke north. I recall sitting, leaning back against a tree trunk, plumb tuckered to the bone, Zeke's head in my lap. Lord, I was tired, dozed off pretty quick. After a spell, Daddy nudged me. 'Come on, boy. Need to get Zeke outta sight 'afo somebody come 'long.' I sat up, looked around in the bright sun. The sight of Zeke's head in my lap took my breath. You see, Zeke was as white as a sack of flower."

Big George tossed his hammer on the steel table. "Daddy paid his debt in full that night. In a way, Zeke was Daddy's brother. Seems to me that the Bustamante family is *your* family."

He picked up the hammer, gave it a practiced flip, it tumbled and twisted in the air, the handle came to rest in his heavy hand. "Folks thought my daddy was no more than a swamp-sucking, black-ass nigger. They were wrong. He proved it. Showed it. Displayed it, like a 1000-karat diamond. I'm the product of that stout man and an adorable woman—my mama.

"You owe Rodolfo, same as you owe each other. My daddy'd say you can't escape who you are, what you are, or what you mean to other folks. I guarantee you that I know what Narlow's papa would do. You two know it as well."

Coot said, "Yes, we dern sure do!"

Big George stood studying his hammer. "But, I'll tell you this. News back in those days traveled mighty slow. The night my daddy and I saved Zeke was less than a month shy of two full, *solid* years since President Lincoln signed his Emancipation Proclamation. My daddy was a free man, but he never knew it. My mama and I found him hanging from a magnolia tree, initials KKK branded on his bare chest, his pants down past his knees, blood all over the place, his manhood and balls stuffed in his mouth."

⊚⊚⊚

Coot and I crossed the wooden bridge to Juarez, intent on a nightcap and a steak.

"Coot, I'd rather bed a rattler than get mixed up in Mexico's revolution. It's none of our business."

He whirled around in the dust of Juarez Avenue. "None of our business, huh? That old woman over there pulling that wee-lad on a board with skate wheels in the dirt is none of our business, huh? While Porfirio Diaz's *politicos* whiz by in a shiny Dodge convertible, the men's tall, black hats flashing like raven wings in the sun, their ladies high ribbon bonnets showing white in the evening sky with not a care in the world. You see that, Narlow Montgomery, and still say that boy's none of our concern?"

"Coot, to quote Shakespeare or Geronimo, don't rightly recall which at the moment, you're what's called *totus porcus*. You're invariably whole hog."

"Naw, Narlow, that's not why you'll finally give in. Just like that legless lad on that board, you never had a chance to be a boy. Your mama stole it."

We stepped into cool dark of Café Central, ordered *bistec* and a bottle of local wine, red on the label, contents green, bearing yesterday's date. Waiting outside in the dim of the evening was one of my favorite people, Alejandrina, an ancient lady selling gardenia blossom corsages *por dos centavos*. I pressed a dollar in her palm, pinned my fragrant purchase to her shawl, her heaven-green eyes invariably reflected a certain "what might have been" glow about them. A tug at my trousers had me looking down into the death-glaze-black eyes of the boy on a board, a tin cup held by pincers serving as fingers. I dropped a dollar in his cup, glanced at Coot, whispered to myself, "Jess-Amighty, here we go again!""

3

Through all those many days of making up our minds on running guns, Big George's story and Papa were heavy on my mind. He raised me even though my mother was always close-at-hand. I should say, Papa raised me *in spite* of my mother being close by. Mean, cruel, unloving, she possessed those traits in such quantity that her own half-brother rode an old brown mule clear over from Texas' south plains. He'd heard of some of her goings-on. Uncle Howard, told Papa out-back in the corral what he'd heard. Papa confirmed it to his satisfaction.

I heard Papa say, "Howard, I just can't walk away from her. I sure can't leave Narlow here with her, and if I left and took Narlow with me, she'd be on our trail until she caught up with us. Then I'd have another choice to make, and I'm no woman killer."

"Abe, not suggesting that you do any such thing. Daisy's a mean one, mean-est of the lot, more venom than a central-Texas ten-foot Diamond back. An old wives' tale pretty well puts the women in our family in their rightful place. She's half-Comanche. You know better than me what happens to a white man when a bunch of Comanche braves captures a white man. Take him back to their women. Many a man has begged to be shot on the way back to their camp. Comanche women's cruelty is legendary. Daisy's mean, not crazy. I just wanted Narlow to know that so he won't be worried about being born into a nervous family."

Uncle Howard's left that night with Papa's promise that he'd repeat his words to his only son. Papa started that conversation early the next morning when we headed out to Brazito Canyon to gather strays. "Papa, you don't have to tell me what Uncle Howard came to say. I was out by the corral making certain that Mama didn't come out of the dugout and overhear your conversation."

Papa also raised Coot for the most part, with a tolerable amount of help from Coot's uncle Doyl. They were about the best men in the West, and Coot and I tried hard not to disappoint them. Doing right was second nature to them. I often thought that trait was further down the line-count for me and Coot.

Our nearly two years at White Mountain Apache Reservation with Many Fast Feet Two Sticks and the medicineman, Na-Tu-Che-Puy, did much to strengthen that resolve. Braves under their tutelage who would not do right, *always* right, and *always* truthful, were soon relegated to the women's campfires and their insatiable need for wood to feed the flames. A brave's word was important, the People's lives depended on that trait, not to embellish or diminish the facts of the enemy or their numbers, simply a statement of the truth without delay. Na-Tu, as he was called when he was not present, was especially critical of my slide on doing right.

When Na-Tu learned of the ways of my mother, his clear black eyes peered deep into my own, he said, "I see much guilt in your heart. You must rid yourself of all guilt, all blame, for it will not serve you well. The fault of the blame is not yours, it is your mama's. You are more man than that."

This thin man sat on a fine buffalo robe under the scant shade of a woven arbor in front of his lodge, telling me of the ways of right and truth was the only way. His solemn manner, his braided hair, the color and coarse texture of pounded pewter that fell to his waist, did much to beat that trait into me. It was hotter than Hades, yet he sat cool as a mountain trout.

He concluded our interview with a single statement that stayed with me. "I believe your mama's critical manner is the cause of your guilt, your blame, why it is often easy for you to stray from doing right. You don't lie to your papa, you lie to protect yourself from your mama."

◎◎◎

Coot made plans to catch the morning train for Socorro, New Mexico, 180 miles north. He'd wired a Socorro wholesaler who was known to have German connections, known to get his hands on German-made rifles and ammunition. On his way to the train, he led me toward the State National Bank.

"How do you know Rodolfo wants that particular German rifle?" I asked. "Probably a dozen varieties just as suitable."

He smiled, his dark eyes wide. "Oh, he'll want those Mausers all right. It's the most sought-after weapon available today. It's powerful enough to penetrate a seventeen-inch tree trunk. Fire as fast as a man can run the bolt. Reliable. Never jams. Ammunition readily available. Cheap."

"But Mexico's war hasn't even started and may never—"

"You heard Rodolfo. We may not be dodging bullets this very minute. You may not hear cannons booming in Juarez across the Rio, but you best be ready to duck."

When Coot said he'd need $230,000 from our joint bank account, I said, "Jees-Amighty, Coot! That'll damn near tap us out. We've developed a Packard appetite, but we'll soon be down to a burro pocketbook."

The bank teller stood behind his golden cage, and counted out the $230,000.

I was still dragging my heels. "That's more than half of our entire account. Every damn penny we cleared when we sold the Sheldon Hotel to those Dallas slicks two years ago. You could buy the whole damn town of Socorro for half that stack of greenbacks. And Jees-amighty, Coot, we can't bankroll Rodolfo's *entire war!*"

"Just an advance. Rodolfo will repay us. Or, do you think that German up there in Socorro will just give me those rifles and cartridges on my good looks and a handshake? He demands hard currency. And by god, we'll give him *hard currency*—$230,000. Right?"

"Well, yeah. *So?*"

"And, *so?*"

El Paso, Halloween 1910

What had we gotten ourselves into? Two, fifty-one-year-old toots running guns? Into a country set for a revolution over stuff that was none of our business? We're *nuts*. Certifiable!

My land and cattle office was off the lobby of the Paso del Norte Hotel, featured an eight-foot window pane facing South El Paso Street. The view offered up through that pane rivaled anything available by Hollywood's bijous. Rivaled? Naw, my private view was far superior.

My bijou offered a menagerie of sights, sounds, colors, and flavors. Like a carnival, a traveling Barnum and Bailey, but they'd be hard-pressed to equal my view. It offered the strangest variety of animals God ever blessed His green earth— two-legged variety—people. People walking to and fro, mainly on their way to or from Juarez. People, along with a few horses, stray dogs, and cats thrown in the mix. People walking in the heat of the day like their creature comforts. Mornings found them on the east side of the street, afternoons swelled the west side as the torrid sun slants from that direction. People, lady-people, standing at a street corner, dressed to the nines, bustled gowns from Dallas, high hats from New Orleans, San Francisco, chatting, waiting for a trolley.

Gas belching automobiles give way to electric trolleys whose overhead power-lead sparked as they turn east on Overland Street, people, horses, buggies, and bicycles, gave way to the larger conveyances. You'd think it would be dangerous, but everyone and everything seemed to ebb and flow, dodging in and out of the other's way, like an orchestrated cotton-candy twister.

My favorite actor among the regulars was a scruffy scamp whose chosen sport was ducking under the belly of a horse, then jumping up to chase after a trolley for a ride that was interrupted by the trolley man chasing him off.

My window pane mirrored the boy's image as he hurried past, caught a glimpse of himself, stopped and pressed his face to the glass to see me gazing back at him. His eyes widened, jumped back, vanished in the crowd.

The boy was a near spitting image of my Alley Boy, a boy who took up residence in a tool shack in the alley behind our house back around 1880, well before Zara and I were married. Alley Boy earned his keep by running errands for neighbor ladies, helping the elderly milkman with his deliveries up steep, concrete steps to his customer's front stoop. Ines, my live-in maid, and me, left a plate of food on our kitchen step that led to the alley three times a day. The lad paid for the privilege by grooming Papa's old mount, Traveler. Alley Boy repeatedly would say, "Traveler's a mighty fine horse." His words haunted me to this day.

Just before Zara and I were married, Alley Boy got wind of that eventuality, said he'd be moving on, saying, "That pretty lady's not likely to want my kind anywhere near her home." The boy didn't even know his own name, but his conversation was pleasant, mirrored good manners, languages, and education. I told him that if he'd spruce himself up a bit, maybe the pretty new bride would warm up to him. I bought him some clothes and he stuck around.

When Zara and I returned from our *Valle Grande* honeymoon, the first thing she did was bring Alley Boy in the house, gave him a converted storage room off the kitchen for his own, a good bed, access to the indoor facilities, a kitchen full of Ines' delights.

Zara said, "That boy has a handsome background. He's smart, intelligent, and from my conversations with him, I'd say he's had a wonderful education. He even has a smattering of languages, European mainly. That boy's going to an east-coast university, and I'm going to see that he's well prepared."

Between bouts with Zara's newfound avocation of gaining full rights for the country's women, she did just that, setting a full curriculum for Alley Boy to digest. Zara was a whirlwind, ever busy, never idle, never a free moment, too busy for idleness.

I told her once, "Zara, if you'll take up gardening, I'll buy you a mail-order miner's helmet equipped with a coal oil lamp so you can garden at night." My humor was often lost on the lady.

Inside two years, Zara had that boy whipped into shape, ready for any university. She grabbed me by the arm. "Come along, Narlow, we're going to pay a visit on Attorney Leighton Green."

That visit to Attorney Green produced an assumed-name document and adoption papers for a no-name, no-past lad of sixteen, signed, sealed, filed of record at the county courthouse.

When we sat him down in the parlor, Zara said, "Will Narlow Montgomery, Jr., welcome to our family. We have legally adopted you and given you Narlow's name. So, Will, what do you think of that? Does that meet with your approval?"

He jumped to his feet, hugged Zara, pumped my hand, swung Zara around the parlor, shouted, "*Will*—Will Narlow Montgomery, Jr. *Yes!* I like that!"

We had us a son.

Twelve short years ago, Zara shipped Will off to Wharton International Business College. Along with his roommate, Jonathon Everstart, he graduated with honors in three years. During their second year summer break, they voyaged to England. Mr. Everstart was impressed with Will and offered to employ him when he graduated. He planned to start a munitions factory in Germany and wanted two men he could trust implicitly—Jon Everstart, Jr. and Will Narlow Montgomery, Jr.

Life had a—

"Mr. Montgomery. Mr. Montgomery? Sir?"

Standing before me in my office was a young lad with a doffed cap.

"Huh? Yes, what is it, son?"

"Sir, Mr. Coot Boldt gave me a whole nickel to come fetch you. He wants you to come down to the Union Depot. Says he has something he wants to show you."

"A whole nickel, huh?" I duplicated Coot's whole nickel and headed for the freight yard.

My partner had returned with a boxcar loaded with 1,666 long, wooden crates marked "Swiss Chocolates," along with a 1,000 metal canisters marked "Swizzle Sticks," all for only $230,000.

"Swiss Chocolates and Swizzle Sticks, huh?" I asked. "What's that all about?"

"Our German-born supplier insists on those labels. Says that's how all of his shipments are received from his Fatherland, as he calls it. It's how all of our future shipments will be marked. Swiss Chocolates will be shipped in these wooded crates. Each crate holds six, brand-spanking-new, 6-millimeter Mauser rifles. Each Swizzle Stick canister contains 500-rounds. Pretty slick, huh?"

"Does he always keep this many rifles and shells on hand?"

"He says his family in Germany shipped them to him last month. Those bastards are way ahead of the game. They know as much about Mexico's unrest as Rodolfo."

"Does this kraut have a name?"

"What do you mean?"

"Kraut," I said. "You know, sauer*kraut*. Does he have a name, or do I just say, Howdy, Kraut?"

Coot screwed his square face around, glaring at me. "No, but you know what, *amigo mio*? Your attitude needs to improve if we're going to be successful in doing this gunrunning for Rodolfo. And your attitude about your Socorro German friend needs a lot of improvement."

"*My* Socorro German friend? Why *my* friend? And you didn't answer my question—What's his name?"

"He's your friend because I've decided you can handle him better than me."

"What's his name?"

"Fritz Hans-Smidt."

"Fritz Hans-Smidt, huh? And, I can handle him better than you?"

"Yeah, I can't tolerate the creampuff little bastard, *that's* why. Most fastidious, mollycoddled pudg you ever laid eyes on. I'd stomp him in the dust inside a week's time. Slimiest fancy-Dan you ever saw. Big, batting-brown, soft, innocent eyes blinking in the moonlight. Has the damnedest habit of pressing his dress pants. Pressing down with those lacy, buttercup hands of his. When we first met, he stuck one of them out to shake hands. I acted like I didn't see it. I started looking around the warehouse, damned if he didn't try to shake me down for a delivery fee. You need to explain that screwing with me, screwing with me—*screwing with me* like that will get his curly head separated from his fat ass."

"Well, gentlemen," Rodolfo said, "I must admit I have been hoping that your answer would be yes. This says a lot about our friendship. What did all of these rifles and cartridges cost, and how much do I owe you?"

Coot said, "Eighteen dollars per rifle, five-cents a round, comes to $230,000."

"Two-hundred-thirty *thousand*? My assistance in this revolution will be far costlier than I imagined. Even that much ammunition will not feed the thousands of rifles in Villa's army for a single hour, but we shall concentrate our efforts where we can accomplish the most. In remote areas of Chihuahua where a little does so much." He shrugged. "But, as to the money I owe you, I don't keep that kind of money in my little bank. I could give you that amount in gold."

"Aw, hell, Rodolfo, don't worry about it," I said. "Coot thinks that we're *ricos*. Money's nothing to us."

"Oh, I have always been impressed and aware of the wealth you gentlemen have amassed, but if you will accompany me to my bank, I will show you that, while I may not have $230,000 in my entire bank, I have other assets to cover my indebtedness to you."

We crossed the lantern-lit plaza to Rodolfo's bank. He bolted the door, drew the blinds on the window facing the street, motioned for us to move his heavy desk. He threw back a rug exposing a trap door, knelt, swung the door up, exposing a concrete stairwell that led to the basement below.

He lit a lantern. "Follow me, my friends. I have something to show you. I think you might agree that I might be able to cover my debt to you."

We followed him down the stairs to a landing that led to the cellar floor. There, laid out in neat four-foot high tiers, were countless scores of stacks of gold bars that measured twice the length of the street level of Rodolfo's bank building.

Coot whistled. "Rodolfo, what in the name of all that's holy is all this? And *where* and *when* did you come by it all?"

I asked, "And, why in the world are you showing us the largest hoard of gold in the United States outside of Fort Knox? You shouldn't have shown this to us, Rodolfo."

"Oh, but I did! I have all the reason in the world to trust you with my secret." He grasped us by our shoulders. "I have known you men for thirty-five years, ever since you were sixteen-year-old boys. You have risked your lives many times in defense of the defenseless, on both sides of the border, less than one hundred meters from this vault. Who else in the world is there to trust when I need it most? Who else but you gentlemen were there when I needed you? When Sarina needed you so desperately? I ask you, *who else?* Who else, my faithful and true friends?"

Coot's gaze locked on mine. My mind raced.

Raced back to that bad time when Rodolfo's daughter, Sarina, had been brutalized just before her eleventh birthday, a girl who was only three when we first laid eyes on her. Back then, word came from Papa that Coot's uncle Doyl'd been killed in a flashflood in Monticello Box Canyon. Coot left Rodolfo's *hacienda* before dawn. I knew where he was headed, and it was not to his mama's farm. I told Rodolfo that I'd be back, but I had to chase after my friend.

Sarina climbed up in my lap and asked, "Uncle Narlow, can you really find my Coot? He says you have a lot of Comanche and Apache in you, and you can see through rocks. Can you *really?* Will you bring him back to me?"

Her hugging embarrassed me, a boy who hadn't been around a young girl since his own little sister died when they were both little tykes. Rodolfo smiled at my unease, made a sign for me to hug her, love her. I did so, then told her that I'd try really hard to bring Coot back to her.

Her emerald eyes gazed up at me. "Good! One day I plan to marry Coot."

Ever since that long-ago time, we made every effort to occasionally spend a few days with them to renew our friendship, a family that had grown so close to us. Eight years after Sarina announced that she planned to marry Coot, we again paid them a visit, as Rodolfo planned a grand *fiesta* to celebrate his beautiful, emerald-eyed daughter's eleventh birthday. We arrived past midnight at Rodolfo's *hacienda*. Not wanting to disturb them, we built a fire by the Rio. We'd stretch out, doze, wait for dawn.

We'd barely settled in, when a shriek brought us to our feet, an anguished cry for help, the voice of a woman.

I asked, "How far away do you think she is?"

"More than a quarter-mile. I swear I heard her say the name Sarina."

We took off running through the heavy underbrush of the *bosque*, limbs whipping our faces, tripping us, trying to get us to the sand.

Coot stopped. "Hear that?"

The cries of the woman were much closer, off to the south a ways. We came upon the woman, someone we knew, Rodolfo's neighbor, Margarita Loya.

"It's Sarina. *Alla!* There!" she screamed, pointing back over her shoulder. "*Esta muerta!*"

The three of us fought our way through the bosque, all the while Margarita assuring us that Sarina was dead. We found the smoldering remains of a fire, kicked life back into it, found a dead branch to serve as a torch.

Strung between two salt cedars was Sarina, naked, upside down, her spread-eagle form was tied by rough lariats to her ankles and wrists, something protruding from her privates. We cut her down, I covered her with my jacket, sat in the sand cradling her limp body. Coot checked her over, slowly removed the object from between her snow-white thighs and threw it aside with an anguished grunt of disgust.

"Nothing broken. She couldn't have been there long, or she'd be dead from hanging upside down."

Coot quickly walked the area with the torch. "Three horses, two of them shod, heading downriver. Come on, let's get Sarina home."

Rodolfo took the news and condition of his daughter far better than I could ever muster. He explained that Sarina had been staying with her aunt across the Rio, in Guadalupe Bravo so that she could play with her visiting cousins.

News of Sarina's tragedy spread along the border. The morning before we arrived, three men, two ruffian-*gringos* and a *bandito*, had killed a wagon driver and his helper as they were hauling meat from a neighboring *hacienda* to Guadalupe Bravo. They killed the mule, turned over the wagon, set it and the driver afire.

Coot said, "There's three of the bastards, Rodolfo. That's good. One of them will start bragging in some low cantina along the border. Stronger, better men, will take care of them."

The women bathed and bandaged Sarina's wounds, and told Coot and me off to the side that her many scrapes and bruises were unmistakable signs of repeated rapes and sodomy.

Occasionally, Sarina was conscious, unresponsive. We took turns sitting with her in three-hour shifts so she would not awaken alone. First Rodolfo, then Margarita Loya, Coot, then Rodolfo's housekeeper, Petra Rodriguez, a lady who'd raised Sarina, then my turn. Sarina never spoke, never ate a thing put before her, only an occasional sip of water, a lifeless, faraway look her blank eyes.

Two days later, a rider called on Rodolfo. Sarina's attackers'd been caught, just as Coot had promised. They'd been stripped naked, strung up in similar fashion, their *cebollas* stuffed in their mouths, ax handles crammed up their asses, left swaying in the soft summer breeze to face the devil.

39

Four more long days and nights crept by. When my late-night shift was about over, I heard a soft rap at the door. I stood, bent over, kissed Sarina's cheek, turned to leave.

"Uncle Narlow."

I knelt by her bed.

"Is Uncle Coot still here?"

"Why, sure he is, honey. You couldn't get rid of your Uncle Coot with a stick. Want me to go get him?"

"Please." She paused. "I wish to speak to him. He's so kind."

Coot's kind? Well, wasn't I kind? No, I wasn't kind. This eleven-year-old girl sees it in my eyes.

Coot didn't come back through that door for yet another six full days. We left a tray of food and water by the door. Sometimes the tray was disturbed, often it was not. When he did emerge with a stubbled face, he told us that Sarina was still somewhat suicidal, at first begging him to shoot her, poison her, *anything* to put an end to her nightmare. She agreed to his suggestion: they would move to a nearby shed that had served as her doll house through the years. She and Coot would occupy the shed for as long as it took to get her through her ordeal, talk it out of her soul. Coot directed that I bring food and water to the shed's door, then leave without inquiry.

A month dragged by, then one morning before dawn, I left the tray of food and water, turned to leave.

Coot whispered through the rough planks of the door, "Narlow, listen to me carefully. Sarina's going to be all right." I heard, maybe *felt* him turn to her. "That's right, isn't it Sarina? You're going to be all right. Everything's going to be sunshine and red roses from now on for you. Isn't that right?"

I heard her infectious giggle. "Yes, Uncle Coot, I will be just fine, *after* you do what you promised."

"Yes, I know," Coot said with a chuckle. "Narlow, don't laugh, but Sarina wants you to marry us. Not the *padre*, not the circuit preacher-man, *you*, The Right Reverend Narlow Montgomery will officiate. Think of something pretty to say. Sarina wants the ceremony at her favorite shady place down by the Rio. Rodolfo knows the spot. Assure him that there's been no shenanigans, no foul play going on in here with his daughter, and—"

"Rodolfo knows that, Coot."

"*I know it!* Tell him anyway. After the ceremony, Sarina will serve tea like

40

she always does, then you and I'll be taking our leave. Sarina'll be ready to get on with life, to work every day to keep the past behind her."

Besides Papa, the Bustamante family was the only warm spot Coot and I'd ever known. They were our family.

Rodolfo grabbed Coot and me by our shoulders, shook us.

I said, "Yeah sure, Rodolfo, who else?"

He gazed deep in our eyes. "Gentlemen, I repeat: Who else could I call on when Sarina was in such horrible need, so desperately in need? I ask you, who else? Who else, my faithful and true friends?"

Rodolfo explained that his father sold his ranch in 1847, the second largest ranch in all of Mexico, a ranch that held more than half of all the cattle in Chihuahua. He sold it to a neighboring *hacendado*, making his ranch the largest in all of Mexico, controlling most of the water in the state. His father sold for $5,000,000 and moved his family to Europe.

The king of the small Kingdome of Beem, between Austria and France, convinced his parliament to borrow $4,500,000 from Rodolfo's father to save the country from certain bankruptcy. They put up the entire country as collateral, the lien held by the Archbishop of Paris, his father's brother. The note given by the king was to be repaid at the end of ten years in the amount of $50,000,000 US. The note was paid in full. His parents perished in a ship crossing of the English Channel, leaving Rodolfo as the sole heir. He invested wisely, then sold his European holdings and moved his family to Tornillo—along with over $100,000,000 in gold.

"So gentlemen, now you know the entire story."

I said, "And all of this gold was sitting right here when we floated the river and you docked us right down there on the riverbank when we first met?"

He sighed. "Yes, this gold has been right here since well before your first visit to Tornillo in 1875. I'd no one to trust. Transporting all that gold in ocean-going ships to the Port of Brownsville was a perilous affair, but nothing compared to getting it here by wagon, over 750-miles. You see, my friends," he said with a wink, "I didn't have trustworthy men such as yourselves back then. It took me over three years, *on my own*, but I did it."

Coot asked, "And why did you decide on Tornillo, Texas? You could have taken your family anywhere in the world with one stack of this stuff."

He leaned over, placed his hands on a pallet of gold, then stood erect. "Yes, that is correct, but Tornillo was not even here, just a cattle crossing. I could have taken my family anywhere in the world, but I wanted my family, and the gold,

41

close to Mexico, but *not in* Mexico. My wife and I wanted our children to grow and mature in a small village such as Tornillo. About the time you gentleman pushed your raft onto Tornillo's river shore, Porfirio Diaz became the *presidente* of Mexico, and her people have struggled under the weight of thirty-five-years of his oppressive dictatorship."

He sighed, rubbed the smooth metal, gazed down the stacks of yellow in the dim glow of the lantern. "This much gold weighs on one man most heavy. I find it distasteful to be in command of the contents of this cellar. For you see, I do not own this gold, I am merely its custodian, this bank-cellar's janitor, *possessed*, rather than the possessor. Astounding, is it not?"

He paused, his brow pinched, then pushed away from the stack of gold. "I must put this treasure to use for the good of Mexico. Its people. The time is nigh. Much has occurred in the short number of days since you were here. Some of those occurrences would seem strange to you gentlemen. For instance, you are no-doubt familiar with the phenomenon known as Halley's comet?"

"Yes," I said. "It occurs every seventy-six years or so, and appeared just last May. Papa remembers seeing it as a boy. Recalls that it scared hell out of a lot of his kinfolk, Apache and Pale Eyes alike."

"Correct, it was not only visible, it was as bright as noon sun in Mexico City. Most Mexicans are quite superstitious. They took the comet's stark white appearance as a sign—a sign that something strange and powerful was about to occur. There has been much whispered talk that the revolution is close to beginning, that the comet was sent by God as a sign for the people to prepare for revolution, or face His wrath."

He paused, crossed his jacketed arms, squeezed, relaxed. "Gentlemen, you will recall that I thought that Francisco Madero would be the catalyst that will lead Mexico to armed revolt. Porfirio Diaz called for free elections, as you know. Madero surprised Diaz, and campaigned in northern Mexico for the presidency. Madero was hugely popular. Diaz had him jailed, the election was held, and Diaz, *who counted the votes*, won by an overwhelming landslide with Madero receiving only a paltry 183 votes throughout *the entire* country. Madero's family pleaded for his release. It was granted. He fled to the US, has declared himself provisional president of Mexico, and has called for a general uprising for November 20, 1910— less than three weeks from today. Your rifles and ammunition have arrived just in time for the first skirmishes of the revolution.

"But tell me—your man in Socorro doesn't require payment in gold? I assumed the suppliers in Germany would require gold."

Coot smiled. "No gold. Cash only. Insists on US greenbacks."

Rodolfo's eyes widened. "How strange. Did he give you any reason for Germany's demand for dollars instead of gold?"

Coot laughed. "Yeah, Rodolfo, but you won't believe it. Fritz says he's a distant relative of Kaiser, Friedrich Wilhelm Viktor Albert. His foreign minister has convinced him that if he sells enough Mausers, ammunition, rockets, and cannon to countries around the world, always demands US dollars for them, he'll corner the market on dollars, bankrupt the United States. Thus, Germany will take over all of Europe and the US. Without firing a shot."

Rodolfo laughed. "He thinks the US cannot run their printing press on a double shift? If the Kaiser goes forward with his own war plans, he may well learn the value of a well-lubricated government printing press. A press that also runs non-stop."

I asked, "So, there is no doubt in your mind that Mexico is headed for a full-fledge revolution that will begin before the end of 1910?"

"Narlow, my dear friend, it is well known in Mexico by the rich and poor, educated and ignorant that the Porfirio Diaz's regime's motto is and has always been, 'Los muertos no hablan.' Can you imagine a regime whose criminal credo is 'the dead do not talk'? I do not believe God will tolerate it much longer."

Coot told Rodolfo that Mexico seemed hell-bent on challenging its master, like a burro charging a locomotive. Rodolfo chuckled. "Well, let us hope the locomotive doesn't hurt our burro too much."

4

El Paso, November 8, 1910

What the hell were we doing running guns into a foreign country at our age? And how could we be over fifty, when just day before yesterday it was 1875, two hell-for-stout, rough-ass boys skinny-dipping in the Black River on the northern edge of the San Carlos Indian Reservation? That could not be. Gotta be dreaming.

It was April of that year, Coot and I'd just turned sixteen, born six days apart. We hadn't a clue what the balance of the year had in store for us—important, life-turning events of great proportions for two boys. Events that grab and hold tight as pine sap stuck to your underarm curl if you're not careful while napping under a big ol' oozing tree. We were tender and tough, bristling with the spirit of youth minus wisdom's anchor.

For as long as I could remember, Coot and I, my papa, Coot's Uncle Doyl, and Coot's daddy before he died, had trailed on horseback northwest out of The Pass, heading for our annual, two-month hunting trip in the White Mountains on the eastern edge of the Arizona Territory. It was serious business as our families depended on the hunt for their year's supply of meat. Leastways that was what Coot and I were led to believe. Papa had over 2,000 prime goats on his 9,000-acre dry, high-desert ranch, land he leased from Old Man Zach White. If we had so many goats, why'd Papa go on an annual meat hunt? Three good reasons come to mind: one, Papa's goats were for selling, not for our table except on special occasions, though my mama observed tolerable few special anythings; two, those nanny goats gave lots of rich milk, and the *asadero* cheese we made from clabbered goat's milk sold for a premium in El Paso; but the third, and *by far* the most important reason Papa took off for two months out of every year, *was my mama*. That was reason enough for any sane man. Some folks said Mama might be a couple of bubbles off plumb, but mean or crazy, it was hard to tell the difference when one was subjected to a daily dose of that woman's cruel ways. Papa's two-month reprieve would put a smile on his face wide enough that you could drive a team of horses through. That grin, and his iron-stout will, had to see him through 'til next spring.

We could count on long hard days, but for two strong boys, it was all fun and challenge, a chance to prove our grit, our mettle. While we were still a long way from our prime, we were strong as Longhorn bulls.

Our destination was the confluence of the Black River and Pacheta Creek, a placid river, a gurgling, clear-running little stream. We called it "The Box," as the place was impassable for twenty miles upstream just a quarter-mile from our head-quarters. The difficult trip on horseback took upwards of eight days, the weather measuring our pace. After crossing the Frisco River, we passed through meadows ten miles wide, forty long, a God-given tread of green. Meadows of unending grasses of all varieties, smells, and tastes, tall dandelions peeking their bright yellow heads through the grasses, while tucked below, strawberry blossoms hiding their white.

We approached Rattlesnake Point from the northeast, trying to gauge our arrival at the Point with enough daylight to allow us to tiptoe the horses and mules down the steep, narrow trail before dark. Spring nights on the Point would always bring heavy frost, frozen water in our canteens. A high promontory that offered a view of forever.

One time, Coot and I were resting our horses before going down the trail to the river. Far below, a mated pair of Mexican eagles, flying golden, playing, darting, daring, catching an updraft, sailing them high above. They reached out to each other, locked talons, falling in a love swirl, a gyrating wheel, talons loosening, parting at the last moment, glided apart, swooped in a high arc above us.

Papa was sitting his horse behind us. "Boys, you just witnessed a rare ritual of play I have only witnessed once before in my entire life."

The narrow trail off Rattlesnake Point went through a crack in a rock ledge that fell off fifty-feet near straight down, then gentled out its slope along a foot wide hogback ridge to the meadow where the Black River ran, its flow flashed between the pines and oaks. From the top of Rattlesnake Point, you could make out a line shack, old beat-up, rusted-tin roof, lonely, forlorn. It housed our meat-drying racks, Uncle Doyl's prized dutch ovens, ropes, and other gear that we left behind last season. The sight of that line shack would invariably bring wet to my eyes. I'd bite my lip, look away from the men. Every year I'd promise myself not to let it affect me so, and every year I'd do the same silly thing, asking myself, *Why, Lord? Why does that dad-gum old line shack strike me down to my knees?*

The line shack's only company was the Black River and Pacheta Creek flowing close by. The Black didn't flow deep, but dark, in places so smooth, little flaws of wind-whipped patches of still water stirred into fleets of ripples. The forest was a vigorous mottle of trees, a true "coat of many colors," mostly Ponderosa pine towering above a sprinkling of maples, aspens, fluttering yellow-lime, heavy-green oak groves along the riverbank. The meadow, shape of a serving dish, would come to life during our early spring visits, grasses lying under a veiled profusion of flowers, red, yellow, blue, purple, and fragrances, heady, pungent, sweet as hay. In wet years, all manner of ferns grew in the deep shadows of the tall pines, like a thick, green comforter. It seemed a shame to ride our horses and mules through that blanket of perfection, as the animals stomped the ferns flat to the ground. Every dad-gum year Coot would catch me fretting over those ferns. He'd grin and call out, "Quit worrying about those ferns, Narlow. They'll grow back in a day or two, and you'll never know we passed this way." But, no doubt, the ferns knew of our approach, our passing, our lack of respect for their private rest.

The Black River formed an S-curve above our camp, flowing north to south at our headquarters area to the line shack, on past to Pacheta Creek. At that point, the river made a sharp turn to the west for 200-yards. There it met a sheer granite cliff, tremendous, unforgiving, that turned the flow back north for a wandering mile, then began its meander to the west past Bear Wallow Creek for a hundred miles, eventually catching up with the Salt River.

Its specialness was visited by no white men, only an occasional Apache, of whom we had no fear in this remote mark. The People'd known our fathers, our grandfathers for nearly a half-century, knowing them to be truthful men who admired the Apache, their ways, besides they had rescued an Apache princesses back around 1830. They had not forgotten. Our only visitor was a tall, lanky Apache named Many Fast Feet Two Sticks. No other visitors came to our camp.

Like most places in the west, Rattlesnake Point and the meadow below was named with a purpose in mind. Rattlers in the usual places waited along game trails for an unwary meal to pass by, most often at the river's edge. The area seemed to be a perfect nursery for the little varmints, a mottled gray-black, the shape and texture of a pine twig. Rattlesnakes during daylight were not much concern to us—it was the town folks who were bitten. While a nighttime encounter with a serpentine of its ilk was a peril to all. Those rattlers were joined by a cautious list of other cold-blooded creatures, black widows, scorpions, centipedes, as well as the common honeybee and wasp.

One hot day, Coot and I'd spied several rattlers before the sun was chest high. I asked if he'd ever wondered about why it was that all poisonous critters are cold-bloodied, the kind that relied on the sun for warmth. He replied, "No, I never wondered about it." I pressed the point, asking him why he didn't know that. He smiled. "Narlow, you didn't ask me if I knew that, you asked if I ever wondered about it." He chunked a rock at a testy mountain rattler. "I've also noticed that a considerable number of the two-legged, warm-blooded variety are also cold-blooded, but I've never wondered about that either."

That night we bedded down. "Hey, Coot, listen to the wind whinny through those big ol' pines. Papa says that every tree has a voice that speaks when the wind passes by. It sure seems to me that pine trees have the most to say by the rush of wind through their high boughs. They know about our past, our future, ancient, coveted mysteries. And they have stories and centuries of secrets to tell. But, you gotta be real quiet and listen close."

"Well, then," he said, "I reckon we'll never hear those centuries of secrets."

I allowed as much that he didn't know all he claimed.

"Like what?" he asked.

I thought a minute. "Well, like you don't know that . . . that . . . that birds ain't got a belly button."

"Heck, I know that." He rolled over, propped up his head. "Everybody knows that."

We hunted every other day, using the off-day to rest our horses and mules while we prepared our kill for the long trip back to the Pass. We jerked thousands of pounds of elk, deer, and bear meat. The jerked meat was much lighter to haul, retained its flavor, richness, its nutrients. Papa saw to it that nothing went to waste, never a man to pick many nits, but he was a certain nit-picker when it came to Nature's bounty, her gifts.

Papa would take on anybody, anywhere, when it came to protecting "his" friends, dumb animals in mankind's care. Like one time, armed only with a barrel stave, he took on two men for shooting a hummingbird with a double-barrel shotgun. Those men got their ears boxed good, making me fearful Papa'd do 'em in.

Papa was lank, knotty, tough as a mesquite rail, hands that never witnessed gloves, possessed the self-confidence of an iron wagon bar.

Papa, Uncle Doyl, and this place we called "The Box," they were all mighty special to Coot and me.

Coot's uncle Doyl, now he was a sight. Straight as a wagon tongue, long as a wagon track, a man whose life mission was teasing us boys without mercy. One scorcher-of-a-day, Coot and me were skinny-dipp'n in the Black River, just little tadpole-boys. That cold water would make you suck up your belly, catch your breath.

Uncle Doyl hollered out over the roar of the water, "You boys don't seem to be too worried about them turtles. Brave little tykes."

We dog-paddled over to the riverbank, tried to splash him. "There ain't no turtles in this river, Uncle Doyl. Ain't nuthin' in this water to be a'scairt of. Don't be a scaredy-cat, Uncle Doyl."

His eyebrows arched. "Oh, now boys, that's just what you think, but they're there, hiding, waiting to sneak up on you. Little buggers, but they be snappin' turtles. Best watch 'em real close-like, that's my recommendation."

We laughed. "Aw, Uncle Doyl, you beat all. You're just funnin' us. Why don't you go skinny-dipp'n with us? Bet you're a'scairt of those mean old turtles, ain't you, Uncle Doyl?"

He jerked up straight. "Dern tootin' I'm sceered of them snappin' turtles. Why, when I was a boy 'bout you boys big, me and this other boy, Henry Hawkins, we went skinny-dipp'n in this very river. Them turtles were sneakin' 'round in that dark water, under them boulders, just like they are this very minute. Anyway, all of a sudden, little Henry, he lets out a yelp you could hear way past the box canyon. He run, holding real tight to his private parts as he run a'shore. I followed him to see what was the matter with my little friend, and do you know that one of them snappin' turtles'd snapped on to little Henry's prune, grabbed a'holt, just a'danglin' there. Had a devil of a time getting that turtle to turn loose of poor Henry's prune—dang near bit it plumb off."

Me and Coot grabbed our prunes, high-tailed it out of there *right now*.

Uncle Doyl laughed at just about anything, saying life's too short to be taken too seriously. He never said he was sorry about a blessed thing, saying apologies wouldn't be fitting for a man. Coot adopted that credo. "Sorry" was a word I never heard him say.

Our headquarters centered on an ancient oak that had fallen at least a century ago, lying right there when our menfolk first came here as boys in 1822. The ground stayed damp under the cover of heavy pines, shielding the ancient oak from the summer sun, the winter months covering it under snow and ice. We covered the oak's heavy limbs with tarpaulins as a rain shelter, where scraps of elk and buffalo hides still draped, dangling from those dark limbs that our very own granddaddies used so long ago. Coot and I were convinced that old tree was the heavy bones and bleached skin of Kipling's *Elephints haulin' teak, In the sludgy, squdgy creek.*

Yep, Kipling's "elephint" might'a been hauling teak in an Indian "sludgy, squdgy creek," but ol' Coot and I were hauling Mausers and cartridges to Mexico behind a coal-belching locomotive.

Tornillo, Texas, November 27, 1910

Rodolfo began, "Things are gaining speed in Chihuahua. It is difficult to know where to begin, but your first shipment of rifles and cartridges could not have been better planned. Madero's men picked them up in Guadalupe Bravo, just across the Rio, and headed back into Chihuahua.

"You remember that Madero called for the struggle to begin on November 20. A man by the name of Toribio Ortega has been arrested in the past for simply planning a revolt. He was arrested again just recently, and released again. Nevertheless, on November 14, Ortega decided to go ahead with his plans. He and sixty men, many unarmed, stormed the residence of the local *politico* at Cuchillo Parado, who fled. Ortega's force has continued to grow over the past week.

"In Parral, and all western and southern Chihuahua, in the village of Namiquipa, revolutionaries gathered before the dawn of November 20. As the sun rose, they began shouting: '*Viva la revolucion. Viva Madero. Muerte a Porfirio Diaz*'. During the day, things quieted down, so quiet that the local police commander went home for the night, but was killed on the way. The soldiers threw down their arms, Namiquipa was taken over. Uprisings are occurring all over the state.

"Two men are emerging as military leaders under Francisco Madero in Chihuahua. A man by the name of Pascual Orozoco, and a man who lived on a *hacienda* near the ranch my parents owned, a man who I have known since his birth, Doroteo Arango. He never cared for his name, and goes by the name of Pancho Villa. If he finds a position of importance—and demonstrates an ability to lead—I will channel our rifles and ammunition to Villa.

"Now, gentlemen, let us discuss how you will be rewarded for your difficult task. What do you think is just compensation for you gentlemen?"

I said, "Fritz Hans-Smidt has already hit Coot up for a ten-percent 'delivery fee,' as he calls it. That's far too much for one man. We've talked it over, and if you think ten-percent is agreeable, that's plenty all right with us. We wired Fritz, not to get his approval, but to tell him what he could expect."

"Ten-percent for each of you and ten percent for Mr. Hans-Smidt?"

"No, ten percent total. To be divided among the three of us equally."

His dark eyes widened. "That seems rather paltry. But do you think that will be agreeable to Mr. Hans-Smidt?"

"Yes, Rodolfo," I said, smiling. "He's agreeable to anything Coot suggests."

"Then, it is decided. We will pay Mr. Hans-Smidt eighteen dollars for each rifle he delivers, five-cents for each cartridge, and ten-percent delivery fee to be split among the three of you when you pick up each delivery. Is that correct?"

Coot said, "Yes, that's it. My ciphering tells me that $253,000 calls for right at 12,240 ounces of gold. Around 760 pounds, no problem for my Reo. It's a six-wheel-drive, one-ton truck. But the delivery fee will not be due until the munitions have been delivered to you here in Tornillo, or any place you direct. You'll give us the gold for rifles and cartridges we are going to pick up. When you need dynamite, we'll buy it in El Paso."

"Well, as you prefer, but will Mr. Hans-Smidt be agreeable to wait for his delivery fee?"

"Oh, he'll go along with it all right," Coot said as he slapped me on the back. "Narlow explains high finance very well."

❂❂❂

Our train pulled into the Socorro depot at 7:45 in the morning. Coot pointed to a man in a pinstripe suit. "There's your Swiss candy man. You're about to find out exactly what pudg is all about."

As we stepped off the coach, Fritz asked, "Did you get the gold? Do you have my money?"

Coot squared around. "*What* did you say?"

Fritz began, "Did you get the gold? Do you have my—"

"Oh, I thought you said, 'Good morning, gentlemen. Did you have a pleasant trip?'" He wheeled around and headed for a warehouse. Hans-Smidt Imports painted in script above the façade, a wide concrete loading dock at the four-foot level, a rail spur ran the length of the dock.

Coot said over his shoulder, "Fritz, this is Narlow Montgomery—you'll be seeing a lot of him. Narlow will pick up most of the shipments and make arrangements with the railroad."

Fritz ran up beside me, offering his pudgy-silk hand. I grabbed it hard, clamped down like I was milking an unwilling nanny. Fritz didn't cry, but the telltale mist in his eyes screamed the thought was crossing his mind.

Coot jumped up on the loading dock, strolled through the double doors like he owned the place.

Fritz scurried up, rubbing his hand. "Hold on there. You'll take possession of those rifles and bullets when I am in possession of the agreed upon $230,000, *and* my one-third of the delivery fee. And you might as well know that ten-percent split between the three of us is *not* adequate, however, I will accept it this time. That comes to $237,666.66."

"Come on, Narlow. Grab the other end of this canister."

We loaded the last canister of ammunition in the boxcar, covered them and the rifle crates with a tarpaulin, tied it all down tight. All that time Fritz was scurrying around, whistle-breathing like an asthmatic.

Coot turned to me and said, "Give him the $230,000."

Fritz added, "*And* my one-third of the $23,000 delivery fee—that comes to $7,666.66."

"No, Mr. Hans-Smidt. That's *not* the way it's going be." Coot clasped his ham hock hands below the back of his hat, pulled his elbows back, stretched, wound tighter'n a Baby Grand. "That's not exactly how we see it. Narlow and I talked it over. We've decided that you get the extra penny. Your share is $7,666.67."

"Well, let's have it," Fritz demanded.

Again, Coot's hands went up to the back of his neck, pulled his elbows back, stretched, teeth clenched. The old goat was about to explode. "Narlow, define the word 'delivery' to this clown." Then he jumped down off the loading dock.

Fritz huffed-up his size-twenty-eight chest. "I define 'delivery' like everybody else, so pay me."

I said, "Fritz, you've pushed this past the safe zone. Watch it! Our agreement with Rodolfo Bustamante calls for the delivery fee to be payable upon delivery of the rifles and cartridges when they are *delivered to our customer*, either to *Senor* Bustamante, or possibly an *hombre* by the name of Doroteo Arango, alias *Senor* Pancho Villa."

"But I just *delivered* 10,000 Mauser rifles, and 500,000 bullets to you. I'm due my fee *right now*."

I handed Fritz the sack that contained the $230,000.

"You'll have to give me time to count all of this," he said.

Coot had not looked at Fritz, either at the train station, or at his warehouse. That could only mean one thing—Coot smelled a turd and had no desire to get a close look at this floater. But, he jumped back up on the loading dock, got right up in Fritz's pudgy face. "Well, Mr. Hans-Smidt, did Narlow explain the word 'deliver' to your satisfaction?"

"Well, I guess—"

"You *guess*? Do you want Narlow to go over it again. Want me to explain it to you?

"No, that won't—"

"No, *what*? Narlow didn't explain it? You don't want me to explain it to you? Which is it?" Coot winked, then asked, "Why don't you like me?"

"No—I mean, yes. Narlow explained it, but I do—but I don't, I—"

Coot jumped off the loading dock again. "Come on, Narlow. Let's get something to eat."

We started toward a Mildred's Café on Market Street, hadn't taken more than a dozen steps, Coot turned around, walked back, jumped up on the loading dock again. *Oh, shit.* And I believe those same two words were plastered on Fritz's forehead.

Coot got back in Fritz's pudgy face. "Mr. Hans-Smidt, we might as well have a clear understanding. *Right now.* We're likely going to be dealing with each other for a long time. Mr. Montgomery and I don't like doing business with men that we don't trust. Don't trust us. He just gave you $230,000, and what did you want to do? You wanted to count it. Good US greenbacks for your Mausers and *bullets.* Sight unseen, no questions asked. *We* have to trust *you. You* are going to trust *us.* We didn't open *one damn crate of rifles.* Didn't shoot off even *one damn bullet.* If we did that, we'd have to fire *every damn* one of those Mausers. Fire off *every damn* bullet in that boxcar. Now let me ask you, shithead. Would that make a lick of sense to you?"

Fritz stood, blinked.

"*Well?*" Coot demanded.

"No, Mr. Boldt, I don't think that would make any sense at all."

Coot jumped down, started toward me, turned again, motioned for Fritz to come down off the loading dock. I laughed out loud when Fritz scurried down the steps, tripped, and fell in the heavy gravel at Coot's feet.

Cook picked him up by his coat lapels, dusted him off. "And, Mr. Hans-Smidt, do you and me a favor. Don't ever piss-off Narlow Montgomery. *Ever again.* That's my recommendation."

5

El Paso, April 1, 1912

Several months went by without a hitch. Made the Socorro trip every two weeks. Not much to it. We took the train to Socorro, loaded a boxcar with rifles and cartridges, took the late train back to El Paso, slept all the way, switched the boxcar to the Southern Pacific rail line, and headed seventy-miles downriver to Tornillo on the early train, while enjoying a plate of ham, grits and red-eye gravy, washed down by a gallon of good, stout coffee. This gunrunning was right pleasant.

Then things went awry. The US government slapped an embargo on all export of guns and munitions to Mexico—just as Rodolfo predicted. Captured gunrunners in Mexico would be shot in the back attempting an arranged escape. If caught by the US feds, the accused wouldn't be shot,, but they'd be looking out through the steel bars of Leavenworth for forty years as their certain reward.

Not wanting the feds dictating our cause, we pressed Rodolfo to go forward. He held fast, saying he had it on good authority that Germans were infiltrating both sides of the revolution. Germany would stop at nothing to keep the US embroiled in Mexico's revolution and out of the political situation heating up in Europe. Unconfirmed reports even suggested Japanese involvement.

Rodolfo said he would notify Fritz Hans-Smidt. Coot insisted that we would take care of that chore for him when we returned to El Paso. I wired Fritz and explained Rodolfo's decision. I closed the telegram telling him that we were certain that we would soon be back in business. Fritz shot back to inform us that he had "thousands of boxes of Swiss chocolates and swizzle sticks. What am I supposed to do with them while you cool your heels waiting for Rodolfo Bustamante to make up his mind?"

Coot snatched the telegram out of my hand and headed for the door.

"Where you off to?" I asked.

"I'm going to the Western Union office. Until Fritz hears from us, he needs to know *exactly* where to store those Swiss chocolates and swizzle sticks."

6

Zara and I enjoyed three months of bliss. Both home at the same time, celebrated Christmas and New Years together, enjoyed a houseful of Papa's cherished old friends who gathered to celebrate his ninetieth birthday. Papa soaked in that day like he faced every day of his life, with warmth and humor.

As a boy, I'd experienced a deep sense of lonesomeness while working Papa's goats at Bishop's Cap. I got over the blues of lonesome as a young man, but became consumed with a far worse dread—*lost*. A full-grown man, lost in his own skin, unsure, mainly about the mysteries of fair damsels.

Women, in general, had stolen my compass. I adored them as a group. Loved being in their midst, surrounded by them, engulfed with their scented essence. There was no doubt about it—women returned my adoration. At mercantiles, on the street, both sides of the border, all sizes, shapes, and ages, I was their favorite. I charmed, teased them, got away with loose talk and flirtation in their company, chatter that would get another man shot. Nothing serious, they knew that far better than me. I was a friend. Their male friend. They trusted me.

I gazed at every available woman on the border, wondering if she was the one I could love. I asked myself a thousand times while talking small talk with one or the other of them, Are you the one I'll allow myself to love? Can I trust you—implicitly?

Never answered my own question. Never asked any of them the question. Never came to grips as to why that could be such weighty question for a full-grown man. Or was I?

But, I did marry Sophie, my first wife, when I was twenty-one, she was twenty-four. Never had any kids. She was frail, so insecure she'd rub the hide off a long-eared mule with her self-doubting. Four long years later, she died of diphtheria. The doc said there was no reason why she couldn't have survived, she *decided* to die.

The night she died, she told me she was tired, thought she could sleep.

I exploded. "*Goddamn it to hell*, Sophie! I'll—I'll . . ."

I left the bedroom, slammed the door behind me, then opened it. "I'm sorry, Sophie. It slipped out of my hand."

I fought the urge to go back in, rip the shades off the windows. Throw back the covers. Yank her to her feet. Shout in her face, "*Fight*, you goddamn lazy bitch, Sophie. *Fight!*" But, I knew her will was about to show itself.

I leaned against the bedroom door, thinking about a line from Nietzsche. I hated that goddamn line. Repulsed me. Reminded me of us. Haunted me since the moment I read it:

It's not the lack of love, but a lack of friendship that makes an unhappy marriage.

I squeezed my brow, my temples, turned to beat on the door, but only sagged, admitted that I didn't like, *hated* what I saw in her. Doubted I ever really loved her. Just wanted someone to coddle. Have a woman to lean on me, to love me. Not me love her. Not to love. Not at all certain I'm capable of love. For God's sake, *why?*

What was I? Why was I so loveless with a woman I married? *Why?* Why was I so hard, so cold? Somebody oughta horsewhip my ass. Mama's damnable horse quirt burst into my mind.

I was beat that night, but I knew going to bed would be a waste of time. I took a couch pillow into the hall and lay down in front of Sophie's door. Dozed, dreamed of a child's scream, a bull elk's call in the fall of the year. Dancing with daffodils. Life bared her bosom to the moon, ropy smoke crawled from under Sophie's door. In the mist, Na-Tu-Che-Puy appeared, dressed in ivory elk-skin britches, adorned in beads and eagle feathers, silver hair, braided, pounded pewter, his finger to his ear as if wanting me to listen. He spoke. I couldn't make out his words, something about his anger that I failed to tell him of the night my little sister died, the cry of the bull elk, something about—

I jumped awake. Bolted through the door, rushed to Sophie's side.

She was gone. A tender twenty-seven years old. Never gave herself a chance. I was guilt-ridden for not being there when Sophie needed me the most. I'd been off with Coot, buying a ranch I didn't need or want. Guilty for not yanking her out of that bed, slapping the shit out of her, talk some sense into her. Guilty for my thoughts, evil, cold. Unlovable. Unloving. Unforgiving.

The morning after Sophie's funeral, I decided not to saddle up, but to walk to town. At the foot of the concrete steps that led down to Utah Street, a petite Mexican woman was seated on the bottom step. Her skin, the color of rich, raw, fresh-hewn mesquite.

I stepped around her. "*Buenos dias, senora.*"

"*Buenos dias, Senor* Montgomery."

I turned back to her. Since I did not recognize her, I asked, "*Senora?*"

"*Senor*, you no know me." She stood, and offered her strong, brown hand. "I am Ines Contreras, *a sus ordenes*." She patted her chest. "Me speak little English, *pero* I read pretty very well. *Yo voy* school many years. Come here my home in Zacatecas. Loose my family *y mi casa* in a bad flood. Come here for work. I work hard, cook good. You paper say—you wife die—she die *estrangulador, verdad? Pobrocita senora*," she said, gripping her throat.

"*Si, Senora* Contreras. *Estrangulador*—the strangler. We call it diphtheria. But it kills in either language."

Worst day of my life, best day of my life, the day Ines Contreras came into my life as my housekeeper.

◎◎◎

Coot's only try at wedded bliss struck during his only semester at the University of Colorado. He came home married to a comely, stout-breasted lass by the name of Geraldine Millsap-Boldt. First time I ever heard of a woman keeping her "maiden" name, as my experience in that regard had been scarce. Her husband's demeanor suggested that Geraldine was also short on experience—as a maiden. Papa and I soon learned that Geraldine came "accompanied by a biscuit in her oven," as Coot termed her condition. Funny thing about Geraldine and that biscuit. While she continued to sport her ill-temper, had the appetite of three wrestlers, she never experienced morning sickness, never produced the biscuit she claimed. Coot knew he'd been had. But why?

They fought, she moved out, leaving Coot at his farm, but never granted him a divorce. She screamed, "There's never been a divorce in the Millsap-Connecticut family going back 200-years, and we're damn certain not starting with *you*, Coot Asshole Boldt!"

Geraldine was from money, bought the biggest, grandest mansion in all of El Paso, just across from my house on Utah Street.

One afternoon, right after she moved in, I heard Coot come through the screen door off the alley, helping himself to what was left of the *posole* and *bolillos*. He stood at the kitchen counter like he took all of his meals, washed it down with a quart of buttermilk. He belched, blew wind, put the dirty dishes in the washbasin, poured not one drop of water on them to soak. He'd shuffle in and say, "What's happenin'."

Zara'd gone upstairs to finish some Suffrage correspondence before Coot arrived, so I took a brandy out on the front porch, lit a *cigarro*, sat down on the swing, put my feet up on the railing. Oh, how could sitting feel so good? The sun was low, warm, drenched orange, sunset wine. I wanted to smoke my stogie, sip my brandy, go to bed for a week.

Coot came out, plopped down hard on my swing. It lurched back hard, spilled half my brandy. He grinned. "What's happenin'." He sat a minute, smiling at himself, then as usual, took his left boot off, then the sock, then his right boot, then the sock.

I always found that unusual in Coot. Most men, me included, take their right boot off, then their left boot, then their socks in the same order. One time as an experiment, I tried taking my left boot off first, then the sock. Found it a strange habit.

He sat grinning, gazing across the street at Geraldine's house, rubbing his feet, "milking" them as he called it. "Got any more of that brandy, or are you going to hog it all?"

"Help yourself." I realized that statement was unnecessary, as well as an invitation. An invitation to say 'good-bye' to an expensive, six dollar bottle of Spain's finest. I was determined to play this out with Coot. Over the years, he'd developed this habit of saying, "What's happenin'," and I'd start blabbing like he pulled a light-chain.

He padded barefoot back out on the porch gripping only the bottleneck of the brandy, no glass, and one of my cigars.

"Couldn't find a glass?"

"Glass's ass." He grinned as he bit off a third of the cigar. He never put a flame to a fine Cuban, constructed so lovingly with such artful pride, blessed by the gods to be smoked, enjoyed by its deserving possessor. But that fine stogie would be chewed up like so much licorice. He took a long draw on the bottle, bit off another third of my fifty-cent cigar, smelled the remainder, then stuck it in the end of the brandy bottle, turned it upside down, let the cigar soak until the brandy dripped off his fingers. He righted the bottle, removed the cigar, stuffed it in his shirt pocket as he took another long swig, licked his fingers, patted his tobacco-brandy-stained shirt pocket, grinned. "For later."

He took another long pull on the bottle, sat his stout frame down on the swing, looking at Geraldine's two-story, yellow-brick mansion across the street. "Wonder who's life she's made miserable today?"

Our veranda was cool, dark, shaded and protected by a swooping overhang of the roof to the west, adorned with honeysuckle vines. So dim, a passerby would have no notion we were there.

Coot motioned for me to look when Geraldine came out on her east-facing porch, dressed in a fine house-gown and silk robe. "Let's see what she's up to. This gal's goofier'n a passel of bats."

We watched her for several minutes. She turned with her back to us, seemed to be doing something with her arms and hands, doing something on the front of her robe, or in it. Coot giggled down to his toenails.

I asked. "What's she doing?"

"She called it, 'cultivating her breasts.' Says her mother showed her that trick. Takes a deep breath, then pushing her breasts up, pushing them up and out, then releases her breath, and strokes them on the way down. Look at her go! She'll have them things waving up in the breeze like mule's ears."

After a bit, Geraldine stopped her breathing and pushing, turned, peering around, up and down the street, then her gaze shot in our direction. She leaned forward, her hand went up to shield her eyes, stepped sideways, never taking her gaze off our veranda, trying to focus-in on what she thought was gawking in her direction.

Of a sudden, she jumped back, pulled her robes tight about her blossoming bosom, whirled around, and beat it back through her front door. Geraldine may have been a menace to Coot, but she was a grand source of entertainment for me.

I never got a firm handle on how he could have ever partnered-up with the likes of that swish of a lass, so shallow that the money her father regularly sent could do little to hide.

My own Zara was a lady, through and through, the daughter of Ambrose Calhoun and his former wife, Betty Bernice. Everyone called him, "Bo," while he attempted to paste the nickname, "BB," on his rather haughty wife. It wasn't long after we met the cooing couple that she announced while we were gathered at Juarez Avenue's Cave Restaurant, that she was leaving him, taking their two daughters back to Dallas. About broke his heart, but she'd made up her substantial mind and caught the next train east. Bo regularly sent money chasing after the three, but his financial support of his family was never acknowledged.

The girls were allowed a three month summer visit with their father in El Paso, a time that they secretly adored. They were free! Free from the starchy existence they endured at Sacred Heart School for Girls. The proctor at their dorm,

Charity Hall, was a young girl from Panama, only four years older than Zara, who had hopes of one day being a nun, a beautiful young lady by the name of Rose. Zara left Sacred Heart, then shortly, the would-be nun got her wish.

Zara attended a New Orleans finishing school for two years, then returned to El Paso the same day that Coot and I returned from Washington. We were honored for our years as scouts for the army near the conclusion of the Indian Wars. When Coot's mama heard that he received an accommodation for reading sign, she said, "*Hummp*! That boy can't read his own fool name."

In spite of our twelve-year age difference, Zara immediately spoke of marriage. She'd always idolized me while she was growing up, but the beautiful young woman who came to town after New Orleans was no little girl in pigtails. I fought the idea of marriage like a starved mountain lion. I'd already failed at marriage, and over those many months of our courting, I became even more determined, more fearful that if we married, I'd spoil Zara's chances for a happy, loving life that she'd so meticulously prepared herself for. I loved Zara so much I just didn't want to take that chance, to spoil a single day of that beautiful lass' life.

Desperation had me by the throat. "Zara, I've told you about my mother. You know how hateful she is, how full of vitriolic copper-acid that replaced her soul so many years ago. I fear that in time, I'll be just like her. You could have any man you desired from Dallas to San Francisco. I'm older, nearly fourteen-inches taller than you. Why would you want an old fly-blown, son-of-a-goat farmer like me?"

"*Hush that talk*, Narlow Montgomery! I'll not hear of my future husband being spoken of in that manner. You're a fine, respectable, loving man. You may have been influenced by your mother, but you reflect far too much of your father to allow that prejudiced view to play any further part in your life. You are far-too-good a man for such foolishness. The only thing that's too short is life. Let us refrain from wasting a second of it. Besides, the difference in our ages is of no concern to me, my short stature should not concern you, for I can assure you that it will not hinder my abilities or performance, whether standing up, or flat on my back."

7

Confluence of the Rio Grande and Cuchillo Negro Creek, May, 1913

IB Crane was a friend of Coot's and mine, a man whose mind never quite made it to adolescence, born between the dates of Coot's and my own birthdates. When Papa was trying to persuade Coot and me to go to college when we were sixteen, I reminded Papa that we could already do our multiplication tables up to fourteen-times-fourteen, that IB and all the other kids couldn't even get to seven times eight. I winced when Papa scolded me for using a simpleton as my measure, a poor lad with both feet in the same stirrup.

IB had a twin sister, whose given name was Shelly Brom. The lass was not only dumb, as ignorant folks called it, mute as we refined people refer to the condition, she had a ruby-red alligator skin layer on the entire right side of her face and neck. The poor girl was plumb hard to look at. But the stubby-legged thing was quick as a cottontail, and regularly set IB's supper table with the snap of her ever-present slingshot.

IB and I sat on the bank of the Cuchillo, our feet dangling in the chill of the stone-cold water. The chill caught our breath. I splashed IB. He grinned.

Squishing my toes in the golden sand, I hollered over the roar of the stream, "*Hey, Bo.* How long's it been since you went barefoot, and squished your toes in sand like this?"

"Not since last spring when IB and I almost had to hogtie you to get you to come along. I don't understand why you always put me off. Like pulling teeth getting you to come up here." He jerked up on his cane pole. "Dag-nab it. Do a little fishin'."

The Cuchillo's flow slows, swirls, foams, as it enters the Rio Grande. There were plenty of bass, clear blue skies, a gallon jug of rye cooling in the Cuchillo. Fresh, cold water off the snow banks of the Mimbres Range forty miles to the west. The hand-sized bass were cooperative. We fished until dark, catching more than we'd ever need, kept what we wanted, gave the balance away to the *pobres* who lived along the Rio.

I was in no hurry to get back to running guns. Doing nothing suited me, giving me time to catch up on my dreaming, recalling old memories. Recollections of the late spring day when Coot and I began our *Hombres de Campo* trek, floating this very creek, the Rio after a major storm and flood, Papa and Uncle Doyl caught in a flashflood torrent in Maricopa Canyon. Uncle Doyl lost. A congregated host of memories of Papa and me chasing goats up Red Rock Canyon, him on Traveler, me on a stout burro or afoot. Memories of Uncle Doyl's way of plastering a mile-wide smile on my face. I looked downstream at Bo, realized how much he and Uncle Doyl favored. They laughed easily, neither of them particularly fashioned for work. Uncle Doyl often said, "I can sit right down close to a chore, something begging to be done. Give me a minute, I'll nod right off."

There was nothing unusual about Bo reminding me of our annual fishing trip, but this time there was a note of urgency in his voice. I didn't think anything of it, just wrote it off as an old man's way of making sure he got his way. He told the same old corny jokes, and after we had a couple of swigs from our jug, rolled up a couple of smokes, we'd both get tickled. Laugh so hard sometimes he couldn't even finish his yarn. We'd roll in the sand, belly-laughing. We had no concerns, just had to keep an eye on IB's consumption of the contents of the burlap-wrapped jug, cooling in the creek.

Something was on Bo's mind, but for whatever reason, he was hesitant to come right out with it. After supper, I rolled back on my bedroll. "Okay Bo, let's have it. You'd have a lot better time tomorrow if you'd get whatever's on your mind out in the open."

He sat up. "What the hell you talking about? I don't have anything stuck in my craw."

"I didn't say anything was stuck in your craw."

IB giggled. "I reckon it be *yor* craw's what's stuck, Nar-low."

Bo lay back, rolled to face me. "Well, I did have a little idea I wanted to kick around. See what you thought. It's been bugging me for months, been thinking about our Mexican *amigos*, that little revolution of theirs. Down Mexico way, you know. You and Coot, you're banging your tails, supplying the hardware they need. I've come up with a plan. Listen to this. We're going to start the MRAF—the glorious Mexican Revolutionary Air Force."

IB bolted up. "Wh-ut?"

I asked, "*You* are going to do *what?*"

"*Hold on, now.* Hear me out. My Dallas contact telegraphed me two weeks ago, telling me that he's located a Curtiss Pusher that's equipped with a 50-caliber cannon mounted in front of the pilot. That cannon can throw a 600-grain bullet over a mile and—"

"Looks to me like you and that Dallas contact of yours have all the kinks out of your idea. But, let me ask you, *Generalissimo* Ambrose Calhoun, what are you going to do for a pilot? Reckon President Wilson will lend you one?"

"Well, I was thinking that's where you would come in—"

"*Whoa.* If you think that I—if you think I—just exactly what do think I'm going to do?"

IB said, "I thinks he wants you'ta fly a air-plane, Nar-low."

"Look, Narlow. My cousin, Jimbo, has an airport west of Las Cruces, training civilians to fly. Success rate one-hundred percent. Hell, flying one of those crates is not difficult at all. Takes Jimbo an hour to teach a man to fly. Fly real good, too."

"Yeah, flying real good around the airport in the cool of the morning, nobody shooting at him. But, let's see Jimbo take on a battalion of juiced-up *Federales*, with every damn one of those bastards shooting at his ass."

A thought crossed my mind. "By the way, does Coot know about this?"

"Well, I did mention it to him."

"And?"

"He said he thought it was a damn good idea. Suggested I talk it over with you."

"Coot said no such thing. You and that bald bastard cooked up this whole thing. Put you up to enticing me to learn to fly. Didn't he, Bo?"

"Well, it wasn't *exactly* like that."

We talked about it all night, and agreed that if Bo would learn to fly, I'd give it a try. The next morning Bo was up early packing our gear.

"Where you going?"

"Jimbo's airport. Be there by noon. You'll be a pilot an hour later."

IB giggled. "I cain't wait. I think Nar-low's skaid."

⊚⊚⊚

Jimbo's two airplanes appeared to be a mated pair of nervous, flopping sandhill cranes.

When I sat in the cockpit, a board seat that Bo'd promised to occupy, I asked Jimbo about the Blackburn Monoplane's brakes.

"Ain't got no brakes. Push the stick to the left, she goes left. Right, right. Pull the stick, up she goes, push the stick, down she goes." Jimbo explained vacuum, how it's the air *over* the wing that keeps it aloft, not the useless wind below. "There are three things that all pilots need not concern themselves with. The length of the airstrip behind, the altitude above, the amount of petro stored on the ground. When you're coming in to land, watch for blowing dust. The wind will pick it up at around thirty-five miles an hour. If it's a crosswind, bring her on in, nudge her like she's your bed partner, buck her windward, bring her down low, slow to a crawl. She'll bounce down like a robin on a birdbath."

IB asked, "How come you don' worry 'bout the air up above?"

"Hush, IB," I said. "I'm concentrating."

Jimbo said that flying was something you either do or don't, can or can't, will or won't. "Your job, Narlow," he said with a wide smile, "is to find out whether it's do, can, will, or don't, can't, won't. Try to do it without killin' yourself."

As Jimbo was telling me all there was to know about man's new venture, Na-Tu's stern teachings and Pythagoras' edict kept buzzing around in my head, *Never do anything which thou dost not understand.* And I damn certain dost not understand what would keepeth me and that stick-and-canvas-flopping-crane in the air.

Wind Mesa, Santa Teresa Land Grant, Five Miles NW of El Paso, May 27, 1913

I went to Dallas by train to take delivery of our Curtiss Pusher. The factory representative, a tall slick, Rupert Thaddeus Kuykendall, sidled over. "How do you plan on getting this pretty thing back to El Paso, mister?"

"Well, it flies. I'm a pilot. Planned on flying her home."

He grinned. "Oh, I dunno about that, Mr. Montgomery. Might take you a while."

"How's that?"

"Well, sir, it's like this. This little baby's equipped with a pretty small fuel tank. Enough to keep her up for only thirty-five miles, *tops.* Now, I may be wrong, but the last time I checked, El Paso's well over 600-miles pretty dern near due west of Dallas. My calculations tell me that's upwards of twenty-five tankfuls. You'll spend more time looking for a place to buy gasoline than flying this bird. Best put her on a rail flatcar. That's my recommendation."

Mr. Kuykendall arranged to have the plane transported to the shipping yard, and loaded on a flatcar. I caught a passenger train, as the freight train would take three days to reach El Paso. I spent my time waiting for delivery of our new toy by helping clear a spot for our airstrip.

We decided on a high sandhill mesa that overlooked the Rio, the Franklin

Mountains of El Paso to the east, Mexico and the *Sierra de Juarez* to our south, a thousand yards from the Mexican border, just out of rifle range. After the greasewood and mesquite were cleared, we dragged the strip until it was pretty level, kinda smooth. Coot pointed out that the sand had plenty of silica, that if we wet and rolled it good, gravel would not be necessary. I talked IB Crane into bringing up his team of mules and a borrowed roller.

I explained to him how we wanted the strip rolled, east to west, no weaving around causing ruts. IB set his mind working through all those confusing instructions, and pretty soon, he grinned, whistled-up his team through the half-inch gap between his buck teeth. "*Hoo-ah*, there. *Hoo-ah*, turn, you sum-sa-bit-ches, turn your asses 'round! *Hoo-ah, hoo-ah, yyuu, yyuu.*" With a great flourish, he got the team turned, and they happily made their way to the east end of the strip.

Bless ol' IB's heart. I recall the first day that he, Coot, and I walked the eight miles to a one-room school house down at Frontera, snuggled up against the Rio. It was our first day of formal schooling, IB's last. The three of us turned eleven the previous March. But this was mid-November, and since our school room had no heat, the teacher took his brood out to the warming sun. That's about the time that IB disappeared. While the city kids were sorting through their tin lunch pails, Coot and I lay down by the Rio. About that time, he said, "Looky yonder." Coming down the lane we'd walked that very morning was IB, skipping along with not a care in his private world, appeared to be hiding something under his shirt. Mr. Pembrooke, our teacher from back east, discovered that IB'd stolen the pencil sharpener right off the wall by the chalkboard while the class was outside. He'd taken his prize home, Mrs. Crane turned him around, told him to return the pencil sharpener.

IB said, "Mis-ter Pem-brooke, sir, Mama tolt me to give you this here pencil shar-pen-er that I stolt whild you wuzn't teachin' on the inside cuz you wuz teachin' on the outside. Mama tolt me to tolt you that I won't be comin' back to school. No more."

◎◎◎

Coot and I met the 6:30 morning train on the third day to take delivery of the Curtiss Pusher. We unstrapped her, eased her down the incline to the rail yard, and pushed her out on Overland Street.

Coot decided that rather than beat up our new airplane dragging it across the Rio, then up to our sandhill airstrip, that I'd fly it over there. I was reluctant, saying it was against the law to fly an airplane off the streets of El Paso. He countered with the logic that El Paso didn't have any such ordinance.

We topped off the tank, pushed her around to the wind. I got in, buckled my lap harness, and was all set to tell Coot to give the propeller a twist.

My heart sank. "*Aw shit.*"

"What's wrong?"

"Look who's walking his cat over there."

"Richard Spency—so?"

"That loud-mouth, prissy bastard will tell everybody in town what we're up to."

"So?"

"Zara still doesn't know anything about me taking up flying, been out of town for two months. But somehow or another, she'll know every detail by nightfall."

"Price of fame."

Coot gave the propeller a mighty twist. She fired up, blowing smoke clear across West Overland Street, right at Richard Spency. His cat hissed, jumped up in his arms, scratching and clawing.

◉◉◉

A week later, the four of us, Bo, Coot, IB, and I, sat eating sausage and tortillas, sitting on the end of our new airstrip. Our perch was a high sandhill mesa, overlooking the irrigated valley that stretched five miles east to the foothills of the El Paso mountains, *Sierra Juarez* to the south. We still had no word from Rodolfo Bustamante as to whether we were back in the gunrunning business. Off to the southeast toward Juarez, we'd heard an occasional rifle shot, smoke from burning buildings. Rumors had been floating around that some of Villa's men were in Juarez, taunting the Federales while sizing up their defenses.

The Curtis was marginal at completing its assigned task. Underpowered, limited range. To test it, we loaded it with a hundred-sixty pounds of sandbags. When I crow-hopped back in, Coot asked, "How'd that feel to you?"

"Like an innocent bystander waiting for a train wreck."

Coot and I talked about removing the machinegun mounted in front of the cockpit, figuring it and its cartridge belts weighed close to a hundred pounds.

IB insisted that we leave it be.

Coot playfully cuffed him, "Okay, boss, if you say it stays, it stays."

We built a shelf at the top and left of the cockpit, rigged a rope looped around my right leg so I could yank the release mechanism, figuring to use it to offload rifles, ammunition, whatever the reason for the flight into Mexico.

That afternoon, a messenger on a big black mule brought a letter from Rodolfo who was hopeful that we could assist a squad of fifteen *Villistas* stranded twelve miles south of Juarez. Rodolfo closed his note with a sentence that caught Coot and I by the shorthair: *I realize that my request may put Narlow and your flying machine in great hazard, but if you feel it can be accomplished without undue risk, my dear deceased wife's family would greatly appreciate it. For you see, Capitan Antonio Munoz is in command of those fifteen men. He is my nephew, the son of my wife's sister. He and his few men have been in Juarez to scout the city in advance of Villa's planned attack in late fall. The information they have gathered will prove invaluable.*

Bo was near violent in his opposition to trying such an outlandish thing. But Coot blew him off, telling him we owed Rodolfo. Coot sent Bo and IB back to El Paso to purchase twenty 30-30 repeaters, 225 cartridges, fifteen rounds per stranded man, ten canvas water bags, and bunch of braised meat and tortillas.

Bo questioned why so few cartridges per man. Coot explained, "Cartridges are heavy. Those men won't be fighting a war. They need help, just enough for a fighting chance to get back to Villa."

IB chimed in. "Fif-teen cart-riches don't seem too tol-erat-ble a load."

While they headed off to town, Coot and I got to figuring how many trips south of Juarez, how many rifles per trip, how many water bags per trip, the cartridges, food. We figured four trips, four hours minimum, and that was cutting it slim. Rodolfo's message said that the men would tie a flag on a mesquite west of the rail line to *Ciudad* Chihuahua. A small white flag, twelve miles south of Juarez, on one of a million mesquites along that long line. *No problema!*

When Bo and IB came back with the supplies, IB jumped out and ran up to us. "Coot, Coot. Guess what? Whiles wes was in El Paso, Bo axd me ta check the oal in the Reo. And I did, 'n guess what? Y'all be right pleased that yor truck don't scarcely hardly don't need no oal."

Coot grinned. "You checked the oil and found out that old truck don't scarcely hardly don't need no oal? Well, thank you kindly, IB. That's a load off my mind. Know who you remind me of, old pal of mine? Andrew Jackson, back in the Battle of New Orleans. He said to his men, 'Elevate those guns a little lower!'"

That pleased IB more than a spoon of chocolate syrup.

We divided the supplies into four stacks, and I took off. Alone again, I thought back to when Coot first found his old Reo in a junkyard. Originally equipped with a chain drive that rattled and groaned its corrupted arrangement, Coot reconfigured the monster with two sets of rear wheels with driveshafts. It proved to be a vast improvement over the factory model—a "race truck," as Coot called it. He'd never hear it from me, but the man was a mechanical genius.

On the return leg of the third trip south, I turned and headed back up the track to Juarez. Up ahead, a track-repair crew. I decided to break the boredom of their day, dropped the Curtiss down to fifteen feet, its propeller appearing as a giant buzz-saw destined to chew them in half. As I flew over, I heard much foul language and a loud thump under the bi-wing, flew back to Wind Mesa, and as I dropped it to the strip, its shadow on the strip cast a strange shadow of something protruding from the Curtiss' underbelly.

I taxied in, cut the engine, Coot came over. "What's that you have sticking out from the Curtiss?" He reached under, yanked something, stood, holding an ax. "What's this?"

IB giggled. "Whur'ja get thet, Nar-low?"

I laughed. "So, that's what I heard when I flew low over that track-repair crew. One of them must have thrown that ax up at me as I flew by."

Coot checked the engine. "Smells like hot metal. Any problem coming back?"

"Yeah, she seemed a bit sluggish. What do you think?"

Coot checked the carburetor, said it smelled like burning metal, asked if I sensed anything wrong, different. I said that it seemed more sluggish than usual. He adjusted the carburetor, thinking the fuel mixture might be off.

We loaded the two remaining rifles and a canvas bag of water, I poured the coal to the Curtiss, but just as the bi-wing was about to lift off, the motor quit, fired up again, died. She and I went over the lip of the runway and slid to the bottom of the dune. To the *very edge* of the Rio, muddy water lapping at her propeller.

I was okay. The Curtiss was okay. IB ran and slid down the steep dune ahead of Coot and Bo, IB hysterical. "Nar-low! You okay, Nar-low? You done wreck'd yor air-plane. We gotta get you to a host-ipal!"

"I'm all right, IB. Take it easy, my friend." I wasn't in any better condition than IB, as evidenced by me sitting still for several minutes while I gathered strength to climb out of that lame bird.

Coot grinned. "Reminds me of you as a scruffy nine-year-old on a burro.

Sliding straight down Red Rock Canyon in hot pursuit of coyote with a newborn kid in its mouth."

Coot pulled the Curtis back up the sandhill with the Reo, slow and easy. Coot admitted that he was no airplane mechanic, that we needed someone who was familiar with airplanes. Like a man named Jimbo. He flew in, sniffed around, looked the Curtiss over with great care. "Ain't nothin' wrong with this contraption. Timing's off, carburetor's *way* the hell off."

Coot grinned.

8

Tornillo, Texas, June 1913

"Rodolfo," Coot said, "you should have seen the look on Narlow's face when he realized a railroad worker'd thrown that ax up at him. Our pilot was a little chagrinned."

Rodolfo laughed. "Well, gentlemen, that is quite a story. I humbly thank you for going to the rescue of Captain Anthony Munoz. He was a favorite nephew of my dear wife. And thank you for flying your Curtiss Pusher down here so I could see and touch a real flying machine. You purchased it with the idea of using this machine in our gunrunning operation?"

"Well, that's what we had in mind," I said. "But I'm afraid that idea has severe limitations. Coot had to drive the Reo down to meet me at the halfway point with petro. Thirty-five miles is about the most I can get out of it. When I landed just now, there wasn't enough fuel to start a weenie roast."

Rodolfo lowered his broad chin to the manicured hand resting on his lapel. "Hmm."

"What?" Coot asked.

"Oh, I was just thinking. It's a shame your airplane's range is so limited. If it had more range, you might save two dear friends of mine from a firing squad in Samalayuca."

"Samalayuca is within my range," I said. "The fifteen men we delivered the rifles to were just south of the garrison at Samalayuca."

"*Splendid*," Rodolfo said, his dark eyes dancing. "Perhaps you and your flying machine could save my friends after all."

"Who are these gents and how do I find them?"

"Oh, you must hurry to save them. A firing squad is scheduled for tomorrow's sunrise. Mexico is never late with their executions. The drama, you know. Soldiers will open the garrison gates precisely fifteen minutes before the first ray of sun appears over the mountains. My friends will be escorted through the gates, hands bound behind their backs. They will be stood before the east wall. The firing squad will march to their positions. The *comandante* will raise his saber and shout, *Preparen! Apunten! Disparen! Fuego! Ya!*" No pomp or ceremony, over in an instant."

I asked, "What can one man flying solo do to save your friends?"

"I am afraid I do not know the answer to your question."

Coot jumped to his feet. "I've got an idea! Most Mexicans have never heard of an airplane, much less seen one. The sight of one would scare hell out of them. But, who are these friends of yours?"

"I met them long ago. Gregorio Gonzalez, a zealot for Mexico's freedom. The other, a confidant of his, Father Estevan, an excommunicated priest, defrocked some years ago. I do not know how, but they could be very useful to us in our own endeavors to help the revolutionaries."

"Is there any way to get a message to them?" Coot asked. "Can you supply them with horses?"

"Yes, indeed. Samalayuca is only a few miles due west of here. I can have men and horses waiting for them near the garrison well before sunrise tomorrow morning. What would be the message for them?"

"Refuse blindfolds if offered. Tell them to expect the Lord. An angel of death will drop from the sky. When they see it, prepare to run like the dickens due north. Have your men and horses waiting 400-meters north of the garrison. Narlow and his machinegun should be able to give them support. Draw attention away from your friends."

Rodolfo smiled when I said, "Yeah, ol' Narlow will be up there like a pregnant *pato*, while Speedy Gonzalez and an excommunicated priest, running like hell from what will no-doubt be shooting *at me*."

Rodolfo laughed. "Well, gentlemen, when you finish that chore tomorrow morning, will you be ready to go back to work? I must remind you that the arms embargo imposed by your President is still in effect. However, you have pressed me, even though gunrunning is illegal. But illegal or not, the Mexican government's troops are still getting weapons from outside the country, *and* they are now producing weapons of their own.

"If you are ready to proceed, then let us load up the 12,240 ounces of gold. Can we assume there has been no increase in the price of the Mausers?"

"No increase in the price," Coot said, "but we won't be needing 12,240 ounces—only 11,500 ounces from now on."

Rodolfo's face broadened, his dark eyes arched. "I do not understand. Has there been a decrease in the price of Mausers?"

"No, just a decrease in the delivery fee. Narlow and I decided not to take our share of the fee. Fee's cut down to Fritz's share of $7,667."

"Why on earth would you be willing to put yourselves in danger. Take yourselves away from your families and business interests, without being paid?"

I said, "Because we leased part of our Camel Mountain Ranch for a hell of lot more than that lava mountain is worth. Coot thinks we're rich, should hire out to you free of charge."

"Rodolfo, what this character means is, we don't need your money. Our way of helping your fight for Mexico. We owe you, owe you more than we have the means to ever repay."

"I have never been so flattered in my entire life, but gentlemen, I must insist. I cannot allow you to go unpaid."

I said, "Rodolfo, our friend of almost forty years, to quote Shakespeare from his, *Winter's Tale*, 'You pay a great deal too dear for what is given freely.' Coot and I have the last word."

Rodolfo smiled. "As you wish. Now, perhaps we should notify Mr. Hans-Smidt that you will be arriving for another shipment. I am certain he is eager to make another sale."

Coot got busy at the telegraph key.

Rodolfo said, "My word, Coot! I am surprised at the language with which you are addressing Mr. Hans-Smidt."

Coot smiled, kept on tapping.

☺☺☺

Coot twirled the prop and came around to me. "I'll see you at the half-way point back to El Paso. Don't push this yellow crate. We're in no rush."

70

When we met at the refueling spot, I asked, "By the way, mind telling me what you think I'll do when I get to Samalayuca? Just fly around, let the *Federales* take potshots at me?"

"No time to explain. I'll pick up Bo and IB and a small barrel of dynamite in town. Road's good. I'll beat you to El Paso."

I flew over, spied Coot's Reo sitting in front of Travis Paul's Pretty Good Hardware Store and Spider Traps. Bo and IB waved up at me.

When the three of them churned up the road to Wind Mesa, IB jumped out of the Reo and took off running, yelling over his shoulder, "I's skaid'a thet dy-no-mite! *Real* skaid. I ain't touchin' the stuff."

Coot laughed. "You don't have to touch the stuff. Come on back, IB." He turned to me. "Narlow, this will work. Put this keg of dynamite on the shelf of the Curtiss. You fly in low, smoking a stogie. Time it, stick the stogie on the fuse. Release the keg so she'll blow when she rumbles through the gate. We'll secure the keg with this stiff hemp rope to this strut under the shelf, bring the rope around the keg, tie a hard slipknot. Being a slipknot, it'll release when you yank on it. Take the rope around the keg, the loose end comes in there with you, tie it to your leg above the knee. When you're ready to drop the keg, your left arm is on the outside of the rope, and all you have to do is jerk both knees to the right, the knot slips, off she goes. Simple, foolproof, efficient, brilliant."

We were back at the strip at 4:00 in the morning. "Now, remember, Narlow, come in as low as you can when you approach the garrison. Being low and in poor light will make it harder for the soldiers on the ground to see what's coming until you're *right on them*. They'll be confused, never seen an airplane before. Line up the Curtiss with the garrison's front gate. Time the release, stick the end of your stogie on—"

"Damn it, Coot, we've been over that a dozen times. Twist that prop!"

He reached up, feathered the machinegun's cartridge belt, pulled back the charging lever and slammed it home. He patted the barrel, winked, he and IB picked up the skirts of the Curtis, turned me into the early eastern breeze. I sailed down the strip and headed south, followed the same rail track south as only three days prior.

Through the early dust haze, I spotted the cream-yellow sands of Samala-yuca, the wooden, block-shaped garrison to the south.

Come in low, keep the nose of the Curtiss lined up with the front gate of the garrison . . .

Off to the west, men with rifles, officer at the ready, two men standing before an east wall. I flew over a tall line of elms, stiff breeze in the open cockpit, cigar blazing in my mouth, brought the Curtiss down just five feet above ground level, lit the fuse, counted to three, pulled the rope, the keg tumbled, I jerked back on the stick, clearing the garrison by a foot. The dynamite explosion shook the Curtiss far worse than I expected. *Must have struck their ammunition storage. Too much damage for a small keg of dynamite.* I came back around, coming in from the sun. The garrison was almost leveled. Two men running north, struggling, their hands bound behind them. Soldiers firing at them. I lined up the nose of the Curtiss, shot a short burst from the .50-caliber machinegun at the soldiers. Missed, but dirt and dust spatted around them, sent them scrambling for a hiding place. When I came back around, Gregorio and the Father had reached the waiting men with the horses. They beat a hasty retreat, heading east for Tornillo and Guadalupe Bravo. I flew over them, waved the wings of the bi-wing, headed for Wind Mesa.

Scared? Naw, but my every fiber was quivering like a moth too close to a candle. Maybe IB was right for being "skaid."

We piled in the Reo and headed for town, went by the State National Bank and made our gold exchange for dollars. Coot said, "Let's get some rest, try to make the 7:30 train for Socorro this evening. That'll put us in Socorro at 3:15 tomorrow morning."

"What's the rush? We'll just have to cool our heels until Fritz gets to his warehouse. Have to wait for the noon train anyway."

"We can have a boxcar loaded, ready to be hooked up to the 6:30 morning train. Back here by noon tomorrow."

"How are you going to find Fritz at 3:15 in the morning?"

"In that wire I sent him from Rodolfo's, I suggested that he bed-down in his warehouse."

72

9

"Narlow, I need to meet with Judge Murdock. Update my will. While I'm tending to that, why don't you take IB to Santa Fe on the morning train. Locate the Santa Fe Capitol building. Find the Taxation and Revenue Office. Have IB apply for one of those new gaming licenses. If he can get a permit, maybe we can set him up in a little business. Manage it and make a few dollars."

"Why don't *you* make that run with IB, *you* take him to Santa Fe, listen to him cough up his toenails, and answer a couple thousand of his questions? *You* take him to Santa Fe while I meet with the judge. I know more about that legal jargon than you do anyway."

"Naw, I need to tend to it personally. Besides, you know how to handle bureaucrats. So, you go on up to Santa Fe with IB, take Shelly Brom along with you. That poor girl never has a chance to get out to see a blessed thing. Nothing to do but keep house for IB and keep rabbit stew on the stove."

When I told IB the reason for our trip to Santa Fe, he said, "Shoot fire, Narlow, I don't need no busy-ness to tie me down. 'Sides, me 'n Shelly Brom's got all the money we needs noways."

"You know what Coot told me about your finances?" I asked.

"No, I rec-kon I don't."

"Coot says you can't scratch up enough money to buy a cough drop."

IB, Shelly Brom, and I made the run to Santa Fe. The girl was wide-eyed as an ostrich, bumping IB, pointing at everything that flew by our passenger car window. Finding the capitol building was not a problem since it was the only substantial structure in town. We found the Taxation Department and newly created gaming bureaucracy. Shelly Brom hurried over and sat on a bench, turning her face away from the clerk. IB asked for an application, but for what sort, he hadn't a clue. I asked the clerk for a gaming application, IB sat down at a desk to fill out the form's three questions. Since IB couldn't fully answer the first question, and I wasn't certain about it, I told the clerk that we'd fill it out and put it in the mail.

The clerk looked up wide-eyed. "But, sir, surely you—"

I smiled and told him we were in a hurry to catch a train.

We hurried back to the train station to catch the 12:15 southbound, but it was already pulling out. The next train was scheduled for five o'clock. I bought our tickets, and the three of us took a stroll around the sleepy village. Santa Fe didn't offer much more than an art colony on the square, assorted taverns and wine parlors, plus a lively assortment and flavors of soiled doves. The sight embarrassed Shelly Brom, but the "flavors" were nothing new to IB since El Paso's district was well-known throughout the southwest. He ignored their advances, and he and his twin sister continued their adventure. I found a park bench in the shade and stretched out.

I slept too hard, dreamed that IB and I were being chased by a jealous husband of one of Santa Fe's "ladies of the night," then awakened with a start. IB and Shelly Brom were nowhere to be seen, but when I took a step or two and peered around a pinion tree, I could see them on the far side of the plaza talking with a dandily dressed man in a brown suit. I resumed my stakeout on the bench.

After a bit, they came along, IB "whistling," as he terms it, more like blowing spit and phlegm through the gap between his buck teeth, with an occasional off-key tweet.

I asked, "Hey, you two, having a good time? IB, I saw you across the plaza talking to a man. Who's your new friend?"

"Oh, just a feller I met a few months ago back in El Paso. Up here on busyness. Tolt me all about his home country. He's a furr-in-er, you know. Nice gentleman of a feller. Nice feller. Of a gent-leman."

"Well, it's good to see you making new friends. Friends are an item you just can't get too many of. Where's your friend from? Did he say?"

"Don't rightly know. I keep axin' and he keeps telling me some-thin' about cologne. But ain't cologne some-thin' what womens splash all over they-selves? Shelly Brom dint like him."

"What's that you're hiding behind your back?" I stepped around to take a look, IB kept turning to prevent that.

"Shelly Brom don't like thet man. Onl-iest 'cause he dint give her nothin."

I kept after him about what he was hiding, finally he gave up, brought his hand around. "That nice man done gaved it to me. My very own pen-cil sharpener, Nar-low. Shelly Brom don't like him cuz he dint give'r nothin'."

I chuckled with the memory of the day IB was forced to confess to our teacher that he had taken the pencil sharpener, "while the teacher was teaching on the outside."

"Why did he give you the pencil sharpener, IB?"

"I dun-no, just a nice man. I dun-no why." He shrugged. "Don' ax me. I dun-no."

Shelly Brom kept pulling at her brother, but IB paid her no never mind.

We made our five-o'clock train, got settled in a compartment with two facing couches, right nice for snoozing. The rocking of the train on the uneven tracks set me to dreaming, with one eye open, peering across at Shelly Brom and IB, asleep like two little children. Me dreaming about two little tykes, me and Coot, he, reading aloud out of a borrowed book, *The Legend of Sleepy Hollow*. Coot stopped. "Narlow, look at these names. They're just like IB and Shelly Brom. Remember Daddy asking us not to call IB by his given name, Ichabod, afraid folks would fun him? Well, looky here. The Ichabod in this story's named Ichabod B. Crane. Reckon my daddy's the one who named him IB?" I confessed I didn't know. Shoot, me and Coot were just learning to read, much less cipher-out something like that.

Coot read on a little further in that Sleepy Hollow book, again he stopped. "By golly, Narlow, looky here. Shelly Brom must be named for this man. His nickname was Brom Bones, and he had his eyes on the lady that Ichabod was courtin'. What do you suppose?"

Coot and I always wondered why his daddy made him promise he'd always take up for IB. Over the years, we wondered why we'd hear folks whispering about how IB's daddy got himself shot at dueling range, why the Territorial Marshall came around asking Coot's daddy about it. But, Old Lady Crane was not widely known as a looker, so we just wrote it off as mischief. Another thing that was strange about that set of twins. Uncle Doyl always said, "IB and Shelly Brom were conceived in the devil's bed."

We got back to El Paso after midnight. The next morning Coot was no where to be found, gone off to Tornillo, so said Big George. He was waiting for us at Rodolfo's hacienda.

Coot asked, "Well, Shelly Brom, how did you enjoy your first train ride?"

She twisted her legs around like a stubby pretzel, pulled the sleeve of her dress up to hide her ruby-colored alligator disfigurement. Coot and I suspected that she had always liked Coot, trusted him for whatever reason, going back to our childhood days.

Shelly Brom signed that her mother only called her by her full name when she was mad, which was all the time. She wished that people called her Shelly Brom only when they loved her.

Coot said, "I didn't mean to offend you, Shelly, and in the future I'll call you

Shelly Brom only when I'm speaking kindly to you, which will be all the time, okay, Shelly Brom?"

He turned to IB. "Did you apply for that gaming license? Ready to go into business for yourself?"

IB looked at me.

"Go on, tell him, IB."

"Well, kinda."

"Kinda? You either did or you didn't. Which is it? Did or didn't."

"We brun-ged the ap-plic-ation with us."

"Why didn't you fill it out while you were there?"

IB looked at me for an answer.

"Because IB couldn't answer the first question on the application, so like he said, we 'brun-ged' it back with us."

"What was the question?"

"*What is your full name?—No initials*. IB couldn't spell 'Ichabod,' and I wasn't real certain about it myself. I told the clerk we were in a rush to catch a train. IB, show Coot the gift that man gave you in Santa Fe."

IB's hand came around, grinning, his buck teeth shining. "Looky heah, Coot. My very own pen-cil shar-pener."

"Well, podnah, you finally have your very own pencil sharpener, huh? Who gave it to you, IB? Did you run an errand for the man, do him a favor?"

"No, I din't do noth'n. A nice man just gived it to me. I don't know why he gived it to me. I dun-no. Just walked up and gived-ed it to me." He turned to his sister. "Shelly Brom don't like him. Don't like him cuz he dint give'r nothin'."

10

On the Road to Tornillo, August 1913

Rodolfo wired us in need of help. Tornillo was left high and dry, the rails being washed out, to the east and west. It would be a weeks before repairs would be completed. He asked that we do what we could to relieve the suffering of the hundreds of starving immigrants out of Mexico into Tornillo. We loaded the bed of the Reo with barrels of dry pintos, rice, and flour, and three barrels of salt pork. Coot threw in a hundred pound sack of candy, "For the little guys." The Reo was stacked high, tied down with a black tarpaulin. Coot said, "Damned if it doesn't look like Two Sticks' black stovepipe hat."

Just as we approached the high ground before Tornillo, Coot slowed the truck to a crawl to negotiate a tight bend in the road, then started coaxing her back up to traveling speed. The tumble of a boulder crashing down the hill to our left caught our attention. We both gave it a practiced glance, but no more noticeable attention.

After we made the first bend in the road, Coot pulled off into a deep arroyo and stopped. "What do you think?"

"I don't know. Didn't see anything."

I grabbed a repeater off the rack and we made our way up a small brushy hill that hid us from view from the point where the boulder began its downhill roll. When we approached the top of the hill, we crawled on all fours, made ourselves comfortable under the shade of a rock out-cropping. The only sound was the stiff breeze cutting through the greasewood and mesquite. It was a scorcher even under the cool of the rock shelf, but a great deal cooler than on the west-facing hill that Coot was glassing with his Army-issue binoculars.

I rolled over to face Coot. "Well, we've been here over an hour. Think it might have been a deer, some animal that started that boulder rolling?"

"If there'd been an animal, you'd'a seen it."

Sure enough, just about the time the sun made its last effort to maintain its reign over the heavens, movement near the top of the hill, 300-yards from our rock ledge. I had been looking at that exact spot for over three hours, seeing nothing. The next second it was apparent why. A man stood, took a long pull on his canteen while he looked around, shook out a gray canvas tarpaulin, folded it, then draped it on the crook of his arm with his rifle. Something about that man was familiar, but I couldn't quite place it at that great distance. Coot passed me the binoculars, but the dirty lenses were a glaze of oatmeal. All I caught was his hat, the back of his head sitting on slim shoulders, topping over the hill.

"Well, I'll be damned, Narlow. What do you make of that? What do you think he was doing up there all these hours? Had to be hotter'n hell's crypt up there."

"I don't know, but he's no hunter."

◎◎◎

"Rodolfo, we don't have a clue who was sitting on that hill," Coot said. "Couldn't have been more hidden or still than an Apache. Narlow looked right at that spot for three hours. If that man had moved an eyelash, he'd'a seen it. No doubt he was waiting for someone to come by. Us? Who knows. He's new to the ambush business, probably spooked himself. Maybe had a foot on that boulder. Pushed it while shifting around."

Rodolfo asked, "What do you propose we do at this juncture? Do you think you are in any peril?"

"Naw, we'll keep at it," I said. "Probably nothing, but if he was waiting for us, then who was he?"

11

Tornillo, September 1913

Revolutions have a way of ignoring neighboring borders. Mexico's brand of bloody upheaval had a unique way of creeping across the silvery sands of the Rio Grande. Overnight, Tornillo was transformed from a sleepy jerkwater border town on the Southern Pacific line to a safe haven and oasis for thousands of daily new arrivals. Poor people, with not a single *peso* to their names. Old people, toddlers, wide-eyed orphans wandering hopelessly along, searching for parents who will never come looking, widowers, war cripples, often limbless, their limbs left bleaching on the Great Chihuahua Desert with the arms and legs of their compatriots.

Foot, burro, and wagon traffic increased in both Tornillo and Guadalupe Bravo, just a hundred yards across the Rio. Oftentimes, the sister villages were unable to supply drinking water and food for themselves, much less the teeming immigrants. The thousands of pounds of beans, rice, flour, and salt pork we transported to them in the Reo was gone before the radiator quit spewing. A whiff off a piss-ant's ass.

Traffic was especially heavy in the town square where Rodolfo's small bank was located. To be as inconspicuous as possible , we timed our arrivals for two o'clock in the morning. Unloading rifles and cartridges into Rodolfo's *hacienda*, transferring gold bars from his bank to the Reo, both risky business. Add to the mix the comings and goings of Villa's men to pick up the munitions, the perilous activity began to verge on suicidal.

Rodolfo was truly *un hombre nervioso*. "Gentlemen, we must find a more secluded place to distribute the Mausers and cartridges. We must suspend operations immediately until an alternative distribution point is found." He paused, peered at the top of the window curtain that was folded over, stepped over and closed it. "I apologize for my overzealous caution, but my nerves have been on edge for weeks. Not so long ago, I knew everyone along the border for thirty miles in every direction. Now, I hardly ever recognize anyone on the streets of Tornillo. The gold, we will leave in my cellar. The risk of moving it far outweighs the benefit. You can pick up the bullion here, but the storage and distribution of rifles and cartridges must not continue here."

Coot turned to me. "What about Judge Murdock's Indian Hot Springs Ranch?"

"Well, the Indian is dern sure secluded, and I doubt the judge has sold or leased that old sulfur and caliche pile of rocks. Fifty-thousand acres of greasewood, jackrabbits, and *candelilla*. It's on the border, the Rio's flow runs by the edge of the springs. It'd be perfect."

"Rodolfo," Coot said, "the man who owns the Las Cruces airstrip, Jimbo Calhoun, has a more powerful engine for our Curtiss Pusher. Almost doubles the horsepower, eight cylinders, what's known as a Vee. With that increased power, we can increase the biwing's fuel capacity and get her range up over four hours. Narlow can fly much deeper into Chihuahua. Jimbo and Narlow can get the engine installed while I go to Dallas on the morning train. I'll have a talk with the judge about leasing the Indian when I get back.

Jimbo and I installed the new engine on steel brackets replacing the factory installed hickory holding braces, beefed-up the three-wheel undercarriage, and at Jimbo's insistence, repainted the undercarriage, "Curtiss orange."

We stepped back. "Wha'da ya think, Narlow?"

"Brand new. The old gal looks like a yellow goose with a pedicure."

"Narlow, I don't think you'll experience any significant difference with this new engine, but I'd keep the rpm down. She's not made to fly as fast as that seventy-five-horsepower will push her. Need to exercise a little caution when landing. Engine's heavier, and remember you've got a lot more weight aboard in the form of fuel."

El Paso's dusty outline soon came into view. I dropped the Curtiss down low, raced along Overland Street. A half-block before Big George's shop, I jerked the stick back, and went straight up. He came out waving his hat, I wagged the wings of the biwing. He stepped toward his old Packard to pick me up at Wind Mesa.

On the road back to town, Big George said, "There's talk in Juarez about Tornillo and Guadalupe Bravo. Rumors that Villa is taking delivery of dynamite there."

"Dynamite? Where did you hear that?"

"A lady who knows everything—our maid, Maria Christina Gonzalez. When she returned from Juarez last night, she told me and the missus about the dynamite deliveries, also said rumors are flying that the *Federales* are set to make an all-out push to rid the border of gun smuggling."

"But the rumor she heard was just about dynamite?"

"That's what she says. The lady's no dummy, but I questioned her to see if she was mistaken. If there was any talk about rifles, she didn't hear it. Nothing but dynamite. She was emphatic, '*No senor, solo dinamita. Nada mas.*'"

"Well, *dinamita* will be close enough to *rifles y cartuchos* to put the fear in Rodolfo. Coot was going to call on Judge Murdock in a few days, but if you'd be so kind, just drop me off at his office."

Judge Murdock's secretary was a man that Coot and I went to grade school with—Ronald Ray Benson. I brushed him off when he asked me to sign his guest registry.

"I only wanted to—"

"Is that you, Narlow Montgomery?" Judge Murdock shouted through the open door, "Come on in here. Let me rest these tired old eyes on you, son."

The judge had always been a favorite of mine and Coot's. If it hadn't been for his connections in the War Department back in 1877, we'd still be scouting for the Blue Coats. The judge stood six-five in his stocking feet, burly, a bush of red and gray hair, eyebrows like full-grown red-breasted finches overlooking a like-colored handlebar mustache, sprinkled with an inch of snow.

"Damn, it's been a long time since I've seen you, boy. What's on your mind, Narlow?"

"I'm in the market for a ranch—big one, private, isolated. I thought of your Indian Hot Springs Ranch. That place would starve a barren cow, but I do have a prospect for that old rock pile."

He laughed. "If you have a prospect for 50,000 acres of rocks and sulfur water, you must have an easterner for a prospect. That right?"

"Yep—New York City. Wants a big, secluded ranch on the border, needs privacy to conduct some experiments. I was on the Indian long ago, but don't recall whether it has a headquarters building where my man could hang his hat."

"No, it has no real headquarters as such, but it does have a hot-springs bathhouse down at the river's edge." He chuckled. "The sulfur stench makes it damn near useless. But, if it's privacy your man wants, and a roof over his head, I've got just the place. A place that I, shall I say, 'acquired' two years ago—the Coal Mine Ranch. It's sixty-odd miles down-river from the Indian. A shade over 70,000-acres, and you can have it for ten-cents an acre per annum. It has an old worthless coal mine and a rail spur that comes down from Van Horn, runs by the coal mine, past the headquarters, meanders down to where it 'Ys,' makes a long gentle loop by the river, then back to the 'Y.' There's an impassable escarpment that protects the east and south, a sheer mountain on the north, the Rio Grande on the west. The rail line goes through that sheer mountain by way of a half-mile-long tunnel. Think the Coal Mine Ranch would suite your man?"

"Seven-thousand dollars. You have a deal, Judge."

◎◎◎

Judge Murdock said the easiest way to identify the Coal Mine Ranch from the air was to follow the Rio Grande downstream 110 miles to a sheer mountain cliff on the Mexican side that resembled a massive dish tilted on its side. The small Mexican village of Los Fresnos sits at the base of the cliff, an unusual circular rail spur to the north of the river. Follow the spur six miles east to the ranch headquarters.

I spied the circular rail, followed it east to the tunnel, then swung around

81

back toward the ranch headquarters. I pushed the Curtiss down low and buzzed the buildings. When I swung back around, a man and woman appeared to be pointing up at me. She only had a broom, but what caught my eye was the man and the glint of the business end of a heavy musket at his shoulder, pointed decidedly at the end of my nose. I pulled the bi-wing around hard to the right, waved its wings, took the long way around to the tunnel, and followed the rail back out to Van Horn.

Coot wired me from Tornillo. On his return trip from Dallas, he had stopped off at Rodolfo's. He wanted me to fly down to show off the Curtiss' new engine and fuel tanks. But the Reo was in El Paso and we'd need it to take a close look at the Coal Mine Ranch. I wired him back to tell him that the Reo and I would be on the morning train, suggested he put some thought into figuring out a way to attach train wheels to the Reo's undercarriage, so we could ride the rails to "my new ranch."

12

Tornillo, Texas, October 1913

"Think the Coal Mine Ranch will work, huh?" Coot asked, crawling back under the Reo.

"Coot, the damned old place is perfect. Coming back to El Paso, I followed the rail line past the tunnel and back to Van Horn. The wagon road that leads down to the ranch is long-gone. Rough, bad-ass country, impassable for the Reo to go cross-country. The rail line crosses several *arroyos*, but the wooden bridges that cross them appear to be in tolerable shape. If we had some way of keeping the Reo on the railroad track, we could use the track to drive down there."

No response.

"What are you doing under there? Asleep?"

Coot stopped banging on the frame of the Reo, crawled out, sat in the dirt. He took off his hat, wiped his forehead with a bandana, cocked his balding head to the side, grinned up at me. "Narlow, can I ask your something? What the hell do you think I'm doing with the wheels off this old rail handcar?"

"Are they stout enough for the weight of the Reo? Pulling a loaded boxcar."

"You kidding? Each one of these steel wheels weighs around seventy-five-pounds. I'll weld a retractable brace to an axle for each wheel with a release pin. Weld the braces to the undercarriage of the Reo. When we're on a dirt road, the wheels will be in the up position. On the rail, we drive her up on the tracks, jack her up, drop the rail wheels in place on the tracks. Set the pin so the rubber of the rear tires ride heavy enough on the steel track to provide power. We can back the Reo up to our boxcar, tie on to it, and pull it to the drop-off point at the river."

By the end of the day, Coot and Rodolfo's forge had the Reo looking like a nursing praying mantis dragging her bag in the dirt. Not pretty, but the steel wheels worked better than even Coot imagined.

The next morning, we loaded the Reo on a flatcar for the fifty-five miles to Van Horn. Coot eased the truck up on the tracks of the spur to the Coal Mine, I jacked it up, set the rail wheels on the track with the rubber tires resting on the rails. Four hours later we were motoring along south to the ranch, coming up to a sheer gray-black rock wall of a mountain. Coot was getting antsy about my lease on a ranch that had no access.

We came around a sharp bend in the tracks that headed straight for a sheer granite wall. No visible means of getting to the other side. The gray wall was brush lined, shaded, the tunnel entrance appeared more like a barn door painted stark-black than a hole punched in a mountain.

"What the hell is *that*?" Coot asked. "Is that a tunnel up ahead there?"

Before he finished the sentence, we were inside that black hole. He grinned in the dim light. "Narlow, I believe it's dark in here, darker'n Big George's long-handles."

We crawled along through the depth of the tunnel, came out on the other side of the mountain, then came to a sharp bend to the right, a barbed-wire fence staring us in the face. The Reo snapped through the wire before Coot's boot made it to the brake pedal.

I said, "Eustacio Tarango's the ranch manager, and he'll be about as happy with you as he was with me when I flew down here the other day."

"No harm done. While I'm fixing his fence, *Senor* Tarango can use you for target practice."

The next bend in the track led us to the headquarters area. We scattered laying hens, jackasses, and a dozen blue shoats in every direction. Eustacio and his wife, Zoila, were sitting in the shade of their front porch as Coot applied the brakes. I waved friendly-like as we sailed by, ground to a stop 200-yards down the tracks.

The Tarangos were a happy pair. Zoila, petite, fair, coal-black hair in a single braid down her back; Eustacio, stout, with the quickest, easiest, toothiest smile that God ever slapped on a man. His friends called him Tacho.

Coot pointed at me. "This man is the pilot who flew his airplane right over your house the other day. Scared you and your wife, I bet."

Tacho looked at me, his wide grin sliding off his leathery face.

"*Como?*" Zoila asked.

Tacho turned to her and said, "He said that this is the man that flew his *aeroplano* over our house four days ago. *Recuerda?*"

The snarl on her mouth, her threatening black eyes, her hands on her hips, told me she had a faultless memory.

Tacho's smile curled back on his dark brown face. "*Un piloto, eh?*"

"*Si,*" I said, "*poco nuevo piloto.*"

"*Piloto pequeno?*"

"*No, poco piloto,*" I said, trying not to get boxed in with him trying to get me to admit being a small pilot, not the little bit of a *new* pilot like I was trying to explain. He laughed and explained my poor Spanish to Zoila in near perfect English. He agreed to join us on our trip down to the Rio Grande on the rail.

Tacho grinned. "This is my first time in *autobus.*" He told us that he was born on the ranch, his father was the mine foreman before it closed down in 1883, same year it opened. He remembered the *Chinos* who worked so hard building the railroad, digging the tunnel by hand. He pointed out the low rock houses the Chinese workers had built for themselves, told us they only lived inside them during infrequent cold spells.

A half-mile from the river, we came to the 'Y' in the track I'd seen from the air. The rail made a long loop down close to the water's edge, then came back up, rejoining the track at the 'Y.'

"So, that's Los Fresnos?" I asked, looking through the salt cedar trees and cattail across the wide, slow-flowing Rio. Los Fresnos was a near-deserted village.

"*Si, senor, fresno* means atch."

"Ash?" Coot asked.

Tacho smiled. "*Si,* atch—sometimes my Spanish ear does not hear English words." He wanted to cross the river and check on his mama if we weren't in a hurry.

"Narlow, without that loop I don't know what we'd have used for brakes. We can bring the boxcar down that track loaded to the gills, make the loop, the Reo will stop when it starts back uphill. We'll build a storage barn for our Mausers over there on that knoll. Ready when Villa comes calling."

I gestured toward the man wading across the muddy river. "What about Tacho? Trust him and Zoila?"

"They seem like good, honest folks. Let's stay over for a couple of days. Get a better feel for them."

We threw our duffel on the screen porch of the frame building that Tacho called the "big house." Zoila cooked our meals, all delicious, hot as Satan's sauna. On the evening of the second day, we were sitting on the shady side of the big house. Tacho had a roaring mesquite fire going in a large metal box that was once a mining car. The fire died down, left over a foot of hard coals, Zoila hung a brisket inside the metal box to a swirl of heavy smoke, then closed the metal lid.

Tacho whispered to Zoila. She smiled, nodded, and went inside and retrieved a gallon-sized burlap-covered jug and four metal cups.

"*Sotol*," he said, "*muy fino. Mi papa* made good *sotol*. Before the *Rurales* killed him."

Coot reached out, patted Tacho's knee. "When was that, Tacho?"

Tacho finished pouring two fingers in each cup, handing the first to Zoila, then to us. He sat down, heavy, ox-like, especially for someone as nimble on his feet as Tacho Tarango. He turned his sad gaze to Zoila as if trying hard to explain something to her. *Especially* to her. "Zoila, *mi corazon*, you recall two years ago when we took *mi mama* to meet your people in Pueblo? While we were gone, the *Rurales* threw a rope around my father's feet, dragged him behind a horse. Back and forth many times across the river. Finally, he drowned. He would not tell them where his brother was hiding—hiding in the hills far to the west of Los Fresnos. They suspected his brother of helping the revolutionaries. The *Rurales* were led by a man whose name was *Capitan* Ambrosio Manzano de Flores. I will *never* forget him. *Mis hermanos* told me that he was a small man, thin mustache, but he made up for his small size with meanness, anger, hate. They left Los Fresnos, then two of them returned, kidnapped *mi tia*, the wife of my father's brother. They heard shouting and screaming from the top of the high, steep cliff behind Los Fresnos. *Mi tia's* begging scream. It was the voice of *Capitan* Manzano. '*Mire*,' he shouted down to them. '*Mire*, this is what this *Rural* does to the women of traitors.' He pushed *mi tia's* naked body off the cliff to the rocks, 300 meters below."

"Forgive me, Tacho," Coot said. "I shouldn't have asked."

Tacho's gaze never left Zoila's. "You should not be sorry, *Senor* Boldt. I am the one who is sorry. Sorry that I am not man enough to avenge my father's death."

"Tacho," I said, "you are but one man against thousands of *Rurales* and *Federales*. What could you do besides getting yourself killed?"

"I do not know the answer to that question, *Senor* Montgomery. But, this I know deep in my heart—if it had been me on the end of that rope, my killer would be dead today. My father would have seen to that."

We sat, each in their own thoughts. I knew what Papa would have done.

Coot read my mind, as often occurs. He reached across, patted the second knee he'd patted in the space of only a few moments.

"Narlow, my friend of fifty-four years, I know right where you are right now. And you're right'r'n rain."

"And, so would you, Coot Boldt. So would you."

13

El Paso, November 1913

After Zara graduated from Dallas' Sacred Heart School for Girls in the 1890s, she and Sister Madeline Rosa had continued corresponding, became a nun after Zara graduated. She'd been the supervisor of Zara's dormitory. Sister Madeline Rosa's letters at first were full of the joy of her calling, about this girl then that, who reminded her of Zara and her older sister. But over the years, her letters began to lose their enthusiasm. Zara always left Madeline Rosa's letters on the kitchen table for me to read. It was apparent. Madeline Rosa was losing her zeal.

A letter from the sister came the day Zara returned from St. Louis. The letter was a thinly veiled request that she be invited out west. Mother Superior Pancretias thought perhaps a sabbatical was in order for Sister Madeline Rosa, to "sort things out in her heart and mind."

Zara and I met Sister Madeline Rosa's train at 5:30 on a cold and blustery Wednesday evening.

Their reunion was as warm and tender as a newborn calf's underbelly, as sweet as its innocent breath. They concluded their long embrace, turned to me. "Sister Madeline Rosa," Zara said, tears streaming down her face, "this is the man I told you about when I was at Sacred Heart. The same man you warned me about when I was that teenage girl in braids. The very same man I pursued until he caught me. My husband, Guillermo Narlow Montgomery."

The sister wiped her eyes, clasped my hands in hers. For the briefest moment, her olive-dark eyes simply gazed up, studying me. "Mr. Montgomery, your precious wife has told me so much about you over these many years. I feel closer to you than my own deceased brother."

We went home, I kicked life back in the sitting room fireplace, excused myself to make coffee. I warmed the cream, set it all along with a sugar cube dish on a tray, got to counting back, thinking, Zara's a youthful forty-one, which put the sister at around forty-six or seven.

I came back through the kitchen door with the tray. They immediately ceased their chatter. "What story is Zara telling on me, Sister Madeline Rosa?"

"Narlow—may I call you by that name?"

"Only if I can drop the sister."

"Oh, please do. I feel I must have relief from the formal world I have lived these past many years. It is so stifling. Zara knew me at Sacred Heart by my given name, which was Rose. Rose Marie Talamantes. I came to the convent from my birthplace, deep in the jungles of Panama, couldn't speak a word of English. Later, when I became a nun, I was given my present name, Madeline Rosa. I wish I could allow you to call me Rose, but that would not be fitting."

I served the coffee, chuckled. "Okay then, it's Madeline Rosa. But, I must say I sense a diversionary tactic often used by my Zara. She was telling her long-time friend about my old Schofield, teaching her to shoot it when she was fifteen years old." I winked at Zara, "Isn't that right, Madeline Rosa?"

Their laughter filled the house. Their mood, their glee to be in the other's company took them back almost a quarter-century. The blush of the fire and candle-lit sconces on either side of the mantle, all around the room, took years off their essence, brushed away the tinniest of wrinkles at their glowing eyes.

They needed space, time alone. Sitting in front of them, I took Zara's hand in my left, Madeline Rosa's hand in my right. "It's unfortunate that men are not as confident, as certain of themselves as women. Not man enough to demonstrate their heartfelt pleasures and emotions. Far too unmanly, that. With one grave exception, I adore most every woman I've ever met, admire their honesty, their openness. You ladies need private time, so if you dear ladies will excuse me, I'll be taking my leave."

◉◉◉

Coot joined Zara and me in cramming more excitement into Madeline Rosa's life in those next four weeks than her entire God-given experience. Coot thought it unladylike, but she learned to shoot my danged old Schofield, only this time, her former student was now the sister's instructor. We took daytrips to see the sights, late lunch at Juarez's Café Central, a *centavo* gardenia corsage from the lady-vendor out on the boardwalk, a special journey and delight for the sister was our daytrip to the Socorro Mission, founded in 1682, destroyed by flooding in 1829, rebuilt 1845, using the same painted, decorated beams; twelve miles up-river, five miles east to Cottonwood Springs where Zara and I did a great deal of our courting, picnicking in the same spot. Madeline Rosa loved Coot's old bronco-busting, butt-banging Reo.

Zara entertained often, inviting all of our friends to dine and meet her dearest friend. Besides me. A different crowd every evening, except for seven specialties: Coot, who was always first in line for "firsts and seconds," Bo and his lady-friend, PeePee, Big George and his wife Marina, and IB and his lady friend, Josephina. Shelly Brom signed that she "lacked the required social graces."

Zara and Madeline Rosa sat long into the night, sitting by the fire, then gradually, Madeline Rosa began to let it flow. Hints, vaguely veiled clues that her steady, unrelenting diet of school children, classes, grading tests, endless church duties, disciplining unruly, spoiled girls, some quite crude with not the slightest glimmer of hope or timber of ever becoming educated ladies. She was not as strong as Mother Superior Pancretias, or her fellow sisters. Her life would be more complete and meaningful if it could somehow change. She thought of mankind often. "A lot," the sister admitted to Zara, "men interest me."

◉◉◉

Coot sent one of his farmhands to tell me that he'd appreciate it if I'd pick up a plowshare that Big George had repaired for him, take it out to his place. *He'd appreciate it.* Ha!

I went down the front steps to my car on Utah Street. *Of a sudden*, I heard the ominous cry of an angry she-dragon straight out of *Beowulf*. A strange, guttural shriek, the ancient call of the wild, springing from across the street. From Geraldine's tiled front porch. My gaze caught her screaming from the top of her ample lungs, summoning, gesticulating with her wings, her forked-tail waving in the warm afternoon breeze, hand signaling me as if to demand, *Come here, you idiot!* It struck my mind to yell in kind, "Alas, Geraldine! 'Tis too late for thee and me. I am already married." I decided to cut her some slack, tried to ignore her.

I opened the door to my brand new automobile—a convertible Packard Twin Six Touring, and stepped up. One big automobile, like stepping into the stirrup of a sixteen-hand horse. But Geraldine was never to be denied. She bunched, lifted her dress, hustled down the steps to the street, ran across and stood in front of my Packard, hatred, fire, and venom screaming from every pore. From my high perch, all I could see of the dear lass was the top half of her sparklingly powdered face, encased in a huge sun hat.

"Narlow Montgomery, you are *not* leaving here until I have my say!"

"Well, what's stopping you? Have your say and cake as well. Or have your cake and then your say."

She came around, the late afternoon sun doing its own glaring—straight into my squinting hazels.

"I know what you're up to, Narlow Montgomery, who put you up to it—your only goddamn friend, *Coot Goddamn Boldt!*"

The sun's glare was intense, so powerful that I could see nothing but her outline, a summarization of a full-bodied something with an enormous parasol perched on its head. I tried to get my own head and hazels under the shade of that parasol-of-a-hat, but could not escape the brittle shine.

"Look at me when I am talking to you! You've been spreading rumors that I am shrewish, garrulous, and a fake. *Answer me*, you baboon. And quit gawking at me!"

"Why Geraldine, why would anyone even *attempt* to paint you in the image of a bad-tempered, aggressively assertive woman, much less an excessively talkative one with spurious tendencies? Can you please explain how a mere mortal such as *moi* could possibly accomplish such a fete? An uneducated man with no hope or promise in this world. 'Twas not I, you may be certain, dearest Geraldine honey."

Her hands went up to her hat, adjusted it just so. "*Well!* As long as we understand each other, I'll let it pass." She whirled around in the street, stopped in mid-twirl. "And damn it, don't call me honey!"

◎◎◎

Zara had heard so much about the wilds of the Coal Mine Ranch. She was eager to see it, show Madeline Rosa what the real west was all about. They decided we would celebrate Christmas there. Coot and I packed up the Reo and the four of us set out for the roughest 70,000 acres in all of Texas.

We bunked in the Big House. Tacho and Zoila had their privacy, but their three-room *adobe* was far too quaint to ignore. The three ladies decided that would be our meeting place, kitchen, dining area. The sun porch offered a place for the men to congregate, "take the edge off the day." Zoila's "hinges of hell's hot" meals were the hit, supplemented by mule-deer steaks and canned vegetables from her garden. The men shared their toddies of sotol, tequila, and mezcal on the front porch, Tacho's own recipes. Occasionally, one or two of the ladies joined us for our evening socials, Madeline Rosa most every evening. She was surprisingly easy around men, a fair hand at an occasional nibble of some of Tacho's "recipes." Coot did not approve.

After our New Year's celebration, we packed up and left for El Paso. Zara would be heading back to St. Louis by mid-January.

As is often the case, important matters seem to always find the back burner. The night before Zara's morning train, the subject of when Madeline Rosa would return to Sacred Heart bubbled to the surface. I stood to leave.

Zara said, "Please. Madeline Rosa is your friend as well."

Madeline Rosa's gaze dropped to her lap, her face in a grimace, cheeks and lips pulled back, teeth slightly clenched. "Narlow, I . . . Narlow, I know you've heard snippets of our conversations. Mainly about Zara's wish that I go with her to St. Louis tomorrow. But I simply cannot. I must be getting back to Sacred Heart. Mother Superior Pancretias will be concerned about me after my absence of almost two full months."

Zara said, "Narlow, I won't press her any further, but I've suggested that she write the Mother, tell her that she'll return by mid-February. Leave it at that. When she's ready to catch the train to Dallas, you can arrange her passage. You, Coot, and Bo can entertain her. Take her back down to the Coal Mine, let her kick the Curtiss' tires, be a girl for once in her life."

Zara turned to me. "And now, my darling husband. Speaking of snippets of conversation, I've overheard bits of your and Coot's brushes with danger. How much longer do you plan to continue this enterprise?"

I couldn't find any tires to kick in our sitting room, not even a rock. "I don't know, sugar pie. Coot and I've talked about quitting, but you know Coot. Coot won't—"

"We're not speaking of Coot, my darling. How much longer will *you*, Guillermo Narlow Montgomery, continue this gunrunning enterprise."

Madeline Rosa started to stand, but Zara patted her hand, nodded her insistence that she stay seated.

"Well, like I was saying, I've tried to get Coot to quit, but he keeps stalling me. I find myself thinking about nothing else but quitting, but with you gone—"

"You're saying that since I am not home all the time, you don't see any reason to quit this insanity, stay home, go back to your own business as you were before 1910. If that's it, I will lay down my shield and saber, as you call it. If that's what it—"

"Oh, no you don't, my dear. You told me the very day that we proposed to each other." I had to smile at those words. I laughed. "Hear that, Zara? The very day *we* proposed to each other. Remember that? Like you said, You chased me until I caught you. A man thirteen years your senior, but you insisted on marrying me, warts and all. Recall that? You also said that you didn't know exactly what you would pursue, you didn't want children, but we have our adopted son, Will. You felt you were bound for something unique in this life. Well, my darling lady, you have most certainly found the niche you sought. Me, I'm still jousting windmills with my friends, Coot Don Quixote Boldt and Bo Sancho Panza Calhoun."

◉◉◉

Zara was off to St. Louis. Madeline Rosa began staying at the Coal Mine Ranch with Bo, Tacho, and Zoila. They took their daily drive in the buckboard down Borracho Canyon to the airstrip, she and Bo would make repairs and patches on the biwing, ask Bo a thousand questions—flying questions. The weight of a tank of fuel, the feel of the controls in flight, how you make it go left or right, up and down. Not being a pilot, Bo didn't have the answers.

A month after Zara left for St. Louis, Coot and I were preparing to go back to El Paso. Madeline Rosa asked me to post a letter addressed to Mother Superior Pancretias. The letter explained her prolonged absence, and that she would return soon. Madeline Rosa was working on the truth of the matter, but didn't quite have the heart or stomach to mouth it, much less reduce it to writing.

Weeks later, Madeline Rosa came up to us as we were preparing to leave, handed me another letter. "Narlow, Coot, you need to read this."

Dear Mother Superior,

I shall always remember and cherish my years at
Sacred Heart, dear Mother, and I need and desire
your blessing and prayers more today than ever before.
You were always there for me at Sacred Heart, took me in when
I had no place to go.
I will always love you, Mother Superior, and remember you in my daily
prayers.
I cannot return to Sacred Heart. I know as I write
those six words that you already know that I will not
be coming back.
My prayers will always be with you. I beg your
forgiveness.
      Rose

I said, "I cannot imagine the difficulty you had coming to this decision, but I believe I understand."

Coot read it, turned to her, smiled. "You should have written that letter two months ago. Saved yourself a lot of misery. So, it's Rose from now on?"

She forced a smile, her eyes a dark sea of torment. "Yes. Rose, my given name. Just Rose." She turned, gazed at the high escarpment to the east for several moments, gazed up at the blue sky and heavens beyond, then turned to us. Her dark eyes swimming for their lives. "I'm begging you. Post that letter the very second you get to El Paso."

As we drove through the gate, Coot glanced in the rearview mirror, and stopped. "Turn around and take a look at that scene." Rose was skipping around the yard, racing after a mean-as-hell rooster, teasing Bo. The lass was home.

14

1914

Coot and I continued exchanging gold for dollars and dollars for Fritz's "bullets" and Mausers. Often, I made those runs on my own when Coot would go off east as far as Atlanta, dead-set on finding an alternative source of munitions.

But, the Coal Mine Ranch proved to be just what we needed. A man didn't just stumble onto the Coal Mine—its remoteness foretold no visitors. We stored most of the munitions in the shed we built near the river where Villa's men picked them up. Other rifles and cartridges were stored at the airstrip. Occasionally, I'd fly rifles and cartridges into Mexico wherever Rodolfo dictated. Tacho Tarango had erected a tall salt-cedar shed over the biwing to keep it out of the blazing heat. Rose took advantage of the shade so she could spend the entire day pulling levers, practicing her imaginary flights.

One evening, she asked, "Narlow, please, can I just . . ."

"Can you just what?"

"Oh, I was just wondering. Would you mind if I taxied the Curtiss up and down the airstrip just once?"

"*Absolutely not*. Never! You don't just taxi that beast up and down the strip like a drive down Fifth Avenue. That's an airplane, not a Model-T."

"You could teach me to push the kill switch so that—"

"No! It's monstrously dangerous. It's *not* going to happen."

Over the next several weeks, she persisted, driving me to distraction with her pleading. I caught the train back to El Paso to make another run to Socorro.

Coot laughed. "You might as well get it in your head that what Rose wants, Rose gets. Wants to fly. Going to fly. Teach her to fly or she'll teach herself. Your choice."

❍❍❍

Coot had a lead on Mausers in Florida, so I took the Reo down to the Coal Mine. On the way down, I decided Coot was right, and while it was still my "choice," I relented. I spent a week explaining to Rose the mystery of the controls, levers, control wheels, theory of vacuum on the top of the wing giving lift, the thousand details that allows a heavier-than-air, seven-hundred pound, glued cloth-to-sticks object to fly. We taxied up and down the strip, me in the cockpit, she standing on the main strut so she could observe. On the ground, a novice has difficulty keeping the prop revved enough to provide wind and vacuum on the upright tail to make it turn without gaining too much speed. The ex-nun was a natural at rubbing her tummy and patting the top of her head, and soon enough, she was happily "driving" the delicate yellow bird up and down the quarter-mile strip on its orange undercarriage.

"Rose, tomorrow I'm driving the Reo out and on up to Socorro. I'm going to trust you with the Curtiss. You can taxi it up and down the strip two times a day. Tell me, 'War Ace,' what's the *first thing* a pilot does when he sits down, straps himself in, even if the pilot just returned from a flight?"

She sat, holding the stick in a death grip. "Pre-flight check." I watched her go through the routine precisely as instructed, smiling up at me like Alice's Cheshire cat.

"Bo, Tacho, stay close and don't let her get into too much trouble."

◎◎◎

A letter from Zara was waiting for me when I got home, chiding me for running guns to a movie star. She enclosed a clipping from *The New York Times* extolling the many virtues of Pancho Villa. The article described the movie that opened at New York's Lyric Theatre, "The Life of General Villa." Zara's closing was typical—"You will be pleased to learn that the movie ends with General Villa becoming the *presidente de Mexico*. Perhaps *Presidente* Villa will give you and Coot a carriage ride around *La Alameda Central* in honor of all your efforts on his behalf."

17

Socorro, New Mexico, July 1914

My train was late. Fritz was standing on the station platform with three *very nice* looking young ladies. Suppose we'd had him all wrong? I drove the Reo off the flatcar and Fritz hailed me down.

"Hop in, Fritz. Those young damsels friends of yours?"

He smiled, straightened his bow-tie. "Uh . . . why, uh, *yes*. Three sisters from a ranch east of here. I couldn't decide which one I wanted the most, so I just sent them all back to their mother."

"Must be nice to be a lady's man like you, huh?"

"Uh, yes—uh, where's Coot?"

"Oh, he had a little personal business to tend to." I reached down to the floorboard, retrieved the bank bag. "Here's your share of the delivery fee for the last shipment."

"Speaking of money, Narlow, you might as well know *right now* that I can't . . . that I simply *cannot* let you have this shipment of Mausers at the old price. The new price is seventy-five dollars per rifle . . . uh, and, uh, bullets are thirty-cents apiece."

I pushed back the warehouse door. "Fritz, seems to me that Coot and I were here not long ago. You need to know that my memory *never* fails me. This warehouse was rafter-full of Mausers and cartridges. What are you trying to pull?"

He reared back on his size threes, eyes bulging. "I'm *not* trying to pull *anything*. That's the new price, a condition of price and demand. I have the supply, and *I have the demand*. If you don't want them at my price, shop somewhere else."

I started stacking canisters. "Are you going to help me load these rifles and cartridges? Get a hold of the other end of this canister."

We loaded twelve canisters of Mausers and started on the cartridges. He asked, "Well, what about the new prices I quoted you?"

"Give me a hand with these cartridges. Sixteen cases—8,000 rounds."

"But what about the new price? They're thirty-cents a bullet, just as I said."

"Stack these boxes tight, Fritz. Don't want them to get away from us. Loop this rope through that slot there. Yeah, there you go—now back around that upright post for me. Give me a hand with this tarpaulin. Damn old rag's almost as heavy as a case of cartridges. I mean, bullets."

We got it tied down, and he started in on me again. I didn't hear him. "Let's see, Fritz—sixteen canisters of Mausers and sixteen cases of bullets. That comes to $88,000."

"*No sir!* That comes to *exactly* $120,000," he said, lifting his chin.

"Fritz, let me tell you how Coot and I see this. You have a warehouse full of fifty dollar Mausers and twenty-cent cartridges. You say the new price is seventy-five dollars for a Mauser, thirty-cents a cartridge. If you're paying that—and you'll have to prove it by the way—we'll start paying the new prices when this warehouse is bare to the walls of the old rifles and cartridges. 'Bullets' if you prefer."

"*Oh, no!* You see, I run my warehouse on what my accountant calls LIFO—Last In First Out—that means these rifles are the last in, but the first out and—"

"Fritz, old pal of mine, Coot Boldt will tag along on the next trip—hell, when I tell him about this he's liable to catch the next train north. He's liable to explain a few of the finer points of your LIFO accounting method, tell you where to stick your LIFO, while explaining that your new accounting method is PDBS."

"PDBS?"

"*Pure Dee Bull Shit.* Best rethink your pricing policy before you see this old Reo again."

16

San Pedro, New Mexico, Downstream from Socorro, September 1914

Coot's trip east was another dry run, unable to find an alternative source for Mausers. We picked up another load from Fritz and headed home. Funny thing—he didn't mention his new pricing policy.

I told Coot about letting Rose taxi the Curtiss.

He grinned. "Might as well give her flying lessons."

"Naw, she's happy as a puppy just driving the Curtiss."

"And how long do you think she'll be happy as that fuzzy puppy just driving the Curtis up and down the strip, want to take her up for a spin?"

"Oh, she won't. She'll be happy just driving it."

He took off his Stetson, glanced up at the sun, wiped his brow on his sleeve, shook his head. "You're dumber'n a stopped clock when it comes to women. And you sure as hell don't know *that* particular woman. *At all.* She'll start with the needle. Badger you. Stomp on your instep." He laughed. "That gal'll be flying in thirty days."

We crossed the Rio at San Pedro and followed the river road south along the water's edge to the easterly trail that leads to Carrizozo. The cottonwoods along the Rio were showing a little gold, but cattails and bamboo reeds were still sending out green shoots.

I settled back, a snooze on my mind, but as we approached a small volcanic bluff that stuck out over the Rio, the cry of a whistling bull-elk in full rut pierced my ears.

"Coot, *stop!* Damn bull-elk just screamed in my ears."

"You haven't mentioned a bull-elk call in years. Your mushroom either, for that matter. What's got into you?"

"I don't know. Turn this thing around! Go back around on the east side of that little bluff up ahead. Something's not right."

"Oh, bullshit, Narlow. There's nothing—"

"Maybe you're right, maybe not. Let's check it out."

We drove around to the eastern edge of the bluff, grabbed our carbines, and climbed the bluff.

Twenty feet below us were four *sombreros. Sombreros* shading four Mexicans with carbines of their own, four horses staked out behind them in the shade of the bluff. The men were intent on watching the river trail, covering it with their weapons.

We backed down the bluff, decided to split up, coming at them from both directions, using the brush and trees to hide our advance.

"Narlow, I don't think these clowns are experienced highway men. If they were, they'd be spread out on both sides of the trail. Don't shoot unless you have to."

When we were in position, Coot shouted, "*Oiga, amigos!*"

They made a motion to swing their weapons around to him.

I shouted, "*No no no amigos!* Let's not do that! *Manos arriba!*"

They dropped their rifles. We questioned them as to their intentions.

The tallest one said in perfect English, "A Mexican friend of ours in El Paso told us that he'd heard a rumor that two men would be coming along this trail in an old six-wheel-drive truck, loaded with many bars of gold."

One of the Mexicans, a small, surly little bastard, kept poking the perfect-English-speaker in the back, telling him in Spanish to tell us to go to hell, that it was none of our damn business what they were doing, who they were waiting for. He giggled something about the possibility that they would be waiting for us the next time we drove by *con mucho oro.*

I pulled out my old Schofield revolver. Shot the surly little bastard in the foot, likewise accommodated the other three in quick succession. They writhed in the sand, holding their oozing-red boots.

Coot threw his hands in the air. "*Goddamn, Narlow!* What the hell'd you do that for? I told you not to shoot unless you had to."

"What else would you have me do? No lawman at hand. The Territorial Marshal is out making his monthly rounds. El Paso's not in the Territory. We didn't cause this. *They did!* And we damn sure don't want them waiting for us the *next time*, like that little bastard just said."

I waved the revolver around. "Get up, you sonsabitches! Yeah, it hurts like the blazes, but you better do what I say or you'll be *dead* sonsabitches. Me and my travelling mate don't kill in cold blood. But if you don't do *exactly* what I say, and I do mean *goddamn exactly*, you damn certain will be dead sonsabitches! *Comprende?*"

"*Si Senor!*"

"Get on your horses. Point 'em south. Don't stop. We'll follow you to see that you *don't* stop. When it's dark, get down. Build yourself a fire. See what you can do about your wounds. Cauterize them if they're still bleeding. After you've bandaged yourselves with your long johns or your serapes, or whatever the hell you have to bandage them with, you get your asses back in your saddles. Get back to Mexico. *Stay there!* If I *ever . . . ever* catch you back on this side of the border, I *promise* I'll shoot you in the other foot, your knees, your gut, and keep shooting 'til you're *dead sonsabitches*. Now, *get!*"

Coot watched them beat a quite hasty retreat around a canebrake, turned to me. "I don't believe what I just witnessed with my own eyes."

"Got a better solution? Want those idiots waiting for us the next time we come down this trail? What would you have us do? Shoot them, dump them in the Rio?"

"Naw." He beat his hat against his leg, grinned. "Come to think of it, you did *exactly* what needed to be done. Getting shot in the foot is no Sunday-school picnic, but it beats floating face down in that muddy river. I bet you just made honest men out of them. And you can bet your ass they'll not be too anxious to meet up with that crazy-bastard-white-haired *gringo*."

As I reloaded my Schofield, he chuckled. "Know what this reminds me of? You remember when we were sixteen, Uncle Abe and Uncle Doyl set us loose afoot in the wilds and we had to make our way back home? Remember one night on that 250-mile trip back home, you told me about your mama hitting you across the neck with a horse quirt? You grabbed her wrists, squeezed hell out of them, made them bleed. You said that after that, you'd catch your mama giving you a side glance, eyes darting back and forth, get skittish, like she was afraid of you. Remember what I told you at the time?"

I holstered my Schofield. "No, refresh my memory."

"I recall it like it was yesterday. I said, 'Narlow, you're meaner'n your mama.'"

Coot drove the Reo to the top of the first sugar-sand hill, stopped, stepped down, wiped his Stetson with his sleeve.

"Damn, Narlow! We can chalk that one up to another failed attempt at getting us dead. Who's behind all of this? Those four clowns had their facts all wrong about us carrying gold out of Socorro, but we've damn certain carted a bunch of it *out of Tornillo*. So what the hell's this all about?"

17

Coal Mine Ranch

All the long miles to the Coal Mine, I fought the dread of the nightmare of Mama hitting me with that horse quirt, wondering if that one episode alone could make me so damn mean. Not brave, but graveyard *mean*. No, it could not be. Mama's mean. I'm just careful.

Coot pulled the Reo and boxcar under the barn. Coot asked, "Tacho, how's it going, *compadre? Mucho trabajo?*"

"*Si, mucho trabajo, poco dinero,*" he said with a toothy grin.

"Where's Rose and Bo?" I asked. "Let me guess. They're down at the airstrip and Rose is driving the Curtiss up and down the airstrip."

"*Si, senor,* something like that," he said, shooting Coot a silly grin.

We unhitched the boxcar and loaded up. Zoila had just gone through the agony of a stillborn child, but she insisted on piling in the Reo for the rough ride down Borracho Canyon to the airfield.

When we drove up to the Curtiss' shed, Rose and Bo were sitting on the rough gravel under the plane, patching a place where a rock had torn a hole in its yellow canvas underbelly.

"*Coot,*" Rose said, jumping up and hugging him around the neck. "I haven't seen you in forever."

"I understand that you skipped learning to drive an automobile, taken up driving airplanes."

"And that ain't all!" Bo said. "Wait'll you hear the rest of it. Go ahead, tell 'em, Miss Smarty Pants."

"Oh, I'll tell them later."

"*Oh no!* Now!"

Rose turned to me. "Now, Narlow, don't get angry. Just let me finish before you start yelling at me."

"What happened? Did a tire go flat, motor quit running?"

"No," Bo said, "a hell of a lot worse than that."

Coot rubbed his hands together. "This oughta be good."

I asked, "Well?"

"Well . . . well, yesterday, Tacho had work to do, so Bo and I came down here in the buckboard like we always do. We packed our lunch so we could spend the entire day down here. The weather has been so lovely and cool and we thought—"

"Quit stalling, Rose," Bo said. "*Tell him.*"

"Okay, okay, I will. I'll tell them." Her dark eyes bubbled over.

I hugged her. "What's wrong? You all right?"

"Oh yeah, she's all right, after I damn near had a heart attack," Bo said. "Yesterday, she went through her checklist, taxied down the strip just like she always does. I stepped around the barn to do my business, and while I was buttoning-up, I heard the Curtiss turn at the end of the airstrip, the engine roared. And I mean *roared*, like it used to do when you'd come screaming down that strip taking off with a heavy load. I figured the throttle stuck. I ran back around and damned if she didn't lift off and fly right over me. Scared the living—"

"Rose, you *flew* the Curtiss? You actually flew it? You flew that thing without a flying lesson, no crack-up, no broken bones, cut lip, chipped teeth? You actually flew the Curtiss and—"

"Yeah, Narlow, I believe you just heard Bo say that very thing." Coot grinned. "And I guess you were right after all. You said she *promised* never to *ask* you to teach her to fly. She didn't go back on her word. Just never asked the question."

Coot grabbed Rose's hands, gazed at her for a full minute. "You've got spunk, pretty Little Miss Rose. A *lot* of spunk." He grinned. "And not bad to look at either. I like both those qualities in a woman."

She hugged him. "Oh, Coot, you always make things right. That's why I love you so."

She turned to me. "You're not angry, Narlow?"

"You're not mad at this hussy?" Bo asked. He jumped up and down, madder'n'a scalded hen. "I sure as hell thought you'd paddle her—"

She hugged Bo, he laughed. "Aw, shoot, Rose. How can a feller stay mad at the likes of you?"

We stayed over to watch her fly. I warned her about being a hot-dog. She just laughed. She really wasn't hot-dogging, she was just danged good at it.

Coot slapped me on the shoulder. "You're jealous. She's better'n you!" I admitted no such thing.

Three days later, Coot and I had to get a move-on. Coot turned to Rose. "Now listen up, young lady. You do exactly what Narlow says about flying that thing. You're too sweet to lose. You're going to limit each flight to thirty minutes. Go through your flight check-off list. Every *single time* you sit in that cockpit. *No exceptions.* If there's any threat of rain, windstorm, you don't go up that day. Stay the hell away from the downdrafts over by the escarpment. Agreed?"

"I promise I'll do exactly what you and Narlow say. And Narlow, don't you dare tell Zara about me flying." Rose squeezed my face in her hands. "I want to see the look on her face when I tell her."

◉◉◉

We stayed over with Rodolfo in his *hacienda.* He was increasingly less enamored with *General* Villa each time we visited with him.

"There was a time not so long ago that Pancho Villa was thought to be Napoleon and Lincoln all rolled into one. He controlled most of Mexico, and favored by the United States. But he is becoming more autocratic, ignores his advisors, makes policy on the wing, but worst of all, alienating the middle class by allowing lawlessness during his occupation of Mexico City, allowing rape and theft among his troops.

"Another thing is troubling to me. His own agents and munitions suppliers are openly cheating him with poor quality munitions—some to Villa, some to Carranza's troops, some to the French. Since the beginning of the European War, his cost for 1,000 rounds of ammunition has risen from $40 to $67. Yet, the price we are paying Fritz Hans-Smidt has remained stationary all of these years. How can that be possible?"

18

El Paso, February 1914

Zara and I enjoyed three months of bliss. Both home at the same time, celebrated Christmas and New Years together, enjoyed a houseful of Papa's cherished old friends who gathered to celebrate his ninetieth birthday. Papa soaked in that day like he faced every day of his life, with warmth, goodwill, and his ever-present humor.

Zara called out from the kitchen, "Narlow, someone's at the door."

I opened it to gaze upon a smartly dressed young man. "Mr. Montgomery?"
"Yes, what can I do for you? Won't you come in?"
"No, thank you, sir. I have a letter for you and Mrs. Montgomery. Good day, sir." He turned and bounded down the steps to the street.
"Who was that?" Zara asked.
"Ha! Expensive, well-dressed mailman. Delivered a letter to us. From Will, London postmark."
Zara read the letter aloud:

Dear Mother and Dad,

I trust the delivery of this letter and the London postmark does not alarm you as there is no call for concern. Conditions have turned ugly in Germany. Preparations for war are becoming more obvious with the passage of each day. Due to the nature of Everstart Industries business, it would be a prime target to be confiscated by the Kaiser. Jonathan and I persuaded his father to sell all of his German business interests. That has been accomplished, and at a tremendous profit, I might add. We arrived in London last evening. All is well. I would very much enjoy a visit home to visit my folks and home, but, sadly, business must come first.

As I said, all is well with Will Narlow Montgomery, Jr. I miss you both. I owe you my all.

With much adoration and love,
Will

Zara and I sat on the sitting room couch, letting Will's letter soak in. Deep in thought, recalling the last time I laid eyes on him, Zara's summer-long visit to Germany, the months he sat on my back stoop, scruffy, dirty, ragtag, refusing repeated offers to come indoors, Zara and I married, she coaxed him in, accepting her invitation to join us, adopting him, giving him my name, his glee to be in our family, Zara's tutoring him day and night for two full years, his acceptance and graduation from Wharton, his position with Everstart Industries, sailing for Germany. Could so much occur in so few years?

I nestled Zara under my arm, held her tight. She turned to me, her eyes misted-over. "Oh, Narlow, my life love, I am so pleased that Will is out of Germany. Thank God. So pleased. So thankful. Our son is far safer in London rather than Dusseldorf."

Two weeks later, I had a visitor in my office. The same smartly dressed young man who delivered the letter from Will.

"Good morning, Mr. Montgomery. Perhaps you remember me. Sir, I am Bryant Pederhoust. A friend and business associate of your son, Will."

He explained that while the letter he had delivered indicated a London postmark, the letter had been retrieved when Will learned that Bryant was on his way to America's southwest. No reason to chance someone getting their hands on the letter's content. He said that after delivering Will's letter, he boarded a westbound train to California in search of a suitable site for construction of an Everstart facility.

"Mr. Montgomery, what Will wanted me to convey to you, without his mother being present, is that my father is in the employ of the British Secret Service. He has it on *verifiable*, authority that German spies have infiltrated much of the United States. Those spies have been on the Mexican border since the day their revolution began. Over a hundred of them are known to live here in El Paso, probably twice that number. Perhaps your neighbors, business associates. It is my father's measured opinion that Germany will do everything in its considerable power to embroil your country in Mexico's revolution. If that is possible, it will forestall any US participation in Germany's planned takeover of all of Europe and Great Britain. My father is aware of your participation in Mexico's struggle. He warns that you and Mr. Edwin 'Coot' Boldt are in danger, *very grave* danger. Germany's spies will go to all lengths to keep America out of the upcoming European conflict. A conflict that will quickly escalate into a continental war, perhaps globally. They will stop at nothing, Mr. Montgomery. *Nothing.* You must trust *no one.* My father wishes you and Mr. Boldt well."

With that, he took his leave.

"So, Coot, that's the story. That's the message from Will's friend and business associate."

"His father knew our names. Your visitor called us by name. That it?"

"By name. *Full* names."

"Hmmm. In great danger, did he?"

"No, I listened carefully to Mr. Pederhoust. He used the term, '*very grave* danger' to describe our present circumstances."

He took off his Stetson, wiped his brow with his sleeve, used the elbow of the same sleeve to wipe the inside of his hat, crammed it down on his head to his ears, spit, smiled. "Well, my friend. We best watch our backsides. Double-ass-careful like."

19

Canutillo, Texas

A soft rapping came at my office door. I figured it was some idiot who didn't know business protocol, so I jerked the door open, prepared to yell, *Whad'a'ya want?*

"Fernando Valdez! What a pleasant surprise. Please come in, have a seat, my friend."

This honorable man had worked side-by-side with Papa every day of his working life. I loved the man, had camped, toiled alongside him all through my youth, milked and tended thousands of goats at his side, figured him to be just a year or two younger than Papa. All through my youth, I knew that if anything happened to Papa, I'd find Fernando Valdez. Go wherever he went.

His gnarled fingers grasped his frayed *sombrero* held tight against his chest, sat erect, somber-faced, clear-eyed, quiet as a church after a funeral. His left hand missed the two smaller fingers but was of no consequence to his strength. My mind flashed back to a day so long ago, Papa and Fernando at the base of Red Rock Canyon, three men came up behind them in the wind, revolvers at the ready, demanding their valuables. Knowing they'd take what they wanted, then kill them, Papa and Fernando fought them off, Fernando grabbed a man by the forearm with his pincer-hand, breaking both bones like a dog on a chicken leg. Somehow my office seemed serene, peaceful as the man's honest, sun-weathered face.

I asked, "So, Fernando, what brings you to town? Going to Mexico for a family visit?"

"Si, *Senor* Narlow, I go to Durango to *mi familia, pero* no visit. All of my time. *Senor* Papa Montgomery, *el es muy enfermo. En su cama.*"

He reached under his *serape* and brought out a leather pouch. "*Senor* Montgomery, he give me this purse. He tell me go back to *mi familia*, he say *para mi trabajo, para nuestra amistad.*"

"Well, Fernando, you've long been Papa's trusted friend, worked long and hard together. You *should* take it easy. But tell me, what's wrong with Papa? I saw him two days ago and he seemed just fine. What's wrong?"

"*Senor* Montgomery, he make a bad fall in the corral with the goats. I run to him. When I help him up, he make a glare at me. Me and he, we know. What he do his pants."

He paused, grimaced. "*Senor* Narlow, *su papa*, he make a chat his pants and he told me so. I never hear him ever use no bad words. He tell me *algo extraño*. He tell me, 'Fernando, *mi amigo*, it over.' He tell me to hitch a horse his wagon. He and me, we go Bishop's Cap, go in his cave where he keep some things. He dig up this purse, give it me. He say it has *mucho oro*. Say it over 3,000 *pesos*. He say same as dollars. *Mucho dinero. Mucho!* He say gold for me. Tell me no tell you *mama*. We go back to his dugout, I helped to his bed. He shake my hand, tell me go home, but first come here tell you this sad story. *El piensa* you better go his dugout."

With that, I shook the gnarled and calloused hand of Fernando Valdez. We shared an *abrazo*, he crossed the street and made his way through the crowd to the bridge. I knew that man. He'd never spend a single *centavo* of that bag of gold, not even for a new *sombrero*.

My greeting at my parents' dugout was the same welcome I'd enjoyed all of my life.

Mother's warm glare aside, she asked, "What the hell do you want? We don't need your kind around here, you worthless son-of-a-bitch. Don't need your money or nothing you—"

"I didn't come here to offer anything. I came to see Papa, and if you don't mind, I'll—"

"Why don't you just *get*? Get your ass off my—"

She was as deaf as a stump, but she heard Papa's thundering voice. "*Daisy!* Leave that boy alone. He came here for a visit. Let him be!"

She turned toward the goat hide hanging at the entry of the dugout, puffed up like she was about to shout back at him, but only turned back to me, swallowing air, gasping for breath, whispering, hissing in a brittle-coarse voice, "Get—*get in there*. Get your goodbyes—get your goodbyes done. Then *get!*"

As I ducked past the goat hide, a flood of Mama's copper-lined memories greeted me. I sat on the side of Papa's bed.

He reached out his hand, we shook hands, but he held on. "Fernando Valdez paid you a visit, son?"

"Yes, sir, he did. Last time I saw that good and honorable man, he was headed for the Santa Fe Street Bridge, back to his homeland."

Papa crossed his arms, breathed deep. "Good man, Fernando Valdez."

Papa seemed as fit as he did two days ago. I had a hard time getting my arms around the reality that he just might be dying. I didn't know where to start, so I kept quiet, knowing Papa would lead us where we needed to go.

My scalp tightened like a drum, my face contorted, my cheeks drawn down and back, teeth clenched, a slight tremor at my lower lip.

Papa laughed. "Look at you, Narlow Montgomery. Looks like you're set to cry. Nothing to be upset about here, boy. Tomorrow's going to be just as sweet as all of my yesterdays. You realize that I haven't seen you cry since the night your little sister passed? Remember Mary Jewell, son?"

I took my first breath since I pushed past the goat hide, took another long breath, tried to smile. "Sure I do, Papa. Sure I do."

I wiped my face. "Come to think of it, that night was the last time I spied any moisture at the corner of your eyes."

We talked and laughed about everything we ever did or said to one another. He asked about Coot, *What's that ornery cuss up to? You two boys still running swizzle sticks to Pancho?* He laughed, asked about a lady he considered his daughter, *How's my darling Zara? I miss that child and you tell her I was asking about her, you hear me, boy?* He asked about his only grandchild, *You tell Will that his granddaddy wants him to get out of Germany. Those Krauts are up to no good. It's dangerous for him to be over there.* When I reminded him that Will had been out of Germany for several months, he laughed. *I'm getting so old, sometimes I can't even remember my own fool name.*

Papa didn't get his dying done for two full months. Mother protested, but I stayed with him, night and day, afraid to leave him alone with his wife. Papa didn't mention it, but I believe he shared my concern. Coot came by every day, visited with Papa for an hour or so, brought food by the carload, always a sack of horehound candy for Papa, a sack of "girly" peppermint for me. They thought that was about the funniest thing they ever dreamed up. They could laugh by the hour over that sack of horehound candy, all the while sucking on that evil stuff.

News of Papa's final days spread across the southwest, both sides of the Rio. His special friends came first: Big George, Bo; two men with whom he'd served as scouts chasing renegades came all the way from Horse Springs, New Mexico; Sly Fox, Na-tu-Che-Puy's nephew, Broken Chain, the son of Many Fast Feet Two Sticks, their elders long past; *tres viejo vaqueros* from Torreon, and on and on. When Coot brought IB out to see Papa, our childhood friend was near a swoon, could not mouth a single syllable, just jabber, so grief-stricken he could barely walk past the goat skin. After a few moments, Papa shook IB's hand, and Coot carried him back to the Reo.

Then after three weeks, Coot told Papa, "Uncle Abe, I've got to cut my visit short today, but I'll be back tomorrow. Have a surprise for you. A *special* surprise for you and this worthless son of yours."

Around noon the next day, Papa and I were recalling me chasing a persistent wolf away from some birthing nannies, when all of a sudden, hell's gate sprang wide open with all manner of mayhem, cussing, and screaming. Just on the other side of that goat skin.

"You get the hell out of here! You—you goddamn little slut. You're the cause—you're the cause of all this. Get! *Get*, before I get a gun and shoot your goddamn fancy-ass ass."

Papa smiled. "There's only one woman in the world that could get Daisy that worked up. Son, I think you best prepare yourself to greet your darling Zara."

He turned his head, "Bring that gal in here, Coot!"

He raised his head. "Daisy, you cut out that cussing! Your profanity in the presence of a lady is embarrassing. If you don't cut it short, I'll get out of this bed and whale you to within an inch of your hateful life!"

Coot held back the goat skin and in ran Zara. She was smiling, but telltale dried tears streaked her pretty face. Her hand brushed mine as she rushed by.

"Oh, Papa, I'm so happy to be here with you!" They embraced for several minutes, Zara sobbing like I had never witnessed, Papa stroking her hair. Coot and I stepped outside.

The "dugout lady" was nowhere to be found. Coot picked up an ax and began cutting lengths of mesquite and cedar. I set about stacking it, replenishing the wood for his cutting.

Mama came out of the hen house, milled around, went over to the dugout, peered around the goat skin, listened, then came over to Coot and me.

"Suppose that hussy . . . suppose that hussy will ever come out of there? Narlow, I want that goddamn . . . that goddamn little bitch-in-heat hussy gone from this place. What the hell . . . what the hell are they up to in there?"

I ignored her, but Coot grinned. "Why, Mrs. Montgomery, if your curiosity has you on edge, why don't you go in and ask Uncle Abe what the hell's going on in there with him and that little bitch-hussy?"

❂❂❂

I read Papa's *King James* through from cover to cover, often pausing to reflect on this or that passage. Papa was an astute student of the Good Book.

When I finished reading Revelation, he said, "There's a message in those words for you, Narlow. Best tend to it, reconcile with your mother. Not for her, but for you, your heart, son."

Caring for Papa forced me to be in the same close quarters with Mama in the dugout. By the end of the first month, we had tolerated each other, spent more time together, than all the years combined since I left this place in 1877. No doubt I riled her, but her discomfort paled in the shadow of my contempt for her, my revulsion of her still possessing the ability to suck air. I hated my thoughts but they were true. A pit of vipers brings fear, but her pit-of-a-grave-heartless soul brought no horror, just the stench of Nature's defect that harbored a vile creature called, Mama. A birthing-being, one who had chased me throughout my youth like a devil possessed, born with scorpion wings instead of a heart.

Here in this dusty dugout, my childhood taunted me. *What childhood?* I asked myself. Though I fought it to a draw, those memories were gaining ground. Then one evening when Papa was resting in a peaceful snooze, I dozed off and went back to that night when I was twelve. Papa and Fernando were off tending nannies and their kids, leaving me alone with Mama.

I was sitting on my milk stool in the milking shed, late in the evening, but the full moon coming through the slats of the shed gave off enough light for my milking. I had just three more nannies. I brought in another nanny, poured a half-cup of grain in the milk stall's trough, started milking her. I was tired, sleepy. I leaned my head against the nanny's warm, soft, velvet-fuzz bag, feeling the rhythm of the foamy-white stream from her tits, hissing, hissing strong into the half-full bucket. I became aware that there was suddenly more light on the gray wall in front of me. A purple mushroom showed itself. Two bobcats caterwauling in the fork of a mesquite, the cry of a little girl, like the night my little sister, Mary Jewell, passed from smallpox. The cry and flash of a nonsensical thing like a purple mushroom were

109

surely caused by me being groggy, dreaming. I shook my head, but the mushroom got bigger, brighter, purpler, garish-like. The high lonesome of a bull elk calling his mate.

I heard a whir. Something stung me, *hard*, hard across my shoulders. I turned to see Mama standing over me. A lantern held above her head in one hand. A horse quirt in the other. Eyes beady, sparking yellow hate. Before I could stand or hoist my arm to fend her off, she swung again, slashing the quirt across my neck. I jumped to my feet, grabbed the wrist that held the quirt. She swung the lantern down at my head. I ducked, grasped her other wrist. Stood squeezing her wrists, holding them above her head, the quirt and the lantern still gripped in her hands.

Of a sudden, her face took on the yellow glow of the lantern, began to turn pink, purple. Her head and face were now in the hand where the lantern was. Like I wasn't squeezing her wrist. Her neck. I squeezed hard, harder, *harder*, with all the might I could muster. Her face turned deeper red. I thought it was because I was squeezing her neck. But I was squeezing her wrists so hard it made my fists, her whole body shake. Until that moment, I don't recall ever wanting to hurt anything or anybody. But there I was, wanting to hurt *this* somebody *real* bad—my own mother. I squeezed harder, like I was milking a nanny, trying to get her to give me that last drop of milk. My hands kept squeezing, wanting her to feel *real* pain, to bleed. I admit I wanted her dead. My own mother—dead.

The boards of the milk shed began to rattle, the ground quaked, eerie purple-pink light all around. Mama glanced down, aware of the ground was quaking. The purple light and quaking mushroom subsided.

I let go of her wrists, jerked the quirt and lantern away. I asked, 'Why? Mother, why? Why did you—'

She gasped for air. "Because. Because *I can*. I'm your *mother,* goddamn you." We stood glaring at each other. She saw it in my eyes—there would never be any more whipping—for *any* reason. Powerless, I suppose for the first time in her life. It showed in her eyes. She backed off, rubbing life back into her hands and wrists, sucking, blowing wind.

She screamed, "*You half-breed son-of-a-bitch*. You should . . . should be real—*real* proud of yourself. I wish I was a man 'cause I'd whip your goddamn ass right where you stand. You oughta be ashamed, picking on a poor defenseless woman. Your *own mother*, damn you. You're just like your goddamn father, and you'll grow up . . . grow up to be just like him. *Weak, worthless*, nothing more than a—a no-count son-of-a-bitch."

110

I started to speak, but there were no words. I looked deep in her evil, swimming-black eyes that spewed a copper stench. All I heard, saw, smelled, tasted, felt was hate, deceit.

Four years drifted by before I ever mentioned that night to Coot. He only said, "That's strange."

"Strange? Why's that?"

He said, "Remember that storybook my little sister had when we were little tykes? The one with a picture of a cow dancing on a rainbow? To me, you've always been that cow, a'dancing around on a rainbow. You've always been easy to be around, a naturally happy boy, and in my mind's eye, I often see you dancing on a rainbow. Kinda strange how you can have a mother like that, yet always a smile plastered on your face."

I told Coot that ever since that night, I'd noticed that when I'm around Mama for more than a minute, her shoulders slackened, her eyes dart back and forth, like she's looking for a way out of a trap, to escape. She backs away, a faint hint of caution in her squinted eyes, then she'll turn and scurry away.

Coot smiled. "Narlow, you don't see it, do you? She's scared of you, terrified to death of you. Thinks you may just be meaner'n she is." He thought a minute, then said, "And I believe you are."

Papa stirred. I bolted up. Mama was hurrying past the goat skin into the dark. No doubt. She'd been standing over us.

◉◉◉

At the close of those so long, yet short, two months, late at night, Papa and I were whispering at his bedside, a single candle burning next to where Mama sat a few feet away, snoring, sound asleep. The odor of burning moccasin leather was thick. I felt Two Sticks' presence and told Papa. He motioned that he sensed it as well, nodded, smiled. He was tired, whispered as much, yet he seemed determined, resolute, about what, I could not discern. He waved, whispered, "Doyl." He lay quiet, eyes closed, his fingers and mouth twitching, occasionally murmured a word or two. We'd talked about everything that needed saying, laughed a thousand times about everything we'd ever done that brought a smile, shared a tear over a couple of issues as well.

Papa's lips flickered, eyes twitched, like he wanted to say he was through with his struggle.

I leaned close. "Papa?"

In a moment, his eyes blinked, smiled.

111

"Papa. You're fighting. Fighting something. Something inside you. Struggling. Know what I think?"

The corners of his mouth flickered.

"Papa, I think you're struggling not to let go."

He woofed air, a smile quivered at his lips.

"Papa."

His body shook.

"Papa, it's all right to let go. If you want to. I'm here. I'll stay right here with you. If you're ready to let go. I'll never leave you, Papa. Always be with you. I want you to know that. You'll always be with me. Always, always with me. Never leave you. Always in my heart. Never forget you. I could never. You and I are always. Always."

He smiled, reached for my hand.

"I love you, Papa."

He whispered, "I . . . I . . ," took a shallow breath, smiled.

He became peaceful, quiet. In the low candlelight, he squeezed my hand hard, then it went limp. Heard him suck in air, air that he never released, witnessed his handsome, tanned face begin to turn gray at his forehead, his ears seemed to curl forward, saw the thin line of gray death slowly recede down past his eyebrows.

In less than half a minute, Mama sprang to her feet. Came over, gazed down in the low light. "He's dead."

❂❂❂

Coot and I were spent, had no interest in running guns. No curiosity in a blessed thing. We talked about it, agreed that Papa meant more to both of us than we had ever realized, all he had done for us, taught us all we knew about being men. About the time I was coming to grips with Papa's passing, Coot disappeared. I drove out to his farm every day, never to find a solitary sign of him. After a week, I figured I knew where to find him. I borrowed a horse from Big George and headed up to the northernmost peak of the mountain range, St. Anthony's Peak, a place we called Abe's Nose. When I was a scruffy boy, Papa and I and Fernando Valdez played in its cave. So much joy for a tyke, fun with my elders. It was a favorite spot of ours as it was the site of Papa's gold mine. It never produced much yellow, but in hard times it got us through.

When I rode over the last rise before topping out on the ridge, I spied Coot at a small campfire off to the north. I should not have intruded, sorry I came. I backed the horse around.

Coot called out, "Narlow, I saw you coming two miles off. Come on down. Bring any whistle wetter with you?"

Fact be known, the only thing I packed in my bedroll was a gallon of prime, sippin' whistle wetter. We camped for two weeks, living off the land, mainly mule deer steaks and last year's prickly pear tunas. No tears were shed. We'd just spent two months taking care of Papa, walking on egg shells because of Mama, and there were tolerable few tears left between us. Besides, Papa would kick our backsides for such silly doings. We laughed, reminisced, mainly about Papa and how he got us through our youth, had a snort of two, giggled and snorted over what I don't recall, ate a deer back strap, climb into our bedrolls, sometimes before sundown we'd watch the orange glow of the setting sun on one side of the ridge, turn over to witness the full, blue moon rise on the other. Peaceful serenity, God's presence. Papa was all over that ridge.

20

Tornillo, Texas

Rodolfo had become increasingly displeased with *Generalisimo* Francisco Villa. Pancho was irritable, vicious with his own men, blaming everyone but himself for his recent battle losses. Rodolfo began to have serious reservations about Mexico's people ever maturing sufficiently to govern themselves. "They are like children," he once said. He was certain that the US would soon become embroiled in Europe's war. Months back, Rodolfo had told us that the seemingly insignificant assassination of Archduke Ferdinand would ignite all of Europe in war. A killing in a Bosnian city by the name of Sarajevo.

As usual, Rodolfo was correct in that prognostication. The Great War was on. The United States would soon be sending troops across the Atlantic. Rodolfo feared our supply of Mausers would dry up for good.

He said, "President Wilson just recognized *Presidente* Carranza as the legitimate head of Mexico. He also allowed Mexican troops to cross US soil to catch

Villa with his drawers down. At Agua Prieto, instead of the 1,200 federal troops Villa expected, there were 6,000, who mowed down the *Villistas* with machine-gun fire and artillery. Villa feels betrayed, forsaken by a country he thought was his ally. He's insane with rage. I fear he will retaliate against the US, seek revenge."

Coot said, "Rodolfo, you have Sun Tzu's book on your bookshelf. You're familiar with him, written around 500 BC. I recall one passage: 'An army may be likened to water: water leaves dry the high places and seeks the hollows; an army turns from strength and attacks emptiness. The flow of water is regulated by the shape of the ground; victory is gained by acting in accordance with the state of the enemy.' Sun Tzu's tactics could have been written by Chief Victorio or any number of Apache war chiefs. When Narlow and I lived with the Apache, we saw it, practiced it firsthand. Apaches believed that no losses in a battle was a win. Sun Tzu or Victorio or Juh or Geronimo or Nana would never attempt to charge their horses through barbed wire, wire strung before well-armed troops with machine-guns in fortified trenches, cannons all around. *Insanity*. Those crazy bastards in Europe haven't learned a damn thing about war in a hundred centuries of constant practice. Villa's doing the same damn thing. What's worse, I don't think he gives a damn."

21

Socorro, New Mexico, Fall 1915

Our train's whistle must have served as Fritz's alarm clock. He was standing tall when we walked up the steps between his loading dock and our waiting boxcar.

Coot chuckled. "Why, look who's up, all bright-eyed and bushy-tailed this bright cheerful good morning."

"Well, you said—"

"Come on," Coot said, "let's get these rifles and shells loaded. Time's a'wasting. Where's your heavy-duty dolly?"

Fritz scurried off, rushed back in with the dolly, wheeled it over to a stack of crated rifles, made a valiant attempt to push the stack back while pushing the lip of the dolly under the load. Coot elbowed him aside, leaned into the crates, slipped the dolly under them, hurried past Fritz on the way through the wide loading doors.

We finished loading, Coot pointed over his shoulder. "Pay him."

I gave Fritz the bank money sack. He asked me quietly if his share of the delivery fee was included for the last shipment.

"What the hell are you trying to pull now, Fritz? You know damn well I wired you your $7,666.67 two months ago. And damn it, I have a receipt to prove it."

"Oh, yes, I must have forgotten. It's been so long ago, you know," he whispered, trying to keep Coot from hearing.

I caught up with Coot, who was talking to the trainmaster. He turned to me. "Track above Albuquerque is washed out. Train's running four hours late. Might as well get a room and get some rest."

Coot gave the trainmaster a dollar, asked him to send a runner to wake us fifteen-minutes before train time. About the time I dozed off, there was a rap on the door. A boy's voice squeaked, "Train time."

As we were boarding, the trainmaster came over and said, "Did Fritz Hans-Smidt find you boys?"

"No, haven't seen him this morning, " I replied.

"Well, he was about to have a hissy-fit about an hour ago when the switch-engine was pulling your boxcar to hook up with the southbound. He was yelling something at the switch engine engineer, about what I don't know. I had to get on the wire to warn the northbound freight to stay at the Elgin spur until your train passed. When I came back, Hans-Smidt was no where in sight."

I said, "I guess I better go find out what's on Fritz's mind."

"Hell with him. Train time."

As the train chugged into Rincon, we were standing on the landing between the Pullman and the first boxcar. The train usually stopped just long enough to drop the jerkwater spout to the locomotive's waterhold, fill it, then steam on south to El Paso.

"Wonder what's up," I said. "Looks like we're being pushed off the main line. I suppose a passenger train is coming north out of El Paso." I looked ahead. "Whoa. Look up ahead. Must be 200 US Army troops and fifty military vehicles. I don't like the looks of this."

The locomotive ground to a stop, a military officer walked up, asked with a toothy smirk, "Coot Boldt and Narlow Montgomery?"

"Yes," Coot answered. "What's the trouble, lieutenant?"

His answer was curt, but not short. "I am Lieutenant George S. Patton, United States Army. By order of the Department of Interior, and under my command, my men are inspecting this train for munitions and similar contraband. Bound for destinations south of the US-Mexican border. There's a presidential executive order in effect banning such shipments to Mexico. I believe you gentlemen have a boxcar on this train. We intend to search that boxcar. Its contents—box by box. Every boxcar. Every farm implement this train's carrying. Every sack of grain. Until we find what we are searching for. And we know what that is." He paused, grinning wide enough to show his tonsils. "Don't we, gentlemen?"

"Be our guest, Lieutenant Patton," I said. I didn't like this smart-ass shave-tail, looking fresh out of West Point.

Never losing his grinning smirk, he said, "I do not require your permission. You are not under arrest, yet. While we are searching this train, please accompany Sgt. Blum to that bench over there in front of the station. The sergeant and his corporal will keep you company while we conduct our inspection." He pivoted sharply and swaggered down the line of train cars.

The lieutenant and his men searched the train's three boxcars, then scrambled over the two flatbed cars loaded with farm equipment, searched a grain car, prodding the grain with long poles, finding nothing. The lieutenant ordered the Rincon trainmaster to dump the contents of the grain car on the tracks. The man argued with the lieutenant, shrugged, removed the safety lever under the grain car, pulled a lever and tons of yellow grain spilled out from under the car, covering the tracks with wheat. Troopers shoveled the grain back until the entire load was out of the car, spread it, kicked the piles until they were certain there was nothing hidden under it. They leaned on their shovels, turned to the lieutenant.

Lieutenant Patton walked back to us, the smirk on his face replaced with a scowl. "Listen here, goddamn it! We have verifiable information that you two characters have been using this rail line to transport munitions to Mexico. However, it appears you have been tipped off. We found no Mausers or cartridges. General John J. Pershing at Fort Bliss has ordered me to advise you that should we catch you running guns or ammunition, the general will have you court-martialed in a military tribunal. Your punishment will not be light. Not as light as your civilian courts charge common criminals. Such as yourselves."

Coot jumped to his feet. "Lieutenant, I don't know who the hell you think you're talking to. You cocky, Mother-of-Pearl pistol-grip, Prima-goddamn-Dona, nettlesome bastard. You are talking to United States citizens. I say you're not only a cocky bastard. You, sir, are a goddamn liar. Either that, or General Pershing doesn't know the law. I don't believe for one damn minute that US citizens can be tried by an Army court-martial, or tribunal. And since generals don't become generals by being the dumbest shit in the brigade, I believe the general knows the law. And you, sir, are lying through your idiotic smirking teeth!"

Lieutenant Patton smiled, licked his lips. "Well. That puts a different slant of things. I've been using that bullshit line to scare hell out of civilians for months. You're the first one to have the courage or brains to say one damn word to the contrary. You are free to go." He turned to the conductor, nodded, and the train lurched forward.

"Cocky bastard," I said. "I hadn't noticed that our boxcar was not on this train until the lieutenant ordered us to sit in front of the train station."

"Fritz must have been tipped off about this train search. Had our boxcar taken out of the line. I don't know how he knew, but I guess that's why he was looking for us in a panic. That frilly bastard probably saved our asses."

"How are we going to get our shipment to Tornillo?" I asked.

"How are we going to get any shipment to Tornillo is the real question."

El Paso

I gave the Western Union operator five dollars for two wires to be sent immediately. One to Fritz asking, You okay? The other to Rodolfo telling him we were all right, in no danger, but that our Swiss Chocolates and Swizzle Sticks had been delayed, that we'd be in Tornillo after we had time to think this through.

The telegraph operator came running after me before we were half a block down the street. He handed me a handwritten note from Fritz. "Your friend must have been waiting for your wire, 'cuz here's his answer, Mr. Montgomery."

In response to my, "You okay?" wire, Fritz's wire read, "Yes, frightfully so."

The next morning, Coot was growling and muttering to himself, looking out of my office window on South El Paso Street. Coot read Fritz's wire, gazed out the window to the street. "I wonder what that bastard wants now?"

"What bastard?" I asked.

"The cocky bastard—Lieutenant George Friggin' S. Ass Patton."

"Oh, that friggin' S. Ass Patton. The Mother-of-Pearl bastard."

"Headed this way," Coot said. "Look at that turd. Strolling across the street in his polished boots. Bloused Calvary field-pants. Strutting like an ostrich hen in season."

The lieutenant stood outside on the boardwalk banging his baton on my gold-leafed glass-paned door.

I yanked open the door. "What the hell are you doing beating on a door that's open for business? You don't knock on a goddamn business door. You open the goddamn business door. Come in, state your goddamn business. Where do you think you are, Lieutenant? Knocking on the general's door, begging for an audience?"

"Ah, Mr. Montgomery, I believe," he said with a smirk. "I have a special invitation for you gentlemen. An invitation from General John 'Black Jack' Pershing, requesting the honor of your company. Luncheon today, 1200-hours. Chow served from the Officers Mess. He asks that you present yourselves at his headquarters. May I presume to say that you accept the General's kind invitation?"

I didn't look Coot's way for his concurrence, as I thought it prudent to accept the general's invitation. If Coot didn't want to join the general's "luncheon," perhaps he might be happy to take his "noon meal" with the general.

"You may tell the general that we shall be happy to accept his kind invitation. We'll be there at noon."

"Don't be late," he said, smirking up at me, expecting my reply. The lieutenant smiled, turned to Coot with the same smirking, toothy grin, touched his cap with his baton, opened the door to the street, turned, and said over his shoulder, his gray eyes sparkling, "I look forward to that luncheon. Far more than you can imagine. Yes indeed. Gentlemen, please—don't be late. The general abhors tardiness."

As we stepped through the door at precisely 1200-hours, the general was on his feet and came across the floor to greet us.

"Thank you so much for joining me on such short notice, gentlemen. I believe you have met Lieutenant Patton. Please seat yourselves and I'll have an orderly bring our trays." He was a strikingly handsome man, gray hair, trim mustache and physique, tanned, manly.

The General strolled to the window, then returned. "I'm so pleased to meet your acquaintance, as I am a great admirer of yours. You men were legendary before I ever came West. Right out of West Point in 1886, my first assignment was with the 6th Cavalry at Fort Bayard, New Mexico. The tracking skills you learned while at White Mountain Reservation have little equal."

I said, "You flatter us beyond our capabilities, sir. We remember you well, General, and my papa happened to be a great admirer of yours as well."

Coot was seated across from Lieutenant Patton. By the time we were served our trays, they were on much better terms. The lieutenant was far friendlier, and Coot never was one to hold a grudge. He ribbed him about his Mother of Pearl pistol grips.

Lieutenant Patton corrected him. "Pure ivory grips, I can assure you, sir. Purchased this silver-plated Colt .45 Peacemaker at Shelton Payne Arms in El Paso just last week. Paid Mr. Payne fifty dollars, which included the superbly crafted engraving he carved himself. I am quite proud of the grips and expect that this weapon will be by my side for the entire remainder. Remainder of my military career."

"Beg your pardon, Lieutenant," Coot said, "but they sure look like Mother of Pearl, all shiny and slick."

The lieutenant gave him a half-smile. "Sir, I am certain only a French pimp would wear pearl-handled pistol grips."

We chatted for a bit, then Lieutenant Patton turned to a more serious subject. "Gentlemen, I'm a curious fellow. Part of my nature. What is it about Pancho Villa. His band of cutthroats that is so intriguing to the revolutionaries. Why do they follow him with such blind allegiance?"

Coot returned the lieutenant's half-smile. "Pancho may be leading a bunch of cutthroats, but after thirty-five years of Porfirio Diaz and his henchmen, Pancho's men aren't so bad. While Diaz and the rich were sipping champagne, smoking wine-soaked cheroots, playing polo on million dollar Arabians, Mexico's *pobres* were slaves, starving to death."

The lieutenant smiled. "Polo, huh? Well, Mr. Boldt, you have just raised *Presidente* Diaz several notches in my book. He can't be all bad—if he plays polo. That's a real gentleman's game, I can assure you. Perhaps you will favor me by a game here at Fort Bliss. That would delight me no end."

Coot grinned. "Sit a horse pretty good, Lieutenant?"

His clenched-teeth-smile brightened. "Quite well."

When we finished our meal, the lieutenant stood and excused himself.

The general watched his lieutenant close the door behind him. "That is the finest officer I've ever had serving with me. Lieutenant Patton is somewhat brash, but he is dead-set certain of himself, and I admire that in a man. He will be an excellent general someday—when our country needs him the most. I wanted a few minutes of privacy with you gentlemen, first to apologize for the lieutenant's action yesterday. He admitted he was a little, shall we say, 'over zealous,' but he was so certain he had you dead-to-rights that he would find you in possession of illegal rifles and cartridges. Well, you know how dead-right we can all be at times, and then have to eat crow when we find we're dead wrong."

"Yes, General," I said. "My papa always said it's always best to eat your crow while it's still warm."

Coot chuckled. "Forget it, General Pershing, and please tell Lieutenant Patton that I apologize for my ill temper. Calling him a liar." He laughed. "Tell him that he is obviously a prevaricator. Never a liar. There's too much gentleman under that tough skin to house a liar. I can see why you're partial to him."

The general leaned against the front of his desk. "What concerns me about this entire scenario is that it appears there is a snitch in my ranks. I don't expect you gentlemen to admit anything, or to even comment on the accusations that have been sent your way, but having a snitch in my ranks, passing on classified information, that concerns me greatly."

Coot stood to leave. "Well, General Pershing, we are not certain about what actually happened at Rincon yesterday. But I doubt very much that you have a snitch in your ranks."

⊚⊚⊚

We caught the afternoon train to Tornillo, found our seats, and I said, "You know damn well this gunrunning's going to get our asses shot, yet you insist—"

"You know, Narlow, if Na-Tu-Che Puy's ghost knew how you wasted almost two years of his time, he'd come back to life and stomp you."

"How's that?"

"Na-Tu taught you not to empower the negative by dwelling on it, saying it negates the possibilities of the positive. How far do you suppose the Apaches would have gone if they didn't believe, believe with all their heart and spirit, in what they were about? Their People, their ancient ways. Huh? How far? Across the first arroyo they came to?"

"Next thing you know, you'll be preaching the Sermon on the Mount, but damn it, Coot, this gunrunning and flying into Mexico is getting to be more than we bargained for. It sure seems to me that we're on a mission that has one final destination—you and me, lying out on some high-desert mesa, nobody knowing

120

what happened to us but the hollow, red-ruby sun. First blow-flies, fire ants, then coyotes and buzzards picking our bones. If the Mexicans don't get us, the US Army will. I hate to leave Rodolfo in a lurch, but this is insanity."

"Narlow, that talk is not like you. What's gotten into you?"

"I don't know. I'm getting spooked about the whole damn thing. I owe it to Rodolfo to tell him that I'm close to quitting this gunrunning mess."

"Stick with me. We've never quit a job in our lives. Never shirked our responsibility to any man."

"I don't like quitting any more than you do, but the threat of twenty years in Leavenworth for gunrunning is another consideration. You want to look through parallel bars until the day they plant your ass?"

"I suppose you have a point there. You're right. We owe Rodolfo. We best tell him what's eating on you. If it's eating on you, it won't be long before it's chomping on my ass."

⊚⊚⊚

When we filled Rodolfo in on the train search, his demeanor turned ashen, his eyes narrowed, as he sat considering what the consequences could have been. He said, "Well, that certainly puts a different slant on our future plans. I would never—"

"Excuse me, Rodolfo, but I have something I need to get off my chest. Coot doesn't share my concerns, but he'll be the first to tell you that it is just a matter of time before it will. I think we've bitten off a whole bunch more than we can chew. This stuff's going to get us killed. It's not our nature to be careless, but you must realize it's hard to keep a violin strung up to concert pitch all the time. You must put that old fiddle aside, loosen its strings, or it'll get flat, become useless. I'm not here to hang up my hat just yet, but you need to know I'm damn close."

"I can certainly appreciate your concerns. I must admit that I have spent many a sleepless night worrying about you two. I have a proposition to make you gentlemen. This is probably an inappropriate time to make this offer, as I know very well that you are not assisting me for the money. Fact is, you have continued to refuse compensation for your efforts. But, I have in mind putting up a million dollars to be split evenly between the two of you and Fritz Hans-Smidt when this revolution is concluded. Considering the risks you are taking, it is not much, but you may want to consider that for your futures."

Coot cautioned, "Rodolfo, I don't see it that way. Don't think that million dollars is a good idea. Fritz is in this for one thing—the money."

"I thought if the three of you had a common goal, perhaps you could act more like partners. You don't think that is possible?"

"Hell no. Fritz's no one you'd want to partner with. Narlow and I don't trust him."

"Well, then, gentlemen, I'll leave that to your best judgment, but the offer still stands. Any thoughts, Narlow?"

"I agree with Coot, but I've never been one to turn down that kind of money. Maybe Coot's plan will take my mind off quitting. Tell Rodolfo your plan."

Coot was sitting on the arm of Rodolfo's heavy, leather couch. He stood, pursed his mouth to one side. "I don't have all the kinks worked out. Basically what I'm thinking about is leaving Socorro and crossing the Rio at San Pablo in the Reo, where there's a good, heavy-gravel crossing that's dern near always passable. We head due east. Skirt north around a heavy, impenetrable lava flow, on into Carrizozo. The Eddy Brothers built a rail line from El Paso to Alamogordo. And plan on extending it to White Oaks, then on up to Carrizozo. Until it's completed, we'll truck the rifles on down to Alamogordo. At that point, we'll load the Reo in a boxcar, a boxcar rather than a flat rail car. Out of view of anyone snooping around. We'll buy a boxcar, paint it typical government gray, to resemble official US property. Forty miles north of El Paso is a spur that serves an active mine at Oro Grande. We'll drive the Reo off there, go cross-country, nearly due south down here to Tornillo."

Rodolfo bowed his head, his chin resting on his hand at his lapel. "Hmmm. Sounds plausible. And what do you think the odds are of not being discovered by a federal marshal or the military?"

I spoke up. "An old trusted friend of ours travels that line between El Paso and Alamogordo. He uses it to transport pine logs for use in making heavy construction lumber, beams, and fence posts. Before this revolution started, he exported everything to northern Mexico, now he ships it on to Dallas for their construction industries. Other than the train crew, he's never seen another soul on that train. No one poking around asking questions, not even a rail detective. That's about all we have to go on, but is seems safe enough."

22

Oro Grande, New Mexico

We rented a barn on the south end of Oro Grande for a dollar a month, figuring we'd need it. We brought IB up to keep an eye on things while we trucked the rifles. IB was not required, or even of much use, but we felt an obligation to help our childhood amigo out, make him feel useful.

◉◉◉

We loaded the Reo on a flatcar for Socorro. We hadn't seen Fritz since the Army searched our train at Rincon. It was late when we pulled into Socorro, so we headed for the Dime Box Saloon. The saloon's fascia showed itself thirty-feet in the air, torch-lit arches declaring its high potent authority in all of central New Mexico. Windowless, dark green, lanterns hung from rafters, their dim light mixed with thick tobacco smoke cast a yellowish-green haze on the crowd. Lit by a single candle, a trio played their string instruments in a dingy corner, dressed to the nines, their chamber music strangely out of place in this rough-and-ready watering hole. But the patrons enjoyed the highbrow background music, causing a powerful thirst in the crowd.

Coot led us to a table in the far corner. Soon, rather than later, Fritz Hans-Smidt found us, ambled up to our table. We needed to talk to him about the train search, but I was hoping that could wait until tomorrow.

He wouldn't go away, just stood there.

I said, "Sit down, Fritz. Take a heavy load off your feet. I do believe you have the daintiest two feet I have ever witnessed attached to a full-grown man. I was born with bigger feet than those. What size are those slippers, Fritz? Threes?"

"No. I'll have you know that I wear a full size-five, narrow."

"Oh, my," I said, pressing my palms to my cheeks. "Such big slippers."

Coot chuckled, stood, bumping the table into Fritz's gut, walked to the bar, ordered himself a drink, called the waitress over, gave her two dollars to send a bottle and glass over to me.

Fritz told the waitress, "Oh, and may I please have a beer? The German Stout you have on tap will do nicely. I just love a bold, courageous European beer. Warm, please."

The waitress smacked her fresh stick of Blackjack gum. "Warm's all we got, sweet lips."

Fritz pressed the tips of his manicured fingers on the table, the half-moons of his fingernails, milky. "I am certain that you are just dying to know how I learned that your train would be searched in Rincon. Well, I have a dear friend that—"

The waitress brought his beer, slammed it on the table, sashayed her wide fanny off into the crowd.

Fritz went on, "Well, as I was saying. I have a dear friend who has a barber shop in Radium Springs, and he has a dear friend in Rincon, who works as a clerk for the Atchison, Topeka and Santa Fe Railroad. Rincon's abandoned, so he gets so lonesome. He told my friend that he had heard, very confidentially, that gunrunners were suspected of using the rail line to transport guns and bullets from somewhere around Albuquerque to somewhere south of El Paso. They did not know exactly where the guns and bullets began their journey, or their destination, but the Army was certain they were destined for Pancho Villa's troops in Chihuahua, which, as you know, is strictly against the presidential mandate prohibiting such activity. And so—"

"For crap sake, Fritz. Skip over this bilious crap and just get to the point."

"I'm getting there, Narlow. For once, just once, can you just be patient?" He threw back his curly head, pressed his sleeve with one hand as if it had a hot iron in it. Satisfied, he went on. "So, anyway—oh, where was I? Oh, yes, my dear friend rode the same train you and Coot arrived on the morning of your last trip to Socorro. My friend was at my home when I arrived there late that night after you checked into the hotel, unbeknownst to me, I might add. But anyway, my dear friend told me that his friend told him—"

"Which dear friend told what dear friend?" I asked. "Can you slap some names on these dear friends? Harry—Mary, George—Shirley?"

"Their names are also very confidential. Well, anyway, the Army suspected the rail line was being used to smuggle guns and bullets, and would be waiting for your train at Rincon. I jumped right out of bed, dressed hurriedly, and began fruitlessly searching to find you. I was so frightened, but then—"

"I get the picture, Fritz." I nodded. "I get the picture. And we thank you for taking our boxcar out of the train line. That would have been disastrous, and on bended knee, we thank you for it."

"Well," he said, ordering another beer, "Coot hasn't thanked me."

"Coot thanks you, his estranged wife thanks you, I thank you, my darling wife thanks you."

"Well, anyway, Narlow, I am so pleased that Coot went to the bar. I have a most important item that we need to discuss. You are so much more agreeable than that beast of a man." His hands flew up, shaking, his head tossed back. "Oh, such a beast!"

He settled down, took a sip of beer, wiped his cherub lips with a white hanky. "Narlow, I must, I just must insist on a larger percentage of the delivery fee. Although I am not involved in the actual details of the transportation of the actual guns and bullets, I am in constant, actually, constant jeopardy, and I must keep my contacts open in my homeland, and, of course, now south to El Paso with my dear friends. There are a host of palms to be greased, as you can just imagine. Therefore, I am due a larger slice of the community pie. And by the way, you owe me $1,000 for two months warehouse storage for the guns and bullets. Of course, you can pay me on your next trip. I'm really, really reenthusiated about my recommendation. Would you like to hear how I propose we split the delivery fee in the future?"

"Reenthusiated, huh? Then you must be really, really fumblgated as well. But, no, I'm not particularly interested in your idea," I said, pouring my bar glass to the brim. "Wait for Coot. Then tell us."

"Well, I have given this considerable thought. A mammoth amount of serious thought. and I believe that a fifty-fifty split of the fee would be quite fair. A generous fifty percent for you and Coot, and fifty percent for me and my mounting expenses. You are such a reasonable man. Don't you think that arrangement would be fair?"

"Fair? What's fair got to do with it? I not only think you've lost your friggin' mind, I know damn well you've lost it. Well, looky there, Fritz," I said, pointing my bar glass. "Your beastly pal, Coot. Coming back in after relieving himself out in the alley. This is your lucky day. He's headed our way. Now you'll have an opportunity to explain all this crap to him to his face so I won't mess it up in translation."

Coot paused at a table where an old gentlemen cowboy-friend of ours was seated. Coot shook hands with the old cowboy-gent using his left hand. He showed the cowboy his right hand, appeared as if he was making excuses for his injured hand, though I did not recall him having suffered an injury. He came back to our table, sauntered around behind Fritz, paused, wiped his right hand on the back of Fritz's neck and ears.

"Damn it, Fritz. Don't you just hate it? Piss all over my own damn hand. By god, there oughta be a law." He sat down, filled my glass to the brim, and poured it down, grinned. "Ah. Hot-damn. That's some damn good whiskey." He slapped the table, Fritz jumped back in his chair, Coot's eyes watering from the damn good whiskey. "What's happenin'."

Fritz gulped down his beer, left a thin dime on the table, beat a hasty retreat out the side door.

Coot laughed. "What did I say to get him jerked off? Need to remember it. Use it again."

◎◎◎

Fritz was waiting for us on the dock of his warehouse before sunup. I walked up the steps to the dock. "Fritz, we're paying you for three loads, but we can only transport the usual load, come back for the other two loads over the next few days."

"But that means my warehouse will be piled to the rafters with your guns and bullets. I will have to charge you a warehouse fee. You can understand that, can't you, Narlow?"

"No, I can't, Fritz. Explain it to Coot. He's a patient listener."

We loaded the Reo, tarped and tied it down, and got in to leave.

Fritz came over to my side of the truck. "When can I expect you to come back for another load?"

Coot looked past me. "Why?"

"I was just wondering. Just curious."

Coot wouldn't cut him any slack. "Wondering, curious about what? Wondering or curious. Which is it? Wondering or curious? Maybe if there's time to take a nap before we get back?"

"Oh, no. Nothing like that."

"Tell you what, Pudg. You do whatever a pudg like you does when there's nobody watching. Just be here when we get back."

Coot turned the Reo and headed for the ford downstream west of San Pablo.

"Better lay off Fritz," I said. "Doesn't do us any good to stay crosswise with him all the time."

"It's the only entertainment I have. That and listening to you take up for your little cinnamon-toast-nutmeg amigo. You've taken a real shine to him, huh?"

23

Gunrunning was slow. Rodolfo sent men he trusted into Mexico to watch Villa, as he was suspicious of the once-great revolutionary, especially his harsh ways with his men, his insistence on fighting the war like the Europeans had for centuries.

Zara was home, anxious to go to "her" ranch, as she phrased it. Open space cures many aches, especially travelling to large cities, living, sleeping in strange surroundings for weeks, months at a time.

She and I, Coot and Rose, piled in the Reo along with a month of groceries and a ton of special treats for Tacho and Zoila, drove to El Paso's Union Depot. I bought tickets, got the ladies situated in a passenger car, while Coot arranged to have the Reo loaded on a flatcar.

Three hours later, we pulled into Van Horn's one-room depot, Coot drove the Reo off the flatcar, got her astraddle the rails of the spur, dropped her rail-wheels onto the rails, locked them in place. Zara and Rose giggled their delight at the sight of that rusty old six-wheeler, perched on the rails, her rail-feet resting on the steel rails. And we were off! Riding the rails to "Zara's ranch."

Our routine at the Coal Mine was the usual. The five of us rode horseback to special places Tacho had in mind, while Zoila rested as she was in her eighth month. Every other day, we piled in Tacho's buckboard for a trip to the airstrip, Rose would crank up the Curtiss and give us a show. Zara was mesmerized. We napped in the afternoon, the three ladies began supper preparations around five, the men retired to the Tarrango's front porch for a toddy. Same, monotonous, tedious, wonderful routine for twelve straight days.

On our last night, we all went outside after supper. Tacho started a mesquite fire by their *adobe*, the six of us sat around the fire, Tacho strumming his guitar, nothing in particular, just soft strumming melding with our conversation.

His broad smile and bronze face flashed in the firelight, indicated that he was improvising, setting the words in place to a love song as he went along. He scooted around on his stool, facing Zoila, his heartfelt song was for her alone. He smiled, the song now formed in his heart.

Coot sat cross-legged on the ground, idly poking an ember with a twig, began softly translating as Tacho went along:

Zolita, eres mi recompensa, mi vida,
Zolita, you are my prize, my life,
Sin ti, no hay nada,
Without you there is nothing.
En tu corazón y en tu cuerpo.
In your heart and in your body,
Llevas nuestro pequeño,
You carry our little one,
Niño, niña, no importa,
A boy, a girl, it is no matter,
Pronto esta revolución quedará atras,
For soon, this revolution will be behind us,
La vida nos llama, nuestros niños serán muchos,
And life beckons us, our children will be many.
Lo que miro en tu cara me dice todo lo que necesito,
The look on your pretty face says all I need,
Todo lo que Dios me pudo haber dado.
All that God could ever give me.

I nudged Zara, pointed with my eyes at Rose. She sat quietly, wide-eyed, gazing across the fire at Coot as if seeing him for the first time. Zara only smiled. She had always expressed sorrow that Coot's only stab at matrimony was with a heartless cur from Connecticut.

24

Well, if this don't beat all hell. Here I was leaning my full length on a pine plank that Tacho rigged up for me. He wired the plank to the back of his buckboard at forty-five-degrees, leaning it on the back of the buckboard so I'd have a view, not have to lie flat on my sore back the live-long day for two months. One month down, one to go in my plaster-of-Paris body cast.

This, the result of an admittedly, self-imposed accident, though the way I see it, it was sorta Coot's fault. He had gone off to St. Louis, yet again, seeking another source of supply of Mausers. I told Coot when he left on the evening train that was a hell of a long trip to keep from dealing with Fritz. Besides, our deal with Rodolfo called for us to deal with Fritz exclusively.

Coot stepped to the Pullman. "Dealing with Fritz can be rearranged. Besides, it would be a lot shorter than the trip to the state prison in Huntsville, and the forty-years I'd get for killing that damn German."

While Coot was gone, I made two trips to Socorro. Fritz asked where Coot was, then added, "Not that I give a damn about that bastard, just curious. He can die and go to hell for all I care."

On my second trip, Fritz was suddenly out of Mausers. Adding to that misery, the railroad bridge south of Carrizozo had washed out the night before, leaving no way to get to Rodolfo's *hacienda*. At sunrise the next day, I was forced to drive the Reo back 250-miles to El Paso on the most unforgiving "Class-A" road in New Mexico. Eighteen hours later, I limped into town, way past midnight. Late, but not too late for a toddy. I headed down to the "We Never Close Pool Parlor and Saloon."

Three hours and several shots of cognac later, I was properly primed for a good night's sleep. I bought the boys another round, paid my tab, and about that time, a pocket-size *mojon* by the name of Bill Fred, started in on the proprietor, Saul Nuninski, calling him "a no-count Mexican-Jew." I abhor anyone getting my hackles up when I'm in a smooth mood, so I asked him to speak easy about my friend, and headed for the door. Bill Fred grabbed my arm, yanked me around, and took a swing at me. I drew my Schofield and gave him a tiny temple-tap, which caused him to hit the floor, his narrow head caught in a spittoon. Much mirth and hell broke loose, so much so that a local copper stormed in, asking what was the cause of the ruckus. Saul explained the situation, and Bill Fred was summarily escorted from the premises.

I stumbled my way back to the Reo parked in the dark alley behind the Parlor, cranked her up, backed out into the dirt street. The next thing I know, the Reo's headlamps are looking straight up at the dark empty sky. *What the hell?* I opened the side door to step out to apprise myself of the situation. Damn door seemed to weigh a ton all of a sudden. But I heaved it open and stepped out, not the two-foot step down where the earth should be, but sixteen-feet back to the Reo's ass-end. She was standing on her tailgate with her front wheels resting on the gravel at street level, head lamps gawking into the night sky, gas gushing out of the gas cap on me at the bottom of the hole.

I must have passed out for a minute, then came around to find myself face down, sucking gasoline-flavored mud, right shoulder screaming. I tried to right myself, and in the struggle, my shoulder slipped back in the socket, and *Jeez-amighty.* Blessed relief crawled down my face, the pleasure like none other, even in the Biblical sense. I realized that I had backed into El Paso's world-class pothole, dug courtesy of the Rio Grande's flood last month.

Next thing I knew, I was on Doc Middaugh's kitchen table with an ether mask on my face. Mrs. Middaugh was setting up to put me out so the Doc could set my leg. I heard Coot come through the screen door, knew he was grinning, could tell by the way his boots scuffed the linoleum floor.

I heard Doc Middaugh say, "Coot, this is the damnedest mess I've ever seen. Likely take me the rest of the night. Worst collection of breaks I've seen in all my years of practice. Everything's broken on his right side at least once, from his big toe up, broken ribs, the whole shooting match. A double-compound, spiral fracture of his right femur."

I could tell by the sudden silence that Coot was standing there smiling.

Doc Middaugh added, "Goddamn it, Coot, your friend is in terrible shape. If you knew just how bad off he is, you'd wipe that silly-ass grin off your face. I've seen men go into irreversible shock from much less serious injuries than Narlow's."

Coot kept grinning. "Aw, Doc, rest easy. I saw Narlow fall off a sheer cliff in Red Rock Canyon when he was a pup. Got up, took off running after a nanny he was hell-bent on catching. Don't worry about losing this patient. He's stronger than a young mule, meaner'n a centipede, couldn't kill him with a brick, has another sixty years of living to get done. I suggest a complete body cast, Doc. Only way he'll stay down so things'll mend."

That was twenty-nine-days ago. Doc Middaugh warned that I had to stay in this damn plaster-of-Paris suit for at least two months. Never experienced such misery in all my life. I itched, was dirty, the cast stunk. I stunk. Claustrophobic, didn't dare sleep. When I dozed off, I dropped off a cliff into the same recurring nightmare, wrapped tight in a long-sleeved white coat worn by the guests at the psycho ward down on 3rd Street, a strange electric sign on the front door of the nervous house blinked with irritating insistency, bright orange, yellow letters: *Gone Fishing—Back in two months.*

Zara and Coot brought me down here to the Coal Mine Ranch headquarters a week after my accident. She stayed and visited with Zoila and Rose for a week, watched her fly the Curtiss with absolute wonder. Before Zara left to catch the train, I overheard her say, "Rose, not to take anything away from your accomplishment, but if Narlow can fly that thing, it certainly cannot be much of a challenge."

Coot came and went every ten days or so. I was stuck here with Bo and Rose, Zoila and Tacho. He moved me and my pine board to his porch.

What was that? My earballs were filled with the creak, rattle, and rolling backfire of the Reo. It had just gone through the pasture gate a hundred yards east of the house.

I yelled out, "Bo, here comes Coot. Just came through the gate, didn't bother to close it. Something's wrong, or heavy on his mind. Best go check on him."

Coot drove into the yard, his clothes tattered and torn, a dusting of white caliche brandished him from head to foot like a fresh-baked raspberry pastry. He stood, blood and white mud caked on his face, mouth, and shirt. He glanced at me, shrugged, turned and headed for the horse trough.

"What the hell's the problem, Coot?"

He waved over his shoulder, stepped in the trough, clothes, boots, hat, and all. In a while, he sloshed back through the yard gate, grinned, said, "What's happenin'. Why so glum?"

"I'm speechless. What the hell happened to you?"

He flopped down and yelled, "*Whiskey.* I feel like cat scat rolled in oatmeal."

Everyone came out on the porch. Rose said, "Coot! What in the world happened? You look *awful.*"

"Why, thank you, Rose. Nothing like a compliment from a pretty lady to cheer a man up. And when I have a full glass of whiskey in hand, I might just tell you what happened to me three hours ago at the spring just off the main road."

Zoila brought out a jug and glasses, Coot helped himself to three fingers, slugged it down, then brought me a glass.

"Narlow Montgomery, you dang near lost your lifelong *amigo* this afternoon." He clicked my glass, touched his finger to his lip, wiped off a spot of blood. "Just attended an old-fashioned ass kicking, me on the receiving end.

"Anyway, I cut off the main—. Naw, hell, let me start all over. I brought down 5,000 rounds of .45-70 rifle cartridges. Rodolfo's people need the cartridges down in a little Chihuahuan town named Carichic, fifteen miles southwest of Cuauhtemoc. Says the town is in the control of a small company of *Federales*. Townfolk evidently have a bunch of .45-70 rifles, not nary a cartridge. Needs the cartridges flown in, but of course our flying ace here got himself drunked-up. The folks at Carichic are dead-set on defending themselves. With the rifles they have, and those 5,000 cartridges, they'd have the wherewithal to get that done. I went to Socorro and picked up the cartridges, put up with Narlow's princess pal, went back to El Paso hoping to find a pilot we could trust. After two days I gave up, loaded the Reo on a flatcar, and went down to Tornillo to talk it over with Rodolfo. Decided to store the cartridges here until we figure out how to get them to Carichic."

South of Van Horn, Coot pulled the Reo off the track over to a spring a hundred-yards off the rails, started filling his water barrels for the Reo's leaky radiator. Had a devil of a time. Every ten-gallon bucket of water weighed eighty pounds, requiring him to lift the bucket to eye-level, set the bucket down on the truck bed, climb up on the bed, then pour it in the barrel. He had one barrel filled, turned to go back to the spring, when he spied a big Indian sitting on the Reo's running board. No idea where he came from, just one big man. Said the man had a long, heavy knife in his belt. Coot had laid his .45-automatic on the Reo's floorboard to get it out of his way. The Indian offered to help him load the water if he'd give him a ride to the border. The giant of a man told him that his name was Yellow Bear, a half-breed—half Comanche, half German, which was damned obvious. He had yellow hair, mustard-greenish-blue eyes, barrel-chested, arms like a gorilla, wore a loin cloth, otherwise he was buckass naked except for his knife and a pair of moccasins sewn to half a tire-tread. Claimed to have escaped from a traveling freak show that had stopped over in Odessa. The show's owner made him act loco, loll his tongue out, grunt, slobber, act crazy. Made him wrestle bears and tigers.

Coot laughed. "I'd bet that big bastard can take on both a bear and tiger at the same time, pick his canines with their ribs."

Yellow Bear stood flatfooted next to the Reo, poured the ten-gallon bucket in the barrel. Coot took the bucket back to the spring and filled it. When he turned back, that big bastard was standing with that long blade in his hand, their friendship seemed to be on the wane. With Coot's .45 on the floorboard, all he had to defend himself with was his old broken-tip Barlow. Pulled it out of his britches, started to open it, the Indian lunged at him with his long knife high in the air. The knife came down, Coot grabbed his wrist while the man grabbed Coot's other wrist with the Barlow, unopened. The big bastard swung him around, lifted him clear off the ground, beating him against the ground like a plucked duck, knocked Coot to the ground, his knees on Coot's shoulders, pinned stout and high, Coot's chin and neck stuck in the giant's crotch. Coot lost his grip on the fist with the knife when they hit the ground, but the man still held Coot's wrist with the Barlow.

Yellow Bear sat holding him down using no more effort than when he was sitting on the running board. Coot squirmed and fought like a wildcat, but was just plumb helpless. The big man sat motionless, his brilliant, flashing yellow eyes telegraphing, *You are a dead man.* The knife went high over his head and he thrust it. Coot heaved to one side with all his might, buried his head in the man's ass. The knife came down, stuck to the hilt in the dirt next to Coot's neck. Coot turned his head, grabbed the man's thumb with his teeth close to where the thumb meets the hand. He bit down as hard as he could and hung on tight. Yellow Bear cussed a war-hoop-blue-streak in three languages, blood spewing out over them. The man released his grip on the knife that was still stuck in the ground, then let go of Coot's wrist, tried to pry open Coot's mouth with his free hand. Failing that, he damn near ripped Coot's face clear off his skull, Coot's teeth still clamped hard on his thumb. Coot started clubbing him with his fist with no effect, but one of Yellow Bear's knees came off Coot's shoulder enough for him to scooted back under the man's butt, still clamping down tight with his teeth on the man's thumb.

Coot was in tears telling the story. "We were in a damn laughable position. Him squatting with one arm stuck back between his legs like he was wiping his ass backwards. Me behind him on all-fours, my teeth clamped onto his thumb, right up close to the cheeks of his ass, blood squirting everywhere. Yellow Bear reached with his left hand for his knife still stuck in the ground. I beat him to it with my boot, broke the knife blade off at the handle, looked down for a rock or a club. On the ground lay my damned old Barlow. I opened it, stuck him in the cheek of his ass as hard as I could jab it, drove that broken blade tip clear to the hilt, several times, but he didn't even flinch." Coot grinned. "Reckon he had his mind on his thumb? He started talking to me in Spanish, promising me that he would go on his way if I'd let go of his thumb. I was breathing like a stampeded buffalo, about to drown sucking blood and air around his thumb in my mouth and—"

"*Oh, Coot!*" Rose said. "You did not! How could you do such a thing?"

Coot laughed, filled his glass. "Then Yellow Bear changed his story, claimed that a man bought him from the owner of the traveling show, promised him his freedom if he killed me. His new owner claimed I owed him an old gambling debt. The man brought Yellow Bear out to the spring, gave him food and water, told him to wait by the spring for a man in a beat-up six-wheel-drive truck. If he'd kill me, he'd go free. I wanted him to describe the man, but couldn't get it done with a mouthful of bleeding thumb. But I wasn't about to give up my slim advantage. He sorta tumbled forward so we could face each other rather than me holding on to his thumb, that was attached to his arm, that was slung under his butt with my nose in close proximity.

"Now we were eye-to-eye. I bit down hard, he jerked back. Tore his own damn thumb plumb off. I beat it around to the my .45 on the driver's side floorboard of the Reo, ran back around, but he was long gone.

"I stood there getting my wind. Puffing and blowing, spewing, blowing blood, couldn't get air. That's when I remembered that I was trying to get my wind around clinched teeth that were still biting onto Yellow Bear's thumb. Teeth clenched so long, I had to pry my jaws apart."

Rose screamed, "Oh, my good Lord! Coot Boldt! How *revolting*. You did *not* do that."

"I didn't, huh?" He cocked his head to the side, setting a place for the devil on his shoulder, grinned at her. "Then how did I get loose from that Indian? Want to see his thumb?" he asked, patting a bloody lump in his shirt pocket.

After a while, everyone settled down, went back to their own knitting.

"Narlow, what do you make of this? Another coincidence?"

"Yeah, another coincidence. Like the half-dozen other times we've been shot at and stomped on. What about Yellow Bear saying you owed somebody over in Odessa?"

"Damned if I know. I remember the train from Dallas breaking down there one time a few months back. Recall playing cards all night in the smoker car. Cleaned them all out, but going bad on a gambling debt? Not my style."

⊙⊙⊙

Coot was cooking pancakes early the next morning, had everyone fed by the time Tacho got around to dragging me and my pine board into the kitchen. Rose was storing away the dishes.

I asked, "What'd you say the name of that Mexican village was that needs those .45-70 cartridges?"

"Why? You're not going anywhere. But if you must know, it's Carichic. Fifteen miles south of Cuauhtémoc, sixty-miles west of Chihuahua on the rail line to the *Barranca del Cobre*. No one knows who controls Chihuahua, so Rodolfo says the *Federales* in that village are as much captives as the villagers."

He flipped a pancake on a plate, stood tapping the spatula on the cook stove. "Another thing's bothering me. Our fearless leader, President Wilson, has formally recognized Carranza's government as the official head of Mexico. He's also embargoed all arms sales to Carranza's enemies.

"Damn it, Coot, I've been in this plaster monkey-suit long enough. You know that I heal twice as fast as any other man. Get me out of this damn thing. I'll take those villagers enough .45-70 shells to start their own revolution."

"Nope. You'd be weak. Wouldn't be able to stand, much less fly an airplane. You stay in that damn thing."

⊚⊚⊚

Tacho had turned the buckboard around at the airstrip so I could watch them work on the Curtiss. Six miles to the west across the Rio, the clouds were building over Mexico, black, heavy, wind gusting grit. Occasionally, Rose and her sidekicks, Bo and Tacho would stop whatever they were doing, look west at the cloud bank, look my way, laugh, go back to their chores. Tacho was busy on the far side of the biwing, back and forth between the airplane and the shed, only Tacho's feet and legs were visible to me under the fuselage. What was he up to?

Rose was dressed in dungarees, the dress of the *pobres*, old, worn-out white trousers and blouse, a silk yellow scarf around her neck. Bo was pumping up a tire on the Curtiss that needed topping off. Something about those three—what were they up to?

Tacho finished his chores on the far side, came around to my side of the Curtiss. I was distracted by an eagle that had a pair of eaglets with her, high overhead. Maybe mama had them out for their maiden flight. The three eagles glided on out of sight in the direction of the brewing storm, and my attention returned to the Curtiss.

"*Hey*. What's going on over there?" I yelled into the wind. "Tacho, what the hell are you doing?"

He was strapping down canisters of .45-70 cartridges on a flimsy yellow canvas-covered wooden frame. Rose climbed into the cockpit, Tacho gave the propeller a twist, and turned the biwing into the wind. I waved my one free hand, blew her a kiss for good luck.

Don't get too smart for your britches, young lady. But she was off to Mexico with 5,000 rounds of .45-70 rifle cartridges. Not a damn thing I could do about it. Coot would shit.

25

I watched the Curtiss go to a dot in the dark sky, then vanished. Bo and Tacho stood looking west, stiff as anchor ice. The harsh cruel ray of reality settled deep in their bones. Tacho hitched up his team to the buckboard, an old white mule and a large burro that was trailing a pretty little colt.

"Bo, just curious, but how did Rose talk you and Tacho into this?"

"I admit it, she talked us into this. Said she'd do it with or without our help. She spoke of the cruelty of her youth, her years as a nun, wanting release from the security of her vows, the safety of the earth. Dang it, Narlow, I should'a hogtied her!"

We got back to Tacho's adobe, Zoila set food before us. Tacho and Bo picked at their plates, I refused the offer.

Bo sat pounding his fist in his open palm. "She knows about the rail line that goes west from Presidio and Ojinaga to Chihuahua. West to Cuauhtémoc. The hazards of going further west to *Barranca del Cobre*. She'll be all right. God, please let . . ."

Bo and Tacho went back to the airstrip. Three o'clock passed. She should have been back by noon. Lost. Shot down. Spark plugs fouled. Fuel mixture askew.

Long hours after dark, I heard Tacho's buckboard rumble through the gate. Tacho tended to his animals, Bo came in with a real hangdog on.

"No sign, huh?"

"Nope, nothing. Tacho's brothers will keep a fire going on each end of the runway." He slumped in a chair. "All night, I reckon."

Tacho joined us on the porch. Zoila followed him in a minute. Tacho hugged her neck, whispered to her. She came back out on the porch with a jug of mezcal and glasses.

Tacho noticed the fourth glass and asked, "*Un vaso por ti saludas, Zoila?*"

"*Si, Tacho—si, por me y Rose.*" She stood tall, head tilted proud. "*Saludas. Saludas a Rose.*"

"*A Rose,*" the three of us answered the call.

26

Coal Mine Ranch, January 7, 1916

I spent the day beating on Bo to cut me out of my plaster-of-Paris suit. He steadfastly refused, said Coot would kill him if he did.

Just before dark, Tacho rode up from Los Fresnos, led his horse to the barn, curried him down, talking to him in low tones. He came out of the side door of the barn, his teeth flashing a meek smile in the fading light. He sauntered up on the porch, plopped himself down on the dusty couch. "*Hola, Senor* Montgomery, *que paso?*"

"*No bueno por* shit, Tacho." I squirmed in my cast trying to find the words that would make him understand that time was working against us. Soon it would be hopeless.

"My brothers can find Rose and they have many horses and—"

"Tacho, that's no good—*no bueno, hombre!* All your brothers will accomplish is getting themselves shot. Tacho, *cut me out of this damn cast!*"

"No, *Senor*, I cannot. *Senor* Coot told me you would—how do you say—*fundira—si fundira*, if I cut you out of that cast."

"*Fundira? Que es fundira? Fundira es* melt?"

"*Si,* Senor Montgomery, you melt."

"No, Tacho, *no!* I won't melt."

"*Si, Senor.* You will be weak. You melt." He turned and headed back to his adobe.

I dozed, fitful, grinding on something I barely recalled. Coot and Big George were carrying me out to the street after Doc Middaugh put me in this body cast, told the Doc that he'd be taking me down to the Coal Mine headquarters. Doc told him to take it easy with me, keep me dry, out of the rain.

That was it! Rain. Water. Any old water would do.

It was far too early for Tacho and Zoila to be up, but I banged on the tin wall beside me as I did in an emergency, and kept it up until Tacho came out.

"Que paso, Senor Montgomery? Quiere pee-pee?"

"No Tacho, I don't want to pee-pee, you *mojon. Quiero un bano—agua.* A bath. I'm about to itch myself crazy. Hitch up the wagon and take me for ride, *por favor, mi amigo mio muy fino. Vamanos por Agua Caliente, hombre!"*

"Loco gringo."

He loaded me up in the back of the wagon and we started out the gate. An hour later we came upon the blistering hot spring. Tacho backed the team and wagon to the edge of the steaming pond, lit a lantern, let the tailgate down, pulled me and my board and body cast over the rough floor boards of the wagon, eased me to the ground.

"Easy there, *amigo. Cuidado con su amigo, eh?* Hey! Damn it, Tacho, don't just push me off in that hot-ass water! Doodle me in there. Don't just push me off in there. *Damn it,* Tacho. Get me off to the side over there where the water has cooled a bit. Yeah, *ooh,* that feels good. Tilt me up over there on the bank. *Ahh*—oh—*oh* that's hot. Feels so good, *amigo. Que bueno, hombre!"*

The water felt good creepin' around in there where it hadn't seen the light of day for oh-so-long. I reached over to the lantern and lowered the wick.

Tacho took off his boots, laid back, soaked his feet, gazed at the stars, began snoring.

After a half-hour, I sensed movement. The cast was softening, the 108-degree water would soon set me free, free as that ground owl out there in the dark.

The first dim pink of day began showing itself over the rimrock. The plaster cast was breaking up fast now. I slipped off my plank, started to sink as the support of the cast began to give way, limp. *Panic!* Before I could call out to Tacho, my left foot felt something solid on the bottom of the spring. I braced myself, began stripping off the gauze and plaster. I was able to work my hands under the cast and break it up. Felt queasy, needed to get out, *fast.* I made slow progress pulling myself out of the spring.

I was on my hands and knees, on dry land, sat, slipped the cast over my ankle, braced myself on a stout salt-cedar limb, stood, white gauze and plaster-of-Paris slime dripping and drooling off. I was exhausted, buckass naked. The red man with his pitchfork goaded me. I picked up the lantern, held it close to my face.

I chanted, "*Woooo—woooo—Tacho—Tacho—ooooo.*"

He stirred, his feet soaking in the water, blinked in the early dawn, seeing nothing at first, sat up, reached for his sombrero, pulled it down to his ears, smiled, tried to focus.

"*Ooooo—Tacho—ooooooo.*"

"*Santos! Senor Montgomery es muerto!*" he yelled as he rolled over, got half-way to his feet, turned, and shot off, forgetting the wagon behind him. He hit the tailgate of the buckboard with his head, knocked his hat off, skidded in on his nose on the floorboard, regained his footing, ran, hit the iron bar over the driver's seat, going as fast as his bare feet could travel. The "gong" of his head on unforgiving iron was sickening. He went down in a motionless heap on the floorboard.

"Tacho. *Amigo,* it's me! Narlow. *Tacho!* Tacho?"

I tried to rouse him. He rolled over on his back, out cold with two bleeding gashes, a skinned nose, a goose egg on his forehead.

He didn't come around. I crawled in on the front floorboard of the buck-board. Nothing for me to do but get the team headed for home. They'd find it. I was chilled to the bone, covered myself with the wagon blanket, shouting for Tacho to wake up but never got the courtesy of a reply.

Bo spied us coming up Borracho Canyon. The team pulled up to the gait, stopped, waiting for Tacho to open it as was his custom. Bo couldn't see me sitting on the wagon floor, leaning against the wagon seat, weak as a kitten. I played with the long black hair that had grown on my leg and the right side of my body. Hair I never knew I had, over an inch long. Fine as silk on a frog's ass. Hair grew like that?

After a bit Bo called out, "You boys waiting on me to come down there and open that gate for you?"

In another minute, he called out again, "Got some hot coffee waiting. Some of Zoila's tonsil-teasin' biscuits all cooked-up with a pound of fresh butter. I'll eat 'em all if you don't get a move on."

"*Bo, get over here!*" I yelled with what little strength I could gather.

Bo sauntered down, opened the gate, blinking up at me, the blinding morning sun coming over the rimrock behind me.

Holding the gate open, he said, "Well, do I have to drive this rig through, and hold this gate open at the same time?"

139

"I believe you better do just that, Bo."

He came around to the side of the wagon. "What the hell? Where'n hell's your cast? You're buckass necked! Where's Tacho? What the hell got—"

There was a commotion behind me on the wagon floor. Tacho labored up, his head and face covered with a thick layer of dried blood. He grinned down at me, peeled a dried slab of blood from his forehead, put the morsel in his mouth, stood for a moment, chewed, spit. He turned to Bo, grinned, his head went back, crumpled back down in a heap on the floorboards.

"What the hell happened to you boys, Narlow?"

"Long story—tell you later. Lead the team in the corral over by the horse trough." He eased me into the green water. "Bo, while I clean myself up a bit, go tell Zoila that Tacho's okay, but he's hurt, need her help."

Zoila had spent her life in this harsh land, well-knew that wailing and crying solved nothing, and from long experience, she also was aware that the mere sight of a wounded, bloodied man, was often far worse than his wounds. She and Bo soon had Tacho stretched out on the porch's daybed. Zoila cleaned Tacho's forehead, then she and Bo came back for me. Zoila looked aside as she handed me a wool blanket to cover my naked self, helped me to the other daybed.

"I'm worried about Tacho. The way he's acting, I believe Doc Middaugh would say he has a skull fracture. Get him on his feet, keep him awake. Walk him around, talk to him, even if he doesn't want to."

Around noon, Bo helped me out to the middle of the yard so I could soak the sun. About that time, Tacho's brothers rode up in a cloud of dust, ready to ride into Mexico to find Rose. From my chair, I told the mounted riders about Tacho's accident. After a solid hour of pleading with them, they agreed to return home and wait for me to send for their able assistance.

We spent the rest of the day keeping Tacho awake. The next day, his head was clearing, but he insisted on saddling-up and checking his livestock. He wouldn't listen to reason, that he needed rest, his head was injured, needed time to heal. I gave up on him, explained it to Zoila.

"Do not worry, *Senor* Montgomery." She smiled. "I have ways to keep him home and safe."

By the third day, I was walking without help. First, by walking around the Big House using its walls and a forked salt-cedar pole for support. I was gradually regaining my strength. Bo massaged my legs morning, noon, and night.

Tacho badgered me about Rose, that he and his brothers could ride to Carichic in two days. Again, his brothers showed up early the fourth morning, packed, ready to take on the entire army of the *Federales*. I prevailed—barely. Tacho was some better, but goofy.

By the fifth day, the four of us walked to view a Nautilus fossil, a relic that Tacho uncovered while clearing mesquite stumps as a boy. A tub-sized sea shell, six-hundred miles from the Gulf of Mexico. The roundtrip walk was two miles. I was making progress.

On the eighth day, I had my plans down pat. All I had to do was get to the SP depot in Van Horn.

"Bo, do you think your cousin Jimbo in Las Cruces would lend me an airplane?"

"Yeah, sure."

"Good. You're going to drive me to Van Horn in Coot's Model-T tomorrow morning, while the dew's still on the gourd. That old Model-T rides the rails just like the Reo, and all you have to do is give her the gas. You don't even have to steer it."

"Now Narlow, dad-nab-it. You know I can't drive that damn—"

"You'll learn on the way out."

At six in the morning, as we were set to ride the Model-T to Van Horn, and my train to El Paso, two riders out of Mexico rode up. They looked spent, their horse near jaded.

"*Senor* Montgomery?" one of them asked.

"That's me. How can I help you."

"We come from Carichic. A lady there, the pilot of the *aeroplano*, *Senora* Rose Talamantes, she sent us here. She wants you to know that she is okay, not hurt. Says to tell you that her *aeroplano* may be okay, *pero* she is not sure. She say when she land, how you say? The thing that makes it go. *Aiii, pardona mi por favor, pero me* English is not so good. The—"

"Senor, el *propulsor*? Tacho asked.

The man smiled. "*Si senor—Senora* Rose, she say *el propulsor*, she may be broke."

Tacho turned to me. "He says Rose thinks the propeller may be broken."

I asked, "But *Senora* Rose, she is okay? Not hurt? Not in any danger?"

"*No, senor*. She is okay. *Los Federales* are in our village, but our *padre* has hidden her. She is safe. The *padre*, he say you know him, know him and his *amigo. Padre Estevan y Gregorio Gonzalez*."

141

"Well, I'll be damned." I turned to Bo. "Those are the same two men I saved from the firing squad at the garrison south of Samalayuca a while back."

"*Senora* Rose, she tell me to give you *este carta*."

I opened it, surprised that it contained several pages.

For Coot Boldt and Narlow Montgomery

Dear Coot and Narlow,

I am entrusting this note to Chico Chavez who is the nephew of Jeromino Chavez, a carpenter in Carichic, a very well respected gentleman. Chico is accompanied by Rogelio Sambrano, also a respected local man. They can tell you more about the daily funerals that are being conducted to confuse and trick the Federales.

My dear Coot and Narlow, I can readily appreciate your disgust with me and my actions. It was a terrible mistake for me to try to do a man's job, but I thought I just had to try to help these people. They stole several hundred .45-70 rifles off a government train with the intention of defending themselves, but as you know, they had no bullets to fire from them. It would take a longer letter than you would care to read to explain that the villagers are burying their rifles in the cemetery next to their church where they've been hiding them. They're afraid the Federales will burn the church down when they leave, but that is another long story. The Federales believe they are burying the dead caused by the plague, a plague that only exists in the minds and eyes of the Federales.

I was forced by low clouds to land the Curtiss. I had no choice as the area south of Carichic forms a bowl. The further south I flew, the tighter the bowl became. After I landed, I had to taxi around trying to find a place to hid it. In the process of turning around what I thought was just a tumbleweed, the front tire hit a small boulder hidden by the weeds. I am not certain, but I believe a part of the undercarriage snapped off and whizzed past me, probably hitting the propeller, because suddenly, the plane began shaking violently. I killed the engine. The propeller has a hairline crack in it from one end to the other. I have no idea whether the engine is sound, but the propeller is definitely ruined. The front wheel is okay, just broken off at the base. I believe it can easily be repaired.

I hid the bullets amongst some large, house-size boulders, a place the locals call, Circulo de Rocas. You will be amazed how similar the place is to Stonehenge in England. Please forgive me for going off on a tangent and wasting your time. I have wasted a lot of people's time since I left Sacred Heart. Perhaps Mother Superior Pancreatitis will take me back into her care if I ever get out of the mess I have created. I pray so, and pray that no one else pays for my carelessness and childish ways.

Where was I? I got off the subject. But Rogelio Sambrano rode by shortly after I hid the bullets. He showed me a wide place between two boulders where we pushed and pulled the Curtiss inside the circle of boulders and hid it under bamboo and sticks. It is well hidden.

I do not expect you to endanger yourselves to get me out of this problem. In fact, I hope you do not, as I have a plan to rid the village of Carichic of the Federales who are terrorizing the villagers. A plan to use the lowly oleander to rid them of this pestilence. I read about the poisonous nature of oleander, and plan to burn it at night near where they sleep, and soon they will begin coughing, throwing up blood, for you see, I read that the peons of Mother Russia rid themselves of Napoleon Bonaparte the same manner back in the early part of the 19th Century.

I'm sorry for getting off the subject, besides, you will not be interested in any further plans that I might have about anything, for I know that neither of you will want anything to do with me in the future. If I had more paper, I would write a letter to Mother Superior Pancretias, and ask you to post it for me, but I don't have any more paper. If I did, I would ask her, no, beg her, to take me back in Sacred Heart.

Chico and Rogelio will return to Carichic after they have rested both themselves and their horses. If you have a message or advice for me, I would love hearing from you.

I love you both and trust you will find it in your heart to one day forgive my transgression against the faith you once had in me. And please tell Zara that I love her.

Rose

Oh, I don't believe I told you, but Rogelio Sambrano is the man who accompanied Chico Sanchez on this long trip. They are eager to leave so I don't have time to rewrite this letter.

Chico and Rogelio explained the non-existent plague, funerals, and how they were getting the rifles to the cemetery.

Chico said, "Our village had a bad plague a year ago. That's when the *padre* and Gregorio came to us, to help us, for our village suffered many deaths. After the plague, the *Federales* came, promised that if we gave them no trouble, that we would be safe, they would only burn our church to remind us of their power. We could not let them burn the church. We buried many rifles under the floor of our sacred church. Gregorio is a very devious man, but he is smart. He came up with the plan. The villagers would cry out as caskets made by our *tero*, my uncle, *Senor* Jeromino Chavez. The caskets were filled with exactly seventeen rifles. Seventeen, because that is what one large dead man weighs. We wanted the *Federales* to see us struggle under the weight of the caskets. We bury the caskets two-deep, for the ground is very hard, very rocky." Chico laughed. "The rifles don't seem to mind."

I wrote a letter to Rose, told her to quit whipping herself, that Coot and I would soon be in Carichic, and we'd lay all the leather required on her backside to help her see the light. I gave the letter to Chico, told them to make themselves at home and not be in any hurry to return to Carichic.

I turned to Bo. "Come on, let's get this Model-T to Van Horn, catch that train."

Rose's letter changed my plans. No need for me to fly into Mexico. Both Coot and I would need to drive the Reo to Carichic, take tools, hopefully salvage the Curtiss.

On the train ride to El Paso, I scratched out a note to Rodolfo telling him what was going on and that Rose was okay. I gave the note to the switchman at Tornillo, asked him to deliver it to Rodolfo Bustamante. I lacked the energy to walk the twelve blocks to Big George's shop, so when the train pulled into El Paso, I sent a runner to fetch him.

"Where's your cast, Mr. Montgomery?" Big George asked. "You're supposed to be in that cast—"

"I know, I know, Big George. You've forgotten that I'm already married. All I want from you is a ride in Mrs. Smith's fine Packard touring car to my house and bed. Seen Coot?"

"He's with Rodolfo Bustamante. Last time I heard from him, he was planning to go to the Coal Mine Ranch."

As Big George was pulling his Packard around to my alley, he stopped. "Uh-oh. Look who's right behind us."

I turned and there he was—my partner of more years than I cared to recall, behind the wheel of his beat-up old Reo.

Big George asked, "Care to wager what is first his first words will be?"

"Think I just fell off the ass-end of turnip wagon?"

Coot came over the Big George's side of the car, pulled the kinky hair on his arm. "What's happenin'?"

I said, "Oh, nothing. Just sitting out here in the alley with Big George, making bets on what your first words would be."

"Rodolfo tells me that Little Miss Rose has gotten herself in a peck of trouble while I've been gone off looking for Mausers. Care to tell me about it?"

"Be glad to—after I've slept the clock out." I stepped out. "Care to join us in a midmorning *cerveza*, Big George?"

"Naw, I'm a working man. Besides, my missus probably already knows you two are in town." He laughed. "She'll soon be on the hunt, looking for the boss of the house."

27

"Coot, I'm sure Rodolfo filled you in about Ace Rose flying those 5,000 cartridges into that little village south of Cuahtemoc, what is it? Oh, yeah, Carichic. Here's a letter from Rose. It's all I know about—"

"Yeah, Rodolfo told me about Rose's little stunt. Is she all right? No broken bones, cut lip?"

"She's okay. Her letter will tell you all about it."

"Well, let's pack up and get to poppin'. We can make the afternoon train if we get going."

"You may change your mind about that after you read Rose's letter, but, my friend, you've obviously not noticed, I'm no longer sporting my body cast. I'm beat to a frazzle. I'll be happy to catch that train with you—tomorrow. As early as you choose to go. Right now, I'm going to bed."

Two letters awaited me from Zara on the dining room table. The first said she was in Dallas, would be home by mid-month. The second gave me a little reprieve as her plans had changed and would not return until the end of the month. Good. Time enough to get Rose back here safe and pretty.

Zara's copy of Robert Service poems sat next to her stack of mail, a bookmarker led me to a page that jumped out of its bindings at me. The poem styled, "Moon Song," brought back boyhood memories of my mother's rage when I told her that I was waiting for the moon to dawn. Papa's brief, incomplete explanation to me was only that it had something to do with her own mother, a full-bloodied Comanche, whose name was Moon Dawn. I read the poem:

A child saw the morning skies
The dissipated-looking moon
And opened wide her big blue eyes,
And cried: "Look my lost balloon!"
And clapped her rosy hands with glee:
"Quick, Mother! Bring it back to me."

The poem and its title again brought back harsh recollections of my mother, her contempt for her son, her dastardly theft of his childhood.

I fell asleep on the sofa, too tired to eat the lunch that Ines set out for me.

At six, Coot was banging around in the kitchen. I took my pillow out on the veranda. He brought the plate that Ines had prepared for me, sat down, took his boots and socks off, helped himself to my supper.

Between bites, he said, "Remember Jorge Jose Umbenhauer. Half-Mexican half-German I went to college with? Daddy owns a million-acre ranch. *Hacienda* down in Sonora. Remember, we called him JJ?"

"Yeah, sorta. Big, hawk-faced man with a Porfirio Diaz style mustache?"

"That's him. I had the misfortune of riding the train with him. All the way from Dallas to St. Louis. JJ's daddy was sending him to St. Louis to pick up what's called an AEG C.II, a German-made biwing, a two-seater reconnaissance aircraft with 150-horsepower and a MG14 machine-gun."

Coot's head was cranking now. Everything on the street was quiet. All the mamas, up and down the block, had called their kids in from their game of kick-the-can. Everything was quiet, except Coot and his cipherin', kept glancing across the street at Geraldine's front porch.

I asked, "How did JJ and his daddy get their hands on a German spy-plane? Wouldn't they need it against the French and Brits?"

His gaze went back crossed the street to Geraldine's front porch light that just flashed on. "Reckon that old hide knows we're over hear spying on her?"

"Probably. After you left on your trip, I ran into Geraldine crossing the plaza. Me thinks the old gal was slightly in her cups, though it was only ten in the morning. Said she was on her way to her Card and Gossip Club gathering. Doubt she made it. Gal was reeking. Breath like a musk ox, hint of cigar, sweet like belched stale cantaloupe, a touch of sherry, mixed with sourdough, maybe half-baked biscuits, rhubarb, and collard greens."

Coot laughed. "That old gal's the one who taught me to drink. Pour that stuff down, she can."

"Well?" I asked.

"Huh?"

"I asked why JJ and his daddy—"

"Oh, JJ's daddy owns the largest *hacienda* in Mexico. Rich man. Has connections all over the world, buy anything he wants. Has a German agent in his back pocket. JJ laughed when he said, 'Daddy can spell *mordida* in any language.'"

Coot tugged at his boots, stuck his socks in his pocket, stood. "Come on."

"You go, I'm going to bed."

"Have you back in fifteen minutes. Need to send a wire."

"What for? Who?"

"Way I figure it, we need another pilot. Get Rose and the Curtiss out. JJ's a pilot, you see with a two-seater airplane."

On the way to the Western Union office, I asked him what he thought of Rose's letter.

"Way I see it, she's whipped herself plumb silly. All that talk about going back to being a nun is just that—loose talk, chatter I won't abide."

"I don't know, Coot, she gets something in her head, she's liable to hop the next train back to Dallas and Sacred Heart."

"I might have something to say about that. I might have *plenty* to say about it."

The telegraph office door was locked. Coot banged on Hank's door until he finally gave up, opened the door a crack to see what fool was doing all the banging. Hank asked, "What do want at this hour? Come back—"

Coot pushed through the door with a not too friendly, "Boy-howdy, Hank, seven in the evening sure is late isn't it? Got an important wire you're going to send for me down in Sonora."

Hank was fumbling with a coal-oil lantern trying to get it lit. Coot said, "Hank, for god-sakes. You mean to tell me that this telegraph office still doesn't have electric lights?"

"Company's too damn cheap to spend the five dollars to hook it up."

"Get to clicking. This wire is for Jorge Jose Umbenhauer in Sonora. He has his own wire unit at his *hacienda*. First message is a question. Ask, 'Safe line?'"

We waited five minutes.

Hank said, "You ain't gettin' a message through anywhere in Mexico."

"Send it again," Coot said. "Send it again every five minutes."

As Hank bent over his instrument, a message came in. He scribbled out the message and shoved it at Coot across his desk, and said, "This gent must know you."

Coot read the scribble, handed it to me. *Safe enough, shit-head.* "I think Hank's right."

"Send another wire, Hank. Tell him, 'Have a little job for you and your St. Louis toy.'"

In a minute, Hank started scratching out another message as it came back down the line, "*Where? When?*"

Coot snickered that certain kind of snicker when he's got his fish hooked that's dying to do Coot a favor so he'll be beholden. They never learned: Coot didn't get beholding.

"Well, what do you want to say?" Hank asked after a minute of silence.

"Nothing just yet. Let him repeat his message." After another five minutes, JJ's message came back down the line, "*Where? When? Damn it.*"

Coot dictated his response as Hank clacked it back, "Need proof you are Jorge Jose Umbenhauer. Identify lady-cousin your daddy shipped back to Germany.'"

"*Hilda*," was JJ's reply.

"Hilda, who?" Coot instructed Hank.

"*Hilda Von Smidt, asshole. What the hell do you want?*"

Coot dictated to Hank, "Bring your St. Louis bird fifteen miles south of Carichic, Chihuahua on the 23rd. Important mission. Rescue fair damsel."

"*Why?*" JJ demanded.

"See you on the 23rd," Coot dictated. He shoved a dollar at Hank, turned to step through the door.

Hank bristled. "That'll be a dollar *and ten-cents*."

148

I flipped a dime at him. I eased my bones back up in the cab of the Reo. "Think JJ will show?"

"Oh, hell yes. Likely be in Carichic tomorrow morning."

Coot parked the Reo in the alley behind my house. I was looking forward to a hot soak and the feathers. "See you in the morning. I've got to get off my feet and to bed before I collapse."

He cut the engine, followed me through the kitchen door, opened the ice-box, peered in for a look-see. "Reckon Ines has any more of that *posole* stashed around in here somewhere?"

"Old amigo of mine, unless you want to see me in Concordia Cemetery pushing up sand daisies, you'll leave me be. I'm beat down low as a one-legged feral cat herder. You've got this thing all figured out. I'll put myself in your capable hands, *tomorrow*."

"Hold on a minute, Narlow. We need to figure on this. How to get Rose and the Curtiss out of there. We've got a crippled biwing and beat-up lady, beat up by herself. Curtiss' engine is probably ruined."

He turned to leave. I asked, "What do you mean, ruined? Damn it, Coot, tell me what you mean. Coot—*Coot*. ."

Seems my head just hit the pillow, when I heard a loud rap on my bedroom window. "Huh? *What the hell*. Who's out there?" I pulled out my pillow-pistol just in case.

"*Don't shoot*, Mr. Montgomery. It's just me, ol' Night Train Big George Jeremiah Washington Smith, at your service, Mr. Montgomery."

"What the hell are you doing out there? What the hell time is it? Must be three hours to sunup."

"Yes, sir, I suppose it is. Mr. Boldt sent me to fetch you down to the depot. He's already deposited the Reo on a flatcar, waiting for the 6:30 to head east."

"Mr. Smith, how did I get myself in this mess? Where'd Coot say we're headed?"

"You're headed for Presidio."

"*Presidio*? Why Presidio?"

"I don't issue the orders, just deliver them. Got that Reo all loaded up with one of my biggest iron contraptions you ever laid eyes on. He and I worked on it down at my shop all night."

Big George and I drove up to the tall, red-brick steeple of El Paso's Union

Depot, the sun began casting a faint pink on the Sierra de Juarez mountain off to the southwest, craggy, deep gorges, green northeastern slopes. We sat for a moment, soaking in the view.

"Big George, every time I leave this old town, the thought crawls through my mind that this could well be the last time. This damn revolution will never end, and if it does, I'll be bent, bald, and blind. We've got men on both sides of this war shooting at our asses, stalking, spying on us. We're blinded to these threats, the more we're coerced, the more lax we become.

"It reminds me of what that English statesman, Lord Chesterfield said about concentration. He said long ago that—"

"Land o' Goshen, Mr. Montgomery, I do believe your troubles are over. Yonder strolls Mr. Boldt, IB, and his twin-sister, Shelly Brom, coming out of the train station, all three of them just a'grinnin' like they had good sense. Look at that walk of Coot's, will you. His walk has that certain knock-kneed, splay-footed way about it that teases the ladies. Man's given me a lot of laughs over the years. Wouldn't trade my friendship with you two for a thing on God's green earth."

"Same holds for Coot and me, my friend."

Coot walked up, pulled hard on the kinky hair on Big George's thick forearm resting on the window opening of the door. "What's happenin'. What are you two yardbird-idiots laughing about? Ready to head to Mexico, Narlow?"

IB whirled around. "Why ya goin' to Mex-ico, Coot?"

"Coot," I said, "I'm not real keen on going anywhere right now, especially all the way to Carichic in that ass-kicking rig of yours. I'm getting damn sick of this damnable revolution. I was in the middle of quoting the great Englishman, Lord Chesterfield, who said—"

Shelly pulled on IB's shirt sleeve until he repeated his question. "Why ya goin' to Mex-ico, Coot?"

"Not now, IB. I called Jimbo just now. He's flying down from Las Cruces with tools we'll need to calibrate the propeller. Copper sleeves to balance her out real fine. Jimbo knows we're in a rush, said he'd just fly over the rail yard, drop the tools and parts in our lap as he flies by."

Coot, IB, Shelly, and I strolled around El Paso's brand new red-brick Union Depot, the grandest structure for 500 miles in any direction.

I asked, "What's this about the Curtiss' engine being ruined?"

"I said it was *probably* ruined."

IB twisted around in front of us. "Why's it ruint? Why ya goin' ta Mex-ico?"

150

"Nothing, IB," Coot said. "Don't worry yourself over it."

I said, "Coot, IB and Shelly are worried about the Curtiss, why we're going into Mexico. They deserve an answer."

Coot answered his questions, resulting in more questions than either of us had answers.

He turned to me. "Satisfied?"

The Reo sat on the last flatcar loaded up with a piece of equipment I couldn't recognize. "What's that?"

IB smiled. "Shelly Brom, me'n Coot 'n Big George done brunged it."

Coot said, "Thought of it in the middle of the night. Big George pounded on it, welded on that hand crank, loaded it up around three."

The contraption in the Reo's bed was a tall hunk of iron, various sand-caked-greasy wheels, pulleys, belts running every which-a-way, with the distinct appearance of an oversized mangy coyote humping a cottontail. "What in the hell is that? And what in the world are we going to do with it when we get it to Carichic?"

Coot's dark eyes sparked with pride. "That, my friend, is a steam-driven auger. Seen it a thousand times leaning up against the shed out back of Big George's shop. A precision instrument, though a little outdated. With the hand crank that Big George fashioned with his forge, we'll use it to drill eight precise holes in a replacement propeller to fasten it to the engine. Cuts slow, but true. Jimbo believes the holes will be close to five-eights in diameter. We want the holes to fit tight. We'll figure it out. Burn the holes if they're too tight."

"If the Curtiss's engine's likely ruined, why are we going through this exercise? And where in hell are we going to get a replacement propeller in the heart of Chihuahua?"

"The engine's *probably* ruined, but that doesn't make it so. We'll figure out another propeller along the way. You worry too much."

Jimbo flew in from the north, circled the train, losing altitude as he came back around, slowing, side-slipping his bird to a near stall, heaved a heavy leather bag over the side. I curled up in the cab of the Reo while Coot busied himself tightening bolts and wires on the truck.

He climbed in the cab, bumped me out of my nap. "Now what's on your mind? You getting homesick on me?"

"What the hell are you talking about?"

"You were telling Big George how sick of this revolution you're getting, quoting some Englishman. What's your beef?"

"Well, I *am* getting sick of this revolution—sick of getting shot at, dodging boulders, sick of worrying about Rose, sick of nightmares screaming at me that we'll never see her again. Sick of worrying about what Zara will do to me if we don't."

Coot eased back, pulled his hat down over his face. "My head hasn't hit a pillow since I found out about Rose, but worrying about her won't bring her back. But, my friend, you can bet your ass that we'll get her back, safe and sound. You'll see. Anyway, what's that got to do with an Englishman?"

"The Englishman? *Oh, yes*—Lord Chesterfield. I read a line he wrote: 'One should always think of what one is about; when one is learning, one should not think of play; and when one is at play, one should not think of one's learning.' I thought that was pretty good."

"What's that got to do with gunrunning?"

"Lord Chesterfield was talking about learning, working, or anything else we do of a serious nature—like running guns into Mexico for instance."

"Yeah, *well?*"

"Lord Chesterfield was talking right at us. We've been working hard at this damnable revolution since the very day it began. Our minds are telling us they need a little play, we're thinking more about play than this damn war and our own asses. At least I am."

"Play? Like with Rose, for instance?"

"What's that supposed to mean?"

"Nothing, your lordship. Take a nap."

28

I started mulling over how we got in the gunrunning business, how we could get out of it as soon as we got Rose out of Mexico. The rocking of the freight car set me to snoozing, going in and out of my nap.

I don't have a lick of sense. We'll get out of this gunrunning the very second Rose is out of Mexico. Taking money for running guns was distasteful. What'd we do? Quit? No. We turned down a half million dollars for a lava rock pile ranch in southern New Mexico. Got $100,000 from the US government for a lease of a worthless lava mountain. I'm just lazy. My Mexican amigos would call me a huevon. Then Rodolfo's promise of the million dollars. More money. We weren't taking money for running guns. But we'd get a bunch of money if we ran guns until the end of Mexico's revolution. Smart? Wasn't the money. Was it the money? Don't think it was the money. Coot and I already had more of the stuff than any ten men within hundred miles of El Paso. Son of a dirt-clod farmer partnered up with the son of a goat herder. Why? Hell, I don't know. Why does a vine produce a grape? Vine gives up its better part to do it again next season and a hundred seasons to come. Why? The vine's nature. It's our nature to run guns? The glory? Factitious adulation? For Rodolfo. Reasonable? Make sense to put life, limb, fortune in the hands of a friend for all these years? A cause that's none of our concern? Hell, even IB and Shelly knows better. IB says, "Don't go bother'n' with some-thin' that ain't a'bother'n ya none," and sister Shelly Brom nods her agreement. Never considered myself a quitter. Coot never quits. I lack will. I remember Papa telling me, "The only thing that conquers will is will." I'm plumb willed out, not the best vine in the vineyard. My grapes are sour, squished.

Rodolfo was waiting for us when the train pulled up at Tornillo. He was worn, tattered, not the usual dapper, confident man we knew. I assured him that Rose was safe and we'd get her out of Mexico, but he had other concerns.

"Gentlemen, I just got word that a Mexican train was stopped south of Juarez. Sixteen American mining engineers were pulled off the train. Shot without cause or ceremony. Their bodies were piled in an empty boxcar and the train was allowed to proceed to Juarez."

Coot said, "That could get the US involved in Mexico's revolution real quick."

"Any idea who did the killing?" I asked. "*Federales?*"

"No, wish it were true. A trusted friend was on that train. He recognized one of the men—General Pablo Lopez. Villa's most trusted general."

"Now what?" I asked.

Rodolfo shrugged. "I do not know. When that train gets to Juarez, the bodies will be taken to El Paso, the news will spread like wildfire. Mexicans living in the barrios of south El Paso will be in grave danger. There will be a riot. Another call for America to go to war against the *revolucionarios*. Conditions will get worse in Mexico, all *norte americanos* will be in jeopardy, you two, more than anyone."

"I was just talking to Coot about that very same thing, Rodolfo. We're liable to be the next *gringos* dragged off a train and shot."

Coot yanked his hat off, swatted his side. "Oh, bullshit, Narlow! Rodolfo, you've got a lot to worry about, but don't concern yourself about us. We'll get Rose out of Mexico safe and sound, then lay low for a spell."

"Well, I know you'll do your best. But since you will not be in El Paso, I'm sending a man to get IB and Shelly. Yes, I know they may live on a farm on the outskirts of town, but I'd never forgive myself if they got mixed up in what may well be a bloody riot."

◉◉◉

Just before midnight our train pulled into Presidio, 200 miles downriver from El Paso. It was dark, cold, wet. A switchman uncoupled our flat car and set it off on a sidetrack. Old man Tupper swung his green lantern, the heavy locomotive began backing its way up the line, caboose first, as there was no roundhouse at the end of the line.

Charlie Tupper yelled out, "Best watch your asses, boys. *Gringos* ain't very popular down these parts." We watched the backing train until it was almost out of sight, Mr. Tupper still swinging his lantern, a fast-disappearing, flittering green moth in the dark chill of the desert air.

Coot parked the Reo to the side of the small adobe that served as Presidio's train station. Across the way was a low, dingy, dark *cantina*, lit by a coal-oil lantern on each end of the bar. Low, yellow-orange light was absorbed by tobacco smoke before reaching the middle of the room. Crowded with border men, Mexicans, except for the burly red-bearded man behind the bar. The *cantina* was hot, muggy, smoky, heavy.

"We should have heeded old man Tupper's warning," I said out of the side of my mouth as we ducked under the low door.

The men parted as we made our way to the middle of the bar. Every pair of surly eyes gave us the once-over. The red-bearded bartender brought us two warm beers, asked through clenched teeth, "You gents heard-tell 'bout the shooting on the train south of Juarez?"

Coot said, "Heard about it. Any news?"

The barkeep wiped the bar with his sleeve, a curve of a smile on unmoving lips. "Yeah, a'plenty. Ain't none good. El Paso's mayor called on the army to stop a riot in the *barrios* of south El Paso. Genteel folks got it in their heads to kill every Mexican in town. Ain't safe for 'em in El Paso. No safer than it is for a couple of *gringo*-in this here *cantina*." His bloodshot eyes held our gaze for a moment, then turned to answer a call at the other end of the bar.

We leaned against the bar, sipping our glasses of warm foam. The crowd parted as a big scruffy-bearded Mexican walked by and bumped me a good one in the gut. The biggest, ugliest man I ever laid eyes on.

"Hey, *gringo*, wha's a'matta you? *Por que—*"

Coot's .45 came out in a flash, rammed it in the man's gut. "*Amigo*, you keep walking like nothing's wrong. Out that door. Do as I say, or your *amigos* will be washing your stinking guts off of them, counting your *pesos*. *Comprende?* Say anything and you're dead—*muy muerto—sabe, hombre?*"

As we headed for the door, the crowd parted, unaware that anything was amiss.

"*Ese, Jorge*," a drunk called out. "*Donde va con sus amigos norte america-nos, eh, Jorge?*" He was thin, scabby, mangy hair and beard. He staggered up as we approached the door, indignant that he had been ignored. Again he demanded to know where his *amigo* was going with the "*pinchi gringos*."

Jorge spat at him, "*No negocio tuyo, pendejo!*"

As Coot and the big Mexican were ducking under the door, the drunk grabbed my arm, swung me around. "*Oiga, gringo.*"

I pulled my Schofield out from under my coat, cocked the revolver in his face, stuck the end of the barrel on the end of his nose.

All hell broke loose. A mad scramble ensued, everyone diving for a place to hide in a standing-room-only *cantina*.

Coot yelled, "*Run!*" as he pushed the man along in front of him. "*Andale pues, mojon! Andale.*"

We reached the Reo. Coot yelled at the Mexican, pointed at the passenger's seat. "Crank her up, Narlow."

I twisted the crank, jumped in the bed of the Reo, we sped off in the dark, the crowd now coming out of the *cantina,* close on our heels. I shot off two rounds over the crowd to slacken their haste. We hadn't gone more than a hundred yards, Coot yanked the wheel hard to the left, pushed the big man out onto the gravel as we sped on.

I climbed over the rack into the cab. "Goddamn it, Coot! I'm telling you, we're going to keep dickin' around like this and get our asses killed. That could have been our Waterloo back there. Right *there!"*

Coot clutched the steering wheel, glancing at the rearview mirror.

We drove north on the cow-trail-of-a-road along the winding Rio. After two hours, we came upon an *arroyo* that had recently flooded. The loose gravel caved in as the Reo's front tires had rolled to the *arroyo's* edge.

Coot asked, "How far you think we've come from Presidio?"

"Twenty miles. Outside, maybe twenty-five."

"Think it's safe to cross the river yet?"

"Who the hell knows. I say we back up, find a place behind some brush, wait for sun, then cross."

At first light, we changed clothes, donned *pobre's* trousers, *serapes y sombreros* we'd brought along, found a break in the salt cedar and crossed the shallow stream into Mexico.

Coot asked, "Where to?"

I pointed southwest. "Head for that far peak. No choice but to go cross-country toward the railroad track that runs between Ojinaga and Chihuahua."

By mid-morning we crossed the Rio Conchos, and headed south for the rail line, got the Reo astraddle the tracks, jacked her up to put her rail wheels in place to ride the rail on west. Before we'd gone a quarter-mile heading up a long hill, heavy coal smoke, chugging, ballooning, coming from the other side of the hill in front of us. A locomotive under full steam, headed our way, judging by the volume of dark smoke was billowing up, the locomotive was close, straining up the other side of the hill.

"Narlow, let's jack up your side. Pull the rail wheels up and clear. Force the shear bolts on the left-side wheels to break as we cross the rail. No time to jack up both sides."

The Reo's right side was up with two strokes of the hi-jack, loosened the shear bolts, released the jack, the Reo's tires were back on the tracks. I threw the jack in the back, Coot yanked the throttle handle down, drove down the tracks to gain speed, then jerked the wheel hard right. We sailed off the track, the left steel wheels hit the unforgiving rail, the shear bolts broke under the strain and flew up on their hinges. We kept going along the side of the tracks in the direction of the locomotive. Coot had his eye on a sizable bridge up ahead where the rails crossed over a deep, dry *arroyo*. The locomotive's stack cleared the top of the hill. Coot dashed the Reo under the bridge.

The train picked up speed going downhill, rumbled overhead, steel wheels clacking past flat, jointed steel tracks, clack-clack, click-click. We peered up through the bridge trellises. Soldiers stretched out, sleeping on the undercarriage of the cars. Several boxcars rumbled and clicked past, churning up speed, the clack-clack like machinegun fire, like a box of ivory dominoes spilled on a granite slab—then gone. We watched the train crawl up a gentle hill to the east like a burnt centipede crossing the baked desert floor toward Ojinaga.

"*Whew*," was all Coot had to say for himself for a minute, then added, "Best keep our asses off this track."

"Reckon those are *Federales* or Villa's troops?"

"Doesn't matter. *Gringos* are an unwelcome commodity in Mexico these days."

I told Coot that I figured we were midway between Ojinaga and Chihuahua. If we cut due south, we might cut across a road I'd heard about, follow it west to Delicias, then we'd be about fifty miles southeast of Carichic. We headed south across a chalk-white dry lake bed. For once, the Reo was on a flat, smooth surface, the ride was easy.

I was humming, singing bits and pieces of a song that I couldn't remember. Switched to a poem that I recited for Geraldine to deflect her ire a month ago:

One day in the middle of the night,
Two dead boys got up to fight.
Back to back they faced each other,
Drew their swords and shot each other.

Coot asked, "What the hell's that?"

"Oh, just a ditty I told your darling, Geraldine a while back. I've never known a woman who used fouler language than that wife of yours. I'm convinced

157

her native language is cuss words, 'Muleskinner adjectives,' as Papa would say."

"That tough ol' gal taught me all I know about the muleskinner language."

"Well, anyway, Geraldine had made another one of her wild-ass accusations about your partner. I said, 'Why, Geraldine, honey, you know me better than that.' She kept fuming and fussing, I repeated that last line, 'Drew their swords and shot each other.' She asked, 'What the hell are you talking about?' 'Why, Geraldine honey, you know darn well that a deaf policeman heard the noise, And came to arrest the two dead boys. If you don't believe this story's true, Geraldine honey, I suggest you ask the blind man, he saw it too!' Geraldine gazed at me in complete wonderment, started looking me over, grabbed my coat sleeve, turned me around right there in front of everybody on the boardwalk. Looking me up and down, I suppose to check to see that I was not only nuts but incontinent, unable to make sense of a thing I'd said. 'Geraldine, honey, it's apparent you don't believe me!' I said, 'Ask the blind man, he'll tell you that a paralyzed donkey passing by, kicked the blind man in the eye and—' With that, she bolted off that boardwalk, got in her Dodge touring car, burned rubber all the way up Utah Street."

I didn't recall Coot laughing that hard in months.

"And you know what, Coot? She was so bumfuzzled she didn't even once demand that I not call her honey."

29

South of Delicias, Chihuahua

We found the road west, which soon stopped at the edge of a heaving black lava flow. We turned north, then came on hundreds of square miles of a blue-green sea of *lechuguilla*, principal source of the stuff Mexicans make carpets and netting. We'd seen Apache women slice the spikes, using the sharp tip as a needle, the fibrous string as thread. Those same knitting needles would make a pincushion out of the Reo's tires.

We were going in circles but had no choice, turned south, forded another river, skirted Delicias, turned southwest. We kept at it all day, planned to keep going into the night, but around nine o'clock Coot jerked the Reo off the trail, and ran over a jackrabbit.

He turned to me and said, "Me kill–squaw cook."

We did our best to get out of the wind and cold. As usual, Coot slept through it, but lately I'd notice my feet being cold at night. Old age creeping up, I supposed. I glanced over at Coot in the cab of the Reo, thinking about how much Coot had changed over the years, I got to wondering how, or if, I'd changed at all, besides cold feet, that is. I imagined if his daddy, Orville Boldt, had not died at the ripe age of forty-two, Coot would look just like him. Not as tall, but stocky, big-boned like his daddy. Papa didn't talk much about him, but they were running mates throughout their youth. Said he was well-educated, honest, hard working.

My grandpapa, Shelby Montgomery, and Coot's granddaddy, Orville Boldt, left their Alabama home before they were half-grown, fought with Old Hickory in 1814 at the Battle of Horseshoe Bend against the Red Sticks. They headed west, became horse trainers, bought a little place on the black mesa above Mesilla. They'd catch mustangs, break them easy, put a mild mouth on them, then *just the two of them*, herd those hundred-plus ponies a couple of thousand miles through Comanche country, all the way to St. Louis where they had an ongoing arrangement with a horse trader for their well-trained mounts. One time on their return trip in 1830, just as they came out of the Llano Estacado and began following the Pecos, they came across a bunch of scalpers in possession of a young Apache princesses. Our grandfathers stormed through their drunken camp, dispatched the scalpers, saved the pregnant girl with the pleasant name of Little Flower, returned her to her father, Standing Elk. From that night forward, the Boldt and Montgomery families enjoyed special favor, a place of honor in the hearts of the Apache People. No Apache would knowingly harm a member of our families.

Those were rough times, times and conditions that didn't change much for their sons, my papa and Coot's daddy. Fact is, from their descriptions of their youth, Coot and I couldn't tell much difference in their upbringing and ours, save the convenience of one thing—wooden matches. But those sulfur-tipped fire-starters cost cash money, so neither of our families ever had them around.

Coot and I were close from the day we came to this grand earth, dern near shared the same birthdate. Never had even a smattering of a spat, looked after each other, always taking the other's side, right or wrong. Many-a-time we had occasion to take on four or more boys, my partner taking care of more than his ample share, me, just the hindmost. Coot was never one to take sass from anyone, while I found other ways, often devious methods, of handling untoward situations.

Coot's mother was not what you might call the typical, loving, proud mother, but she was a sight warmer in every regard than my own. He was always certain about himself in the presence of grown men and women and their children, even around girls, where I about needed smelling salts if I caught sight of one of those things a mile away. Until we were well up in years, Coot favored his daddy's attitude about women in general. Too bad Geraldine happened to be the first grown girl he was close to. A bad union that was a train wreck from the get-go.

Coot only had a vague memory of his daddy, but Papa always assured Coot that his daddy was a smart man, known to go to town only a couple of times a year, raise a little hell, drink a barrel of rye, back home well before sun, following a team of mules around his cornfield in the blistering heat. That being said, he was best remembered by the valley's old-timers for his disdain for the fair sex, telling his *amigos* down at some no-name *cantina*, "Boys, let me tell you about women, 'cause I'm an expert in that regard. You see, I'm married to one of them, don't you know. It's my considered opinion that if it wasn't for their pretty sex-stuff, there'd be a bounty on every damn one of them."

It wasn't so long ago that Coot still pretty-well mirrored that position except for Shelly Brom. He'd never admit it, but Zara had a lot to do with changing that rather sexist attitude. He'd come a long way, while I only suffered from cold feet at night.

Late the next afternoon, we had to be getting close to Carichic. I'd studied Chihuahua maps when flying into Mexico, but found them unreliable. On the ground, they were worse than useless, nothing was familiar. Then it all looked the same. Every hill, every mesquite clump, canebrake, chinaberry tree looked familiar. A mighty sandstorm beat us in the face all afternoon. Coot stopped, retrieved some oily rags from the toolbox to wrap around our faces and necks to ward off the stinging sand. "Damn this wind. It's blowing hard enough to peal the hide off a mule."

I said, "Yeah, if it'd ease up a little, I might get my bearings."

I stepped out, arched the ache in my back, cupped my hands to hold the grit at bay, peered around, saw the sand sift and tingle against the metal sides of the Reo, got back in, Coot glaring across its cab.

"You're lost aren't you? That's not like you. There was a day you had sight beyond the horizon. Usually know pretty much where you are—all the time."

"Jeez-amighty, Coot! We've been going in circles for days, changing directions, going around lava flows, *lechuguilla* barricades, stumbling around in blinding sandstorms. But, yeah, I'm guessing. That mountain up ahead looks like something we should head for, but then, that mountain over there to the southwest looks even more inviting. But it's too far south to be the mountain near the Curtiss' hiding place."

We drove on. I hit the dashboard. "Damn, Coot, we're not getting anywhere. Pull up. I want to climb that small hill over there, stretch my aching legs, take a look around. Maybe I can get my bearings from up there."

"I'll go with you" he said. "My old legs are starting to cramp."

We'd never get the Reo cranked up if we killed the engine, so we left it running, climbed to the top of the hill, Coot leading the way. Just before we topped out, Coot froze in his tracks. Arms outspread. My mind flashed back to Coot and me when we were sixteen-year-old boys, stumbling on a small band of Apache women and children on top of a hill as they tried to start a fire in a strong sandstorm. I didn't know if it was Coot's signal, or my earlier admonishment for him not to cuss the wind that brought instant understanding to me. No doubt—we were close to an enemy, an enemy that was probably only a few feet in front of Coot. He signaled me to walk back away from the top of the hill. When we got a few feet downhill, he turned, hustled past, waving me to come on, his eyes telling me to watch our backside.

He eased the Reo away. "I damn near stepped on a *Federal* soldier up there. Asleep, probably a lookout. I saw a church. Sizable number of adobes. Think that's Carichic?"

"Gotta be. If it's not Carichic, we're sure as hell lost. That mountain to the south must be where Rose hid the Curtiss, the place she called *Circulo de Rocas*. Let's head for it."

As we neared the mountain, Coot took a swing around and come up on it from the east. We came out of an *arroyo* and there it stood—*Circulo de Rocas*. The wind stopped as suddenly as it came on. "Rose is right about this place," he said. "It sure as hell does look like Stonehenge on Britain's Salisbury Plains."

As we stepped between two boulders, he said, "Well, I'll be damned. These boulders are square as a block of ice, thirty feet tall, thirty on a side."

We searched the plaza formed by the boulders.

"Coot, there she is! Little Miss Curtiss, all covered with bamboo and limbs.

No worse for wear, if you don't count one split propeller, a bunged-up undercarriage, and that ruined engine you mentioned."

"You're not listening. I said it's *probably* ruined." He reached in front of the engine, dislodged a piece of heavy wood, painted orange. "This is what whizzed by Rose's head. The front corner of the undercarriage. If hadn't been for that corner brace, I doubt it would have split the propeller."

We bedded down, figuring to approach Carichic tomorrow.

☺☺☺

The next morning we sat around sipping hot coffee and cream, munching tortillas and jerky we didn't have. Coot inspected the Curtiss' propeller, cranked it over, didn't hear anything that would give suspicion that the engine was damaged. I told Coot that a good woodman with a sharp plane could fashion a propeller—if he had a long, straight piece of strong wood.

Coot said, "Well, now what? Need to find Rose, make sure she's all right. Think we should foot-it to Carichic or drive the Reo? We haven't seen any sign of a burro, a cart track, let alone a tire track."

"There's no use hiding the Reo here, going on afoot. I say we get moving."

Coot drove the Reo inside the circle of rocks, tied a chain to the drill press, around a boulder, then drove forward, easing the press to the ground on skids. The monstrous drill press teetered, then settled. We cut cane and brush to drag along behind the Reo to cover our tracks, headed north.

After an hour, I told Coot that I thought we should stop and stay out of sight until dark. He drove the Reo off the trail behind a canebrake. A minute later he was snoring. I walked to the top a knoll to the north, peeked over the top. Carichic, less than a half-mile away.

After dark, I punched him. "We're close to Carichic."

"Huh? How do you know?"

"I climbed that little knoll over there, that's how. Let's hide the Reo."

He took the Reo on a long sweep around the cane, brush still trailing along on a chain. When he got to the far side of the cane, he gunned her and damn near went all the way through the heavy canebrake before he let off on the gas.

As we walked to the village, we wondered how it would be laid out, where the church would be, where we'd find Rose. We felt confident that the *Federales* would be headquartered in the middle of Carichic, probably close to the church.

We made our way through a *bosque*, orange light from the campfire flickering, dancing on the walls on the front of a large *adobe* across the way. Had to be the *comandante's* headquarters. Women's screams of grief filled the night air. The night was young, and there were still .45-70-caliber rifles to be blessed, grieved, buried.

I said, "Those Carichic women take their grieving seriously. If I was a *Federale* in this village, I believe I'd cut them a wide birth."

"Are we going to stand here jawin' all night or go find Rose? I've heard nothing but blabber out of you for four days and nights." He pushed me ahead.

We stumbled, felt our way through the cemetery. Up ahead, we witnessed a funeral procession coming through the gate, led by a man with a torch. Father Estevan followed him swinging a smoking pot of incense. Father Estevan passed without a glance. We dropped in behind the last of the group, our *ropa de pobres* concealing our identity. Gregorio was the last through the gate, he closed it, turned to be face-to-face with Coot who was standing, grinning a menacing smile in the low light.

"*Aiiii—chinga tu madr—*you shit chicken, Coot. You scared me down near enoff to make me make the pee in my pants."

Coot grabbed the small man in a headlock and playfully scrubbed Gregorio's head with his knuckles. His way of saying he liked you, as close as he ever got to touching a man.

Gregorio stood, face flushed, tears rolling down his face, grinning. "You bigger than me. You a shit chicken!"

"Where's Rose, you two-bit pimp?" Coot asked.

"Chico brought Narlow's letter. We have been expecting you. Rose lives at the home of *el carpintero, Senor* Jeromino Chavez, Chico's uncle."

I said, "That's good. We're in dire need of a good carpenter. Is he any good?"

"Oh, *si senor.* Very good. Wait until you see the crucifixes he has carved for the church. They are so real, no one will even touch them. You will see, *poco tiempo. Pero primero*, we must bury these poor rifles, *eh?*"

"*En el nombre del Padre, del Hijo y el Espirtu Santo,*" Father Estevan chanted as he turned from the burial sites, and led the mourners back out through the gate.

"Wait here, *por favor,*" Gregorio said. "We got plenty more caskets full of dead rifles. We be back *muy pronto*, then me and Father Estevan, we take you see Rose, *bueno?*"

From the shadows, we watched Father Estevan say last rights over another two caskets of .45-70-caliber rifles. The mourners filed out of the cemetery to the front of the church. The father disbursed the mourners after blessing each of them as they knelt before him, then Gregorio led the *padre* back into the church.

Coot nodded at the *comandante's* headquarters, only fifty steps away. "How are we going to get to the front of the church without showing ourselves to those bastards?"

"I don't know. Guess we just wait for Gregorio. He and the *padre* will soon show themselves."

The scratch of wood on gravel came low at the side of the church as Gregorio and Father Estevan threw back a wooden door, crawled out through a hole that led back under the church. The unlikely pair led us down to the cemetery wall and one by one we climbed over and scurried off into the dark toward Jeromino Chavez's place.

"*Coot. Narlow.*" Rose screamed. She ran to us, hugged us. "I know you both want to spank me. Please forgive me. It was foolish. I am truly sorry for my actions and realize I put everything you have worked for at jeopardy, and I can only—"

"Shut yourself, Rose," Coot said, grinning. "Yeah, I oughta spank your butt with a razor strap. I read your letter that Chico delivered and you might as well clear your head of all that crap about returning to Sacred Heart. You showed a lot of spunk flying down here. Go easy on yourself. Hear me?"

She introduced Jeromino Chavez.

I turned to Chico, a tall, strong man with a ready smile flashing a gap between his front teeth, the man who delivered Rose's letter to me at the Coal Mine. "Chico, I want you to meet my partner, but watch him! As you see, he's not near as handsome as me and he's completely untrustworthy."

Coot smiled up at him. "*Chico?* You're sure a big man to be called Chico."

Rose led Coot by the hand, then me, back to Coot, as Jeromino showed us the crucifixes he was carving for another wall of the church. Precise in every regard, lined along the wall, each one proportionally smaller than the one closest to us, the allusion of a hundred-foot wall in the space of fifteen-feet. Gregorio's description of the man's carving ability did him no justice.

I told Jeromino that we needed a propeller for our *aeroplano*, explaining that the cracked one was made from five layers of laminated walnut.

"But, *senor*, I have no way of laminating wooden. I trained in engineering at your University of California, so I appreciate the strength that laminating offers over a single piece of wood. I can only offer a piece of mahogany that I have saved for many years. Perhaps it will fill your purpose."

He pulled a tarpaulin away and there lay the longest, straightest piece of rough mahogany that I'd ever seen, over twelve-feet in length.

Coot said, "Jeromino, you can rest assured that this will work. If we brought the propeller here to your shop, do you believe you could carve one exactly like the one we take off our airplane?"

"I have never seen a propeller, but even so, I can carve anything to exact proportions. *Exactamente!*"

I said, "That's grand. Sure wish the Curtiss' engine wasn't ruined like Coot says."

Rose turned to him. "Ruined? It won't work?"

He smiled. "Rose, I've told this clown a hundred times—it's *probably* ruined."

◎◎◎

Rose, Chico, Gregorio, Coot, and I piled in the Reo and headed for *Circulo de Rocas*. On the way, Coot asked Rose about her plan to rid Carichic of the *Federales* with burning oleander. She recounted her memory of reading about Bonaparte's invasion of Russia, of following their army across the frozen tundra of that great wasteland. The Russians burned every house, barn, fence, and crop as they retreated, leaving nothing, not even a bird nest to burn in a futile effort to stave off freezing. The French supply lines were stretched for over a thousand miles, every mile they advanced added another mile of ever-increasing difficulty of supplying their troops. Bonaparte was desperate. He ordered his men to dig holes to get out of the wind and cold, but the ground was frozen several feet down. He then ordered them to seek shelter in hollows where the lowly oleander flourished. They built fires from the twigs and branches of the dead brush. Throughout the night, the men fed the flames, and all that long night, the French soldiers began coughing, wheezing, throwing up blood. Increasing numbers died before dawn.

"And the very next day, Bonaparte ordered a retreat out of Mother Russia. Can you imagine his disappointment? How he would be received when, or if, he ever made it back to Paris."

Rose tapped the dashboard. "One thing haunts me. The success of my plan depends upon a young girl to feed the *Federales'* fire a small amount of oleander, slowly, for if their men begin coughing, maybe even dying, and they see the smoke, they'll quickly figure it out. Her name is Mercedes, a girl who wants these unwanted guests dead. Not to leave, but *dead*. They murdered her mother and father when they first arrived here, made her bury her mother with nothing but a

165

spoon. But, if she goes slow, one or two of the soldiers will begin coughing late at night, worsen by daylight, perhaps recover, but the next night his symptoms will worsen, and with any luck, he'll die."

She clasped her face with her hands. "Would you listen to me? Do you hear what I just said? I'm wishing a child of God an agonizing death! What have I become?"

Coot grabbed her, pulled her to him. "Don't start that, Rose. That child of death will kill every child in Carichic if it suits his purpose. Go easy on yourself. It's not too late for that razor strap."

We removed the cracked propeller and headed back to Jeromino's shop.

"As I said, *senores*, what I carve for you will be *exactamente* as this laminated one."

Coot asked, "Jeronimo, can you give us a guess as to how long will it take to carve it? Days? Weeks?"

"Oh, no no no. Chico's ability is approaching my own at the end of a carving knife. Give us three days. It will be ready for you."

Coot squeezed Rose's shoulders. "Well, War Ace, Narlow and I are heading back to *Circulo de Rocas* so we won't be spotted. We'll fix the undercarriage while we're waiting. No reason for you to hang around here and get in the way. Care to come along?"

"I thought you'd never ask."

The three of us loaded up, ready to head south. The village ladies furnished us enough food to last three months, much less three short days. A good spring at the edge of the boulders furnished all the water we required, an item that we didn't require much of, just enough to cool off our evening whiskies.

The second evening, Rose got a little deep in her cups, began opening up about her past, her childhood.

"There were nine of us in our small hut at the edge of the jungle. My father was gone a lot, worked as a stevedore at the port on the Pacific side of what is now the Panama Canal. Often he'd be gone for months. He rarely gave our mother any money for food, a *peso* of two, only came home to rest, to sleep with me or one of my sisters. He was a lecherous bastard—*lascivo!* We were penniless, starving. My mother did the only thing she could do. When he did come home, he was cruel, a drunkard. One night, he called our mother a whore. He hit her, *hard*, with a cast-iron skillet. My older brother went to her defense. My father opened my brother's skull, killing him with the same skillet. Said nothing, just kept drinking, laughed when Mother died that same night, wouldn't allow us to bury our own mother, our brother."

She stood, glanced down at her cup. "How can I drink this insanity? Why do I love it so much after all the dreadfulness it's caused. I'm as sick as my father, just as heartless, just as cruel."

Coot hugged her. "Rose, don't be hard on yourself. You're as bad as Narlow about that sorta thing. Give yourself a little room, grant yourself a little grace, forgiveness."

She warmed to him for a moment, pushed away. "Only God can forgive what I've done in my life," and went on with her story. Her father finally passed out, her other brother came to her saying he wanted revenge. They found their father passed out in a tool shed, crept in, found an ax and a sledgehammer. Her brother hit him with the sledgehammer. Rose slashed out with her ax. They were young, frightened, certain the police would come and take them away, as their father's favorite drinking *amigo* was the chief of police. They took turns with the ax, stuffed their father's body parts in gunny sacks, his head in another. They were covered with their father's blood. When their little sisters came to see, they shooed them away. They dragged the sacks to where the French had built a dam before giving up their failed attempt to cross the isthmus. They loaded the sacks with rocks, then heaved them over the side of the dam, then buried the head deep in the dark earth of the jungle.

Coot and I sat quiet, didn't utter a word, dumbstruck.

Rose sighed. "I've only told that story to two others, both sisters at Sacred Heart, not even to Zara. But, now you see that I'm not that pristinely perfect package in a hooded, white and black frock like you thought."

Coot knelt by her, took her hands in his. "Rose, my dear lady, let's get this straight. No one's perfect sitting around this stick-fed fire. Fact is, the one man who was perfect found himself gasping for breath nailed to a crossed post. I know God's working on Narlow's soul, patching it up a bit. You see, Rose, Narlow's mama is meaner than your daddy was, but, you see, Narlow didn't have any little baby sisters to protect like you and your brother did. I know my friend here, known him all my life. Had there been any little ones in their dugout, that woman who birthed him would not still be sucking air. He'd'a put her in the ground when he was twelve years old."

Rose came close to sobbing, but held back, glanced at me, tried to force a smile, then stood. "But that's only half of that horrid tale. A week after we threw my father in that putrid swamp, the chief of police came to our home, asking where our father was. He didn't look for him, he already knew he was dead. None of us said a word. He picked up our youngest sister, said that a Nicaraguan patrol had found a sack that had floated to the top of the lake. He was called, inspected the contents of the sack, saw a familiar tattoo on the man's arm. Our father's arm. He got tough, mean, kicked us around, then dragged our sister away, shouted over his shoulder that he would have his way with her until one of us talked."

Once again, she and her brother found the sledgehammer and ax, took off in the direction the man had dragged their little sister, heard him breathing in the heavy undergrowth, silencing her, said he wouldn't hurt her, that he had something he wanted to show her, a pretty present for her. When Rose and her brother came up behind him, he was pulling down his pants. She hit him at the base of his neck with the ax, her brother pounded him to the damp earth with the sledgehammer.

They left him there but they had to flee. They fought their way through the jungles for two days and nights until they came to the Gulf of Panama side of the narrow isthmus. Her brother found a freighter, heard sailors speaking a strange language, something about America, that they'd be home in only three weeks. They sneaked onboard, hid behind bales of straw for many days. The ship dropped anchor. Her brother slipped on-deck, overheard sailors talking about going ashore, ashore to a place called Belem. A seaport. Said their ship would enter the mouth of the Amazon River, sail a hundred miles inland to the sailors' home. Her brother and sisters didn't know much, but knew they didn't want to sail into the innards of Brazil.

Their ship stayed at anchor for more than a week, all the while, they lived on raw rats, putrid, the underside of their hides, ulcerated, vermin-ridden. Shore was only a hundred-yards away. They slipped over the side of the freighter and helped each other to the docks. Brazilian shore authorities tried to take them into custody. They ran, became separated in the heavy crowd at a fruit market.

She sighed. "I never found them. After so many years, never a trace. I found my way back to the shipping docks. God took me there. I *know* He did. There was a group of nuns waiting in an outdoor café nearby. I crept up behind them, listened. They were going home, home to Sacred Heart for Girls in a place called Dallas, taking four young, orphaned girls with them. One of the nuns caught sight of me hiding behind a low wall, edged over and sat, told me not to be frightened, and we began to talk. I told her my story, that I had no place to go. She asked about my parents, and when I began recounting that gruesome story, she put her soft, white hand over my mouth. '*Shush*, child! Never repeat that to anyone.' Her name was Sister Juana Tsagaris. I told her my name was Rosa Marie Talamantes. She took my face in her hands, gazed deep in my eyes, then said a marvelous thing. 'Child, I don't know one thing about you, but I see truth and goodness in your eyes. They reflect kindness, honesty, a touch of righteousness, a gentle, but somewhat troubled soul.' She embraced me, then said, 'Brazilian authorities are very strict about taking their young people away. I will speak to Mother Superior.' She patted my hand. 'I'll see what I can do.'"

Rose said that Sister Juana spoke to another of the nuns, one dressed in a different frock, appeared older. She gazed at Rose for several moments, nodded to Sister Juana. Sister Juana picked up a small bag, told Rose to follow her. She led her between two rickety buildings, handed Rose a sister's frock, told her to put it on, that until they were safely on US soil, her name was Sister Rosa, told her to speak to no one except her and the nun she was talking to, a nun known as Mother Superior Pancretias.

"A month later, I found myself cleaning floors in a dormitory at Sacred Heart School for Girls, dressed in a long checkered skirt and a long-sleeved white blouse, scolded, told to only speak English. Mother Superior Pancretias sent for me, asked me to tell my story completely, to leave nothing out. When I finished, she said, 'Dear Child of God, I want you to sit quietly and write down on paper everything you just told me. Skip nothing. Do not embellish it, nor make light of anything that occurred.' I told her that I wanted to forget it ever happened. She said, 'No, child, you do not want to forget it, *ever*. You must remember it. If you fail to write it down, time and your imagination will work on your memory. It will soften. Do not seek softness in life, choose reality.' So, I wrote it down, gave it to Sister Juana to read and safe keep for me. Every month, she brought those pages to me, sat by my side as I read them aloud."

Rose glanced up. "What are you smiling about, Narlow?"

"Mother Superior Pancretias must have been reading Papa's mail. Those are the exact words and advice he gave me when I was a boy. Things were never good between my mother and me. Papa did not want a boy's natural inclination to soften his mother's harsh ways, her ill-treatment of him, but to recall the truth. After a particularly harsh time with my mother, I sat down in the milking barn where it occurred, wrote it all down, stepped up on a milking stall, hid it on a dusty, cobwebbed rafter. I still read it from time to time, especially those times when I began to doubt my own memory of it, my sanity, my mother's cruelty."

Rose smiled. "Well, Narlow, you'll want to know that a short time later, Zara came to that very dormitory. I'd been promoted to proctor, but I was still mopping floors. A long voyage, my friends. Now, look what I have to show for it."

She stood, threw her cup aside. "Now, look at me. I've proven to the entire world that I cannot successfully live anywhere except inside the walls of the place I was taken as young girl. Taken from the malaria and yellow fever-ridden jungles of Panama. I'm as narrow as my isthmus birthplace. If Mother Superior Pancretias will have me, and if we ever get out of this mess I caused, I'll board the next train back to Sacred Heart."

Coot stood, arched his back, locked his fists behind his head, stretched like he did when set to explode, bent over, and got in Rose's olive, oval face. "Young lady, you've undoubtedly had a long, rough row to hoe, but you'll catch that train back to Sacred Heart over my *very* bloodied, *very* dead body. You'll likely find I don't die easy.

"No doubt you're a firm believer in God, but right now, He's testing you. And, I'll tell you something else, something you best consider. Narlow's papa often told us that God provides the wind and rain, but if you only offer up a hanky for the wind, a thimble for the rain, that's about all you'll get."

30

Back at Jeromino's Shop.

Coot grinned as we stepped up to Jeromino's prize. "Say now, Jeronimo, this propeller looks like it could fly by itself."

Jeronimo said, "Over here is the propeller that was taken from your *aeroplano*. It is the same length, dimensions, slope, curve, and twist. *Exactamente* as the one I carved for you."

Jeromino smoothed his hand over his work. "This propeller is as ready as I know how to perfect it. I believe it is balanced and will work for you. All you need to do is to drill eight precise holes to match the broken propeller with the big drill press you brought with you."

Rose smiled when Coot turned to her. "Well, Ace, are we going to spend the night here 'ooing' and 'aahing' over this propeller? Or get in that tail-bustin' Reo, and go mount her up?"

Jeromino beamed. "With your kind permission, I would like very much to see your flying machine, how this propeller draws it through the air."

When we drove up to the Curtiss' hiding place, dawn's rosy fingers were stretching across the eastern sky. The day was crisp, bright, but by eight, we were all up looking for shade to escape the hot sun. Rose was back to her old self, jabbering at me, scolding Coot for his wayward ways, chastising him for having so many lady friends.

We set the metal facing-plate in place to serve as a template for the drill. Gregorio and Chico had a devil of a time getting the weight of the wheels, straps, and pulleys turning with the hand crank, but once in motion, the drill became a one-handed task. The augur bit slowly, cutting its way through the propeller, and within the hour, it had cut eight smooth holes. Coot used the calipers to measure the holes and the bolts at the front end of the Curtiss' engine.

"Close, but no cigar. Holes are a tad tight."

We built a fire, got a five-eighths inch bolt white-hot, and with the aid of a pair of blacksmith tongs, Coot grabbed up the bolt and pushed it through the holes in the prop in eight fluid motions. Just a whiff of smoke caused by the slight burning of the hard wood. We hoisted the propeller up in position in front of the crankshaft, and Coot taped it in place. "Like a silk glove."

Jeromino held the facing plate in place while Coot tightened the nuts on the prop. "Well, Narlow, should we crank her up?"

Chico had stepped over behind some bushes to relieve himself. He ran back to us waving his arm.

"*Senores!*" Chico whispered, his finger to his lips, "*Escuchar!*" In a moment we heard men's voices coming from the direction of the trail.

Coot hurried past me. "Come on, Chico, you too, Narlow. Grab a rifle. Let's see who our visitors are. The rest of you keep out of sight."

When we got to the edge of the boulders, three young men and an older, smaller man appeared, talking, chunking rocks up the trail ahead of them, heading south away from Carichic, preoccupied with their game.

One of them stopped, not thirty yards away, sat on the ground, removed his *huaraches*. "*Espere, amigos—una piedra.*"

They all laughed and sat down while their friend found his source of irritation.

Chico crept up behind us, squatted down, peered through the bamboo and mesquite, whispered, "*Los hombres*—I know them. The *hombre* on the right, the small, older man, I do not know. *No problema, pienso.*"

They stood, still laughing, talking, something about *agua*.

Chico whispered, "He is thirsty, thinks there is water here."

They started walking toward us.

Coot said, "Come on. We've got to show ourselves. Chico, you do the talking. Narlow, make certain you show that rifle." We walked out, my rifle in-hand.

"*Hola, Gordo, Seco, Pepe, como le va?*" Chico called out.

"Bueno. *Quien son sus amigos, Chico?*" Gordo asked.

"*Son del Ciudad de México. Son hombres de negocios que vinieron a buscar pajaros,*" Gregorio answered proudly.

"*Cazadores del pajaros? Es su guia? Tiene un tonto por una guia!*" Gordo said, his friends laughing.

I wasn't following the conversation word for word, something about me and Coot being from Mexico City, here to do some bird hunting. Gordo said something about us having a fool for a guide.

Coot piped up in a strong bull voice, "*Guarde sus muchachos de la boca. O pregunta el alcalde de su pueblo en el final de un palo por un asado este noche!*" Coot told Gordo to shut his mouth before he asked the mayor of Carichic to stick him over a pit and cook him for supper.

"*Favor de perdoname, senor. Signifigue ningun dano. Nos vamos. Gracias. Muchas gracias, senores,*" Gordo said as he backed off, their smiles disappearing as they turned to leave.

"Well, what do you think?" I asked. "Think they suspect anything?"

"I don't know," Coot said. "Chico, *que piensa usted?*"

"*No se, pero no piensa problema.*"

Coot whistled, and the others came out.

Rose asked, "Who were they? Is it okay?"

"Four men. Chico knows three of them," Coot replied. "Not certain about the older one." Coot turned to me. "Narlow, we can't chance firing-up the Curtiss. To give the propeller any kind of test, you'd have to rev it up tight and loud."

"Yeah, darn near have to chain her to a tree and pour the coal to her to get her up to maximum rpm."

Coot agreed. "Guess we'll leave the testing till Rose flies her out."

"*I'm* flying the Curtiss out?" she asked, her feathers in an instant kink. "I'm not leaving without you two. I got us in this mess, and I'm not leaving *you* to clean it up. I am *not* going without you and *that's that.*"

Coot squared around to her. "The day after tomorrow is the twenty-third day of the month, right?"

"Well, I guess, but what's that got to do with it?"

"Well, young lady, you'll be pleased to know that on that particular day, we have a friend flying in here. He'll either lead you and the Curtiss to El Paso, if the propeller problem is under control, or he'll fly you out in his two-seater biwing."

"Coot, did you hear what I just said? I am *not* flying out of here with anybody. *No sir.* All of us, or none of us, my dear man."

"*Settle down,*" I said. "You're going to do as we say."

"I told you, I am *not* leaving without *both* of you."

"Rose," Coot said, his finger at the end of her nose, "let me tell you something, dear darling lady of my heart. Narlow's papa used to say, 'two men can ride a horse, but only one can ride in front.' Somebody in this outfit has to be the boss, and that *somebody* sure as hell isn't going to be *you.* Quit your yammerin'. *Right now.*"

I asked, "Rose, the cartridges you flew down here—how are they boxed?"

"They're in wooden boxes with rope handles, in metal canisters marked 'Swizzle Sticks—Ship to USA.' My bullets are right over there between those boulders."

"Narlow, what do you think?" Coot said. "Those cartridges are still fifteen miles from the closest friendly rifle, buried in a cemetery. What do you think of bolting the canisters in the wheel wells of the Reo? We can hide them close to Carichic."

Rose showed us her stash, Coot positioned himself in the crevice and handed out the canisters.

When he handed out the last one, he glanced down between his boots, motioned for Rose to come over. "Did you see what was lodged in here?"

"Well, no, I was in such a rush and I was frightened half to death so I didn't . . . *oh my God.* Bones! A skeleton. Is it a man or a large animal?"

173

Coot said, "Well, it may not be the bones of a man, but they sure have the shape of a man with all the man scraped off."

I asked, "What's this? There's several loose .45-70 cartridges on the ground. Why's that, Rose?"

"One of the boxes spilled. I thought I replaced them all. But I don't recall."

The cartridges were passed around so everyone could take a look at them, feel their heft.

Gregorio said, "Oh, they are so beautiful! *Hijo*, so heavy."

Jeronimo hefted them, put them in his tool bag.

We carried the canisters back to the Reo, Coot took Rose by the hand, pointed up over the back tires. "See that deep wheel well? That's where we're going to stash your bullets. We're going to bolt these canisters right there to the frame of this ol' truck. Safe, out of sight."

While Coot bolted the canisters in place, Jeronimo brought a bucket of dark clay from the spring.

I asked, "What are you going to do with that, *amigo?*"

"For the metal canisters. This brown clay will hide the letters on the canisters. If by chance a *Federal* or *Rural* saw those words printed there, and reads, 'Swizzle Sticks—Ship to the USA,' he might ask to see your swizzle sticks. Embarrassing, don't you think, *senor?*"

Coot and I drove the four of them back to Carichic, told Rose we'd pick her up at the same spot in two days, noon sharp, to meet JJ Umbenhauer and his biwing.

Coot waved his finger at Rose. "Don't be late, Ace Rose, for I'll come looking for you. If you're on time, I'll give you a lesson in the finer art of cartridgeology."

"'Tis not an art, sir—'tis a science. And I shall tell you more about *bulletology* than you ever knew about cartridges."

31

Two days later at noon, we drove up to the cane break.

"Ace Rose! Are you there?" I called out into the brush. "You better be, or Coot'll come hunting for—"

Rose sprang from the cane, arms raised, face flushed, wretched, inflamed, distraught. "Oh, my God! *Oh, my God!* Chico's dead. The *Rural* shot Chico. Shot him like a hydrophobic coyote. Shot him because he wouldn't talk. Wouldn't talk about the *norte americanos.* As Jesus is my witness. I will see that bastard die. For his sins. I will go to my—"

Coot jumped out of the truck, grabbed her, held her tight for minute. "Rose! *Calm down.* Sit down. Tell us what happened. Start at the beginning."

She pushed away. "I *hate* myself. I hate—"

Coot hugged her, pulled her down on the running board. "*Shhhh.*"

She sobbed for a moment, wiped her eyes, sat erect. "I really don't know where to start. When this all began, I was down by the *bosque* with Mercedes. I wanted to be absolutely certain that she understood about the oleander. When to begin putting small amounts in the *Federales'* campfire. We heard a pistol shot, then Gregorio ran up, said that a *Rural* came into Carichic, a *capitan* of the *Rurales*, demanded that the *comandante* bring Chico to him. The *Rural* was standing on the *comandante's* porch, ordered the villagers to be silent. The *sargento* dragged Chico to the steps of the porch. Gregorio said the *Rural* began questioning Chico, confusing him, twisting his story. Chico's story changed. The *Rural* put the barrel of his pistol under Chico's chin. Asked him what he knew about the *norte americanos*, the ones at *Circulo de Rocas.* Chico refused and the *Rural* . . . pulled the trigger."

Rose's head went down, her mouth and cheeks tightened, lost her voice, trying to breathe around her grief, waved us off when we tried to console her. "I'm all right. Please, just give me a moment."

She began again. "After the *Rural* murdered Chico, Gregorio told us what he knew, told me to run, to hide here where you were to pick me up today, told Mercedes he would help her with the oleander. He turned and ran back toward the square. I came here and hid in the cane.

"After just a little while, Gregorio ran back here to where I was hiding. He said the *Rural* grabbed up a little girl, began prancing around the villagers with the little girl on one arm, pistol in his hand. The girl's mother ran to her daughter, the *Rural* put the pistol in her face, telling her to shut up, to back away. He began screaming, demanding that the villagers tell him about the *norte americanos*. Threatening to kill the little girl. To send her ghost chasing after the ghost of Chico. The villagers were confused, no one spoke.

"Gregorio said he told the *Rural* that he knew what was going on here, that the villagers were stupid, afraid."

Rose sniffed, dabbed at her nose with a hanky, sniffed, composed herself. "Gregorio said he told the *Rural* that he'd heard about the *norte americanos*. The *Rural* and the *comandante* began arguing, went inside his headquarters. That's when Gregorio ran back here to tell me to go with you back to *Circulo de Rocas*, not to return to the village, that the *Rural* was insane. He turned and ran toward Carichic."

"Come on," I said, "let's get started back to *Circulo de Rocas*. You can tell us the rest on the way."

Coot said, "So, when Mercedes feeds the *Federales'* campfire with oleander, what's to keep the entire village from dying?"

"She needs to be very careful, to feed the fire slowly. The *Federales* are frightened to death thinking the plague is all around them. When villagers are near, the *Federales* wear cloth over their faces. It won't take much oleander smoke to convince the *Federales* that they are getting the fever and plague. I cautioned Mercedes to only put a few small limbs on the fire, or the *Federales* will figure it out. There is seldom any wind at night, so the smoke stays close to the ground, just like it did in Russia. I can only pray that Mercedes doesn't overdo it."

"Well, let's hope it works," I said. "We expect JJ to be here by the time we get back to the Curtiss. If it's okay, you can fly her home today."

She glared at me, then Coot. "So, you make all the rules, and you expect me to obey them without question. I'll be leaving you here to make the most of my horrible mistake. And Chico—poor Chico. That's *my* doing. Just as if I'd pulled the trigger that scattered his brains in that courtyard. I wonder how many others will die because of my—"

Coot said, "Rose, damn it, we had more to do with Chico's death than you did, but you don't see us blaming ourselves, boohooing over it. We all did what we thought best at the time. And, yes, we make all the rules, and rule number one is that you are damn certain flying out of here today. Whether JJ shows or not. If he doesn't, and the Curtiss' engine is okay, you'll fly east until you cross the Rio Grande, then follow it north to El Paso. But never fear–JJ'll be here."

A far-off hum. Coot cocked his head. "Listen up. There comes JJ. Right on schedule."

"Damn he's flying low," I said. "Wonder why he's coming from the east?"

JJ taxied up, unbuckled his seat harness, stepped off without cutting the engine, his heavy mustache waving in the stiff breeze of the propeller. A tall man, an inch taller than me, his step, slow, sorta sauntering, lumbering along.

"Damn, JJ, that mustache of yours is about to sprout wings of its own," Coot ribbed his old classmate.

JJ smiled and said, "You know what the Mexicans say about a woman kissing a man without a mustache, '*Un beso sin un bigote, es el mismo que un huevo sin sal*.'" His gray gaze settled like a warm blanket on Rose.

Coot squared around to him. "JJ, let me tell you something about this pretty lady you're gawking at. She's spent most of her life in a convent, impressionable as hell, unskilled in the ways of the world, at least not in *your* world and ways. No reason for you to add this lass to your bevy. You lay a hand on her and you'll answer to me."

"*My* world and ways, huh? I didn't know you'd taken up the ways of the cloth, Mr. Boldt. And certainly, my friend–*certainly*. Never occurred to me to do otherwise." He turned to admire Rose again. "A woman of the cloth, huh?" He whirled around to me, stuck out his hand. "Coot's an impolite bastard. Howdy! I'm JJ Umbenhauer."

"Howdy, yourself, JJ, I'm Narlow Montgomery. Met years ago."

He turned back to Rose. "So, little Miss Rose, you can fly, huh? I never heard of a girl-pilot before."

"Well, mister, whether it's a girl, woman, or lady-pilot, you're looking at one now."

"Didn't intend to ruffle your feathers, sweet thing. No cause to get your drawers all knotted up."

I asked, "JJ, just curious, but why did you come in low from the east? I figured you'd be coming in from the northwest."

"Well, I did come in from that direction, way the hell up there at 12,000 feet, just to get the lay of the land, see what the air tasted like at that altitude, but, hell, up there, there's damn little air to taste. And what there is, is colder than an Eskimo's tit. Oh, beg your pardon, miss. Hard to breathe up there, *cold*. Anyway,

I saw your Curtiss hiding in those boulders there, about that time, I saw a small bunch of *Federale* cavalry and infantry headed your way, on this very trail, about three miles to the north. Looked like a uniformed officer, maybe two of them, riding old, scrawny, broken-down Indian ponies, half a dozen or so soldiers with rifles, running along behind. I turned this kite around, took a long sweep around to the south, then dropped her down like a spent dick on a Saturday night—oh *damn*. I mean—beg your pardon, young lady. Not accustomed to being in the presence of fair damsels. Anyway, I came on in real low-like." He turned, grinned down at Coot. "Podnah, I think you're likely to have some more company pretty dern quick now."

"You two get going. Get out of here," Coot said, shuffling them toward their airplanes.

JJ said over his shoulder, "Whoa there, Mr. Boldt. I don't think that would be the prudent approach. By the time we get your Curtiss out here and cranked her up, I believe we'll be within rifle range of those military men. Even for a Mexican."

"Why in hell didn't you say that before, JJ?"

"Because you've been chewing on my ass and threatening me about this lady-pilot since I stepped off my biwing.

Coot started cipherin'. "JJ, cut your engine. Rose, grab up a stick of bamboo, do what you can about brushing out these tire tracks. Let's get JJ's plane on the other side of these boulders, push it in with the Curtiss. *Get moving!*"

We no more than got JJ's plane hidden when the men on horseback and soldiers came over a rise less than a mile to the north.

"What do you think, Narlow? Think we can hold them off?" Coot asked.

"Yeah, we can hold them off until dark, then what? Reckon they'll come sneaking around these boulders, cut a few gizzards before dawn?"

"All right. Here's what we're going to do. Check me out on this. We have to hope they know nothing about the Curtiss. Rose and JJ, you stay here with the planes. Narlow, tie your vest on a stick. We'll wait until they're about a quarter of a mile out, take off in the Reo toward the east like we're making a run for it. Still be out of effective rifle range. When the *Federales* start shooting, you stand up, start waving that vest around like we're surrendering. We'll stop and wait for them, but by then, we'll have led them away from these boulders. Upwards of a half-mile away by that time. Miss anything?"

I grabbed up a stick. "Let's do it."

"JJ, watch us. With luck they'll just arrest us. Head us back to Carichic. Fire up the Curtiss right where she sits. If the propeller is true and runs smooth, taxi her out of here. Both of you skeedattle. And JJ, if you're not absolutely certain, even *sense* a problem with the engine or propeller, don't chance it. Put Rose in your biwing and fly out—"

"Coot," Rose snapped, "if the Curtiss doesn't go, I don't go, and—"

Coot pushed her around behind him. "And JJ, if she doesn't go willingly, tie her up, sit on her." He whirled around. "Damn it, Rose, you gotta learn to do as I say!"

"If you force me to do this, I'm going back to Sacred Heart. You may depend on it, sir!"

"And you can depend on this! You do and I'll come get you, embarrass hell out of you in front of the sisters and Mother Superior!"

I said, "Rose, Zara will be home in a few days, probably already there. Tell her what's happening, everything. Don't sugar-coat it but tell her I'm okay, that Coot and I will get out of this mess and be home as soon as we can. Tell her I love her—always will."

Coot's plan worked almost too well. We came out of *Circulo de Rocas* and took off fast in the Reo. Only problem, about that time the advancing soldiers and the two on horseback went down into a shallow valley and didn't see our exit and dust until we were way the hell out of rifle range. We could see the soldiers stop, shoulder their rifles and fire, hear the report of the rifles seconds later.

"Start waving your vest!" Coot barked.

"*The cartridges*. Coot, we forgot about those damn cartridge canisters. We're sitting on five-thousand rounds of rifle cartridges. We could make a run for it. They'll never catch us."

"Naw, we best wait here. Can't chance it with Rose so close by."

Two men on horseback rode up, one in uniform, the other dressed as a *po-bre*. They kept their distance until Gregorio and the weary soldiers ran up. Coot whispered that the man out of uniform was the same man who was with the three boys who walked past *Circulo de Rocas* the other day.

Gregorio ran past the two men on horseback, pointing at us. "Those are the *norte americanos, mi Capitan, mi Comandante*. They are the traitors. *Traidores!* Be very careful. They are *muy peligroso*, very tricky, *senores! Traidores!*" Something about Gregorio's repeated use of the word "traitor" caught my attention.

The man out of uniform pushed his horse up to the Reo, its nose in my face.

"Gentlemen, let me welcome you to Mexico. Though I am not in uniform, I can assure you that I am *Rural Capitan* Ambrosio Manzano de Flores." He turned to the other officer, "And this is *Federal Comandante* Horacio Bienvenides."

This had to be the same *Rural Capitan* Ambrosio Manzano de Flores who killed Tacho's father. The same bastard who pushed his aunt off the cliff above Los Fresnos. His name couldn't have escaped Coot's ears.

"Tell me, *senores*, how has the dove hunting been for you? I hope your hunt has been successful. And do you remember me, *senores*?"

I began, "The high point of any day. How could we forget you—"

"*Si senor*," Coot said. "You were walking with three boys the other day, correct?"

"*Exactamente, senor, exactamente!* I was just telling *Comandante* Bienvenides that you gentlemen must be expert shots to go hunting *palomas con sus rifles*. Very good shots, indeed."

I spoke up, grinning. "Oh, I wouldn't go so far as to say that we're the greatest shots in the world. Now, my papa, *he* was the greatest, *then* me, *then* my hunting-friend here."

The *Rural* asked, "Tell me, *senores*, I have *un amigo—un Aleman*. He says to me that he knows three old *gallos—gringo* roosters—that have been running guns into Mexico for many years. One of the *gringo* roosters even flies *un aeroplano*. He flies his *aeroplano* into Mexico delivering *rifles, cartuchos, dinamita*. But there are only two of you. Could it be that you are two of the three my German friend told me about? Could it? Those two *gringos* have an old friend, *un amigo* that is a Mexican *con mucho oro*—very much golds that they buy *muchos rifles, cartuchos y dinamita* to bring to our country. Would you know those *gringos, senores?* Would you know them and the Mexican man *con mucho oro?*"

Coot said, "*No senor*, we do not know those men you speak of. We've heard the same story."

"And I assume you will deny being in Mexico running guns to the *Villistas* as I suspect. Is that correct?"

I asked, "Running *what?*"

"*No senor*, we are not running guns," Coot said.

He clucked his brilliance for the benefit of the *comandante*, then said, "Now *senores*, your guns—all of them, *por favor*. Please do not hold back from my request. If you do not give me all of your guns, I will find them. You have this *Rural's* word that I will shoot you with the guns I find after this one request."

I reached back behind the seat and pulled out the rifles, and handed them to the *Rural.*

"And the *cartuchos, senor—todo por favor. Y senores, estoy seguro que tienen pistolas, eh?* Please give them to me."

As I reached under my coat, I realized this was the first time I'd ever handed over my sidearm to another man in my life. I handed him my Schofield. Coot grimaced as he surrendered his .45-pistol.

"*Bueno, senores.* I like this one—what you call it, S*enor* Boldt?"

"It's a Colt .45 automatic—actually it's a semi-automatic. Take extra-special care of it, *por favor.* Had it a long time."

"Oh, indeed, *senor,* you can trust me with your prize. Do you have more *cartuchos* for this *pistola?*"

"Only the cartridges in the clip. I use that pistol more to beat men over the head than shooting them. Haven't bought a box of shells for that pistol in years."

"*Por favor, senor,* show me how this *pistola* of yours works. I am curious, and I would appreciate a lesson from you. How do you make it shoot?"

My smile fought for audience. We had a Barnum and Bailey cooking.

Coot came around to my side of the Reo where the *Rural* was admiring his new weapon.

"Perhaps you would do me the high favor of unloading the *pistola* first, *senor,*" he said with an all-knowing curl at his lips.

"You are familiar with this pistol, *senor?*" Coot asked.

"*No, senor.* It is strange to me."

Coot held up the automatic, released the clip, it fell in his hand. He handed the clip to the *Rural.* "This is the clip. Holds seven rounds. *Siete cartuchos.* With one in the chamber, you have *ocho cartuchos.* This is the slide. It will only move to the rear when the weapon is not on safe. When the slide is moved to the rear like this. The cartridge in the barrel is ejected, falls to the ground—like that. When the slide is released. The hammer stays back. All you have to do is pull the trigger. It will fire as fast as it is pulled."

Coot retrieved the cartridge at his feet, gave it to the *capitan.* "This pistol was engineered to be handled with only one hand. If the hammer is back, and you want to uncock it, you reach up with your thumb, and pull it back all the way like this, then pull the trigger, let the hammer go forward a little bit, then take your finger off the trigger, let your thumb guide the hammer on to its home position. Takes a little practice. You'll get the hang of it."

I winced as the *Rural* tried to uncock the big .45 with his small hand, and I almost ducked when he touched Coot's hair trigger. I had to fight a broad smile as Coot convinced him his .45-Colt was the world's first one-handed semi-automatic.

"*Aiiii, Senor* Boldt—that is very hard to do."

My jaw contorted in a futile effort to restrain a grin. Coot told that man everything there was to know about that automatic—*except* the built-in safety in the grip. As long as he didn't squeeze the grip thus releasing the safety, the gun would not fire.

The *Rural* handed the pistol and the clip to Coot. "You will load the gun for me, *senor?*"

Coot replaced the loaded clip, pulled the slide back, let it slam forward, loading a round in the chamber, released the clip, crammed the round in place, slammed the clip home, uncocked the weapon using only one hand, smiled at the *Rural*, handed it back to him, safety off.

The *Rural* grinned, enthralled with his one-handed killing device.

"*Bueno, bueno, senores,*" *Comandante* Bienvenides said. "We are many kilometers from our village. Perhaps you have heard of it—Carichic. Would you be so kind as to take us there in your truck? We will have the ladies of our village prepare a feast in your honor, then we can talk further."

"Why, certainly *Comandante*," I said. "Hop on. We'd be right pleased to give you a lift back to town. Here, let me offer you my seat up here in front, and I'll ride back there in the bed of the truck. This old beast is fast, but intolerably rough on a man's backside."

"*That* will *not* be necessary, *senor,*" the *Rural* said, a smirk on his lips. "Keep your seat."

The *comandante* and the *capitan* climbed in the back of the Reo and the *comandante* ordered four of his men to get in with them, leaving two men to ride the horses back to town. And Gregorio—who stood looking up at the *Rural*.

"Gregorio Gonzales, you called these *norte americanos* traitors a few moments ago, do you remember? *Eh?* Perhaps they are *traidores,* but to whom? *Eh?* That is to be determined, but you have already proven you cannot be trusted. You have already proven your ability to betray—*sus amigos y familia.* No, *traidores* do not ride, they walk. *You* walk. The fresh air will be good for your traitorous heart." He bent over laughing at his own humor.

The hot, rough trail leading back to Carichic, the drain of the day's excitement, the drone of the Reo's laboring engine, the monotonous squeal of *Capitan*

Manzano's biting voice, melded together for a strange, lazy combination, making it a losing battle for me to keep from dozing off. I was aware of another far off drone, but my sleepy condition could not distinguish one senseless drone from another.

Coot bumped me hard with his elbow as we were coming out of a steep *arroyo*. He motioned with his eyes. I didn't understand. His eyes blinked up repeatedly. He shrugged as we glanced up in the direction of a solo biwing, flying high. JJ was making it clear to us that only one airplane left *Circulo de Rocas* this afternoon. Rose was up there with him. Safe.

"*Mire!*" the *Rural* screamed as he pointed Coot's .45 at the biwing. "*Un aeroplano!* I do not believe that is *un aeroplano* of our government, *senores*. Whose *aeroplano* do you think it is, *amigos? Que piensan, senores?*"

I started to reply, but Coot raised his hand. "We do not know whose airplane that could be."

"I have not seen the *aeroplano de los gringos*, but I have heard of them. The *aeroplano es de estados unidos, pienso*. Yes, I think it is. *Generalisimo* Hugo Garcia de Gomez is certain the *norte americanos* are flying *cartuchos y rifles* to the many enemies of our country. The *generalisimo* is a very smart man." He scratched his nose with the .45. "And, he is my mother's older brother, *mi tio*." He repeated, "*Mi tio!*"

Capitan Manzano smiled down at me, his gaze shot up as he watched JJ turn the biwing back to the southwest toward *Barranca de Cobre*.

As we neared Carichic, the *comandante* ordered us to drag several heavy timbers into the village, then directed his men to remove all six tires and wheels. We jacked up the Reo a few inches on a side at a time until she was blocked up over seven feet in the air, presenting a most unladylike appearance, like a barefooted, six-legged javalina stuck on a tree limb with her skirts hiked up.

Coot motioned for me to look up, a most unwelcome sight. The heavy dust of the trail on the Reo's belly, the smear of mud on the canisters that Jeromino applied at *Circulo de Rocas* was the only thing covering the black on green lettering—*Swizzle Sticks*—*Ship to USA*. The lettering was covered except a portion of USA on one of the canisters. My heart sank. I looked around the village square—every bullet-riddled adobe wall seemed to have our names stamped on them.

Among the *comandante's* soldiers was an orphan-of-a-boy, Juanito by name. A full-grown, hate-filled man all wrapped up in the skin of a twelve-year-old boy, no more than a doorknob in height. Bottomless, yet piercing bright eyes, black as pitch. Eyes that appeared to see nothing, then at another angle, to be absorbing everything in his view. Nothing childish or boyish about Juanito. Nothing light about his step, no *huaraches*, only heavy, purposeful shoeless steps, his every movement, every action, a resolute duty. Over his tattered *serape*, he wore two cartridge belts that crossed in the middle of his chest in *bandalero* style, a single live .45-70 cartridge in the top cartridge ring of each belt, several spent casings in other loops. He carried a beat-up, single-shot rifle, only leaning it against a wall when he was helping Mercedes with her chores or doing the *comandante's* bidding. On his waist was slung a beat-up .45 Colt Single Action Army revolver with three live .45 rounds in the belt loops. Juanito repeatedly hiked-up the heavy revolver to keep it from sliding down his narrow hips.

The *comandante* told us we were free to come and go at your liberty, but to be careful. "Do not wander too far. My men might suspect you are making your escape. You would not want me to have to send Juanito after you. He would find you, but he would not bring you back."

Juanito's gaze fell on Coot, then locked on me. The boy's eyes never blinked. He bore the essence of a lost child with a tarantula gnawing at his innards.

We headed down the winding trail to Jeronimo Chavez's shop. Coot said, "Rose and JJ should be in El Paso by now. Reckon they're all right?"

"Sure they are. She's probably got him on the end of leash by now. Don't worry about her. Save your concern for your old lifelong chum."

As we stepped to the shop door, we heard the rattle of hammers on nails. We tried the door, bolted from inside. They did not hear our repeated raps over the noise of pounding hammers. Father Estevan's voice was loud over the clatter of pine planks and hammers. We couldn't make out what the *padre* was saying, but he was pleading with someone to listen to reason. I found a rock and banged hard on the wall planks and called out his name. The *padre* quieted the others, then unlocked the door.

Jeronimo Chavez eyes were low and hollow.

Father Estevan said, "First, Gregorio Gonzalez deserts his own people, now Jeronimo Chavez is intent on certain suicide. Ignores me, has vowed to kill the *Rural* for murdering Chico. The *Federales* will kill him, and for what? One more dead *pobre*."

"It is of little matter," Jeromino said. "I will avenge my Chico's death. The *Rural* dog murdered my Chico as if squashing a gnat. Chico was all I had in this life.

This *Revolucion Gloriosa* sickens me. Tired of the killing, tired of looking at death from the outside. I wish to know it closer—from the inside."

Coot squatted down beside him. "Jeronimo, *mi amigo*, we all want the bastard dead, but if you will give us just a few days, we'll find a way to trick the *Rural* and the *comandante*. Then we'll stand that *Rural*-dog bastard against a wall. You can shoot him, before you stuff his *huevos* in his mouth, or afterward. Promise me you will give us three days. If we don't have *Capitan* Manzano standing against the adobe wall of your choice, you can go after him in your own way. Okay, *amigo*?"

"*Manana* or three days. The *Rural* will die."

⊙⊙⊙

The next morning we made our way back to the *comandante's* headquarters. *Capitan* Manzano had shed the clothes of a pobre, now donning black trousers bloused at the top of laced black boots. He stomped around the plaza, glaring at a banner hanging on a side wall of the headquarters, strutting under the banner, practicing cocking, uncocking Coot's .45. The banner read: *Libertad o Muerte.*

"*Bah! Comandante,* don't you realize that banner is against the very government you represent? Me, *Rural Capitan Manzano* says, 'Give them what they want—*muerto*, death!' And you have done nothing to secure yourself from the villagers. If they have guns, and you can be certain they do, they could march into this plaza and kill us all in less than a minute."

"*Capitan* Manzano, we have been here for over a month and had no difficulty with these people. The man who put up that banner was the mayor of Carichic, he became insolent, he and his wife were shot. I told these people that the banner would remain to remind them that they must behave. If not, I would give them their alternative."

Capitan Manzano wandered off.

The *comandante* asked Mercedes to bring food. She reappeared with rabbit stew and tortillas, Juanito close behind with bowls and spoons. After we ate, Juanito helped Mercedes clear the table. She touched his hand as a way of thanking him, his eyes met hers, the slightest curve of a smile on his wide mouth. A smile that contented itself only at the corners his mouth. *Only* his mouth, a smile I had not witnessed before. His face, eyes, showed no pleasure in Mercedes' touch. That boy would never possess an authentic smile, a hearty laugh, a woman's touch, caress, her love. I recalled my own youth, never easy by any measure, but I had not lived the horror that was mirrored on Juanito's face, the ghastliness that was forever his, a slate never to be wiped clean. I was one known for my ready smile, laugh, while Juanito did not hold a single laugh in his entire being, hadn't a notion as to how to tickle his giggle box. His essence was hate, deceit, killing, the stench of death had him gobbled up.

"*Comandante*," Coot said, "if it is agreeable with you, we are going to the *carpintero's* shop and give him a hand. He's got a twelve-hand job to do with only two hands, building caskets night and day."

"*Bueno. El carpintero's* workshop then. If I need you," he paused, smiled, "I will send Juanito for you. Do not go astray."

On the way to Jeronimo's workshop, Coot laughed. "I wonder how many more times does that insipid little bastard-*Rural* have to cock and uncock my .45 one-handed before he blows his damn head off."

"What worries me are those canisters hanging down from the skirts of the Reo like balls on a rooster."

"Aw, hell, there's so much caked-on dirt and mud you can barely make out the lettering. And as far as we know, none of our hosts can read English."

"It doesn't take a certifiable genius to read USA in *any* language."

Jeronimo was glum, sitting, facing the wall, his back to the others, throwing a knife in the dirt between his feet, sticking it close to his *huarache*-clad feet.

"Hey, Jeronimo," I said. "Looks like you're playing a one-handed game we call mumbly-peg. Mind if I join you, *amigo*?"

He remained intent on his knife and *huaraches*.

Father Esteban said, "He's been like that since you left here last night, never laid down to sleep. I expect him to walk out of here any minute with his rifle. He has *cartuchos* as well."

I asked, "Where did he get the cartridges?"

"He told me that he got them at *Circulo de Rocas* when you went to install the propeller."

Coot said, "I remember him putting them in his tool bag. Narlow, I'll try to keep his attention. You take a look in his bag."

"You will not find the cartridges," Father Estevan said. "Jeromino told me that he was tired of seeing his rifle empty. Tired of seeing the *Rural* alive, while his Chico sleeps in the *cementerio*. He has hidden his rifle and cartridges."

32

Coffee With the *Comandante*

We were invited for coffee on the *comandante's* porch. Mercedes and Juanito served, she with the coffee, he with a wooden tray laden with proper fixings for
such a delicacy. After Juanito passed the warm goat's milk and honey, first to the
comandante, the *Rural*, then Coot and me, he ducked into the building, returned
with his heavy rifle—always at the ready, forever tugging at the belt holding the
heavy revolver on his hip. The coffee was not coffee at all, only boiled roots and
strips of cedar bark. But the brew was warm, pleasant, reminded me of Papa and
his goats.

Coot stepped off the porch, reached for a rusty cut-nail in the dirt. He came
back on the porch, motioned for Juanito to come to him. The boy looked at the
comandante for direction, who nodded. Coot spoke softly to the thin lad. He again
glanced at his superior who again nodded. Juanito unbuckled his gun holster,
handed it to Coot after removing the old Colt. Coot winked, gave him a broad
smile, then began twisting the nail into the belt, gouging another hole in the dry,
cracked leather. Coot draped the holster belt around the boy's thin waist, pulled it
tight to the new hole, then tugged at it to test its snugness. Satisfied, Coot smiled,
scruffed the boy's coal black hair. Juanito stepped back, reholstered the revolver,
glanced at the *comandante* again, smiled at Coot, then his gaze fell to his feet.

After a few pleasantries, the *comandante* turned to the *Rural*. "Capitan
Manzano, I have been considering your concern regarding our security. I have a
solution to that problem. Observe that wooden table there at the edge of the plaza.
The one with the concrete base. It serves as a table where the villagers display their
produce. I was curious about that concrete base, and had my men remove the
tabletop. I found that it is an abandoned well, very dry, five or six feet wide, fifteen
feet deep."

"Very interesting, *Comandante,* but how does a dry well solve your security
problem?"

"*Capitan* Manzano, do you suppose our safety would be in good hands if we
were to place two village women in the bottom of that dry well, and two children—
not children of the two women—children of *other* women of the village. We will
post a guard, allow nothing for them to eat or drink, allow no conversation for two

days and nights. Then we will exchange those women and children for four others. Do you not agree that would be adequate protection?"

"*Si, mi Comandante, si!* That is a superb idea! Wonderful. *Felicitaciones, Comandante!* Congratulations!"

The *comandante* called out, "Juanito, go and ring the church bells. Spread the word that every villager is ordered to assemble here immediately. Ring them long and loud."

The villagers gathered as if they'd been called by their maker. The *Rural* took over like it was his idea, relishing the choosing of the two women and two little girls. He had the villagers playing a childish game of choosing their favorite woman in the village, that woman's favorite little girl, then the woman most respected in Carichic, and that woman's favorite little girl, little ones who were not their own daughters. It was a game that put a smile of the faces of the villagers, and glee on the *Rural's*. He ordered the soldiers to remove the table from the top the abandoned well.

Confusion replaced the villagers glee when the *Rural* explained that those chosen would have the honor of serving as security guards for their unwanted visitors. He ordered a boy to fetch a rope, then told the first woman, Maria Santoscoy, to hold tight on the rope. She did so, he motioned for her to get in the hole. A murmur went up. The *Rural's* game was becoming clear.

He pushed the woman toward the well, screamed, "You will climb into the well, Maria Santoscoy, *ahorita!*"

The villagers milled around. Their dark eyes became menacing, darting glances at the *Rural*, trying to keep each other steady.

The *Rural* called out for the *comandante* to push them back. The crowd settled down, the two women were lowered into the well, but when the *Rural* tied the rope around the little girls, shrieks of horror erupted.

The *comandante* shot his pistol in the air several times. "Listen to me! *Escuche!* No one will harm these women and children if you do as you are told. They will stay in this well for two days and nights. You will not talk to them. You will not feed them. You will give them no water. *Nada!* Their lives are completely in your hands. If you do not do as you are told, they will die! Their blood will be *on your hands*. Anyone disobeying these orders will be shot. In two days, they will be lifted from the well, then four more of your number will take their place. If anyone attempts to harm me, *Capitan* Manzano, or any of my men, the guard posted here will shoot the women and children at the bottom of the well. Now go back to your homes."

Two days after Chico was shot by the *Rural*, Gregorio Gonzalez hobbled into town using a forked branch as a crutch. *Capitan* Manzano was questioning Coot and me on the *comandante's* porch, ranting about the necessity of a dictator's iron fist at the controls of Mexico.

"The *pobres* of Mexico are stupid, stupid and dumb. Only five out of one hundred of them can read or write his own stinking name."

Gregorio Gonzalez came in view across the plaza, his face contorted, limping, dragging his right foot—step, drag, step, drag. He hobbled to the plaza well, filled the gourd several times, and drank, poured water over his head and face. Gazed around the plaza, leaned his crutch against the well, began dragging himself toward us. A long step, then a short step, his hands on his knees for support.

I called out past the *Rural*, "Why, *Capitan*, looky yonder who's finally shown up. Your little pencil-thin mustachioed pimp, *Senor* Gregorio Gonzalez himself."

Gregorio crippled on up, helped himself to some of the shade offered by the *comandante's* porch.

Capitan Manzano was on him in an instant. "*Oiga, pendejo!* No one gave you access to my headquarters! Get out of here! *Quitate, mojon!*"

"*Perdone, mi capitan, pero yo pienso—*"

"You think nothing! Stand there in the sun. Drink the dust until I decide your fate."

Capitan Manzano stomped back and forth on the porch, picked up a large rock that served as a doorstop, reared back, hurled it at the headquarters' door, not three feet away. The rock bounced back at him, he stepped aside, stooped, picked it up. We all ducked, then he tried to cram the fist-size rock into his pants pocket. Failing that, he set it down on the floor with great care, nudged it with his foot to the door. He stepped to the edge of the porch, jumped down, glared at the villagers, stepped back up on the porch. His gaze came back to Gregorio, the man that he'd forgotten had led him right to us at *Circulo de Rocas*.

"*Pendejo!* Where have you been the last two days? You only had twenty-five *kilometers* to walk. Have you been spying all this time?"

"*Mi capitan, yo—*"

"No lies! Answer me, *traidore!*"

Gregorio stood on one foot. "My foot—I twisted my foot, *senor*. It hurts very badly and is swollen. I could not walk and—"

"But you did walk! I saw you with my own eyes! No lies!"

"*Capitan* Manzano, I have a plan for you that—"

"*Bah!* No more of your lies! *Silencio!* I cannot think while you are jabbering like a fox. You must learn that people who talk all the time, and say nothing, have a sickness in their heads. *Muy mal!*" The *comandante* shot Coot and me a glance with a faint smile. The little shit was almost as laughable as he was treacherous.

At noon, the *comandante* directed Mercedes to serve our meal. She and Juanito brought *frijoles* and *tortillas* covered with a folded burlap sack, and a clay pot of warm goat's milk. Juanito held the tray as she set the rough table with four plates and spoons, then scurried off the porch and past Gregorio still standing in the sun.

I sat facing Gregorio standing in the dust and heat, whose narrow eyes were straining up at the bottom of the Reo trying to make out the stamped lettering on the canisters. Coot and I still had not figured out this small man, but somehow in our gut we knew he'd not really double-crossed us. We supposed that he must have seen Rose and JJ, probably talked to them, or at least saw them take off. He kept studying the bottom of the Reo.

I called out to Gregorio, "Hey, *amigo*, aren't you hungry? How long has it been since you had anything to eat?"

He remained silent, glancing nervously at the *Rural*.

"Do not be impolite to our guests!" the *capitan* screamed. "Answer him this instant!"

"But I thought—"

"Answer him this instant!"

"I have not eaten in three days. Only roots—no water and—"

"*Senor* Montgomery asked you nothing about your thirst!" the *Rural* screamed as he sailed a tortilla over Gregorio's head in contempt.

The villagers were busy with their chores, wearing cloth over their faces to ward off the plague that did not exist. Coot and I felt compelled to do likewise, but we thought it strange that the *comandante* and the *Rural* never bothered wearing their masks on the porch, as though the plague hadn't the strength to climb the two steps to their shade.

Gregorio stood there for over four hours as his shadow quartered around and pointed our way. His right ankle was an ugly shade of purple at the instep, turned black as the swelling rounded the front and up his ankle. He occasionally put a little weight on it to relieve the other foot from bearing his weight. I didn't know what to make of the man. On the one hand, he did indeed tell *Capitan* Manzano that Coot and I were hiding at *Circulo de Rocas*, but he said nothing about Rose, JJ and his biwing or Curtiss. Coot figured Gregorio recognized the futility of standing by while the *Rural* shot yet another villager as he'd dispatched Chico, so he blurted out our whereabouts and just made the best of a sour situation.

We thanked our host and found two empty benches on the far side of the plaza for a *siesta*. I was glad to get away from the Reo, the glaring black on military green letters, as if distance absolved us from the damning guilt those canisters contained.

"Coot, our time will soon be up. Jeronimo will likely be coming to this plaza to fulfill his promise. Got any ideas on how to get that *Rural* against a wall so Jeronimo doesn't get himself and a lot of other folks killed?"

"No, I've been doing considerable thinking about it. But the *comandante* keeps a guard posted night and day, seems to trust Juanito more than the others. There's also the matter of two women and two children at the bottom of that well. Juanito's sitting on the edge of the well right now, his rifle across his lap. I haven't found a crack in his defense. All we have is several hundred rifles buried in the cemetery and beneath the church's floor, with five-thousand cartridges stashed in the wheel wells of the Reo in plain view, save a little mud and road dust."

"Well, maybe Jeronimo has thought better of it, given up on shooting the good *Rural*."

Coot shook his head, smiled. "I read that dreaming's good for a man. Keep it up."

33

At mid-afternoon, I was startled out of my nap by the screaming *Rural*.

Coot was sitting up on his bench. "I've been watching that cocky little bastard for the past half hour. Parading up and down in front of the *comandante's* porch. Stops in front of Gregorio. Gets right up in his face, glares at him, stalks off. Comes back, glares at him again, pushes Gregorio off balance. Kicks him until he gets to his feet. He said something to Gregorio a minute ago. Couldn't make it out. Just now he screamed at him, something about Gregorio being a traitor.

Before that, Gregorio was trying to convince the *Rural*, said he knew where *rifles y cartuchos* are buried, but he—"

The *Rural* kicked Gregorio's swollen ankle. "*Aiiii! Senor, por favor! No!*" He fell to the ground from the pain.

The *Rural* continued kicking Gregorio. *Comandante* Bienvenides walked out on the porch to witness the scene, simply stood shaking his head, slapping a horse quirt against his bloused trousers.

The *Rural* turned to the *comandante*. "This lying traitor of a dog now says he has hundreds of *rifles, escopetes y cartuchos* buried along the Texas side of the *Rio Grande*. That we can use the truck of the *norte americanos* to travel to the border and save ourselves from the *Villistas* who control the state of Chihuahua. What do you make of this dog, *Comandante?*"

"I assure you I would not know, *Capitan* Manzano. I do know that I fear that if we stay here in Carichic we are inviting certain disaster from this plague that is killing many of the villagers and my men, and an equally certain death at the hands of the *revolucionarios* if we stay. The *Villistas* will come. They will kill us all with dispatch—assuming this plague does not consume us before they arrive. You should listen to Gregorio's claim of *rifles y cartuchos*, but you will not. You will shoot him before the setting of the sun."

The *Rural* spat. "*Bah!* You are afraid, *Comandante* Bienvenides. I thought better of you, thought you brave, but you are afraid!"

"Brave? No. Afraid? Perhaps. Realistic? To a fault. I was taught much, but never a word about dying for our country. We were taught to *live* so we may lead."

The *Rural* blew his nose on the dirt, wiped his nose on his sleeve, glared up at the *comandante*. "You are nothing but a woman in officer's uniform!"

The *Rural's* screaming seethe, disgusting behavior, ground on my nerves. I lay back down on my side, sleepy, gazing at Juanito guarding the women and children in the well. Thinking how much he would gain with a father like my papa.

I fought it, but the warm sun combined with my wish to be shut of the *Rural's* fuming voice pushed me over the side into a dreamy sleep. I drifted back to when Coot and I were just a few years older than Juanito, we were with Many Fast Feet Two Sticks and Na-Tu-Che-Puy. To a time when Papa sent word that he would be where the Black River and Pacheta Creek met, that he'd enjoy a visit with us if we were of a mind. The Box canyon, our special place where we spent the happiest times of our youth, hunting elk, drying meat on racks, making jerky and pemmican. It was thought that I had Power, could learn to be a medicineman.

A medicineman! *Humph!*

My dreaming deepened. I sat on Uncle Doyl's all-time favorite stump, suddenly ill at ease, striking this pose, then that, trying to look grownup and manly, tilting my seventeen-year-old chin up in a mature, all-knowing pose, wanting Papa to be impressed when he rode down the steep, narrow trail.

Why did Coot refuse to come with me to meet Papa? I couldn't make any sense out of it. Coot was a burly boy, stout, heavy black hair, curly black eyelashes. I recalled the day he mimicked a school girl he caught giving me the eye. He blinked his heavy dark lashes, winked, closed his eyes, held his head down low, opened his eyes again, blinked a couple of times while sucking in a breath of air for effect, raised his head to the side. "Oh Narlow, I declare, you are the handsomest boy in the whole world."

Voices and sounds, images and flavors of those many trips to this mystic place swirled around me at that old campsite. Coot belching, *"Enjuh,"* mimicking Two Sticks when he stood to leave our fire. Uncle Doyl telling a yarn as he made up a Sunday morning apple pie in his iron oven. Papa reminding us of our manners when we eased one off. Horses snorting on the picket. Mules braying, the smell of damp earth and horse dung, new grass and flowers—

Huh? *Papa. Papa—mounted, leading a packhorse, just dropped off the top of the trail at Rattlesnake Point.*

I glanced down at my loin cloth, felt my shoulder-length hair, wondered what Papa would think of his son. I was the same boy, but that was only partially true. For one thing, I didn't talk as much, learned to hold my tongue, didn't play pranks on anyone with the elders present. So much had happened since the spring before. So many things would never be the same. I sat up straight. Papa would be following my pony's tracks down here, would likely assume that I was not mounted on Traveler because something bad had happened to that fine animal. How would he understand that I rode a bony Apache pony when I had Traveler? Papa would have to understand that Na-Tu had not allowed me to ride that grand animal until I proved my manhood. Loincloth, knife belt, moccasins on my feet were all I wore.

I stood and waved at the tall boulder at the top of the bend in the trail just before Papa appeared, mounted, leading a packhorse. He was several hundred yards away, but I took off at a dead run to meet him. As I approached, he stepped down, and met my embrace. Papa was never comfortable about men hugging or touching, but this time the mood held him.

"Let me look at you, son. Good lord, I do believe you've grown a foot, brown as a bronze juniper."

"Traveler is just fine, Papa," I blurted out, realized my outburst, and hugged him again. "Traveler's such a fine horse. Oh, I'm sorry, Papa, but I'm so proud to see you I'm about to bust. You look just the same, Papa. Just the same."

"Well, I could say the same for you, son, but that would be a mighty stretch of the truth. You're a fine specimen of a man, Narlow Montgomery," he said, his slate-blue eyes glistening.

"Aw Papa, you sound just like Two Sticks, calling me Narlow Montgomery like that."

We walked down to our camp, both too full to speak. My eyes formed a lake that I could barely see through. We sat around the fire, Papa said that Fernando Valdez threatened to go home to Mexico when he learned I'd gone off to an Apache Indian reservation to learn to be a medicineman.

"Coot's with me. Did you know that, Papa?"

"I supposed he was. His aunt Beulah wrote me asking after him. She and Coot's mama don't see eye-to-eye. I wrote her back, told her that Coot's plans had changed, that I'd let her know more about him when I saw him. I figured he'd be with you today."

"He backed out, telling me that you and I would need a private conversation, some such nonsense."

Papa thought a minute. "I don't suppose Coot is over the loss of his uncle Doyl. Coot's lost all the menfolk on his daddy's side of the family—his daddy and both uncles, all dead before they were fifty years old. You and I've taken him in as family. Coot's your brother."

"Coot feels the same way, but he can be a stubborn cuss."

For hours I told Papa about my training, training that had not included much about being a medicineman or learning much about Power. Papa concluded that was the Apache's way of making certain that I could be trusted. I told him the story of Na-Tu-Che-Puy naming me Kicking Bear in honor of the mama grizzly that cornered me on a high ledge. He thought that was a right fitting name, and he really got a kick out of Coot's new name, Running Duck, so named for shooting coots down on the Rio when were just little shavers.

"I tell you, Papa, the Apache know how to train their boys to become warriors. They're tougher than iron, can endure anything, *never* flinch, and they're all just like Coot—they *never* quit. We were taught to endure pain, cold, heat, thirst, hunger, sleepless nights for days-on-end, to do without everything the Pale Eye must have in abundance. We're growing, Papa. We may not be full-grown men yet, but Two Sticks says it won't be long."

"You boys are experiencing something that no white man or boy will ever experience or witness. I've seen warriors outrun horses in rough, boulder-strewn country, and the very next day, that same bunch of warriors were up and gone, the horses, lame for days. I've seen Two Sticks do that for many days running. I'm proud of you boys' decision to go to Two Sticks and Na-Tu-Che-Puy."

"I've sure missed you, Papa. And Papa, everyone on the reservation knows about you, and I bet I've told the story about our granddaddies saving Little Flower from those scalpers a hundred times. Those people couldn't hear that story enough if I told it every day. Both Coot and I speak Apache, but the People like to hear that story in English as well. I tell it in English, Coot repeats it in Apache. They believe what our granddaddies did for them was a gift from Ussen."

Papa reached behind him, handed me a long package wrapped in oil cloth. "Well, speaking of gifts, here's a little something that will make you and Coot heroes with the ladies back on the reservation."

I peeled back the oil cloth—a bolt of bright red cloth with a touch of orange.

He said, "Vermilion—the Apache's favorite color. Brighter the better."

"Thank you, Papa. As Uncle Doyl would say, 'That's right thoughty of you.' And speaking of gifts, here's a little something for you." I handed him the journal he'd packed for me when I caught the stagecoach to Austin to go to the new university, then doubled back for the Arizona Territory. "I filled that journal plumb to the brim, Papa—not an empty line remaining. There's a lot of stories in there that I imagine you'll enjoy reading. When you have the time, that is."

"Oh, I'll have the time real soon, son. Thank you, and you can be assured I'll take good care of it. One of these days you'll want your sons and daughters to have this—to read their daddy's journal."

"Aw Papa, I'm not going to have any children, get married, all that stuff. Shoot, I'm scared to death of girls."

He chuckled. "Oh, you'll figure it out. The Lord has mysterious ways of helping a young man figure out things such as that, explain things to you, my boy."

"Papa, do me a big favor. Turn to the page I folded over in the journal. I want you to read the part about our Apache concealment training. I'm kinda proud of that story."

Papa opened the journal. Mid-February 1876—This morning before sunup, the elders came for us, and we ran behind their ponies for many miles. They stopped at a frozen lake, packed ice in their fists and had us hold it under our armpits until they melted, then broke the ice on the lake, told us to swim. My heart felt like a walnut bouncing around in a peach basket. By mid-morning we were out on an open plain, only large clumps of grass scattered around, no trees, bushes, a few scattered yuccas. Far off to the south, the elders spied a herd of antelope. They dismounted, hid their horses in a low area of the plain. Each of the elders took two of us boys, each group loped off, spanning out in the direction of the herd. For the next hour, we were on our hands and knees, on our bellies, getting as close to the herd as possible. Our elder, Standing Elk, tore off the corner of his red bandana, and tied it to a yucca stalk. He told me and the boy with me, Lukey No-No, to hide ourselves, cover ourselves with grass and sand. Standing Elk waved the stick with the red cloth above him, real slow, back and forth, then stuck it in the sand. I watched him take up tufts of grass, place them on his body, then sprinkled just two handfuls of sand over himself in a certain way, disappearing before my very eyes. In just a bit, I could hear the soft treading of four antelope, sniffing their curiosity at the red cloth on the yucca stalk. Standing Elk reached up with his knife, slashed the throat of a large buck. The others shied away a few steps, but came right back to the red cloth. Lukey No-No lay hidden on the far side of Standing Elk. I saw his knife come slowly out of the earth, the antelope standing almost on top of him slumped to the ground. The other two antelope scooted away, hesitated, then came back over me. I reached up less than a foot with Two Sticks' long knife, and cut the throat of a doe. The other young doe stood stamping her front foot at the fallen doe, but showed no fright. I thought, *If she would come just one step closer.* The herd panicked and ran off. We shouldered our prizes, and joined the other groups of elders and boys who gathered and counted the kill. Sixteen antelope. Our group's count of three was the most of any group, but every group got at least one of the animals. It won't surprise Papa when I tell him that Coot got two nice-sized bucks. Dern it's hard to best that boy. We dressed out the antelope and carried them back to the reservation, arriving just before dark. Plenty of fresh meat for all the People. The elders said it was good, like the old days when the people shared. I have never been prouder to be alive as I am this day.

Papa closed the journal. "Son, that's about the most profound story I've ever read. Ol' Coot got two, huh? I have to admit I sure do miss that boy."

The stars came out bright .We had our supper, hinted around about getting into the warm blankets Papa brought.

He said, "Well, we've talked about everything under the sun today—what else? Oh, and your mama's fine, son."

I hadn't even asked about my own mother. I was supposed to be a man, but acted like a spoiled town boy. "Oh, Papa, I'm sorry. I should have asked about her."

He poked a small oak limb in the fire, his gaze shot up to a bright star, sat for a moment, even when sad, his slate-blue eyes shown bright as marigold at the sun's edge, flashing in the firelight. "Don't worry yourself, son. Your mama doesn't worry about anything, not even herself. I wish I could say she sends her love, but she still thinks you are in Austin going to college. She was about as warm as a hen laying eggs in a pail of cold water when she came to grips about you going 600-miles away just to go to school."

The next morning we awoke early. I'd just returned from the Pacheta Creek to fetch a bucket of water. Papa gathered an armload of oak, squatted down, poking the fire back to life. I set the bucket of water on a stump, got down close, blew on a warm ember to help get the fire going. I smelled burning leather. First, I thought it was just the campfire. It was this same campfire we always had, but not *this* fire. What I smelled was a fire nearly a year old.

I jumped to my feet. "*Papa!*"

"What is it, son?"

"Nothing, Papa. Sorry to shout at you like that. It's just that ol' mushroom-medicine-man stuff acting up again." I smiled. "But, you might like to know that Two Sticks and Coot just came over the rimrock on horseback. What do you reckon they're up to?"

In a minute, they appeared around the boulder at the top of the trail, the sun at their backs outlining them and their ponies as they quartered down the trail and stopped. Two Sticks handed Coot what looked like a leather pouch, pointing down to us. He raised his arm, saluting Papa, who returned the greeting. Coot turned his horse, starting down the trail toward us as the tall man with the red bandanna and tall hat started back up the trail.

Coot rode into camp, slid to the ground, wearing nothing more than a loin-cloth and a sheepish smile. He strolled up to Papa, stuck out his hand. "Howdy, Uncle Abe—sure good to see you, sir."

"Mighty fine seeing you, my son. I understand it's Running Duck now."

"Yes, sir, it's about as good as Coot, I reckon. Either one of them suits me a lot better than the one I was born with."

I asked, "What made you change your mind about coming down here?"

"Tell you later," Coot answered with a hint of a sheepish look on his brown face, shining in the early light. He turned to Papa. "Uncle Abe, when Narlow and I showed up at the reservation, I gave Two Sticks this pouch of gold to safe-keep for me. He gave it back to me just now, saying I should give it to you, so here it is."

Papa hefted the tote. "Well, I'd say it hasn't lost half an ounce. I'll safe-keep it for you, son, but the gold is yours."

We told stories for another hour, munched jerky, and drank a gallon of coffee. Papa stood. "You boys excuse me, but while it's on my mind, I need to tack a shoe on my pack mule. Cussed old fool. I swear she kicks her shoes off just to spite me."

I turned to Coot. "You going to tell me what changed your mind about coming down here to meet Papa?"

"Yeah, lemme tell you. I'm here to witness that tall gentleman with the stovepipe hat changed my mind. After we left you at the Frisco River, I showed up at his lodge. He asked where you were. I told him that you'd gone to meet your papa. He asked why I hadn't gone with you, and I told him that Abe Montgomery is Kicking Bear's daddy, that I didn't want to impose. I tried to explain, but that tall Apache just got madder. 'Abe Montgomery you daddy now. Uncle Doyl dead. You daddy dead. You go to Black River, see you daddy Abe Montgomery.' I tried to talk him out of it, but he dug in his heels, black eyes flashing a storm. Took me by the arm, walked me back to my pony, grabbed me by the nape of my neck with one hand, my knife belt with the other, tossed me on that pony like a half-pound rag doll. 'You big boy, but just boy. Papa Abe tell me long ago you and Kicking Bear were brothers joined at hip like he saw one time long ago. You go to Papa Abe Montgomery. Many Fast Feet Two Sticks go with you, make *sure* you go see Papa Abe Montgomery.' That was one mad Apache, smoke coming out of his black eyes, steam out of his wide ears."

Such long ago happy times, oh, so long—

"Narlow." Coot's voice, interrupting my revelry. "*Narlow!* Wake up. Here comes Jeronimo Chavez. And I don't believe that is a crucifix I see poking out from under his *serape*. Looks more like the thick barrel of a single-shot .45-70 rifle to me."

I stood, took an involuntary step toward Jeronimo.

Coot's arm shot up in front of me. "Hold on. Jeronimo's going to do what Jeronimo's going to do. Nothing we can do about it."

Jeronimo walked up behind the *Rural*, pulled his *serape* aside, cocked and breasted the heavy .45-70, tapped the *Rural* on the shoulder with the end of the rifle. The *Rural* turned to Jeronimo. An unbelieving smile formed on the *Rural's* lips. His tongue rolled over their thin, chapped surface.

Jeronimo screamed, "I want you to know who I am before I send you to the devil! I am the *tio* of Chico Chavez, the innocent boy you murdered in this very plaza three days ago. *Go to hell!*"

A blur flashed from the direction where Gregorio'd stood as Jeronimo pulled the trigger. With the crack of the rifle, the barrel end jerked skyward, the muzzle jumped, smoke and dust billowed. *Capitan* Manzano was knocked to the ground as if hit by a wagon iron.

No one moved. On the porch, one of the soldiers stood, pasted against the wall. Then the young soldier's body toppled forward to the porch floor, stiff as a domino, a horseapple-sized hole gaped between his shoulder blades, struck in the breast by the same bullet that glanced off the top of the *capitan's* head.

Juanito cocked his rifle and pointed it down the well. The crowd gasped, muffled shrieks from the bottom of the well.

"*Juanito! No, Juanito! Todo es bueno!*" *Comandante* Bienvenides shouted, The boy's hard gaze turned sour as he sat back down, his rifle on his lap.

Jeronimo stood with the rifle in his hands, Gregorio still holding the end of the rifle in the air, the *Rural* lying at their feet. The sergeant and three of his men materialized out of the milieu, rifles at the ready. The sergeant turned to the *comandante*, looking for direction. Gregorio yanked the rifle out of Jeronimo's hands, handed the weapon to the sergeant. The sergeant searched Jeronimo and removed six cartridges from his pockets, posted two guards to watch him.

Capitan Manzano lay face-up on the ground. He twitched, rolled over on his stomach, elbows on the ground, hands grasping the top of his bleeding head. He rolled back, sat up in the dirt, gazed around to get his bearings, still holding the top of his head, blood running through his fingers, down his face. His eyes crossed to look at the blood dripping off his nose, studied that for a minute, then tilted his head back, stuck his tongue out, blood dripping into his mouth. All eyes were on the *Rural*. He sat in the dirt catching blood on his tongue, his throat flexed as he drank.

He spat, stood, staggered, fell back in the dirt. He stuck a finger in the pool of red on his lap, peered at it, started to taste it, then wiped his finger on his shirt, blood streaming down his face.

The *comandante* had his revolver out. He yelled at the villagers to stay back, not panic. The sergeant motioned to his men to circle, their rifles leveled point-blank at the villagers. The *Rural* rolled over on his hands and knees, and as he got to his feet, it was apparent what had happened—as Jeronimo pulled the trigger of the .45-70, Gregorio shoved the barrel up, the bullet glazed the top of the *Rural's* head, hitting the soldier on the porch in the breast bone. The bullet gave the *Rural* a permanent, deep part in his heavy black hair, the gash was yawning, wide, would require several stitches. One thing certain—Gregorio'd saved *Capitan* Manzano's life.

He struggled to his feet, stumbled, weaved around the plaza as if in a drunken stupor. The villagers backed away from the crazed man, keeping their little ones hidden. He reached behind one of the women and tickled the chin of the little girl hiding behind the folds of her mother's skirt. He pushed the woman aside, grabbed up the little girl, reached for Coot's .45, fumbled looking for it, not noticing that it lay in the dirt in front of him, still cocked. He motioned to the sergeant for his pistol. The sergeant glanced to the *comandante* for approval. He nodded.

The *Rural* screamed, "And who will save this little girl from the same fate as Chico? Do you want her to follow Chico's ghost? *Eh?* Answer me, *pendejos—ahorita!* Or I will call for another of your daughters to follow this one's ghost. There are *norte americanos* here in our country posing as hunters. Where are they hiding? Tell me before I shoot every child in this village!"

Coot glanced at me. The villagers looked at us. The *Rural* was crazy. Gregorio tried to talk to him, but the *Rural* brushed him aside, then turned back to Gregorio, raised the pistol, his hand jerked, then he lowered the weapon, then turned and began screaming nonsense at the villagers. He wiped the blood out of his eyes and peered at the blood on his hands.

Jeronimo heaved his weight against the two soldiers who held him.

Comandante order, "*Sargento!* Get that man down on the ground. Have your men sit on him."

Coot said, "Come on. Maybe that crazy bastard'll remember us before he shoots everybody in this plaza."

"*Senor Capitan Manzano! Hola—que pasa, amigo?*" Coot hollered as we approached him, the pistol muzzle pressed hard against the little girl's throat.

The *Rural* turned as we approached. He squeezed his blood-filled eyes, attempting to recognize the man who'd called his name. He turned and gazed at the *comandante*, then the villagers. His expression changed to recognition, peaceful, as his eyes returned to us. He looked at Coot for a full minute, smiled as he looked me over, tilted his head down and wiped the blood on top of the little girl's head, a red smear in her long, raven hair. He raised the pistol from the child's throat, rubbed the bleeding gap in his scalp with the pistol barrel, started to speak, his head fell back as he crumpled in a heap, the pistol falling to the side.

The *comandante* shouted to the villagers, "Do not run! Stay where you are!"

I asked, "*Comandante* Bienvenides, you seem like a peaceful kind of man—would you mind if I gave the *capitan* just a little light tap on his head so we can have a few more minutes of quiet? That 550-grain bullet was just a little too light, a wee too high to keep this ornery cuss down—and quiet."

Gregorio spoke up. "*Por favor, mi comandante*, may I speak? *Capitan* Manzano will not let me speak to defend myself."

"What do you know of these *norte americanos*?"

"*Nada, senor*, but may I respectfully remind *mi comandante* that it was I who told you and *Capitan* Manzano about the *norte americanos* hiding at *Circulo de Rocas*."

"You and I will talk further tomorrow," the *comandante* said. "You will tell me more about the guns you say you have buried along the border."

The *Rural* groaned, rolled over on his stomach, still holding his bleeding head. He lay peering up through bloodied eyes, wiping them with his bloody fingers. His gaze focused on Jeronimo. He was on his feet in an instant, grabbed the .45-70 rifle out of the sergeant's hands, and demanded the cartridges. The sergeant's dark eyes again went to his *comandante* for approval who again, nodded. The sergeant gave him the six cartridges he'd taken from Jeronimo.

He loaded the single-shot rolling block rifle, screamed at the *sargento* to get Jeronimo on his feet. He cocked the hammer, danced around, circled Jeronimo, poking him with the rifle, taunting him. "You want to kill this *Rural, eh? Eh?* Well, *you* will die today. You will die but *not* for killing a *Rural*. Not today and not tomorrow—not for killing this *Rural!*"

He shouldered the rifle, leveled it at Jeronimo, lowered it as he wiped the blood running into his eyes. He raised the rifle again, aimed at Jeronimo's head. Jeronimo clenched his teeth but never closed his eyes. The *Rural* grinned, lowered the end of the rifle barrel, and when the rifle was pointed at Jeronimo's ankle, he fired. The force of the heavy bullet on bone wrenched Jeronimo's leg up behind him like a rag doll. He fell on his face, his foot dangling from his leg, held only by skin and tendon, blood spurting out in an arc.

201

Women and men shrieked in horror.

"*Silencio! Silencio, pendejos*, or you will be next! *Rural Capitan Ambrosio Manzana de Flores* makes that promise! *Arriba!* Stand up!" he yelled down at Jeronimo, still wiping blood out of his eyes, reloading the single-shot .45-70 with another cartridge.

Jeronimo rolled over on his belly, labored up, stood on his one foot, blood gushing from the stub of his other leg. Again the *Rural* leveled the rifle at Jeronimo's head only ten feet away, lowered the rifle and fired. Jeronimo was down again, another ruined foot. This time not one cry came from the villagers. Many turned their gaze away from their friend lying in the dirt, while none could contain their contempt as they glared at the *Rural*. They could do nothing. Helplessness is a most unmanly stance.

Gregorio stood behind the *Rural*, and for an instant I thought he would spring on him. But the *Rural* circled Jeronimo in the dirt, screaming down, "Kill a *Rural*, eh? *Arriba!* Maybe another *Rural*, but never *Rural Capitan* Ambrosio Manzana de Flores. *Never!* Get up!"

Jeronimo lay writhing in the dirt that was fast turning the sand to red.

"Get him up! Stand him up!" the *Rural* screamed. "You two there—stand him up, *ahorita!*"

They helped Jeronimo up, he fainted, becoming dead weight between the two men.

"*Agua!* Throw water in his face! I want him awake!" The *Rural* screamed at another man who quickly brought a bucket of water and heaved it in Jeronimo's face. The *Rural* reloaded. Jeronimo was conscious, limp in the arms of the two men who held him. The men were on either side of Jeronimo, their shoulders under his armpits, his arms straight out to his sides.

Again the *Rural* raised the rifle, the villagers pulled back, getting themselves and their children as far away from the madman as possible.

"*A donde van, pendejos?* Where do you think you are going, *amigos?* My fun is just beginning!" the *Rural* taunted them, waving the rifle shells in the air.

Coot approached the *Rural*. "*Capitan* Manzano! Aren't you going to let me show you my skill with a rifle?"

The *Rural* turned, smiled. "Ah, *Senor* Boldt—who could deny a world-class rifleman his one great opportunity. A shooter of birds in flight *con un rifle* should not be denied. Certainly—be my guest by all means." He handed Coot the rifle, then warned, "*Pero por favor, senor,* do not miss and kill *Senor* Chavez. That will be my pleasure—*mas tarde.*"

I grabbed the rifle out of Coot's hands. "*Senor* Boldt is a poor second to my skill as a marksman, *Senor Capitan.* He might miss, but I sure as hell *will not!*"

I wheeled around, leveled the rifle at Jeromino's wrist that was only inches from the head of one of the men holding Jeronimo upright. The man winced, ducked his head, eyes closed tight. I fired, hitting Jeronimo square in the chest, ripping his body from the arms of the two men, driving him back to the edge of the *comandante's* porch.

All was quiet except the sobs of a woman who could no longer contain her anguish. Everyone glanced around, trying to understand what they'd witnessed. Coot turned to me, grimaced, yet a faint smile graced his gaze.

I turned to the *Rural.* "We all miss sometimes."

The *Rural* began to stomp up and down. "You spoiled my fun, *gringo!* This *Rural* does not like—"

I shoved the rifle hard into the *Rural's* chest. "Mister, you've certainly got your aliquot of vituperative, carrion-cold insides. Jeronimo suffered enough for trying to kill you—even if you are a *Rural.*"

The *Rural* started to protest, but the *comandante* intervened, "*Basta! Basta!*"

He was right about that. Enough. *More* than enough.

We buried Jeronimo in one of his own caskets. No one said a word as we lowered him into the grave, dirt slowly shoveled in on the pine box. Father Estevan said a rosary for his soul, a rosary that did little for Jeronimo's friends.

I said, "People of Carichic. I must explain why I killed Jeromino. He could not—"

"*Senor* Montgomery," a woman said. "It is not necessary for you to explain why you shot Jeromino. He could not be saved from the bastard *Rural.* You did what any of the rest of us would have done—if we had your courage. The difference is that you did it—while his friends stood lifeless, witnessing his suffering."

"But I—"

"Narlow, rest yourself," Coot said. "I've always been the down-in-the-dirt sorta fighter, but you're not built that way. All our lives, I've seen you step up when no one else could or possessed the means to do what needed to be done. Rest yourself, my friend."

He turned back to the villagers. "*Senor* Montgomery is good with words.

203

Maybe he'll say something over your friend. Something to send him on his way."

I stood motionless, my brain as empty as my hat.

After what seemed an eternity, they turned to go, I said, "Wait, *amigos—espere por favor.*" The villagers turned back to me. "For his heart was in his work, and the heart giveth grace unto every art. Jeronimo Chavez was a carpenter *lo mismo de Jesus Christo*, he was an artist. His many crucifixes that adorn your church will remain after his death. They will live with you as a reminder of his life with you."

Coot came up beside me. "*Mi amigo, Senor* Montgomery *dice, 'Por su corazon estaba en su trabajo, y el corazon hacia cada arte.' Jeronimo Chavez era carpintero gusta su salvador que encanto y el que Jesus Cristo es un artesano. Los crucifijos que adornan su iglesia quedran despues de su muerte y viviran con ustedes como un recordatorio de su vida con usted.*"

Coot's words were a lot prettier.

On the way back to the *comandante's* porch, he said, "Narlow, don't go getting hard-ass on yourself. What you did just had to be, so don't—"

"Yeah, I know. Just like those four men in *sombreros* a few years back, the ones I shot in the foot. It had to be. *This* had to be. Whadda ya think, Coot? Think my mother's close by?"

❀❀❀

Capitan Ambrosio Manzano did not wake up the next morning, not for *several* mornings. We assured *Comandante* Bienvenides that he'd suffered a concussion from the rifle shot, and would wake in time. A village woman, a *curandera*, sewed up the *Rural's* scalp. She concocted a goo from boiling the leaves and roots of a greasewood, and applied the paste to the wound. She cleaned it daily, kept it plastered with the greasewood paste. The wound never swelled or festered, but the *Rural's* black hair had a ghoulish-green cast, the wound itself, a bright yellow smudge down the middle of his scalp. Fresh and spring-like as an April posy.

Gregorio spent every opportunity trying to convince the *comandante* that his buried guns were the only way out for he and his men.

Mercedes' evening oleander burnings were effective. Four of the *soldados* died a hacking, painful death, six others lay in agony. *Comandante* Bienvenides' command was down to eight men, a twelve-year-old boy, his sergeant, and himself. I counted the shells in their cartridge belts, figured that, counting the rounds in their Mausers, Juanito's nine, they only had fifty-six rounds of ammunition. If the *Villistas* came, their ammunition would be quickly spent, making short work for their enemies.

"*Sargento!*" the *comandante* called out. "Father Estevan just led a funeral procession to the graveyard. When he is finished, send Juanito to tell him I would like a word with him. When Juanito brings the *padre* to me, escort Gregorio Gonzalez away. I want to interview the *padre* without Gregorio present."

We stood to excuse ourselves. The *comandante* stopped us. "*Por favor, senores*, I want you to stay. I will interview Gregorio Gonzalez again tomorrow, and I want you to hear what the *padre* has to say about his guns and ammunition. Gregorio claims to have many guns and abundant ammunition, that the *padre* was with him. He says you gentlemen can take us there in your truck. We will let Gregorio sleep on his story, and we shall see if it changes tomorrow. *Por favor*, keep your seat."

When Juanito escorted the *padre* to the *comandante's* porch, he was offered a chair, and cool water. He refused both, standing in the sun, head turned, watching Gregorio being escorted down the path.

"Father Estevan," the *comandante* said, "thank you for giving me a few moments of your time. Gregorio Gonzalez claims to have guns and ammunition buried along Mexico's border with *Estado Unidos*. That you were with him when he buried several *caches* of arms in many locations along our border with Texas. Tell me, *Padre*, is Gregorio speaking the truth? If I knew for certain that his story was true, I would leave Carichic tomorrow morning. We would not return, and I would report most favorably about you and the people of this village to my government. I will not burn your church as I promised when I came here. No *Federales* will ever come here again. You have my word as an officer."

The *padre's* eyes darted back and forth, glanced at us. Then he said, "In the past, I have always found Gregorio Gonzalez a trustworthy friend. If he told me that story, I would believe it."

"I see, *Padre*. Tell me, please—how did you and Gregorio come to be in Carichic? I learned that you and Gregorio came here a few months ago, perhaps from a neighboring village. But you came together?"

"Yes, we came here from his village, *Ojos Azules*, to the north. We came because of this dreadful plague that has claimed hundreds of our people. He came as my assistant. He has been close to the church since he was an infant. The nuns reared him, as I recall."

"And tell me, *Padre*—a man of your years and obvious education—why would the church allow you to stay in such a place as this? You are much too qualified to be here, unless you are a spy, and I do not think that is the case, I assure you. Your speech is flawless, your manner with your people is without equal. You should be in Mexico City, New York, Paris, Rome—but Carichic, Chihuahua? Does that make sense to you, Father Estevan?"

"As to why I am here, I was an ordained priest, but confess I had a certain weakness for some of my flock—a horrible weakness—for women. I thought I could overcome it in time, but I could not, did not. I was caught, deservedly thrown out of the church. I have grown to overcome that weakness here in Carichic. That should adequately explain my presence here, unless you insist on hearing some of the details of my exploits, *mi Comandante*."

"That will not be necessary, *mi padre*. I can easily appreciate the heavy burden your vows must have been for you as a young priest. I imagine there are countless of your brethren who share your guilt, but do not share your shame—yet. So now, *Padre*, tell me about Gregorio, the guns. Then you may go."

"When I was quietly removed from my duties in Guadalajara, Gregorio learned that I was leaving. He was on the train with me on my way to Juarez. We worked in Juarez for three years. Gregorio became possessed with the notion that we would form another country. Named it—*Libertad*. In 1908, we traveled by train to San Antonio, Texas. Times were poor, no work for *pobres*, so we decided to return to Juarez. He insisted on buying a mule and a burro to ride back to Juarez, giving up the luxury of hot food and warm beds, to give his dream time to germinate, grow. Our journey took three months, but we finally reached the *Rio Grande*, hopelessly lost, but thought we were at the big bend in the Rio, and soon we came upon the mouth of the Santa Elena Canyon. We rode our mounts many miles over great mountains to the point where the *Rio* enters Santa Elena Canyon.

"Shortly, we came to a wide crossing of the river, a place called Lajitas. The river had flooded the lowlands forcing us to seek higher ground. We rode up an *arroyo* and to our astonishment, we came upon a wagon loaded with scores of .44-40 repeaters, thousands of cartridges. Gregorio's prayers were answered. The skeletons of the horses were still hitched to the wagon leading us to believe the wagon was a runaway, that the wagon lodged between the boulders of the narrow *arroyo*. We pulled the wagon backwards out of the boulders, then pulled the wagon with our animals back to the river. The road was so muddy we could go no further, then came upon an ancient dry stream, I recall it was called *Terlingua*. We went up the *arroyo* for many miles, very rough, but we made it to the top of a high *mesa* where we buried the guns and cartridges in a very deep hole. That was our first *cache*. We found other guns. or simply stole them, but we ended with many *caches*.

"Will that be all, *Comandante*?"

"Fascinating, *padre*—absolutely fascinating. If you just fabricated that story, you are to be congratulated. And tell me, *padre*, you say you buried the first *cache* of guns in a hole. Could you find where you buried that first cache of guns?"

"No, *Comandante*, we could not. A few days after we buried the guns, we became fearful that they somehow could get wet, become rusty, ruined. We turned around and found the same dry stream bed, but all the *mesas* looked alike. We searched for many days, finally gave up. After that, I kept an exact journal of the location of guns, cartridges, and dynamite. There is no doubt that we can find every one of them with our journal."

"*Bueno*, keep the journal safe, however, soon I will send for you, and I want you to please bring the journal along with you. That will be all."

The father turned to leave. The *comandante* said, "And, *padre*—you have my word that the reason you are no longer ordained will go no further. For you see, *mi mama* had planned for her son to be a priest, but I took care of that ill-conceived idea. Our neighbor's fourteen-year-old daughter was shipped to her aunt in Argentina when I was sixteen."

34

Can I Trust This *Pobre*?

The next morning, the *comandante* sat, his finger lazily outlining his pistol in the dust on the table.

Juanito ordered Gregorio to stop when they approached the foot of the porch.

The *comandante* said, "Gregorio, come up here, sit down across the table from me. Look me square in the eye. Now, recite for me again exactly what you plan. If I suspect any treachery, I will empty this pistol in you where you sit."

"*Si senor, Comandante, si!* I will tell you my plan, and how *mi rifles y cartuchos* can save your command."

Gregorio's description of how he originally acquired guns and ammunition tracked the *padre's* tale almost word for word. The particular *cache* of munitions he wanted to lead the *comandante* to was buried on the Texas side of the *Rio* above Ojinaga and Presidio.

Gregorio went on. "The *cache* is high, on a very dry mesa overlooking the *Rio*, buried at the bottom of a Sycamore tree—a very big, very old tree, like that one over there on the far side of the plaza. You will see, *mi comandante*, you will see."

Coot and I weren't certain of Gregorio or his story, but if the *comandante* would fall for his scheme, Carichic would at least be free of the *Federales* and one bastard *Rural*. And another plus—we weren't making any headway of getting out of this jam on our own. Our biggest concern was the crazy bastard *Rural*, *if* he ever came out of his coma. But most of all, those black-on-military-green letters shouting *USA* was the compelling reason for our haste to get the Reo back to ground level.

One of the soldiers, Jesus, tall, muscular, began coughing early in the evening. Juanito brought him water, but he refused it. By midnight, he was coughing up blood, complaining about his burning lungs, Juanito still at his side. The *comandante* never went to bed, concerned that he would have one less man by dawn. He ordered Jesus to move away from his porch. Juanito helped the man to his feet, handed his rifle to him, and he turned to leave.

The *comandante* called out, "Jesus, leave your rifle with Juanito. You will not need it tonight. Juanito will take your guard duty."

"Your men are soft, *Comandante*."

The *comandante* jumped to his feet. "*Que?* Where are you, *Capitan* Manzano?"

The *Rural* stepped from the side of the adobe, his hair casting a ghoulish yellow-green glow in the blue moonlight.

The *comandante* said, "My men are not soft! Let me tell you how many of them have died while you have been sleeping the past six days—"

"*Seis dias?*"

"*Si, Capitan* Manzano, six days. I should think you will find ample evidence in your pants to prove my point. During your slumber, my men have been dying of this plague. Do not accuse my men of being soft. The mettle of my men is not your concern. I am in command here. If you wish, you may leave on your own, or stay here, wait for the *Villistas* if you care to. But I am in command of Carichic."

At sunrise, Coot and I joined the *comandante* and the *Rural* on the porch.

The *comandante* asked Juanito to check on Jesus, who hadn't coughed for many hours. We heard Juanito call Jesus' name with no response. He rolled the stiff body over.

I said, "Lies the warrior, dead his glory, dead the cause in which he died."

The *comandante* said, "*Senor* Montgomery knows Tennyson."

"*Bah!* The soldiers of the *comandante* have no cause!" the *Rural* screamed.

The *comandante* ignored the insult. "*Capitan* Manzano, your *amigo*, Gregorio Gonzalez, has been telling me about *caches* of rifles and cartridges that he and the *padre* buried in Texas. I have decided that my men and I will leave Carichic and go to the border. *Senores* Boldt and Montgomery will take us in their truck. We are nearly out of ammunition and—"

"You and your men are soft and afraid. I am ashamed of you. *All of you!* I am relieving you of your command, and I will not—"

"You are *not* relieving me of my command. My men will shoot you if I give them the word. They despise you. What is worse, they are afraid of you. More afraid of you than the plague."

"I will have you all shot when we get to Mexico City, *mi comandante.*"

Coot and I thought they needed privacy, and we stood to leave.

The *comandante* said, "No need for you gentlemen to take your leave. There is nothing more two officers of the Mexican government can say or do in your presence that could possibly be more unbecoming as what you have already witnessed. Please take your seats."

He turned back to the *Rural*. "Your threat to have me shot when we arrive in Mexico City is just that—a threat! But if either of us are to ever see that beautiful city again, we must first get back to friendly forces. I fear the state of Chihuahua is in the hands of *Villistas*. If they overran Carichic, they would shoot you *first*. Do not question my authority!"

His sergeant approached the porch. "*Mi comandante*, I regret to report to you that two of our men are missing. I fear they have deserted."

"*Deserters?* We will lose the rest of our men if we do not leave this place."

The *comandante* faced the square. "*Senor* Boldt, *Senor* Montgomery, you understand that after we find the guns and cartridges, that you will still be under arrest. I cannot, *will not* release you. We will then make our way down the *Rio Grande* to Matamoras on the coast of *Golfo de Mexico*, board a steamer to *Veracruz*, travel overland to Mexico City." He turned back to us. "What will become of you, I do not know. You will be tried. I will speak on your behalf, but promise nothing. We have a long trip before us, *senores*. If you try to trick me, I will have you standing before a convenient adobe wall. Juanito has my every confidence, expert with his rifle, revolver, in spite of his youth, he has no peer behind a machinegun. Do you understand my position in this matter, *senores?*"

We nodded.

"*Sargento*, have your men get this truck on the ground. Remount the wheels. Quickly, *Sargento, andale por favor*."

"*Por que, Comandante?*" the *Rural* asked.

"Because, *Capitan*, we are leaving Carichic. My command now consists of the *sargento*, four men and a twelve-year-old boy. We will ride in *Senor* Boldt's truck to the *Rio*. We will find Gregorio's *rifles y cartuchos*. We will then make our way south into Mexico and find friendly forces."

The *Rural* stomped, the yellow in the part of his coal-black hair gleaming in the morning sunlight, screamed, wanting to question the *padre*, angered that he was being ignored.

The *comandante* turned from the *Rural*. "Juanito, fetch Father Estevan and his journal. We will be ready to go when you return. And Juanito, if the *padre* does not wish to come, persuade him."

We loaded two wooden barrels of water on the bed of the Reo. Word swept around Carichic that we were leaving. A feeling of relief spread through the village like applesauce heaped thick with a butter knife. Women brought baskets of tortillas, clay pots of *frijoles* and *bolillos*, dried fruit, smiling as they offered the baskets up to us in the high bed of the Reo.

Sergeant Porras asked, "*Comandante*—the church. Do we burn the church?"

"*No, sargento*, I am tired of burning churches. Besides our *norte americano amigos* would think we are uncivilized. I told the *padre* that it would be spared."

Capitan Manzano's hands went up, his eyes widened. "Burn the church? *Magnifico, mi comandante! Magnifico!* Yes, we will burn the church. Adobe walls do not burn. But the roof! It will burn. So will the floor and benches."

The *comandante* said, "*Capitan!* Burn it if you must, but be quick about it."

Capitan Manzano ordered an old man to gather dry straw and kindling.

The man refused, turned to the *comandante*. "*Por favor, mi comandante*. Our church and the crucifixes that Jeronimo Chavez carved for us, they are all that we have left. P*or favor, senor!*"

The *comandante* called out, "*Capitan* Manzano, allow this man to gather the crucifixes from the church."

The *Rural* started to complain, then pushed the old man through the door. In a few moments, the man reappeared, his *serape* slung over his shoulder bulging with the carved treasurers.

Straw was gathered, the *Rural* ordered an old woman to bring a burning stick from the firepit. The *capitan* entered the church, pushing the old woman along. Smoke began billowing out the door, just as quickly the roof was ablaze, crashing within itself in minutes, leaving only *adobe* walls, blackened, smoldering.

Capitan Manzano and the *comandante* were standing on the porch of the headquarters, watching the fire die down to a smolder. The villagers turned toward their country's representatives, held their tongues, but found it impossible to hide their disgust.

Sergeant Porras said, "*Y, mi comandante,* the women and children in the well. Do you want me to bring them up?"

"*Si, sargento, por favor.*"

"*Bah!*" Capitan Manzano screamed. "Shoot them and cover them up. Do not weaken, *Comandante.* I shall shoot them!"

"You will do no such thing, *Capitan* Manzano! You burned their church though I told the *padre* that we would not. Those women and children fulfilled their side of the bargain. We will do the same. *Sargento,* pull the women and children out of the well."

The *comandante* turned. "*Capitan* Manzano, if you are going with us, get in the truck."

Giving up his role of authority did not come easily for *Capitan* Manzano, but it did come with a surprise. The *Rural* perched himself on the load bar at the front of the truck's bed, looking forward above the cab. He shouted his order that Coot move out.

I turned to the *Rural*. "*Senor Capitan,* you best screw yourself down real tight, 'cause Coot Boldt is a wild-assed bull rider and a Barney Oakley behind the wheel."

Rurales are known worldwide for their horsemanship, but there is a marked difference between the response of a horse to the touch of a spur, and that of a Reo six-wheel drive with her motor revved up and her clutch popped. We didn't look back, but we heard a decided "thump" when the *Rural's* head hit the floorboard behind us.

35

On the Trail to Texas, February 28, 1916

We spent four rough, uneventful days getting to the Rio Grande. I figured we were about fifty miles north of the crossing at Ojinaga. We'd not seen a solitary soul, boring, laborious, freezing cold, and the constant rasp of *Capitan* Manzano's brittle-chalk-on-a-copper-sheet voice grating on our nerves. When he was not extolling the virtues of the Diaz thirty-year regime, and Marx's *Manifesto*, or swearing at Gregorio Gonzalez, he simply muttered to himself.

It was rough riding back in the bed of the Reo. When the going was particularly rough and slow, the *comandante* and his men, Gregorio, and the *padre* got out and walked, leaving the *Rural* to guard his prisoners—unarmed Coot and quitter me.

Zara was heavy on my mind. She would have been home within two weeks from the day we crossed the Rio going in after Rose. Didn't even leave her a note as to my whereabouts or the reason. Rose would have told her all that, but that too was weeks ago. By now, Zara has cause to think she's probably a widow lady. May well be the case before this has played out. Damn revolution's sure as hell a widow-maker.

We approached a particularly steep hill, upward of 400-feet straight up. Coot stopped, asked the *comandante* and his men to walk, to push the Reo. I did as well, pushing on the fender next to Coot's side of the truck. Half-way up, I heard the grind of metal on metal, a loud bang. Coot and the Reo careened backward, a scream of pain came from beneath the truck as it continued its jolt to the bottom of the hill.

"Jeez-amighty, Coot, what happened?"

"Busted u-joint. *Comandante*, let's see if there is anything we can do for your man."

The soldier's head was crushed. *Capitan* Manzano screamed at Coot for backing over the soldier, accusing him of being careless because he was only a greasy Mexican. The thought crossed my mind, *Senor Rural, you're about to have your very yellow and green head separated from your very brown ass.*

I stepped between them. "Sir, *Capitan* Scorpion-puss, you remind me of a goose I have back home. Name's Bubba. Me and my wife, Zara, thought ol'

Bubba was a girl-goose until he commenced to want to mount me from behind. That's when Zara and I started to think he was a boy-goose, named him Bubba. The point of this story is to inform you that Bubba may be just a goose, but that long-necked creature's got a lot more gray-matter in his narrow cranial cavity than a dozen of you. And you need to exercise a little caution with my friend, *Senor* Boldt here. The man is hard to rile, but once he gets pushed over the edge and commences to swingin' and kickin' a scorpion-puss's ass, there's only one thing he won't do—*quit!*"

The *Rural* looked up at me, looked at the dead soldier, turned to his fellow officer. "*Comandante*, what is all that talk about a goose named Boo-boo?"

We found some of the parts of the broken u-joints, Coot stole from this truck part, then that, and two days later was able to piece together a workable replacement.

We climbed out of another deep *arroyo*, topped over a high, rough pass through the *Sierra la Esperanza*. Far below lay a broad, green valley and the faint, tree-lined silver line of the Rio Grande.

Coot stopped and said over his shoulder, "Down yonder is the river you call *Rio Bravo del Norte*—Rio Grande to us *gringos*. We've been looking for that mighty river and there she flows."

"*That* is the *Rio Bravo del Norte?*" the *comandante* asked. "It cannot be. I have heard of that great river all of my life, but it looks to be a bare trickle. Are you certain that is the river that separates our two countries?"

"Yes, sir, that is the magnificent river you have heard about," I said. "If the name Rio Grande or *Rio Bravo del Norte* doesn't tickle your fancy, perhaps the *capitan* would prefer to call it the *Rio Chico*. You remember Chico, don't you *Capitan* Manzano?"

The Mexican side of the Rio was one deep arroyo after another coming off the *Sierra*, while the US side showed a wide plain, offering easy riding, but the *comandante* feared being captured by the Texas border guards.

At mid-afternoon the next day, Coot stopped, killed the engine, stepped down, stretched. "*Senor Comandante*, this old Reo may hold together through another week of this. But hanging onto her by this steering wheel and the cheeks of my ass, have my hands and ass about worn down to the nub."

The *comandante* stood looking across the Rio, the gentle plane beckoning him to cross.

He turned to Coot. "You may proceed."

We crossed the trickle of water and motored along the smooth plain at a good clip for an hour, then topped out on a rise.

Gregorio shouted, "*Comandante! Comandante!* There it is, *mi comandante!* My sycamore tree! There, *Comandante*, on that high *mesa!* Look, *mi padre.* Our tree!"

Coot drove around the sycamore tree, stopped. "Gregorio, I think *Capitan* Manzano is correct. This looks like any one of a hundred sycamore trees I've seen myself. *Amigo*, you better be right about this or I'm making a gift of this Reo to the *comandante* in exchange for the first shot at your skinny ass."

Gregorio jumped down, grinning. "O, ye of little faith. None of you have faith in me, *pero, si, Senor Comandante,* this is the tree I told you about. Isn't it, Father Esteban? You, *padre*, my old *amigo*—you were the very first to question me, but you taught me to forgive."

With a shovel and pick and Coot's water bucket and rope we started digging. Coot and I got on the business end of the pick and shovel. It was slow digging in the hard caliche. Coot lit his coal oil lantern. Our progress slowed to a hard grind. By nine that night we were down to the eight-foot level. More correctly, I was down to the eight-foot level, and Coot was up on top because he reasoned he was more suited to pulling the load to the top.

Juanito started a fire and warmed some of our remaining food. The soldiers spelled us while we ate, then we resumed our chore. Soon we were in loose gravel and our progress hastened.

When we dug down to the ten-foot level, Gregorio called down, "Okay, *Senor* Montgomery, you come up here, and I will go down there. You might strike my treasure with that pick."

The heavy gravel of the ever-deepening hole began caving in, showering down on Gregorio as we pulled the bucket up.

Coot said, "*Comandante,* I believe we should build a ladder for Gregorio. The sides of this hole may cave in and bury him and the rifles. And, he'll need the ladder to bring up the guns."

The *comandante* agreed and had his men build a crude ladder of dead limbs tied with wire. Soon we heard Gregorio's shovel clang on metal. The *comandante* smiled. The *Rural* frowned.

Gregorio yelled for us to pull up a wax-covered tarpaulin to get it out of the way. Coot asked the *padre* about it.

"That is wax from a plant called *candallia*. We melted the plant down in a large copper caldron, then spread the wax over the tarpaulin. It will keep everything dry forever."

Gregorio continued working at the bottom of the hole, but the faint yellow light and dust did not reveal what he was up to. He called up, "*Mi papa*, he was a traveling peddler. 'Don't peddle your goods from an empty cart,' he always said."

The *Rural* screamed down into the dim dusty, yellow light, "*Que dice*, Gregorio Gonzalez? Speak up!"

"*Capitan*, you cannot sell scissors and pots and salt if they are not in your cart," Gregorio said. "It is a famous old saying—from Italy, I believe. You should look it up, *Senor Capitan*—it serves a lot of purposes. You could say that about guns with no bullets, I think, *pero quien sabe?*"

Coot and I glanced at each other across the hole, faint dust drifting up in the yellow haze.

Gregorio's high-pitched voice ground on the *Rural*. "A stitch in—in—a stitch in—in—something or other—*Aiii!* I forget, but you save time if you put a stitch at it. At least that is what I heard a woman say in El Paso."

Again the *Rural* screamed down into the dusty yellow light, "*Que dice*, Gregorio Gonzalez? What are you saying, *pendejo?*"

"*Nada, senor Capitan—nada*. I was just talking about a woman." Gregorio had our attention, but Coot and I could only grin across the top of the hole at each other, not getting the point of his palaver.

"*Oiga, pendejo!*" the *Rural* screamed down into the yellow hole. "Where are the guns?"

"*Si, senor*—I am tying the rope around two of them now. There. You can make a pull at them."

Coot pulled up the guns and handed one to the *comandante*, and said, "Muskets. Maybe we could use them for firewood, or the *Villistas* could use them for crutches."

The *Rural* screamed at the *comandante*, "Automatic weapons? *Bah!* What do you think of Gregorio's weapon cache now, *Comandante?*"

The *comandante* called down, "Gregorio! These are ancient muskets. They will not serve us against the *Villistas*. Where are the modern weapons you promised? Answer me before I order my men to bury you where you stand!"

"*Si, senor comandante, si! Por favor*, a small measure of patience for me, *eh?* I will throw them up to you one at a time, but first I must make a check at them."

All was quiet around the top except the faint sound coming from the bottom of that fifteen-foot hole. The solid metal, rhythmic click of a heavy .45-70 rolling block rifle being cocked—a soft, muted, strong click, the throw of the click of a hammer. He threw the rifle up and I caught it, handed it to the *padre*. The *Rural* grabbed it away and inspected it. It was brand new, no worse for wear for having been buried all those years. Gregorio cocked another rifle and threw it up, and again I reached out, grabbed it, handed it to Sergeant Porras. Gregorio continued cocking and tossing several rifles out of the hole, I handed them to the soldiers as I caught each one. I handed Father Esteban a rifle. The soldiers stacked them as directed by the *comandante*. Juanito took one of the .45-70s to the side, sat, admired the bright metal and polished wood, comparing it to his beat-up rifle.

I heard the unmistakable muffled clatter of the slide of a Browning Auto-5 being pulled back, the hushed pad of an ejected shotgun shell hitting the rocky bottom of the pit. Gregorio released the mechanism, its heavy spring shut the bolt with a telling clatter—a unique, *heavy*, *solid* clank that anyone who ever heard it would instantly recall.

"*Mi papa*, he did not like guns," Gregorio called up from his hole. "He always warned me that a wise man treats all guns as if they will make a kill at you. 'Guns are always loaded,' *mi papa*, he say. Catch this, *Senor* Montgomery. *Senor* Boldt will appreciate this fine *escopete*—a shotgun you call it—one that shoots five cartridges, now maybe four. Cartridges what you call double-OO something. I don't know those *gringo* words."

I caught the shotgun and tossed it to Coot, whispered, "Forward the Light Brigade! Cannon to the left, cannon to the right. And that cannon in your hands is damned sure ready."

Gregorio cocked another .45-70 and tossed it up. I caught the rifle and stood with a sudden urge for invisibility.

After a few long moments, the *Rural* took a lantern over to the edge of the hole, got down on his all fours, and screamed into the dim hole, "*Oiga, pendejo!* What are you doing down there? You are too quiet! Answer me, you traitorous sonavabitch!"

From the depths of the pit, the heavy slicing sound of the levering action on a 44-40 carbine drifted out of the pit, the lever pushed down with a faint clatter of metal parts separating, handling a cartridge, then metal on metal slammed home as the lever was returned to the ready position.

"Oh, *Capitan*, I am just checking the sights on this Winchester so I don't miss your stinking, murdering, yellow-streaked *cabeza!*"

The rifle boomed from the bottom of the hole. *Capitan* Manzano's body flew back from the mouth of it. I turned to the *comandante* with the .45-70 as if to present the rifle for his inspection. He fumbled to get his pistol out of its holster. As his pistol came up, I shot him point-blank with the single-shot rifle. Coot swung the shotgun around in an arc, shot the sergeant. The double-00 buckshot caught him in the gut, cutting him almost in half. Coot turned to the soldier to his right and behind me and fired. Something hard and strong hit me in the ass, spun me around to the ground.

Father Estevan had his rifle to his shoulder, pointing the weapon at a soldier across the hole. The soldier pointed his rifle at the *padre*.

Juanito screamed, "*No padre! El es mi hermano!*"

The soldier fired. The *padre* went down. Gregorio scrambled up on the ladder. He had the ladder in one hand, the .44-40 in the other, shooting the soldier.

The remaining soldier pointed his rifle at his fallen *comandante*, then at the *padre*, then at the body of the sergeant. He eased the rifle to the ground, shock, disbelief, confusion plastered his face. Before anyone could move, the soldier went down on one knee, stuck the muzzle in his mouth, pulled the trigger.

Juanito gazed around, at his *comandante*, the *Rural, su hermano,* his fellow soldiers, all dead. He backed away, tripped and fell, his rifle slipped from his hands. He turned and ran.

Gregorio yelled, "*Esperete, Juanito!* No one will hurt you. Come back!"

Juanito was gone in the dark of the wilderness. We talked about chasing after him, but dismissed it. He was only armed with an old Colt .45, besides, we'd never find him in the dark.

Three standing where nine men and a boy stood only seconds ago. I stepped over to the sergeant's body, retrieved my revolver from his gun belt, took Coot's .45 from the belt of the *Rural*, uncocked it, smiled, handed it to Coot.

Gregorio turned the *padre* over on his back, cradled him in his arms, hugged him. "*Senores!* He is breathing. The *padre* lives!"

Coot took a look at his wound. "Gut shot. Doubt he'll be with us come daylight." Coot covered him with a *serape*. He turned to me. "What happened to you when you fell down during all this fracas?"

"Hell, I forgot all about it. Now that you mention it, my ass aches like it was hit by a sixteen-pound sledge."

I dropped my drawers, tried to turn myself around enough to take a look in the lamp light. All I could see was a stream of blood flowing down the back of my leg. "Coot, you blind bastard! You shot me in the ass when you shot that last soldier. Sure as hell, there's a double-OO b-b stuck in there. Take a look at it for me, will you?"

"Well I don't know, Narlow, sure don't know about this. You *know* people'll talk. I haven't seen your white ass since we last skinny-dipped the Black River at the Box. Yep, Narlow, you sure as hell got hit in the ass. Now, if that was my ass, I'd want to get that piece of lead out of there. What do you think, Gregorio?"

"Poor *Senor* Montgomery, maybe so he die from the poison of the lead. What do you think, *Senor* Boldt?"

"Poor, poor *Senor* Montgomery. I fear you are right, Gregorio."

"You two shut up and build up that fire. I've got more than a little lead in my ass to worry about. Like being gone for two months and one worried, angry wife."

Gregorio dug out the buckshot, Coot made a coal-oil poultice with rags and tied it in place.

The two of them sat around the fire and we talked about what we were going to do. I was on my belly to give my backside a rest, let the coal-oil-soaked rag do its magic. The wind came up from across the Rio, Gregorio covered the *padre* with another *serape*.

Coot said, "Gregorio, you sure had our asses fooled. The *padre* wasn't in on this with you?"

"No, he knew nothing. Now, maybe so I am afraid *mi amigo* maybe so he die thinking I betrayed him, our people."

"I don't know so much about that, Gregorio," I said. "As soon as I heard you cock that .45-70, then pulled that Browning's action open, the shotgun shell hit the rocks in the bottom of that hole, the whole thing crystallized in my mind. You sure had the wool pulled over our eyes. Us, probably more than the *comandante* and the *Rural*. You have to believe that Father Estevan realized the truth."

Gregorio stoked the fire. "Mercedes did not believe me. When we were leaving, I tell her, I told her I would return for her. What do you think, *Senor* Montgomery? *Senor* Boldt says you have a way with womens, that you know how they think. Do you think she will believe me?"

"You do me no favor saying I know how women think. The law would have me committed, but don't doubt yourself Gregorio. She'll believe you because she's a woman and women just naturally want to believe in their man. Mercedes is a good woman, make you a good wife, lots of babies."

Coot said, "Speaking of women, you know what I want right about now, Narlow?"

"Naw, let me guess. Judging by that grin and how long you've been without, I'd say a woman might be at the head of your list. That, maybe a jug."

"No, I'd get to all that in due time. First, I'd like a hot, day-long soak, then I'd like a dozen fried eggs mounted on two burnt steaks washed down with that jug you mentioned. Then I'd like to climb into a big four-poster and sleep for three days, wake up all sweaty and tangled up with a big-titted gal, my nose buried in her hairy armpit."

With the rising of the sun, my ass was stiff and tight as a hound-fed tick, felt like I had a bullet up my ass, not figuratively. Getting on my feet, moving around in the warm sunshine loosened me up. The coal-oil-soaked rag had worked its magic. I felt a tad better.

We carried the *comandante* and his men to the pit, lowered them in with the rope, and started the chore of filling in the hole. The *padre* came around. He motioned for Gregorio.

The *padre* struggled to sit up, tried to wave his hand, but it fell limp in his lap. "My friends, I know I will die very soon. But please do me . . . the honor of allowing me . . . to bless those men who were our enemy."

Father Estevan sat leaning against the sycamore and blessed the men. Then he said, "I have sinned much in my life. My worst sins . . . was my hatred for these men. I hated them. Now, I pray for Juanito. That young boy has seen too much death, tasted . . . tasted too much blood, heard the screams of too many dying men. If he makes it to manhood, he will be dangerous, murderous. Last night I recalled a poem. A poem that helped me get through my hatred of these men. I do not recall the name . . . of the poem or who wrote it. I fear I cannot remember it precisely, but it was something like:

I came in haste with cursing breath,
And heart of hardest steel;
But when I saw thee cold in death,
I felt as man should feel.
For when I look upon that face,
That cold, unheeding, frigid brow,
Where neither rage nor fear has place,
By Heaven! I cannot hate thee now!

The *padre's* gaze shot up, his head fell to his chest. He was gone.

Gregorio said, "That *soldado*, the soldier the *padre* had his rifle pointed at—the one that shot him. Remember, Juanito screamed that the soldier was his brother? I saw Father Estevan praying with him last night as you were making the dig for the rifles. He heard his confession. The *soldado* said he was afraid to die. If he was to die, he wanted to die in Mexico, not *Tejas*. Father Estevan told him, he say he would have a plump wife and many children."

"Father Estevan died honorably, Gregorio," Coot said. "He could have shot that soldier as easily as the soldier shot him."

"*Si, Senor*, he died honorably. More honorably than his life—at least that is what his church would say."

When the hole was almost filled, we took a break. Coot asked, "Gregorio, what about those cartridges in the wheel wells of the Reo? Rose flew them all the way down to Carichic from Texas. Now we've brought them all the way back to Texas."

"*O senores*, we will put them in the hole. I will come again one more time to my sacred sycamore tree, take the bullets to Carichic."

We lowered the canisters into the partially filled hole, covered them with the tarp, finished filling it, then carried five large rocks to the gravesite to serve as markers for the *comandante* and his men. Gregorio insisted the *Rural* and Father Estevan not be buried with them.

"*No no no, senores*, I will make a deep grave for *mi padre*, with nice sides, a view across the Rio to Mexico." He motioned at the *Rural's* body. "Then I will scratch out a shallow trench for that shit chicken *bastardo pendejo*."

Gregorio asked that we take him as far south as Presidio. He would wade the Rio to Ojinaga, hop the rails to Cuahtemoc, walk to Carichic, to his Mercedes. Coot found the rock ledge where we stashed our slickers and clothes when we crossed into Mexico. Shedding the white cotton pants and blouse of the *pobre* felt good, my old trousers and shirt, rough but welcome.

When we were on the outskirts of Presidio, Coot pulled off to the side of the dirt road, smiled back at Gregorio, and said, "This is the end of the line for us, Gregorio. We're not welcome in Presidio. *Senor* Montgomery got us in a little trouble in a dingy *cantina* with the biggest Mexican in all of Chihuahua and Texas."

Coot pulled a wad of dollar-bills out of a metal box under his seat, handed them to Gregorio. "This should be enough to get you back to Carichic. Maybe even a little extra to buy your bride-to-be a pretty little something."

"Gracias amigos! I will send you an invitation to our wedding."

36

On the Road to Tornillo. March 1916

We drove north on a cow path that would get us on the main road to Tornillo, came on a pointer sign to the west—"Shafter Silver Mine." Under that the notation—"Notararary Public."

Coot grinned. "Any mine that has its very own 'notararary' public has got to have a working telegraph. Let's take a look. Need to wire Rodolfo so he'll know we're all right. Wire IB to tell him we'll be in El Paso in three days."

We found the mine headquarters, a 'notararary' public sign prominently carved on clapboard, twisting in the breeze, dangling at an angle by a single strand of rusty wire, a telegraph line trailing off up a steep hill behind the headquarters building. Abandoned a short time ago. Coot sat down, started clicking the keys of the instrument. In a few minutes, he was busy writing Rodolfo's return message: "Happy you are safe. STOP. Expect you late tonight or early tomorrow. STOP. Shelly Brom is with me. IB nowhere to be found. STOP. Safe travels. STOP. Rodolfo Bustamante.

"Wonder where IB got off to. Remember, Rodolfo going to send a man after IB and Shelly before we went into Mexico."

I asked Coot to wire Big George. "Tell him to deliver the telegram to Zara. We're in Texas, that we're safe, be home soon. It'll mean more if Big George delivers it. Comfort her a might, make it more believable."

I banged on the side of an overhead fuel tank, satisfied myself that it was half-full of petro. "I'll fill the Reo and the fifty-five gallon tank in the bed."

Coot pulled off several feet of insulated wire hanging on the wall. "I'll rewire the lights on the Reo. Liable to be doing some night driving so we can get on home."

Coot left a ten-dollar bill for the mine owner under the telegraph unit. "I imagine that's more silver than that old mine ever produced," he said as we headed back to our cow trail.

We needed to check-in with Bo and Tacho, but Rodolfo was our main concern. From what the *Rural* said, they were on to him, every passing day put him closer to danger.

At near dark, two days after we'd left Presidio, we drove into Tornillo, Rodolfo standing on his porch, Shelly Brom playing in the dirt with a little girl. "Welcome, gentlemen. It is so good to rest these tired old eyes on my friends. You have quite a story to tell I understand."

Shelly's only greeting was turning her disfigured face to the side.

When Coot asked about IB, Rodolfo said, "As you recall, I sent a man to fetch him and Shelly, but he was not there. I questioned her, but she only shrugged and ran down to the Rio. So much has happened in the past few days. First, Germany has given the United States all the reason they will ever need to enter the European War—on March 7, they sank the British ocean liner, Lusitanian, with one-hundred-twenty-eight Americans lost. Then on the morning of the 9th, Villa forces attacked Columbus, New Mexico. General Pershing is gathering 8,000 troops to enter Mexico to capture him. You got out of Mexico just in the nick of time as the *pobres* of Chihuahua will come to the aid of their old hero.

"But let me tell you about Rose and your friend, Jorge Jose Umbenhauer. They paid me the courtesy of flying down here soon after they flew out of Mexico. Mr. Umbenhauer is organizing a group of fellow pilots to return to Carichic and rescue you gentlemen."

I moaned, "Jeez-amighty, just what we need."

"I tried to get them to wait and give you gentlemen an opportunity to get out on your own, but Mr. Umbenhauer is a persistent man. I finally persuaded him to wait until Saturday before he would—"

"Saturday?" Coot asked. "When is Saturday?"

"Tomorrow, I am afraid."

"Narlow, we best beat it to El Paso. Maybe that big German hasn't flown back into Mexico."

Coot stood. "Rodolfo, we'll be back to fill you in on everything. Right now we need to make tracks."

"Gentlemen, surely you will stay over with me until morning. It has been raining upstream steadily for the past two days. The mesa road is washed out north of here, and the prospects of the river road being passable are not good. If you are up to it, I have a little chore for you. I thought perhaps you'd have time to take a load of gold with you for another shipment of rifles and cartridges. The armaments would be at the Coal Mine Ranch should we need them in an emergency. But that can wait. My days of arming Villa have probably ended for all time."

"Won't take a half-hour to load up the gold," I said. "We've got time for that, for whatever good it will do. Rodolfo, my gunrunning days are a thing of the past."

When we were ready to head out, Rodolfo said, "Shelly wants to go home, and since you will be around, it's safe for her to return home now. She won't hand-sign me where IB is, but I feel she knows his whereabouts. She seems afraid, but won't sign anything. I was planning on sending her home on the morning train, but perhaps she could go with you gentlemen."

He turned to Shelly who was playing with the little girl, mending her rag-doll. "Shelly, your friends will take you home if you're ready to go. Would you like that, dear child?"

She shook her head, stood, ready to bolt, leaving no doubt she was *not* getting in the Reo. Rodolfo assured her, pressed her to go with us. She took off running.

Coot said, "It's hard to keep in mind that Shelly and IB are our age. No telling why she won't go with us."

Rodolfo turned back to us, shrugged, smiled. "A woman's privilege, I suppose."

Coot turned the corner at Rodolfo's bank, started for the river road. Shelly ran out of an alley, waving her arms, muffling the indecipherable. We figured she'd changed her mind and decided to go with us, but when we got out, she backed away, staying away from any possibility of catching her. She pointed at the river road, shook her head, pointed and shook several times, then ran off in the dark, her stubby legs pumping like locomotive drivers.

"Damn, Coot, what do you suppose? Maybe she wants us to wait, that she'll go home with us tomorrow."

"Hell, I don't know, but I don't think that's it."

An hour out of Tornillo on the river road, I peered ahead into the dark, then turned and looked into the black, blurry mist behind us. "I wonder what happened to that Model-T pickup that pulled out in front of us in Tornillo, taking off in such a hurry. That old bucket of rust would have a hard time getting up to five-miles-per-hour, but we haven't caught up with it yet. Wonder how she's kept ahead of us."

"I wonder," was Coot's invariable wise-ass reply to my habitual wondering.

"Do you ever wonder about anything, you old bald-headed fart?"

"Yeah, I do. I'm wondering what the hell's wrong with Shelly. Wondering where IB might be, what's happened to him. Shelly's always appeared to be smarter than her twin brother, but maybe she's reverting."

The Reo slid sideways in the mud before Coot could get her straightened out. "That Model-T is ahead of us. Caught a glimpse of her tracks in the mud when we swerved just now."

The light mist was just enough to muddy the windshield, the vacuum wiper blades hadn't worked for months. In a few minutes the mist and fog turned to a heavy shower, turning the windshield to a mass of streaked red mud.

Coot stopped, stepped out, wiped the glass with his bandanna, and got back in the cab. "I need to fix that vacuum pump when we get to El Paso."

"Maybe he turned off back there a ways," I said.

"Maybe *who* turned off a ways back there?"

"That old Model-T pickup we saw leaving ahead of us in Tornillo, the tracks you saw a while back."

We sat there for a minute. Coot peered through the front glass, wiped it with his shirt sleeve, peered again, then turned, peering back through the back window. "I don't know whether that old Ford is in front or back of us, but when I stepped back up on the running board just now, I saw headlamps behind us a ways, then suddenly they went dark. Bright lamps. Bright-white. Not weak and yellow like a Model-T. Like the headlamps of a big new automobile."

"What do you make of that? Another coincidence?"

"Maybe. I hadn't noticed any lights in my rearview mirror. Maybe I didn't look, but there's not two cars a week that travels this road. Hardly ever at night. Tonight there's three vehicles out here. The Model-T ahead of us, a touring car behind us, and this Reo."

"You're thinking that maybe when you stopped to wipe off the windshield, the car behind us caught up, then backed off? Not wanting to get too close?"

"I wouldn't have thought much about it except you were talking about the Model-T that we should have caught up with. Adjust that side mirror so you can keep an eye out for lights coming up behind us."

When we got to within three miles of the near-deserted village of Isla del Rio, we relaxed a bit, but the next bend in the road brought us to a bypass around a washed-out bridge. The detour led us up an arroyo, then down the other side back to the river road. We drove on in the rain for a mile, expecting another washout any minute, rounded a slow bend in the river and the road disappeared into the black.

We stopped, lit a bull's eye lantern, and stepped out into the rain. There were narrow vehicle tracks going up the shallow *arroyo*, then crossing it, then back to the road on the far side of the washout.

Coot stood peering into the dark, his old Stetson drooping in the rain. "Come on. If that old Model-T Ford can make it, we sure as hell can."

Just as we got across the *arroyo* and back on to the road, we came on the Model-T sitting in the middle of it, leaving no room to pass on either slippery side.

Coot took off his hat, wiped his puckered brow. "I don't like this one damn bit. Get your Schofield out. Watch our backsides." He tapped his .45 on the dashboard. "I'll watch front."

My scalp tightened.

A man shouted out from Coot's side of the Reo, "Hey friend. We need help. Just some petroleum if you have any to spare, friend."

Petroleum?

Coot cut the headlamps. "*Watch your ass,*" he whispered.

Coot hollered out into the dark rain, "Sure, friend, we've got *petroleum* to spare for you. But I'd sure like to see who I'm talking to. If you don't mind, *friend.*"

"Yes, assuredly so," the man said as he walked up. "Didn't mean to frighten you, friend. Don't blame you for that. Very spooky country, wouldn't you agree?"

"I didn't say a damn word about being frightened, *friend!*" Coot bellered. "It just makes a man a little nervous to come up on a parked truck. *In the middle* of a goddamn isolated, slick-ass road. In goddamn *pitch dark. Goddamn driver* standing over there out of sight. Like an orphan highwayman."

I didn't like being in the Reo. Coot and I were on the ground in the same instant. Another man was approaching the rear of the truck, crouched, creeping along the side of it. When he got close enough to touch, I yelled, "*Howdy!*"

"*Aiii!*" he screamed and jumped back. "*Buenos noches, senor.* It is raining very hard, *eh?*" he said, wiping his wet sleeve across his forehead. He was a stern, compact man.

Bright headlamps showed from around the bend behind us. I barked, "*Coot.*"

The man on Coot's side of the Reo said, "Allow me to introduce myself. I am Harrison Kohl."

We made no reply.

"Say friend," he said, "those are our traveling companions coming behind us in their touring automobile. I doubt very much they will be able to traverse that

225

creek back there. Could we impose on you gentlemen to assist our companions should they not be successful in driving through the creek? Perhaps your truck can pull them through."

Coot frowned. "*Friend*, there's no such thing as a creek in west Texas. That's what's called an *arroyo*. But, first you wanted petroleum, now you want us to pull your traveling companions across that *arroyo*. We're not running a mechanics shop out here in the middle of nowhere. And, how the hell do you know those lights are your traveling companions, *friend*?"

"Well, of course I cannot say for certain. I only assume the bright headlamps belong to the touring car of our companions." His English was good, though stilted, forced, strange.

The light thrown by the headlamps of the vehicle was stark white, not yellow as Coot said, the heavy gravel in the *arroyo* reflecting wet and white in the light, falling rain drops sparkling in puddles.

Coot squared around to the man. "Well, *friend*, why don't you gents go talk to your companions. Decide what you want to do. Want to do that, *friend*? We've got to get a move-on, so if you want our help, you need to get your ass poppin', *friend*."

"Yes, certainly. I'll have my man run back and see what they want to do."

He turned to the man who'd sneaked up on my side of the Reo. "*Pedro, pro favor, pregunta al Senor Mueller si quiere se llevar a cabo el arroyo o si el y sus companeros preferirian andar al lado del barro.*"

The Mexican man turned and ran back to the car. Kohl's Spanish sounded as though read from a primer, but why did Kohl speak Spanish to him? Pedro spoke English to me when I got out of the truck. Mueller, or was it Miller? Mueller had a definite European ring to it. As in German. So did Kohl.

In a minute, the Mexican man came running back yelling, "*Si, Senor Kohl— Senor Mueller dice que van andar al lado del barro.*"

What was this shit? Mueller was coming over to our side of the muddy *arroyo*. What happened to the other companion that Kohl said was in the touring car?

Coot stood in the dark rain, his hat pulled down to his ears, brim drooling down. His glance echoed my concern. We didn't like it, but the men hadn't really given us any reason to suspect anything, didn't appear to be armed, but they probably thought the same thing about us, standing in the hard rain, our cocked weapons under our slickers.

226

Mueller walked up, fumbling with a lamp, trying to get it lit in the middle of the downpour. He was a good-sized man, wearing no hat, appeared to be blond, but in the dark I was not certain.

"Good evening, gentlemen. Thank you for stopping to assist us. I am afraid we will have to take you up on your offer to pull our automobile through the mud. It is a splendid conveyance, but I fear it has a propensity to high-center rather easily. Beg your pardon, sirs, I am Kevin Mueller."

Kohl asked the Mexican, "*Donde esta, Jorge?*

"*Jorge viene,*" mumbled something else but I didn't get it.

The pounding rain drowned out most of their conversation. I guessed another man named Jorge was joining us on our side of the washout. Why were they sloshing through the mud to be on our side of the washout? Why were they speaking Spanish to the man when he spoke English? My biggest question was for me and *my* driving "companion." *Why the hell don't we get back in the Reo, dropkick that Model-T in the ditch, and get the hell out of here?*

Kohl asked, "Do you think this rain will maintain itself for much longer?"

The question struck me as a stall. I shouted the first thing that popped into my mind, "Coot, we're pissing on a flat rock. I fear we are amidst a fair amount of duplicity." I got in Kohl's face. "And, *friend*, why would you give a rat's ass whether we thought it would rain much longer? That seems like a—"

Something big and fast as a locomotive blurred past me, hitting Coot broadside, thumping him off the road, tumbling him down the slope to the river. Mueller ran after Coot and whatever hit him. The Mexican and Kohl were on me. My revolver was in my hand, but Kohl had my arms pinned to my sides under my slicker. The Mexican man tried to trip me. Kohl was intent on wrestling me to the ground. I didn't go down easy but when I did, I went down with all the force as I could muster.

When we hit the mud, I was on top. The force knocked the wind out of Kohl. His grip, strong as a bear's, slackened. My revolver came up. I fired at the shadow of the Mexican in front of me. Kohl was trying to get to his feet while attempting to get at his pistol. He grabbed my other hand, we went around in circles in the dark and mud, holding onto each other with one hand, jerking each other trying to make the other fall, slipping in the boot-sucking mud, half falling, trying to get a bead on the other. I took a wild shot in the dark. Kohl shot his automatic twice in quick succession. The bright flash blinded me. I tripped and went down hard on my face. A pistol report rang out. Coot's .45 automatic?

227

I struggled to my feet in the mud. Couldn't see Kohl or the Mexican. I heard splashing in the river. Coot let out a shout, grunting in the mud at the bottom of the embankment. Mud in my eyes. I ran in the direction of Coot's voice. A hulk of a man was on him at the edge of the river, straddling him with his hands at Coot's throat. I hit the man's head as hard as I could with the Schofield. The heavy iron had no effect on him. I hit him again. Again.

"*Coot*. Hang on, Coot. Where's Mueller?"

"Think I shot him. Shoot this big bastard. *Shoot him*, goddamn it, Narlow! Shoot him!"

I groped around but was afraid to shoot in the black rain.

I reared back and swung that four-pound piece of iron revolver as hard as I could swing it. Nothing. I holstered my revolver, grabbed Coot's leg, tried to pull him away.

Coot yelled, "My other leg's stuck under a root. Shoot this big bastard. *Shoot him*."

"I can't. Can't see, might shoot you!"

"*Shoot him*. Shoot him in the ear!"

I felt around in the dark, found his wet, bloody ear. Put the muzzle of the Schofield between my fingers, fired. He fell away.

"*Son-of-a-living-bitch, Narlow!*" Coot stood, clawing for breath. "I shot at that big bastard, but know damn well I hit Mueller. Did you get Kohl and the other Mexican?"

"I guess I got the Mexican, but I didn't see his body. He was close when I shot. Probably hit him. Kohl and I were wrestling around in the mud. Dancing. Holding hands, shooting at each other. I fell, got free of him. Got to my feet, eyes plastered with mud. I never saw him after that."

"Let's get a lantern and see what's left up there."

The rain started a downpour. We cranked up the Reo, turned on the headlamps. The first thing we saw was the pitch black road ahead—minus one rusty Model-T.

I said, "Didn't hear him crank it up. Too much excitement."

"Looks like Kohl ran out on his traveling companions. What about the Mexican named Pedro?"

The lamp helped us find him, lying face up in the mud.

"Narlow, let's go back down to the river, see if we can find Mueller. Need to know if Kohl's the only one left."

We found the big Mexican, missing the left side of his head.

"Coot, you need to retire from the ring. Never seen you bested by any man until Yellow Bear came along, now this monstrous bastard."

"You don't recognize him? Remember the *cantina* at Presidio just before we first went into Mexico? The Mexican that elbowed you at the bar. His friend called him Jorge, remember?"

"Well, kiss my . . . sure as hell is."

"Somebody's sure after our asses. We've been a whole bunch luckier than we deserve. By all counts, we oughta be the ones face-down in the mud."

I took the lantern downstream. "Here's Mueller at the edge of the water. Let's take a look at their touring car."

The car smelled brand new. I turned off the headlamps and slid the driver's side window closed. Coot grinned and asked, "What the hell are you doing that for? Let's get a move on. Leave these bastards where they lie, see if we can catch that bastard in the Model-T pickup before he gets to town and lose him."

We followed the tracks of the Model-T up the river road for another slow muddy mile where it ended at a major washout, tracks headed up a rocky hill toward the mesa road. When we got to the top of the hill, the Model-T's tracks made a beeline for the main road.

Coot said, "Kohl knows exactly where he's going. Talks strange, terrible Spanish accent, but knows this country. He can drive that old Ford, too, only hits the road about every thirty feet. May be driving a bucket of rust, but I bet the motor under that hood isn't the one that left Detroit."

It struck me. "That damn *Rural, Capitan* Manzano. Remember him saying that the *Rurales* were close to narrowing down the location of the man on the US side that was bankrolling the gunrunning into Mexico?"

"Yeah, so?"

"It seems to me that Kohl and Mueller started this chase in Tornillo."

"*Oh shit*. We gotta get Rodolfo out of Tornillo pretty damn *pronto*."

"We'll wire him when we get to town. Tell him to catch the next train to El Paso, bring Shelly with him. Plenty of room for him at our house."

The rain had cleared, the sun was peeking up when we got within sight of El Paso. I said, "Turn off the road up there at the top of the hill. Let's swing by Too Slim Glardon's airstrip. Maybe JJ is using it to gather his fly-boys. Won't take a minute, and we may learn something that'll save some time."

No sign of JJ, but we found Too Slim. He laughed. "Yeah, JJ's stirred up a

229

hornet's nest. That big bastard had every flyer in the southwest ready to fly into Mexico. But General Pershing impounded their airplanes, put them in the stockade until they settled down. Twelve of those crazy bastards were ready to follow him to Mexico, their goddamn planes got machineguns all over 'em."

"Are they still in the stockade?" Coot asked.

"Well, yes and no, maybe so, maybe no. Yesterday I heard that the general let them out, and one of his lieutenants, a Lieutenant Patton, followed them and damn if they weren't at your airstrip west of El Paso, ready to fly south. So he arrested the whole lot of them. I suspect they're still in General Pershing's pokey."

We got back on the river road and headed for town. I got to wondering, then a miserable thought hit me. "Coot, what about Shelly's panic about not wanting us to go down the river road last night. Think she knew something?"

"Aw, hell no. Neither Shelly or IB can tell the time of day. She just couldn't make up her mind whether to go with us or play with that little girl."

"*Whoa*, Coot. *Stop*. Kohl's Model-T pickup is sitting behind that mesquite at the bottom of the bar-ditch."

We drew our weapons, and approached the truck. Deserted.

Coot said, "Probably ran of gas sure enough this time." He screwed off the gas cap, stood on the running board, and gave it a heave to get the truck rocking back and forth, put his ear to the filler neck and listened. "Dry. Out of gas. Five miles from town."

He opened the hood on one side of the motor compartment and whistled. "Take a look at this. I don't have a notion what this is, but I can tell you what it's not. It's not a four-cylinder Model-T motor. Six-cylinder job—foreign made. And look at the transmission housing and running gear. Stainless, maybe aluminum. This is no Model-T—it's a rusted body of a Model-T, bolted to the chassis of a European-made hotrod. Likely German."

"So, they had the Model-T in front of us that was fast enough to keep ahead of us, followed by their touring car. The Ford stopped, boxing us in. That the way you see it?"

"Yeah, and like you said, we should have called their hand when all that got started."

We followed Kohl's footprints leading away from El Paso for a half-mile, then curved around to the north, then due northwest toward town.

I said, "Looks like he's wearing house slippers. I was having a hell of a time staying on my feet back there in the mud, but he was having a worse time of it."

Coot started out on foot tracking Kohl to make certain he didn't head into Mexico. I beat it to El Paso, gave the sheriff our story and a description of Kohl. When I got to Union Depot, I found my third-grade classmate, Ronaldo Giloloni, SP's ticket master. Never made it out of the third grade, speech patterns made it difficult to understand, but I concluded that a man fitting Kohl's description came slipping and sliding across the depot's fresh-moped tile floor wearing shoes similar to house slippers. Bought a ticket from Ronaldo, then slid over to the Western Union counter, sent a wire, waited around, appeared to get a return wire. Came back to Ronaldo wanting to trade-in his ticket to Socorro for one just to Rincon. I got back on the Isla del Rio road and found Coot, flat-splay-footed and knock kneed, hoofing along.

On the corduroy road to Rincon, I brought up quitting, a sore subject to Coot, but quitting was the only thing on my mind. That and a guilty conscience. I leaned forward on the wooden bench seat of the Reo, easing my weight off my sore butt. "Hell of thing, killing a man. Even a bad one. The *comandante* wasn't a particularly bad one, and Pedro, the Mexican man with Kohl and Mueller was just trying to make a buck. Besides, it was dark, couldn't see his face when I shot him. I've tried to convince myself that shooting Jeronimo at point-blank was for mercy, and it was, that it couldn't be helped, but another killing none-the-less. Then, there's the four men with *sombreros* at the San Pablo crossing that I shot in the foot to chase them back to Mexico, also just trying to make a buck. But the *worst*—the *very worst* thing was cramming my goddamn Schofield in Jorge's ear and scattering his brains in the mud, the side of his head, *gone!* Good God Almighty, Coot! What sort of man have I become? Even my heartless goddamn mother never stuck a gun in a man's ear and blew his brains out."

"Ease up on yourself," Coot said. "Shooting those men couldn't be helped."

"Wonder how brave I would have been if it had been full light when I shot Jorge? Huh? Tell me that! Would I really stick my revolver in his ear and pull the trigger? *No.* Don't have the stomach for it. Don't have the grit for it. One thing to blast a man's head off you can't see—"

"You've got more grit than a peeled hen-egg rolled in sand, and you're as brave as they come, Narlow Montgomery. Change the subject, would you?"

"Brave as they come, huh? I'll tell you what's brave. Boys that will soon be lining up to be shipped off to France pretty dern quick. Boys who know they'll likely not come back. But Coot and Narlow won't be in that line. *Oh, no.* Too damn old. But we weren't so old at the outbreak of the Spanish American War in 1898.

We were what? Less than forty years old. But, damn it, you didn't see me pushing anybody out of line down at the recruitment office."

"America shouldn't have pushed itself in that damnable war, and, no, we didn't push anybody out of line. But then back when we were less than twenty, still wet behind the ears, I don't recall anybody fighting for our spots as underpaid, unappreciated scouts for General Bourk's Blue Coats either. Shot at for nearly two years, day and night, by Apaches who had nothing to lose. I'll say it again, Narlow, you've got more grit than a thirty-pound turkey gobbler's craw, brave as they come."

"*Bull shit*. Brave as that boy, Juanito, back on the *comandante's* porch? An unsmiling, cold-black stare of a twelve-year-old boy. Twelve-years-old stuffed in an old man's skin, who'd cut your heart out and stuff it in your mouth to watch you choke for air. That little waif sure set my heart strings to twanging. Reminded me of son Will when he first took up sleeping in my alley. Of course, Will never witnessed the horror of death like little Juanito. That boy'll never have a chance. Be surprised if he makes it through this damn revolution, ever reaches true manhood. But if he does, *if he makes it*, he'll be one dangerous *hombre*."

"Ease up on yourself, Narlow. You're gonna drive yourself—"

"This damn revolution and I are way the hell out of tune. Hate each other! Damned old hateful bitch. Likes blood too much for my taste. We've heard her cannons roar, the deafening, blinding flash of her exploding shells, the rhythmic tattoo of the bitch's machinegun fire. It's sickening. This whoring-bitch-of-a-war's served up too much blood."

Rincon was a small, worn-out old town with a few scattered shacks and a vacated red-brick schoolhouse. Coot pulled in at the front of the Santa Fe freight station. Locked. Deserted, just like everything else in town. We went in opposite directions looking for Kohl's slippered tracks. Coot gave a shout. Kohl's unmistakable tracks led in the direction of an abandoned store—Ryno-Bear's Outfitters Feed and Seed. The tracks lead to the boardwalk at the front door.

Coot banged on the door with his .45, hollered for Kohl to come on out, motioned for me to go around back. I came back around when I found no door or window. Kohl still hadn't answer Coot's call. He reared back, charged through the door, but we found nothing. Searched the back room, rafters, and storage bins. Kohl wasn't there, but he had to be. We went outside and looked around again, walked both ways on the boardwalk. Nothing. Vanished.

Coot pointed the nose of the Reo south, and we headed for Fort Bliss. We needed to check on JJ Umbenhauer and our would-be-flying-war-ace.

The general met us as we came through his office door. "Well, gentlemen, we meet again. I understand you've been traveling in Mexico. Down there on business, I assume."

The general smiled, waved off his own remark. "No doubt you're here for Miss Rose and Mr. Umbenhauer. They, and a dozen of his fly-boy friends. Mr. Umbenhauer told Lieutenant Patton that he could not arrest Miss Rose as she was a nun. That was all the lieutenant needed to hear. A real Panama hell-cat, that Miss Rose, but the little lady came along peacefully." He turned and barked at the closed door, "*Lieutenant Patton.*"

Lieutenant Patton came through the door, clicked his heels, saluted, barked, "Yes, sir."

"Release Miss Rose and Mr. Umbenhauer and the others to these gentlemen."

When Lieutenant Patton led his detainees through the gate of the barricade, Rose's face broke into a smile as broad as a sunrise. "*Coot. Narlow.* Thank God you're safe. Zara's worried herself sick over you two. Let me assure you of something, Mr. Narlow Montgomery—you're traveling days are a thing of the past. So are Zara's. She hasn't budged since she returned in January."

JJ sauntered over. "Well, it looks like me and my *amigos* won't be flying into Mexico after all. All my plans and effort, up in smoke like a fart in a stiff breeze."

Coot said, "Well, Lieutenant Patton, I understand that you and the general are going after Villa. Better watch your step down there in Chihuahua."

"We'll have that criminal squealing on the end of a pointed stick within a week's time."

"West Point no doubt schooled you on knowing your enemy. Given that any thought?"

"Scant thought. Villa fights like warriors of the Fifth Century. We'll overpower him with might and lightning force."

"Maybe, but you best put something else in your equation. The people of Chihuahua don't like *gringos*. You'll offer cash rewards, probably sizeable cash rewards if you are lead to his hiding place, but no one in northern Mexico will take you up on your bribes."

"We don't need cash rewards to find Villa. We'll find—"

I turned to him. "Your ass, Lieutenant! *Barrancas del Cobre* alone mocks the size of the Grand Canyon. Sheer cliffs, freezing cold, blistering days, no dependable water, caves sprinkled all over the range, some with entrances that are hidden from view a hundred feet above the plain. Find Villa? Ha! Give me and Coot four of your best horses, an hour head start, and you'll *never* find us in southern New Mexico, much less in the harshest territory in the western hemisphere."

The lieutenant licked his lips. "Oh, how I would relish the opportunity of tracking you two down." He stepped away, turned, tapped his baton to his cap. "Another day, gentlemen. Another day."

Rose climbed upfront with us in the Reo, JJ and his fly-boy pals loaded up in the back, and headed for town. She was all atwitter. "We tried to fly the Curtiss out, but JJ thinks something may be wrong with the motor. We cranked it up, it started shaking and jumping all over the place, so I hit the blip switch. About that time, Gregorio showed up. I'm so sorry for taking that beautiful airplane into Mexico. My mistake cost so much. Poor Chico—"

Coot said, "You can add Jeromino and Father Estevan to that list if you just have to. But all of that whining won't do you or them any good."

Her head jerked up. "What happened to Jeromino and Father Estevan? They were such a dear men. And, Gregorio?"

"Gregorio's on his way back to Carichic—tell you about Jeromino and the good *padre* later." Coot put his arm around her neck, pulled her to him. "But let me tell you this, young lady—instead of whining and beating yourself up, think of the good you accomplished. The people of Carichic are rid of the *Federales* and the bastard *Rural capitan. Plus*, with your 5,000 bullets, they're no longer defenseless."

37

Seeing, holding, touching Zara after so long a tough time was like the comforting delight of the desert after a summer shower. We stood at the front door in each other's arms. She shooshed me when I started to speak. "Just hold me. I'll tell you when I've had enough."

That evening, I told her about the danger Rodolfo was in, that we had to get him out of Tornillo, hide him somewhere. I knew she had regained her old control when she smiled, "We must insist that he come here with us."

Coot and I met Rodolfo's early train. "Good morning, my friends. I am quite eager to hear about your emergency. Is it Fritz Hans-Smidt? Or has Rose gotten herself in another difficulty?"

"No, nothing like that," Coot said. "Rose is safe and sound at Narlow's house. He reminded me that in all the years we've known you, we've never entertained you here in El Paso."

As we drove to my house, we told him about *Capitan* Ambrosio Manzano's remark that the Mexican government had been suspicious of the Tornillo, Texas and Guadalupe Bravo, Chihuahua areas. They suspected it as being the center of the *Villistas'* source of guns and munitions. More to the point, the millions of dollars required to fund the operation was being funneled through the area. Rodolfo's bank was an automatic suspect. He didn't share our concern until Coot told him about our run-in with Kohl and Mueller that began when the Model-T pulled out in front of us, the touring car that followed, both vehicles with four killers, out of a quaint border town by the equally picturesque name of Tornillo, Texas.

"*Hmmm!*" Rodolfo crossed his arms, flicked a spot on his sleeve. "Well, Narlow, it is obvious that your concern for your lives has been well-placed. Isn't it strange how much more succinct a situation is when it occurs near our own front door? You have been telling me all this time about the threats on your lives, but until this very moment, I must admit I did not pay close attention to your plight. I apologize for my lax attitude."

Coot parked the Reo in the alley.

"No apologies necessary," Coot said. "Hell, it's just now sinking into my head. But tell me, my old friend," he picked up Rodolfo's valise and held the kitchen door open, "how does it feel to be under house arrest?"

"I beg your pardon."

"Zara's idea, and a good one. Rodolfo, using your word, it is as succinct as the dickens to us. Not only are we in danger, but you, my friend, are now in the crosshairs. German spies and the Mexican government would dearly love to get the man paying for all the munitions we've been supplying Villa. Until this blows over, you're staying here, free to come and go as you please. As long as your coming and going is done inside these walls. Don't show yourself outside. Trust no one. Don't even go down the steps to the street to get the morning paper. Zara, Rose, and Ines are here. They'll fetch your paper, do your shopping for you. Your only task will be to stay completely out of sight."

I said, "Mexican and German operatives want us delivery boys, but the moneyman is who they really want."

Rodolfo smiled. "You use the term 'delivery boys.' That's how Mr. Hans-Smidt referred to you gentlemen when he visited me in Tornillo."

"What? *Fritz* visited you? In *Tornillo?*" Coot asked. "When? Why? He wanted to go around us, didn't he?"

"Fritz visited me quite unexpectedly in Tornillo. I assumed his visit was to discuss the million-dollar offer I made to the three of you. And, yes, he said he and I could deal directly with each other. He reasoned that you gentlemen were just 'delivery boys,' as he phrased it, and that we could make our own deal more favorable to us. He didn't mention not knowing about the million-dollar bonus offer, nor did he give me any indication of surprise. I also told him that you'd refused to participate in the delivery fee since you leased a portion of your Camel Mountain Ranch back in 1912. That bit of news caught him off guard, became suspicious, and wondered why you would refuse your share of the delivery fee."

Coot smiled. "I bet Fritz messed his britches when he heard the sound of a million dollars."

"Delivery boys, huh?" I asked. "We weren't trying to cut him out of anything. You know us better than that, Rodolfo. We didn't say anything to him about the million dollars for two reasons. One, it was not our place to tell him anything. Secondly, we just thought you were trying to get us to stay, that you weren't worried about Fritz. He'd get his one-third of the million dollars when this revolution is over, and it'd just be extra icing on his German-chocolate cake."

"Well, it seems we all assumed too much." Rodolfo shrugged, smiled. "What *can* be misunderstood *will* be misunderstood, especially as it concerns love or money."

We told Rodolfo about some of the particulars of the threats and near misses on our lives. He interrupted when Coot related his encounter with Yellow Bear and Odessa.

"Coot, you mentioned Odessa and the Indian man. When did that occur?"

"Early December. Yellow Bear claimed to come from Odessa. Said he was in a traveling freak show, that he was bought by a man who took him by train to the rail siding thirty miles south of Van Horn, described me and my Reo. So Rodolfo, why'd you ask about Odessa?"

Rodolfo stood, walked to the window, then returned and sat. "I gave Mr. Hans-Smidt my word that I would not share this episode with you gentlemen, but I must. I recall that it was the morning of December 15 of last year. I am certain of the date, as I always go Christmas shopping in El Paso on the 15th. On that date, I received a wire from Mr. Hans-Smidt asking that I send $500 to the sheriff of Ector County. He'd been jailed in Odessa, and the money was to be used to make his bail. I caught the eastbound train that morning to personally deliver the $500. Mr. Hans-Smidt was highly embarrassed about the entire ordeal, explaining that he'd been falsely accused of supplying, shall we just say, 'soiled doves,' to the roughnecks working in the oil fields. He'd been charged with fourteen counts of soliciting."

I laughed. "Ol' Fritz was caught *pimping*?"

Coot laughed so hard he about lost consciousness.

"Now gentlemen, please, remember I gave him my word that I would not disclose that embarrassing misadventure to you. He and I caught the westbound afternoon train, I got off in Tornillo, he went on, saying he was returning to Socorro. He assured me that he would repay the $500, which he did."

I said, "December 15th. This house was broken into late on the afternoon of that exact date. Whoever it was took nothing except Zara's mail stacked up on the dining room table. The house was empty, as Ines was off shopping. She always separates Zara's mail into three stacks—newspapers and periodicals on the corner of the dining room table, her Women's Suffrage correspondence in the middle, her personal letters on the far corner of the table. Nothing was disturbed or taken except her personal letter stack. Whoever came through the alley door, picked up that stack, and was gone by the time Ines returned from her late afternoon shopping. But who would want Zara's personal mail? And if it was Fritz, why would he want it?"

38

Socorro, New Mexico

It was becoming increasingly obvious that Fritz was somehow involved in the several attempts on our lives. Coot drove the Reo off the flatcar at Socorro's train station.

"Coot, we're not dead-certain that Fritz is behind all of this, so let's—"

"*I'm* as certain as sun."

"Let's not just storm into his warehouse and beat him senseless. If he's in bed with the Germans, he's more frightened of his bed-fellows than us. We won't learn a thing."

"I don't give a damn who he's bedding. Let's arrange a little accident. Be shut of him."

"Damn it, Coot, let me handle this. I've been having claustrophobic dreams lately—of being buried alive. I suppose that damn plaster-of-Paris cast brought them on. Those nightmares have given me a Jim-dandy of an idea on how to make ol' Fritzy talk."

"Fine with me. What do you have in mind for that weasel?"

"Don't have all the particulars ironed out. Pull in over there at Momsen's Hardware. Won't take a minute. Keep the motor running."

I came back out on the mercantile's porch.

Coot grinned up at me, his head cocked to the side, Lucifer thumping the scriptures on his shoulder. "Plan on doing a little fence repair with those posthole diggers?"

"Naw, these are for your friend, Fritz. Has little chore to do this afternoon."

We moseyed the Reo on down Socorro's only street.

"There's your ol' pal, Fritzy," I said. "Pull up over there in front of his emporium. And damn it, let me do the talking for a change. Coax him out of town a ways."

Our man stood on his warehouse landing, a turkey-pomp manner about him.

"Hey, Fritz. Haven't seen you for a spell. Come on, get in. Take a little ride, have a little chat. Out yonder in the desert a ways, so our conversation won't be overheard."

He pressed his trousers down. "You two don't—you don't have a thing to say to me that can't be said right here. And if—and if you're looking for trouble—uh—I've got—*yes*, I've got a lot of friends here that will back me up." He turned to go back into his warehouse, his turkey feathers dragging.

Coot called up in a flat tone, "*Fritz!* Sometimes Narlow talks too damn much. What he really meant to say was, 'Fritz, get your frilly-dilly ass in this truck *right now*. Sidesaddle Sally, you've got five seconds."

Fritz consulted his pocket watch. Coot said, "*Four.*"

Fritz straightened his speckled gold-on-dark-blue bow tie, pressed down his trousers with his chubby soft hands. "Oh, all right. But I've got to be back here in half an hour to help Manny close up shop."

I said, "*No problema*, Fritzy. Come on down."

He came down the stairs, got in the seat between Coot and me. We drove south of town five miles.

Fritz said, "I told you I had to be back in a half-hour. We've already been gone twenty minutes. Turn this damn thing around and take me back to town."

"Shut up, you damn pimp," Coot barked.

"I am *not* a pimp. And where did you hear about that false charge? It is *false* and—"

Coot jabbed his elbow in Fritz's gut. "You being Odessa's prize pimp is all over town, heard about it in a saloon. I said *shut up*. If you don't, I'll stop this truck *right now*. Shut your goddamn ass up real permanent-like. *That's* a promise, pimple-princess."

"Well, I, uh . . ."

"Fritz," I said, "best listen to your partner. Or did you forget that Coot's your partner? Coot, turn off to the right past that big flowering yucca. Follow that cow trail that leads off to the west a ways."

Coot pulled in behind a heavy mesquite mound, killed the engine.

I said, "Fritz, the three of us have us a little conundrum we need to work—"

"We have a what?"

"A conundrum—a quandary. You know, a dilemma. An impasse. Aw, hell, Fritz, we've got a problem. Coot and I've been experiencing a lot of strange goings-on lately. Boulders rolling down a hill west of Tornillo a few years back for no apparent reason."

Fritz shook his long curly locks. "That—that holds no interest for me. I insist that you take me—"

"And I suppose you wouldn't have any interest in a yellow-headed giant German-Comanche from Odessa who paid Coot a visit at the spring south of Van Horn. Did you know that ol' Coot bit that giant bastard's thumb clean off? Then on the way out of Tornillo a couple of days ago, two big stout Germans and two Mexican henchmen tried to do us in. Like to killed ol' Coot, and would have, too, had it not been for my expert marksmanship. I was successful in killing both of the Mexicans, but Coot shot only one of the Germans."

"I—I don't know anything—"

"Then, a while back, there's the four novice Mexican highway-men who were waiting in ambush just south of here at the San Pablo river crossing. They proved to be inexperienced in the highway robbery business, so we didn't kill any of those *sombrero*-wearing hombres. No sirree! I just shot every damn one of them in the foot, sent them packing to Mexico."

Fritz squirmed, stammered, "What—what's that got to do with me? Come on, please take me back to—"

Coot snapped, "You pimping, diddless bastard. Narlow, quit wasting time. Shoot this goddamn skunk. Leave him out here for the buzzards."

Coot's eyes were down to pinpoints, working up a pizen-mean. He bolted out of the Reo, came around to my side of the truck, grabbed Fritz by the collar, dragged him over me, out through the truck window. "*Delivery boys*, huh? We're just delivery boys. I'll 'delivery boy' your fat ass, you cocktail goddamn waitress."

"Gentlemen. *Gentlemen*," I said, stepping out of the Reo.

Fritz sat cross-legged in the dirt where Coot tossed him, still as a birddog on point.

"Make yourself comfortable, Fritzy," I said, smiling down at him. "You know, Fritzy, Coot and I are easy-going sorta fellows. *Se la vie! Lais sez faire,* all that rot. But the threats on our lives have gained momentum and size like a snow-ball rolling downhill.

"Now here we are, the three of us, gloomy, suspicious, a shadowy sorta feeling between us. We understand you were suspicious of us when you learned we weren't taking our share of the delivery fee. Now, may I ask you, is that a good commentary on your character? Now, there you are, sitting in the dust and gravel. Coot with a 'dare-you-to-blink' scowl on his otherwise handsome face, and me, in the untenable position as an arbitrator between the former factions of our once-friendly alliance. You planned, spun into action a most wicked, nefarious plot to dispose of us, your once erstwhile *amigos*, confidants, partners.

To be concise and forsaking rhetorical verbosity in *toto*, let me simply say—"

"For chrissake, Narlow! Shut the shit up. For the past half-hour, you've forsaken everything but simplicity. Tell this mawdicking, kraut-breasted son-of-a-bitch what needs to be said. That this bastard has been trying to kill us. Get on with it!"

Fritz kept dabbing at his bleeding brow with his white hanky. I thought, Fritz, if you don't stop that sissy dabbing with your silk hanky, you won't have any blood to bleed, a brow to priss at, a prick to piss with, only a white hanky poking out of your ass.

"Well, Fritzy, you heard the man," I said. "Best start talking while you're still drawing oxygen. By the look in Coot's narrow eye, and the way he's rubbing those big ol' knuckles, I'd say you have under five seconds to start explaining. You're not the mastermind behind this. Who is?"

"I can't—*I mean*—I don't know who—*I mean*, I don't what you're talking about, Narlow. I swear if I—"

"You can deny it all you want," I said, "or call it a T-bone steak if you like, but no matter how thin you slice it, Fritzy, it's all baloney."

Coot grabbed Fritz up by his bow tie, lifted him off the ground, his sledge-hammer fist cocked, ready to turn ol' Fritz's lights down real low. His brown eyes, wild, bulging, blinking with fear, lost all color, only the white showing.

"Mr. Boldt. *Please.* Settle down. I have an idea I want you both to consider."

Coot pushed him down, uncocked his fist, but maintained his grip on Fritz's starched collar and blue and gold polkadoted bow tie.

"Now then, Fritzy, I suppose if you say you can't talk, I guess you can't, or won't. But, I've got an idea for you, an idea that will get you out of this little pickle, and satisfy me and Coot all at the same time."

Coot was losing patience. He scrambled Fritz, knocking him facedown in the gravel, his arms crucified. The sun was down, the high desert cooling fast.

I stepped to the bed of the Reo and came back. "Now, Fritzy, get on your feet. Here, grab a tight grip on these spanking-brand-new posthole diggers. I want you to dig us a hole right there. Right where you're standing. If you please, *deep*, two feet wide."

"I'll dig you a hole to China if you want it, Narlow, but that doesn't mean I'm talking. Those Germans play rough, they'll kill me for sure."

"*Germans?* You have German friends? *Oh my.* They do play rough, play marbles for keepers. *Get digging.*"

241

A tell-tail shine of wet began to form in Fritz's lower eyelids. I thought he'd break, but he blinked it away.

"Well, Fritzy, if you're not going to tell us who the mastermind is, then get with it! Get yourself on the blister-end of those posthole diggers and commence to begin digging. Sun'll be down soon. Start digging. *Now*."

After fifteen minutes, Fritz'd made his way laboriously through the top sward of dry sand and gravel. The metal spades of the diggers struck rock and gravel, producing more clatter and sparks than results. I lit a coal oil lantern.

As the hole deepened, he had to squat, then forced down to his knees, trying to fill the opposing blades of the diggers, bring them up before they lost their trifling load. It was slow, hard going. Two hours passed.

"Okay, Fritzy, take a breather. While you're relaxing, I think I'll step over here to the floorboard of the Coot's fine traveling apparatus, get my jug and take a little pull. *Ahh—damn-nation.* That Straight American whisky is some kind of tasty. Want a swig, Coot?"

I handed him the jug. He grabbed it by the ring at the neck, swung it over his elbow, and took a long pull. Coot giggled his infectious way. "Narlow, what in the hell do you have in that pea brain of yours?"

Another half-hour, Fritz was tiring appreciably, sweat soaking his coat. He laid down on his stomach to reach the handles of the posthole diggers, his hands bleeding from open blood-blisters on the web of his hands. Coot and I were jawin', passing the jug, watching Fritzy claw at the gravel in lantern's yellow glow.

Fritz whined, "How much deeper, Narlow?"

"Let me have a look-see. Too dark down there. Coot, light that bull's eye lantern so I can check the depth of Fritzy's hole."

Coot brought the lantern, sucking on the jug.

I peered down. "Naw Fritzy, I believe you better take her on down the better part of a foot."

Fritz's snowflake butt was sticking up fat, his shirt tail pulled out of his britches, a goodly length of his crack showing in the yellow glow.

"You know, Coot, I always did enjoy the mellow bouquet of burning coal oil. Reminds me of my youth, and don't it go right-tasty with good whiskey."

I took the lantern to the hole. "Okay, Fritzy, I think that'll do. Too bad for you if it's not. Get up."

Fritz's face was a pool of dirty sweat, his nose dripping red. "Narlow, can we please just go on back to town?"

"*What?* And waste this perfectly good hole? No-siree-a'Bob'a-rhubarb-pie. *Get yourself in that hole.*"

"Get in there? *Why?* I'm not getting in that—"

Coot shoved him, shouted in his ear, "Get in that goddamn hole like he says. I'll put you in there head first, you limp sack of lily-livered cat shit."

Fritz fell, one foot in the hole. "*No.* For God's sake, no! *Please*, Narlow, don't do this to me! I'll—"

Coot yelled in his ear, "I'll see your bones vitrify in hell, if you don't tell us what we want to hear!"

Coot was on him with both boots, kicking, stuffing him in the hole. Fritz put his hands on the edge of the hole, set to boost himself out. Coot stomped down on his hands, screamed down at him, "You keep your goddamn hands *down*. I'll take an ax to them. You damn sissy Little Lord Fauntleroy pimping bitch."

Fritz stood in his hole with the top of his head barely clearing the ground, his eyes reflecting somewhat timorous. "Narlow, *please*. What are you doing, for god's sake? You can't just bury me alive. Are you?"

"Nay, nay. Do you think us barbaric? No, we're not going to bury you like an old hound dog's prized bone. But, I must apologize. Your hole is too deep."

I scooted gravel back into Fritz's hole, told him to tamp it down.

Coot grinned, then stepped back, cocked one boot back. "I'd kick your damn fancy-Dan head in, but Narlow's peaked my interest. Believe I'll take another pull on this jug, see how this plays out."

"Fritzy, just hold your arms straight down at your sides. If you don't, ol' Coot's liable to drop-kick your teeth through your ear-balls." I pushed sand and gravel in and around Fritz, got him buried up to his ears. He started crying. I stomped the loose sand and gravel down tight.

I got down on one knee, took a swig. "Fritz, quit your boohooing. Why don't you turn yourself into a skink, slither right of that hole."

"A—a skink?"

"Yeah, you know—one of those smooth-bodied lizards, short arms, just like yours, slippery as a watermelon seed. You could pop yourself right out of there."

Coot started for the truck. "Come on, let's go."

"*Go?* Go where? Narlow, you're not going to leave me out here all by myself, are you?"

"All by yourself? *Oh, my.* Fritzy, what do you take us for? Inelegant, ignoble clods? With you in your tight cocoon, me 'n ol' Coot can go on about our business, come back out here every night or so to check on your progress, see if you're ready for that little chat."

"Narlow, for the love of god-almighty, think about what you are—"

Coot kicked a wad of grit and gravel in Fritz's face. "Come on, let's go."

Fritz's expression assumed a smirking "ya-ya" appearance, closing his brown eyes, blinking them, pursing his lips. The bastard thought he'd out-foxed us, thought he had the upper hand. His head seemed to be perched out here on the desert floor, enjoying the cool air and lantern light.

I looked down at Fritz. "Got any 'next-of' you want notified?"

"Next-of what?"

"Next of kin. You know, brothers, sisters, your mama, maybe an uncle, a favorite aunt back in Berlin, old boyfriend maybe?"

"*Hell, no.* Know why? I'm not talking! Not now, not tomorrow, the next day, or the next. You think you'll scare me into talking, but you won't let anything happen to me. The dead don't talk."

We drove off in the dark, Fritz's words following us in the night sky, "*You sons-a-bitches!*"

39

Are You Lonesome Tonight?

It was dark by the time we got back out to visit Fritz. As we approached the yucca I'd used for a marker the day before, Coot sped up and churned the Reo over a low hill, stopped, backed around, the headlamps flashing over the dark sky above Fritz.

We drove back down the road to the yucca. Coot gunned the Reo on past, stopped, turned, our lights again sweeping yellow over Fritz's dugout. As we came up to the yucca, Coot slowed to a crawl, again passing the turnoff. "Reckon that will give Fritz a little fright?"

A horrified scream in the cold night air, "Over here! Narlow, over here. *I'm over here.*"

Coot and I took turns on Fritz. Coot threatening, me smooth talking. But he didn't budge, just promising us a bigger cut of the million dollars. "Hell, you can have all of it!"

When he cried that we could work something out, Coot bellered, "You'll be working my boot out of your teeth if you don't start talking!"

Fritz had visitors during the night and following day—said coyotes were close by, a badger warted him, "a damn cow and her calf about licked my face off." When he asked for water, I teased, "No talkee, *no agua*."

The next evening we left Socorro a little earlier, stopped at the bottom of an *arroyo*, and loaded the Reo down with the biggest boulders we could lift. River rocks, round, smooth. Just at sundown, we turned off the road at the yucca, around the mesquite mound, and damned if Coot didn't drive that Reo astraddle of Fritz's head, skidded to a halt just passed him. Fritz must have been dozing. We heard him scream as we passed over.

I strolled over to him. "Top of the evening to you, Beelzebub! Got a load of boulders for you. Circle 'em all around you, snuggle 'em real close to your pumpkin head. Whew, Beelzebub, you're wafting pretty strong, know that?"

We started setting the boulders around Fritz's head in a circle twelve feet across.

"Mr. Wolf and Miss Coyote might try digging you out of your cocoon. Can't have that, huh? These boulders will keep them at bay—for a spell. But don't worry yourself none, we'll be back in a couple of days."

"Narlow, please—*please*. What good will those rocks do me after I'm dead? They'll just bite my head off—"

"You know what, Fritzy? Coot pointed out something that makes no sense—no sense at all—you're committing suicide in self-defense. Looky what else Coot thought of. What's this, Fritzy?"

"A wooden bucket."

"With a what?" I asked.

"With a barbed-wire bail."

"A wide-mouth, five-gallon wooden bucket to fit over your head, a barbed wire bail for you to hold the bucket on your head by biting the wire with your teeth, *real* tight-like."

"No! You can't do—"

I slammed the bucked down on his head. "Best open your mouth, shithead. Grab that barbed wire. *Got it*? Good. See you in a couple of nights."

245

His muffled screams followed me back to the Reo. I slumped on the hard seat, staring blank through the windshield into the dark. My mind, racing like the driver wheels on a locomotive.

Coot started to reached for the gear lever, but I raised my hand. This postholing scheme was supposed to get Fritz to talk. It wasn't working. Why was he willing to die in that stinking hole? All he had to do was talk. Why die for certain, when a choice was offered? I'd missed something here. Something critical.

"Aw, shit," I said as I grabbed the canteen and stepped out. "Better give him some water or he'll never make it."

I kicked Fritz's bucket. "Let go of the barbed wire, *now*."

I kicked the bucket aside, crammed the canteen in his mouth. "Here, asshole—take a long drink. Got to last you a spell, so best drink deep."

Fritz sucked down the half-gallon canteen, I slammed the bucket back down on his swollen head. "Get a grip. Best get a *firm* grip, Fritzy lass."

40

My Bucket

Two mornings later, I walked up to Fritz. Heard not a sound. I glanced up at the sun, admiring the ring it was sporting around its circumference. Seemed that ring had been following me all my days, then just recently, I read where the ring was formed by ice crystals, but I didn't know so much about that. Papa's forbears sure didn't put much stock in such scientific hogwash, and my personal experiences with that ring around the sun told me better.

"Hey, Nicodemus! Hey, Fritz, wake up. I want to describe what you'll see when I take your bucket off. A blighted, ominous sky. Sun has a ring around it, like a circular rainbow. The Pale Eye on my papa's side came out of Louisiana, his mama a swamp medicine-woman healer. Those folks believed that a ring around the sun foretold floods, impending death, all manner of mayhem. It's ominous, I tell you, *ominous!* Reminds me of the time long ago when my pal Coot and I rented a skiff from an old man down at Lajitas on the Rio, Big Bend country. Old man had a dimwit helper who advised his master not to rent that beat-up old skiff to us. Kept chanting, 'Ring around the sun. Ring around the sun. Floods a'coming. Ring around the sun. Floods a'coming.' Sure wish that old man had heeded that dimwit's advice. That night, me and ol' Coot got ourselves all tangled up in the skirts of the mama of all floods. There we were in the middle of Santa Elena Canyon, all our gear lost, food, the old man's skiff, our jug, *everything* gone. Tried to walk out when the water got down to knee deep, but the swift water made the riverbed a sea of quicksand. Bog a saddle blanket, it would. Dern near starved to death, had to wait ten damn days for the flood to recede so we could walk the bank out of that steep-walled canyon. We learned to pay attention to the ring-around-the-sun, the chant of that dimwit idiot. You best do the same, *you dumb sonofabitch!*"

"Wa-wah, Narwo—wa-wah . . ."

"Want wa-wah, huh? Want Narwo to get you some wa-wah? What'd you do with that half-gallon of water I gave you two days ago? Didn't save a damn drop. Just stood there and peed it all out. Mighty wasteful of you, Fritzy."

"Nee' wa-wah, Narwo. *Yeow.* They're af'er me. Wa-wah . . . oooh, *yeow. Aiiiii.* Lord save me . . . *Yeow* . . . got me . . . ."

"Acting kinda queer this morning, *amigo.* Know that? Bet you don't even know your own damn-fool name. Somebody pilfer your rudder, Fritzy?"

Silence.

"Hey, you in the bucket! I'm talking to you, goddamn it. What's your name?"

"Fwitz."

"Fwitz? Fwitz, who?"

"Fwitz Hen-Shit."

I laughed. "Fwitz Hen-Shit? *Hot-dang.* A few days ago your name was Fritz Hans-Smidt, now you tell me it's Fwitz Hen-Shit. Okay, Fwitz Hen-Shit, I just wanted to be sure it was you. Thought maybe somebody traded you out of your bucket."

Fritz's wooden bucket showed a lot of nail scratching by his nightly visitors.

"Fritzy, let go of your wire bale." I yanked Fritz's bucket off. "*Look up there!* This is your last damn opportunity. That frozen ring up there—up there circling around the sun in that dreaded—that dreaded sky serves as your last goddamn warning. You kraut-breathed son-of-a-bitch. Goddamn it, *start talking.*"

The bright sun had Fritz's blinking like a mule in a hailstorm. "Oh, pwease. Wa-tah. I need wa-tah."

"*Jeez-amighty*, Fritzy. You look like a *piñata* that's been beat with a tire iron. *Whew-ee.* All cut up, greasy, dirty, ulcerated. If your mama could see you now, mouth all red-puckered, she'd likely think you've been sucking on cherry licorice. Your mouth's kinda cloven, sorta vulval, if you know what I mean."

I uncorked the canteen, poured half of it on his head. He lapped up what he could, blood and all, then I let him drink what remained.

"Oh, tank you, Narlow, tank you. And, yes—yes— but pwease, more wa-tah. Worms—*wattlesnakes, and* "

"*Wattlesnakes?* Must have great big wattlers, huh?"

"Yes! Somethin' got . . . God, they're aftah me. For god's sake. On my back—arghhh! Aiiii! Scop-ions *on my nuts. Squeezing.* Squeezing my pwune—crawling around down there, dwiving me *insane!*"

"*Uh-oh.* Sounds like that awful old claustrophobic bug done bit ol' Fritzy. Warned you about that. *Whew.* You're getting a little ripe. Forget to wash your privates this morning, Fritzy? Know what you remind me of? Martha's brother, Lazarus in the Good Book. Remember Martha telling the Lord that Lazarus had been dead four-days, and 'he stinketh'? *Ha!* That's my most favoritist King James verse of all."

I dribbled the few remaining drops of water in the canteen on the ground in front of him. "Now where were we?"

"Wa-tah—Narwo, wa-tah. . .'"

"Speak up, Mr. Hen-Shit. You're babbling again. Can't understand a damn word you're saying."

I went back to the truck and retrieved another canteen, let him drink half of it.

"Oh, tank you, Narlow! Tank you, tank you. Coyotes all night wong. All night wong. Hun-wreds. *Mil-yuns!* Scwatchin', pawin' at me, my woodun buck—"

"Shut the shit up! I don't give a flying shit about what's pawing at you and your wooden bucket. I came back out for one damn reason. To hear who's behind all this crap. Start confessing, *now.*"

"*Pwease.* Get a shobel. Dig me out. More wa-tah. Coyotes all night and—"

"You're not listening, you goddamn—"

"*Coot.* Whuur's Coot? He's gnot here? *He's gnot . . . here.* That's good, *weel good.* That's smart, Narwo. Weel smart. Dig me gout—dig me gout of here. Coot's gnot here. You and me, we're fweinds," his voice a clicking, rasping croak.

"Yeah, Fritzy, we're real *amigos*. I don't dare let Coot come out here. He's real sore at you, Fritzy. Know why?"

"No, I—mo wa-tah—"

"Cut the more water crap! You ain't gettin' any more."

I kicked a rock, my face flushed redder than Fritz's. "I came out here. You mother—. By myself. For one damn reason. Warn you. Your thread of life is getting *mighty damn thin*. The only thing separating you from an eternity spent in your stand-up grave is *me. Me*, goddamn it! *Me!* You lying Kaiser-boot-licking son-of-a-bitch. I'm leaving. *Right now*. Not coming back. By god-almighty damn. What'll it be? *Answer me. Right now!*"

His brown eyes were blinking fast. I needed to kick something—*anything*. I plopped down on the bucket, gave him more water.

"So glad Coot's not here. He scares me to death. You'll see my pwan will . . . ."

The hopelessness in his coffee-brown eyes told me all I needed to know. He was beaten. Or was it me? I sat looking at him as he kept clicking and clacking words. I gambled, Fritz called my bluff, aced me with an empty hand. Beat me. He was a sad, hopeless, misguided godless coward son-of-a-bitch, but he'd proven impossible to break. *Me*, with all the cards.

Good God Almighty. I thought if I came out here by myself, that he might trust me. I'd dig him up after he told me what I wanted to know. Shouldn't have come out here. Bluff failed, a bluff I couldn't take back.

Fritz's rasping voice began to register again, his voice clearing a little from the water. ". . . and tank you for coming by yourself. Just bewieve me when I say you will be rich—"

"*Look up there*, you deaf bastard! See that ring around the sun beginning to disappear? That's just like your chances if you don't start talking. When that ring disappears. In less than a minute. You are one dead son-of-a-bitch. You hear me! One dead *son-of-a-bitch!*"

"We'll boff be wich, you'll see, and—"

I was shaking. Picked up the bucket, fumbled it on the rocks. Grabbed it up, slammed it down on his head for the final time.

"Okay, Fritz, you win. You beat me, fair and square. I lose. But I'd suggest you keep your teeth clamped down *real* tight on that rusty barbed wire." I bent over, thumped his bucket with something hard, heavy in my hand. "Just wait, *you son-of-a-bitch*. Wait until your parched tongue lets loose of that barbed wire bale and sticks to the *blistering hinges of hell*."

249

I kicked his bucket, still shaking, turned, began picking my way clear of the rocks.

I heard his muffled scream from under the bucket, "Pwease! Narwo, okay, I'll twalk. I sweah. Come back—*pwease*. I'll tell you. *Come back*. Pwease, Narlow. *Pwease*. I sweah I'll twalk."

Lying bastard. I turned, looking back at the coyote shit scattered among the boulders with the bucket in the middle, covering what was left of a man who had tried so many times to kill me and Coot. *To hell with the bastard. Let him rot with his tongue stuck to hell's gate.* I stood with my boot on a boulder, knowing I'd shoot him if I lifted that bucket one more time. I couldn't trust myself. I needed to get the hell away from him. I glanced up. The crystal ring around the sun had vanished, disappeared in the harsh blue of eternity.

I squatted, yanked the bucket up with my left hand. My Schofield in my right, hammer cocked. I looked at that ancient piece of heavy iron, wondering how the hell it got in my hand. Fritz's eyes were crossed, fixed on the dark hole at the barrel-end of my Schofield.

I smiled. "Fritz, take a second to look up at your vanished ring around the sun. Just like you, if you don't start talking. You're dead in a scant two seconds."

41

The Day After the Untimely Passing of Fwitz Hen-Shit

Coot and I kicked around the next day. I caught him watching me. "Narlow, you all right? Never known you to be so quiet. You haven't said two words all day. This thing is weighing pretty heavy on you, isn't it?"

"Naw, I'm all right. Let's go down to the Dime Box, let you buy me a drink. Spending your money always cheers me up."

Late afternoon of the second day after my last visit with Fritz, I was sunning myself, napping on a park bench. Coot came out, sat on the bench across the walkway. "You awake?"

"Am now."

"Reckon it's time to check on that kraut-head? You need to know something before we go back out there. This is the last damn chance we're giving that bastard. If he still won't talk, we're going to dig him up, tie a rope around his neck, drag his stinking hide down to the Rio. We'll see if I can't force enough muddy silt down his gullet to make him puke river water and everything he knows. I've a good mind to just go on out there right now and—"

"Coot, ol' Fritz's ring around the sun up and melted on him."

"What the hell is that supposed to mean?"

I sat up. "Fritz is dead."

"*Dead? Fritz is dead?*" He stood in front of me, bent over gazing in my eyes for the truth. He stood erect, went back to his bench. Studied me for a minute, his brow furrowed like a mile-deep *arroyo*. "*Dead?* How do you know that? Go back out there without me?"

"Yep."

"When?" he asked.

"Two mornings ago."

"Dead. How? Coyotes get him?"

"Nope."

"Then how?"

"Shot him."

"Shot him?"

"Shot him."

"Shot him how?

"Shot him with my Schofield."

Coot gazed down the row of benches to the side door of our hotel. "Shot him. Telling me you shot him?"

"Yep, shot him."

"Shot him with your damned old Schofield."

He walked around me in a wide circle, trying to get a handle on it all. "Why'd you do it?"

"Why you reckon?"

"Wouldn't talk?"

"Yep. Wouldn't talk. You can add another man to my killing list."

"Did you bury him?"

"Already buried."

We grinned at each other across the boardwalk.

"Died with his boots on? Well, kiss my ass. Fritz finally did something right. Something almost honorable." Coot took off his Stetson, wiped his brow, flipped his hat round and round in a circle on a finger, wiped the headband with his bandana, jammed it down to his ears, sat in a pensive mood for a minute, jumped to his feet. "Well, kiss my white ass."

We were quiet for a spell. Coot's eyes narrowed. He gave me the once over, as if for the first time in all our years. Shook his head, a thin smile pasted over his face, started chuckling. I got to belly-laughing at that mental image. About laughed ourselves sick. Fritz dying seemed to wash the stress away. Before my confession about killing Fritz, Coot and I'd planned to give Fritz one more chance, then head southwest to San Augustin Plain, camp, do a little deer hunting like we did when we were boys.

Coot snickered. "Let's go over to the Dime Box and have a beer. I'm buying."

We had a couple of beers, then switched to whiskey. We'd make a night of it.

Coot leaned his back against the saloon's bar, his elbows resting on the edge. "So, how did you get back out to Fritz's dug-out? You didn't take the Reo. You saying you hoofed it all the way out there?"

"Nope. Borrowed Travis Turner's truck.

"So, tell me. What happened out there."

I sighed, gulped hard. My nerves shattered. "Not much to tell. You were right about that worthless bastard. But the thought of him out there all those horrifying days and nights, thirsty, scared shitless. I gave him a sip of water. Just a drop, thinking the taste would coax him into talking. It damn near worked. Oh, how he relished that tiny sip. You'd think he was sipping single-malt Scotch. The expression on his blistered face, lips. God, he looked red-awful, stunk to high heaven.

"*He would not talk*. Suddenly, it was me doing the pleading. I slammed the bucket back down on his head, yelled, '*See you in hell*,' and walked back to Travis' truck. Got in, sat there a few of minutes, waiting for Fritz to scream out. But he didn't. I drove the truck over the first hill, left it, sneaked around on the other side, tiptoed up behind him, thinking he would cry out any second.

"But he didn't. Every now and again, he'd sniff, clear his throat, hawk, try to spit through the barbed wire, his mouth brittle, ladle-dry. I stood there, beaten. I knew he wouldn't talk, now or ever. I pulled out my Schofield, cocked the hammer.

Shot through the bottom. The bottom of that goddamn wooden bucket. Cocked that goddamn revolver again. Shot that goddamn wooden bucket two more times. Two more times to be certain. The rocks, my boots, pants, the lip of the bucket. Everything splotched, dotted red, strangely reminded me of his goddamn polka-dot bow tie. God, what a bloody mess."

I sighed, grimaced. "He's dead, Coot. *Real* dead. Another man added to my list."

He sat on a barstool, stood, then sat. "Narlow, I—well, I want you to know I don't blame you. Not a damn bit. Bastard deserved it. But I know how hard this whole thing has been on you. Leaving him out there to suffer, waiting for that pack of coyotes. That's no way to go out for *any* man. Come to think of it, Fritz didn't need to talk. We already knew *damn well* he was in cahoots with the Germans. Forget it. Not worth the bother."

I stood, thinking it sacrilegious, maybe blasphemous, to sit while talking about a man's death, a death I caused, then realized that was about the stupidest idea I ever came up with. Plopped back down, my boots on the top rung of the bar stool, my arms drooping long between my legs, both hands holding my bar glass. "I don't think I can forget it—*ever*. Coot, this shit is making me mean. Cruel as a mama wolf with a passel of starving pups to feed. My breath tastes brittle, like sulfur, copper-soaked-kerosene. Flesh, cold as iron ice. When I look in a mirror to shave, my eyes refuse to look at themselves. They've gone numb. *Numb* cold. Exactly what I see when I look through them. Like I'm looking at life from somewhere behind me. I'm in that vision, but I'm not the one doing the looking. Understand what I'm trying to say?"

"No, can't say as I do. Then I never understand half of what you ever had to say."

"Well anyway, I'm quitting this crap. I read the other day about a man on the loose in Boston, killed a bunch of women, strangled them. Senseless, in cold blood. Know who he reminds me of? *Me.* I've lost count how many men I've killed in cold blood, point blank, cold-goddamn-hate-my-guts blood. Now, I can add Fritz to my list. I keep thinking about that twelve-year-old boy back in Carichic. That boy, Juanito. He's killed. Saw it in his eyes. He's killed and he's seen more killing in his short lifespan than a hundred of me. Yet he haunts me to this day. And my damn old mushroom is driving me nuts again. Everyday, *all night*, it flashes red at me, flashing, 'Eat at Joe's.'"

"Damn it, Narlow, there won't be any more killing. And if there is, *I'll do it.*

Your imagination is running away with you. You're beat down. Physically, mentally. We need to change the way we're doing things. Change our routine. We'll be needing a new source of Mausers. I'll find a source in San Antonio. Maybe New Orleans. That would cheer you up, wouldn't it? Change of scenery. How does that—"

"Damn it, I said I *quit*. You deaf? What I sorely need, and aim to have, is my little darlin' Zara. I didn't think I'd ever miss her as much as I do right this minute. We've been married over twenty years now. Can you believe that? Twenty years."

The Dime Box was Socorro's favorite watering hole, "The Dime," as the locals reverently referred to it. We closed the place up, hell of an evening that lasted 'til dawn. Coot gambled all-night, busted the whole damn town. I drank, danced the night away with an old blister, Marisalinda Lou Parish, by name. She was a regular, a hanger-on at that dusty ol' tawdry gin mill. I swear that old hide's predacious eyes threw me a kiss when they met mine across that dingy saloon floor. The gal had the face of a Boston terrier, bulging nose, caved-in manner about her forehead, bringing to mind the homeliness of a plowed field. But—but she had a certain comeliness about her, rather dulcified, yet mawkish like a warm beer. The Dime's chamber music trio wasn't much at playing the honky-tonk two-step, but with Coot's encouragement in the form of twenty dollar gold pieces, the threesome livened up and got in the swing and mood of the evening.

Marisalinda Lou kept drooling, swooning, pulling at me. I had a dickens of a time convincing her that I was only interested in a tango partner. "Marisalinda Lou, I'm a married man and—"

"Well, shoot, Narlow-sugar, I was a married woman myself—once, on three different occasions. That didn't slow me down even half a notch. Why would being married put the brakes on a man like you? Saying 'I do' blind you or something? Lose your desire for a gal like me?" She pulled at me, grabbed at me, rubbed them things all over me, tugged me by the cheeks of my ass, all the while assuring me she'd long had her eye on me, how much she loved me. I even quoted George Washington, "More permanent and genuine happiness is to be found in the sequestered walks of connubial life than in the giddy rounds of promiscuous pleasure."

Marisalinda Lou's learned comment was, "Is that so? Well, I don't know so much about all that," and went right back to her reach, pull, rub, grind.

At dawn, a velvet bar of white light pierced the saloon through its batwing doors, dust dancing in the delicate, dry ray. I made it out to the boardwalk, but Marisalinda Lou gave it one more try. Coot, waiting in the Reo, me, trying to disentangle myself from Marisalinda Lou, a gal dead-set on keeping me raveled and tangled.

"Come on, Narlow, honey, you're not going anywhere special. I've told you how much I love you," she swooned, batted her shady-greens. "I'll make you glad you went home with me, honey bun—*promise*. Come on home, give your darlin' some sugar. Want to?"

"Lordy, Marisalinda Lou, I'd swap my prize horse and dog for a gal like you, but—"

"But?" she asked smiling up at me.

"But—but, Marisalinda Lou, like I said—"

"That's all right, honey. I understand," she said, smoothing her cotton, feed-sack-dress, flicking a bit of lint off my lapel. "You can't help how you don't feel, and you sure can't make your heart beat what it don't."

Now, *that* was a scholarly thing to say.

I got in the Reo. Coot laughed. "Damn, Narlow, ol' Marisalinda Lou was sure putting the heavy-hurry on you. One time when she had you pinned against the bar, I'd bet the house she was going to, as they say, 'have her way with you,' right there if front of me and the boys."

"Shut up and drive."

❂❂❂

The next morning was a spilled-milk-mist of a day, not suitable for traveling. Then came Thursday morning, we gassed-up, headed south out of town. For whatever reason, Coot drove off the road at the yucca, pulled the Reo around the mesquite mound.

There it was—Fritz's tomb. An eight-foot-high mound of rocks and boulders, the posthole diggers running horizontal through them near the top.

"God-amighty, Narlow. Fritz's tomb is a real shrine isn't it? Graven. You stacked those boulders up there as a tribute to Fritz Hans-Smidt? Hell, you even stuck his posthole diggers in there to form the Cross of Calvary. If that don't beat all. I damn sure would have shot that turd, but damned if I would have gone to the bother to build him a shrine. Why'd you go to all that trouble for that prissy bastard?"

"Hell, I don't know. Maybe I figured we'd leave the day after I told you I shot Fritz. You'd stop here just like you did right now. And without this shrine, you'd soon figure it out. You'd see nothing but the boulders thrown back, Fritz's empty hole, you'd turn to me and ask, 'Narlow, you didn't' kill Fritz, did you?'"

255

"Well, did you?" Coot asked.

"No."

"You didn't?"

"No."

"You didn't shoot Fritz like you said?"

"No, I didn't shoot Fritz like I said."

"You didn't pull out your Schofield, shoot him through that wooden bucket. Splattering blood all over the place?"

"Nope, no shooting. No blood."

"You dug him up, let him go after all the time we wasted. And you didn't learn a damn thing from him?"

"I dug him up, let him go after all that time, but our time wasn't wasted. He told me who he was in cahoots with, why he thought he deserved Rodolfo's entire million dollars, why he wouldn't talk."

"Why did you wait until now to tell me this?"

"Made Fritz a promise. *One* promise. A promise he knew I'd keep. I swore an oath on Papa's soul before Fritz would spill the kraut. I promised him a forty-eight hour head start before telling you he was still alive. Gave him my word, even though his word isn't worth a tinker's damn."

Coot beat on the steering wheel. "But, hell's bells, Narlow. You gave him what? Seventy-two hours, when you start counting back. Why did he want a head start?"

"Why you suppose?"

"Guess he thought I'd hunt him down."

"That's right, Coot. Right as spring rain. His only concern, from the *very beginning*, was his fear of talking, spilling the beans, then you'd shoot him, drown him, beat him to death. He told me that if it had only been him and me, and you weren't in the picture, that he would have told me what I wanted to know the very first night we were out here. Even before he dug that hole. He was scared to death, but figured that as long as he didn't talk, you wouldn't kill him. I got to figuring as much, and that's why I came out here by myself. I had to work every angle, and you were a kink I had to work around. And I was right. He did indeed, 'spill the kraut.' I tell you Coot, Fritz had the most cravenly look in his eyes. The epitome of abject fear. Yet he would not talk. *Damn.* This won't make a bit of sense to you, Coot, but if I hadn't been in that plaster-of-Paris body-cast all that time, I would have *never* figured this out. *Never* made him dig that hole. *Never* dreamed that hole would break him down. It was just circumstance. Pure chance that brought the broth to a rolling boil."

We sat there in the truck looking at the pile of rocks. Me, admiring my handiwork, Coot gazing first at the shrine, then at me.

"Well, Narlow, you said Fritz spilled the kraut. Are you going to fill me in on that conversation, or do you want to dig yourself a hole with Fritz's posthole diggers?"

I laughed. "Naw, believe I'll pass. When I got back out here, Fritz was in bad shape. You think he looked bad when you last saw him, Jeez-amighty, his head was swollen up like an over-ripe melon, blistered, cankered, lips split to his chin, tongue swollen, bleeding, torn all the hell from the barbed wire. He got himself in a real nest of tarantulas with the Germans. As we've known all along, the Kaiser figured if he could keep Uncle Sam's attention on what was going on south of the border, that would keep us out of his business of trying to take over Europe. Then news leaked out that the British had intercepted a wire transmission, the so-called Zimmermann Note, a wire from the German foreign secretary to the German minister in Mexico, indicating that Germany would renew its unrestricted submarine warfare, and would form an alliance with Mexico and Japan if the US declared war on Germany. As a reward, Mexico would get back Texas, New Mexico, Arizona, and California. That telegram was all Uncle Sam needed to get his long nose right in the Kaiser's crack. So what happened? We declared war on the krauts. While that was going on, the Germans really started cooking things up along our border with renewed earnest in a last-ditch effort to try to divert America's attention from Europe. That's when the Germans dangled the bait, Fritz snapped it up. The Germans wanted Mexico's revolution to have all the guns they needed. But not too many to sway the balance too far in one direction or another—some for the *Villistas*, some for the *Zapatistas*, some for the *Federales*."

Coot asked, "So, he first tried to kill us that day when the railroad was washed out. We drove the Reo down the river road and the boulder rolled down the hill. That was his first attempt?"

"I asked him about that. Said he had been waiting on that hill for two days when we showed up. Fritz knew about the rail being washed out on both sides of Tornillo, and that we were trucking in emergency supplies for the Mexican immigrants. If he'd been more experienced in such matters, he'd'a have killed us both,. He bought a 30-30 repeater from one of Socorro's drunks. Fritz didn't know it, but the rifle had a spent casing stuck in the chamber that would not eject. He said he had you square in his telescopic sights, squeezed the trigger, but nothing happened, just a click. He thought the bullet must have been a dud. In his excitement levering the Winchester, he pushed too hard on the boulder at his feet, it came rolling down the hill at us. He had no idea we were still down there after all those hours, but he was afraid to move for fear that we might be. You're blind at that distance, even with field glasses, but damn it, I should have recognized him. The way he neatly folded that gray tarpaulin he'd been hiding under, the frilly way he gazed around with his hands on his hips. Fritz realized he was not cut out for the ambush business, and that's the last time he tried anything himself. After that, the Germans called all the shots, where and how to do it, buying and paying off everyone that needed greasing.

"Remember when Fritz claimed he couldn't get any more Mausers from Germany? Well, he *could* and *did* get more Mausers, he just didn't sell them to us, but to the *Federales*. The Germans paid him $100,000 to temporarily drop us, ship the guns and ammunition to Mexico by way of Baja California. The temptation was too much for Fritz. He bit, the hook set. But he had to spend a lot more than what they paid him.

"He swears he had nothing to do with those four Mexicans who ambushed us at the San Pablo crossing."

"Bull shit!" Coot said. "If not him, then who? Why would he deny that?"

"Damned if I know. Didn't make sense that he'd deny that, but he would not change his story. Denied it bitterly. Tell you something else that he denied. He swears he never breathed a word about the Curtiss. You and I suspected that he told the *Rural*, or someone in the Mexican government, but Fritz adamantly denied that. Doesn't make sense, and like you said, if not Fritz, then who? Fritz admitted that he kept his German buddies informed about our every move, including our going into Mexico, but he swore he never told them about our having an airplane, or about us flying into Mexico, *ever*. He was afraid we would have to know it was him who was tipping off the Germans, who in turn, were feeding information to the Mexicans. He figured they would get us in Mexico, and they damned near did. We just lucked out with Rose's oleander scheme, the plague, Gregorio's rifle stash."

We sat there thinking back on all those months, all those years, wondering, kicking over rocks in our heads, trying to recall something we'd let slip, hadn't considered.

Coot's head went to the side. "You don't really think that someone else was after us on their own? Someone we know, maybe?"

"Doesn't make sense, I know, but we better put some thought to that prospect." I shook my head. "Naw, Fritz swore that while he knew Kohl and Mueller, he didn't have any idea that we were out of Mexico. Swears he didn't tip them off that we would be coming out of Tornillo that night. Fritz says the first thing he knew about them and the two Mexicans was when Kohl wired him from the El Paso train station, told him that Mueller was dead as well as one of the Mexicans, assumed the other was killed too. So, when Kohl telegrammed Fritz about what happened on the river road, Fritz wired Kohl right back, told him to meet him in Rincon, hide in the outfitter's store until he got there. Told him some lie that he had information that Kohl'd been waiting for. Kohl was the missing German who knew about Fritz's deception. Knew that if we got our hands on him that we'd make him talk. So he met Kohl in Rincon.

"Fritz was at that abandoned outfitter's store just hours before we showed up. You and I knew that German *had* to be in that feed store, but he wasn't. But, Kohl was *dead*, buried under the dirt and straw at our feet. Shot dead and buried by a fellow Kraut."

"And what about Yellow Bear?"

I laughed. "That's when Fritz damn near got his petticoat in a wringer. First, he buys Yellow Bear from a freak show in Odessa, takes him down to wait for you at the spring, goes back to Odessa, writes Zara an anonymous letter, warning her that I'd be dead in a week if I didn't quit running guns. He mailed the letter, *then* he gets thrown in the pokey for pimping girls for the Odessa oil-field roughnecks. He wired Rodolfo for the bail money, Rodolfo caught the train to Odessa, made his bail. Fritz feigned embarrassment, asked Rodolfo for his word that he won't mention anything about his pimping, which of course, Rodolfo being the gentleman he is, assured him that he would never mention it to us. But Fritz couldn't chance that. If Rodolfo even *mentioned* Odessa to us, then Zara gets the letter with an Odessa postmark, the cat would be scratching the bag. So what does he do? He breaks into our house and steals Zara's personal mail off the dining room table. That bastard had his web so tangled up, he couldn't find his own damn ass.

"By the time I had him convinced to talk, he was as much afraid of me as he has been afraid of you all along. And, he damn sure should have been, because I was some pissed-off gunrunner. My temper was not to be trusted. Fritz saw it in my eyes. The *exact* minute came when I made him look up and watch the disappearing ring around the sun. I'd already determined I would kill him just like I told you I did. I hate killing in cold blood, but shooting a wooden bucket kinda takes the edge off killing a man, having to look him in the face, his eyes, and all. Like shooting a man in the ear during a black downpour. I was through with Fritz, but I didn't want him dragging on my conscience any more."

I sighed. "So, Coot, that's Fritz's story, and I believed him. Every word of it."

We got out of the Reo. Coot yanked the posthole diggers out of Fritz's shrine. "Want to save these for a memento? Might miss them."

"Naw, I don't need anything to nudge my memory of what happened here."

Coot tossed the diggers aside, arched his back, took off his Stetson, wiped his brow, came back to me. "Then what happened? And, *damn it*, Narlow! We gotta find out who else was feeding the Germans information about our whereabouts."

"That's a mystery all right, but when Fritz finished his story, and I convinced myself that was all there was to it, I threw back the boulders, started the gagging chore of digging him out with my bare hands. Tried to use the posthole diggers. After getting down past Fritz's shoulders, I threw-up all over him and hit him hard on his shoulder with the diggers. He may have been bone dry, but he still had plenty of blood left to bleed. I didn't use the diggers again until I couldn't reach any further, then got enough dirt and gravel off his lower legs and feet that he could sorta move them. The gravel around him was wet with piss and all manner of bodily fluids. His arms and legs swollen double as were his hands, feet, neck, and head, everything about to split like an over-ripe pumpkin off the back of a produce wagon. I suppose that was caused by the lack of circulation all that time, standing there motionless. I finally got him uncovered and tried to drag him out, but it was no use. Pulling on him was like tugging on lemon meringue, his flesh, loose, hanging limp like chicken skin on a soup bone. Then I had to use the posthole diggers to dig the hole wide enough for me to get down in the hole with him, slowly lifting, doodling him out on the ground, getting his slime and putrification all over me. I puked until I gagged on my socks. I dragged him by his ankles over to the shade of the truck, gave him a little water. Bastard got piss and shit all over me lifting him into the back of the truck, and I damn near puked in his face before I could close the tailgate. His stench'd peel the scales off an armadillo. I gave him a little more water, then went to stacking up these boulders. I glanced over at Fritz, who was chugging down water from the canteen that I carelessly left too close to him. I thought about you, knew you would have given him a barrel of water, but I took it away from him before he busted a gut."

"Why'd you do that?"

I laughed. "Anyway, I finished making this shrine, thinking it would throw you off."

"Where is he now? Did he say where he's going?"

"Yeah, that's why he wanted forty-eight hours. I made him ride way in the back of the truck. Thank god the wind was out of the east that morning. But, the wind stopped momentarily, the stench grabbed me by the tonsils and ankles. Gag a maggot's only child. I gagged, threw-up on the dash and windshield of Tom' truck before I could get it stopped. I took off my shirt, wrapped it around my nose and face to hold off the stench.

"When we got back to town, I drove him around to the rear of his warehouse, dropped the tailgate to let him out. Weak as a newborn kitten, could barely stand, much less walk, but I wasn't about to touch him again if he *never* made it up those stairs. Told him I'd be back in an hour, that I'd take him to the train. I drove down to the river, soaked for half-an-hour, clothes and all, scrubbed my hands and arms with river sand until they bled, cleaned up Tom's truck, then went back for Fritz. He struggled down the back stairs, all duded-up in a blue-stripe suit, carrying only a leather valise. He'd washed up, must'a poured a quart of cheap cologne all over himself, but I could still get a vulgar whiff of him, like smelling shit through a piss glaze. I *still* can.

"Anyway, old friend, to answer your question about where Fritz is going, he's headed back home—to Germany. They promised to take him in, be one of their 'chosen golden hair few.' I told him not to go to the trouble. He asked why not. I told him that if he wanted to die, Coot Boldt'd be happy to oblige him, save him the expense of a long train and boat ride. He couldn't believe he'd be dead on arrival if he went back to Germany. How can one lying bastard think he can trust, and out-fox, another lying bastard? In a couple of days, he'll be onboard a Swedish freighter, crossing the waves from whence his ancestors came.

"When you think about it all, that's kinda poetic, ain't it, Coot?"

"Poetic? Yeah, if you say so." He wiped the sweatband of his Stetson, pulled it back down to his ears. "But who else is feeding information to those Germans?"

42

Gunrunning was a thing of the past. Zara and I relished our time together, spending many afternoons picnicking on the slopes of Mount Franklin as we did when we were courting back in 1893.

Rose accompanied Zara to St. Louis to attend a benefit in her honor. When they returned, Rose began spending long weeks with Tacho and Zoila at the Coal Mine. They rode the low foothills that lead to the base of the escarpment and up through a crack in the wall to the overhanging high, rough mountain overlook. Occasionally, they took along a pack mule for an overnight stay, riding south on the rim to the point where Capote Falls tumbles its beauty to the valley below, mist rising, casting a golden sphere in the desert air. From the height of the escarpment at the ranch headquarters, the view across the wide valley to the Rio and Los Fresnos' platter-shaped mountain was a rainbow's blend of breathtaking hues, patches of blue-green spiked cactus, stark-white caliche-salted dry lake beds, pink and orange clay spikes in all manner of shapes, Tacho's gray-green "atch" trees along dry arroyos and the Rio.

Rose often said, "This is a time of reflective growing for me." Heaven offers few settings more conducive.

Coot's mood soured every time she took the train east to the Van Horn depot where Tacho would meet her with horses to ride to his headquarters. Coot worried that she was spending too much time grinding on her childhood. "She should put all that crap behind her, forget about it, get on with her life. Next time she shows up, I want you to lay down the law to her, get her straightened out."

I laughed. "Lay the law down, get her straightened out. *Ha!* I'd pay top dollar to be present when some dirt clod takes *that* chore on. Your hand, Pedro, does all your farming, leaving you with not a damn thing to do but worrying about Rose. Why don't you get yourself down to the Coal Mine, ride a horse up Soldier's Peak with her, impress her with your cowboy outfit." That always burned him, poking fun at his flop-eared Stetson, his worn-out jeans, his love for horses and cattle.

"Cowboy outfit, your ass. Besides, she's not looking for company, least of all *my* company. If she was, she'd stay here, not go wandering off like she does.

I say she's still gnashing about her childhood, killing her no-count father. Bad habit."

Weeks on end without a word from Rose, then one day I'd walk in and find her and Zara in the kitchen. The two of them spent a couple of days shopping in El Paso, Juarez during these intermittent times of peace along the border. She'd then dedicate several days writing her "other family"—her old friends at Sacred Heart. Then, just as I became accustomed to having her around the house, she'd leave us a note saying she was returning to the Coal Mine, signing off, "See you soon! Love you both."

❂❂❂

Coot pulled the Reo under Big George's ivy and honeysuckle-covered awning. When we walked through the double front door, Big George was sporting a wagon-wide grin. "Well, look who's here. Mr. Montgomery and his sidekick, Mr. Boldt, the almost ex-husband of his almost ex-wife, Miss Geraldine."

Coot grinned. "What's got you tickled, you old black fart?"

"Oh, nothing really. Just that my missus had a visit from Miss Geraldine this morning. Asking questions, trying to get my wife to say that someone's been fooling around with Miss Rose." He laughed. "Maybe a *someone* like your partner, the Right Reverend Monsieur Narlow Montgomery."

"Is that so, Mr. Smith? Why me? Why not Coot. He's only sorta married. Besides, Zara's not traveling anymore."

Big George grinned. "Miss Geraldine claims this little romance has been going on since the very day Rose showed herself in El Paso."

"Is that so? Well, if that's what's going around, I better head off that nonsense before it takes root. Funny. Geraldine didn't have her stinger out yesterday when I helped her out of her Saxon Six Tourer, took her hand on the sidewalk, walked her through my office to the Paso del Norte's lobby. Then three hours later, steadying her as she climbed back in that beast of an automobile. She'd complained about her back, said she had an appointment with a chiropractor on the mezzanine floor. She was dern sure hurting, but not enough to keep her from bragging that she paid $785 cash money for her Saxon Six." Coot and Big George laughed when I grinned, added, "I'll think of something to get her off this rumor mongering."

Next morning before sun, I crossed the street to Geraldine's yard, all dressed up in my pajamas, housecoat, and house slippers. I stationed myself behind her geraniums close to her front porch—within easy sight of the bottle the milkman left earlier.

On schedule, ye ol' erstwhile damsel came out in her slippers and silver, silk house robe, leaned over, peered across the street in the dim light at my west-facing veranda. Spying nothing, she picked up her milk bottle, turned to find me standing *right behind her.*

She jumped back, shrieked a cussing blue streak, dropped her milk bottle, pulled her robe tight to her bosom, screaming for the world to hear, "Narlow Montgomery, you goddamn shit-hooking, mother-humping orangutan! *Goddamn it to hell!* You scared the shit out of me, you contemptible son-of-a-bitch! What are you doing hiding in my geraniums? Lurking around a lady's home to see what might be exposed. And *what the hell* are you doing dressed only in your goddamn pajamas and housecoat?"

I licked my lips, cocked my head, leered at her, indicating that I may have had a look-see at something enticing under the back of her robe when she stooped for her milk bottle.

She glanced down behind her, turned and screamed, "*Well! Answer me* before I call the sheriff!"

"Easy, Geraldine. *Easy.* Zara might be watching us from across the street. You know she's a horrendously jealous woman. If she saw us together here on your lawn, all decked-out in the same outfits, before dawn, I might add, why, she might find out about you and me and—"

"What do you mean, 'find out about you and me'? There's *nothing* going on between you and me, and goddamn-it-to-hell, *you know it!*"

"That's right, Geraldine. *I* know it, and *you* know it. But Zara doesn't know any such thing. She certainly has her suspicions, but I don't think she has any hard evidence. At least I don't *think* she—"

"She has suspicions? Where did she hear anything like that? Why, I've never had a single thing to do with the likes of—"

"I confess, Geraldine. I was the one who got Zara to nosing around in our affair and—"

"*What* affair? We're not—"

"That's what I told her. *Exactly* those words, Geraldine. I told her, 'Zara, you gotta believe me. Geraldine and I just appear to be paramours, but I promise we're not. Geraldine and I are just good friends. *Close, dear* friends, but we're not—"

"Goddamn it, we're not close, dear friends! And what the hell is a paramour?"

264

"Well, Geraldine, *you're* married, *I'm* married, just not to each other, and please remember that we were seen by half of El Paso just two days ago when you stopped your Saxon Six Tourer in front of my office door to the street. I invited you in and—"

"You *did not* invite me into your office! My back was out and I was on my way to a seminar presented by a chiropractor. Instead of me walking all the way around to the Paso del Norte Hotel's main lobby door, you offered to let me go through your office to the hotel lobby and that was all—"

"That's *exactly* what I told Zara! But, dang it, she just wouldn't listen. Some of her friends said you didn't come back out of the hotel to your automobile for *three hours* and—"

"You know very well why I was so long in the hotel. I was in horrible pain. My goddamn back was out, you son-of-a-bitch! I was wracked with pain all the way down my right leg. I was on the chiropractor's massage table *all those hours* and—"

"I suppose that explains your hair being messed up, looking all disheveled, face flushed and all. That's what I told—"

"My hair messed? *Disheveled?*"

"I dunno, Geraldine, honey. That's what the ladies reported who said they saw you—"

"*Who? Who* said they saw me? *Who?* I demand their names this instant!"

"Well, Geraldine, you know I can't divulge—"

"Was it Sally Schoolpepper? Linda Armstricker? Or—"

"*Uh-uh*, Geraldine honey, we're not playing that old 'twenty questions' game. But I can tell you who it's *not*. The ladies who saw you coming out of the Paso del Norte are not the same ones speaking ill of a lady who was a nun for nearly thirty years, nor are they the female gossipers who are spreading unfounded rumors about that dear lady and me during Zara's long absences. I can assure you of that. If that's helpful to you. Helps you narrow your suspects down."

Geraldine's face dropped with the decided slap of a kitchen trapdoor to the cellar. She started to speak, but turned slowly and went back up the steps to her front porch. I put her milk bottle by the porch pillar.

Strange. She didn't scold me about calling her honey.

☺☺☺

Not long afterward, Geraldine dropped my office, handed me an envelope from an attorney. "Don't worry, it's not a summons for you or Coot to appear in a lawsuit. It's something he's wanted since the day we were married."

Coot read the contents of the envelope, then said, "The old gal's giving me up. Divorce agreement. All I have to do to rid myself of that scourge of a woman is sign this and file it with the county." He smiled. "I believe I'll just hang onto this for a while, see what she's up to. Maybe she's come into millions. If that's the case, I know she'll want to share them with me."

45

May 20, 1916

Something startled me out of my nap. Coot. He parked his truck out back in the alley and slammed the iron door of the Reo. Door didn't catch, never did, unless Coot slammed hell out of it. He opened it, slammed hell out of it, then stepped through the kitchen screen door, slammed hell out of it.

"*Hola, Ines!*" he said, greeting the best housekeeper on either side of the border.

"*Que pasa, Senor Boldt? Todo es bueno?*"

"*Si, Ines—gracias.*"

He stepped to the icebox, opened it, then the sharp click of a drinking glass striking the tile drain board, followed by the clunk of a milk bottle on tile. The thick, plopping of buttermilk pouring into a glass. The icebox door slammed shut. He sauntered down the hall, knock-kneed, splayfooted as ever, coming toward the living room where I take my usual nap on the couch. My peaceful repose was at an end. I could already hear what he'd say when he came in here and sat down.

"What's happenin'." He plopped down in his favorite easy chair. After all these years, it just occurred to me that he plops like buttermilk. He wiped his chin on his sleeve, belched, smiled. "Narlow, it's been two months since we postholed Fritz. And we never did find out who else was feeding information on us to the krauts."

"Yeah, I know. You reminded me yesterday."

"Don't you think we should go back to Carichic. See what we can do about getting the Curtiss out of there? Haven't heard a peep out of Gregorio Gonzalez."

"I don't have any use for that biwing. Besides, if we did, we can damn certain buy one. We're rich, remember? As far as Gregorio's concerned, we're not likely to hear from anytime soon. Probably took him a month just to get back to Carichic from Presidio. Gregorio's busy courting Mercedes. And Coot, you know damn well that I gave Zara my solemn word that I'll not step foot into Mexico until their revolution is dead and gone."

"Have you seen IB and Shelly Brom lately?"

"No."

Coot stood, slapped his Stetson against his leg. "I haven't seen them in a month. I caught the train up to Orogrande thinking he might be holed up in our storage barn. His cot's still there, no sign of him being there. Came back to El Paso, crossed the bridge to Juarez, went by his girlfriend's house. She wasn't there, but her mother was. Seemed uneasy, maybe frightened. Wouldn't tell me a damn thing. Told me to go away. Slammed the door in my face. What do you think?"

"Lover's spat, I suppose. Maybe IB's with child."

"Real funny. The last time I saw IB, he was at Tornillo, still playing with that damn pencil sharpener of his. Grinding up sticks when there isn't a lead pencil handy. Where'd you say he got that thing?"

"In Santa Fe when we went to get his gaming-permit license application. Said a man bought it for him. A foreigner, as I recall. I remember Shelly didn't like him, least that's what IB said."

Coot stood, handed me an envelope. "This is for you," and went back out the kitchen door to the alley.

I opened it. A note from Rodolfo. It read:

To my esteemed friend of forty years, Narlow Montgomery,

> *Coot assured me that you would not accept this, but I insist. If you do not choose to accept it, you may give it to charity. Or as your lifelong friend offered with a smile, "Tell Narlow to give it to me. I'll spend it for him."*
> *You've earned every penny of this money, perhaps a hundred times more.*
> *I hold you in the greatest part of my heart, your friend,*
> > *Rodolfo Bustamante*

I shook the envelope and a bank receipt dropped out—$500,000. I ran out in the alley, but Coot was long-gone. Wouldn't do any good to argue with him anyway.

A week later, Coot and I went to the Central Café in Juarez late one afternoon. We talked about everything that had happened to us since late 1910. We were concerned about IB but clueless about where to start looking for him. Shelly was another worry, a strange worry.

Why Rodolfo chose Pancho Villa as the benefactor of his several millions of gold for munitions was still a mystery to us, though Rodolfo's dedication to him had waned over the years.

Coot said, "Rodolfo Bustamante may not have had the best reasons for backing Villa, but Rodolfo's the most unshakable man I've ever known."

"No more than you, Coot Boldt."

"Nor you, Narlow Montgomery."

44

June 1916

Things were mellow and peaceful out my office windowpane. Two lady-friends of Zara's, Hanna Rae and Mia Helene, were standing at the corner, chatting about this or that, a shoeshine boy busy spittin' 'n shinin', folks all abuzz, refreshing my bijou screen at every turn.

Coot broke my peace. "I just got back from Juarez. Went over there again looking for IB's lady friend, Josephina. No Josephina, but her mother was there. Wouldn't talk to me, wouldn't tell me where Josephina was, or a damn thing about IB. Kept craning her neck, looking over my shoulder, eyes darting back and forth, kept saying she was not frightened. If she didn't have anything to be afraid of, why'd she beg me to leave?"

He leaned over on the edge of his chair. "I've been watching the Crane Place for the past three weeks, going by at odd hours. No sign of IB, but there's plenty of indications of Shelly coming and going. I've got her schedule down pat. She always shows up when there's irrigation water in the canal for her garden. There was water in the canal when I went by on the way to town just now, so I'm heading back out there. Something's up. Come on. Maybe the two of us can make sense out of all this."

The Crane Place was one-hundred-ninety-seven acres of blow-sand that formed a high sandhill that dropped off at the edge of the irrigated bottomland. Only a three-acre plot rested in that low, fertile area, Shelly's garden, a plot she'd tended since we were all kids.

Coot drove the canal road to the edge of the sandhill, gunned the Reo fast up to the top to a trail that led a quarter-mile on north to the Crane's clapboard shack. The place was a mess—kitchen door ajar, a foot of sand on the floor.

Coot forced the door back. "She's been here today. Wind's been blowing, but those are fresh tracks."

"Coot, look here," I said, pointing to a stack of *New York Times* newspapers on the kitchen table, a butcher knife stabbed in the headlines dateline El Paso, "German Operations Believe Headquartered El Paso, Texas."

Coot studied the neat stack of papers. "A subscription to the *Times* is not cheap. Suppose Shelly can read?"

"Damned if I know. We've always known she's mute, just assumed she was as slow as IB. But thinking back to when we were leaving Rodolfo's, remember she was playing with a little girl, mending the girl's ragdoll. Shelly Brom's our age. At first I thought she was playing, but the thought crossed my mind, 'She's not playing as a ten-year-old, she's *playing along*, observing the little girl, not really playing.'"

As we wandered through the four-room shack, Coot hollered out, "*Come here*. You won't believe this!"

I went through the door to what must have been Mrs. Crane's bedroom. On every wall was a crudely crafted bookcase, crammed to the rafters with books. Not cheap *novellas*, but walls of poetry, classics, geography, world history, dictionaries, science, medicine, the gamut. A library suitably owned by an elite professional.

I said, "Remember, IB sallied along with us to the first grade with us when we were eleven, but Shelly never attended a day in her life. My god, Coot, what do you make of this?"

Coot was studying something on the back of the library door. He pushed the door back against the wall of books, then hurried out to the sandhill overlooking the valley below.

I pulled the door back so I could see what had his attention—two genealogical family trees. One headed, "Boldt," the other with the name, "Crane" scratched at the top. A single pencil line drawn from the name Orville Boldt across the door to the name Sarah Sweat Crane—Coot's daddy and Shelly Brom's mama.

By the time I got to the lip of the sandhill, Coot was already sloshing through the irrigation canal next to Shelly Brom. She was squatted on her stubby legs, siphoning water out of the canal, watering her garden. As I walked up, she stood, appeared to be set to run.

Coot said, "Easy, little sister. There's nothing to be frightened of. Narlow and I've come to help you, help IB, too."

She turned her head so as to hide her ruby-red alligator-skin layered face, squatted, went back to tending her siphon tubes.

Coot squatted beside her. She shuffled away, duck-like. "Shelly Brom, we saw your beautiful books, your wonderful library. Have you read all those books?"

She duck-walked to the next row of her garden, set the tube to watering. Coot followed suite.

"Shelly Brom, we're worried about IB. Haven't seen him for several weeks. Wouldn't say a word the last time we saw him, like he was afraid to say anything. I went to Juarez looking for Josephina. Couldn't find her, but found her mother. She's afraid to talk, kept looking over my shoulder behind me, like she thought someone might be watching. I asked her about Josephina, about IB. She closed her door, told me to go away."

Shelly, still squatting, duck-walked backward to set the next watering tube, still facing away from Coot.

"Shelly Brom, you're a very smart girl. We had no idea until we stumbled on your library. Please forgive me. And—and, Shelly Brom, I know—dagnabit, Shelly Brom, I know it's been a long time coming, but I want you to know that I'm proud to be your brother. Really want you to know that. *Believe* that, and Shelly Brom, you've just got to forgive me for not acknowledging that long ago. Too full of false pride to admit it. I shamed myself, but, Shelly Brom, you'll find I give more than I ask. You have my word that I'll make it up to you."

She went down on all fours, her calloused hands in the shallow canal, groping for something. She pushed back to a squatting position, holding a siphon tube, flashed Coot a faint smile.

I had never witnessed Coot speaking with such tenderness. He reached out and touched her shoulder. She tensed, then softened. "When we get all this trouble behind us, we'll do something about patching this up between you and me." He cupped his hand and poured a bit of water on her sunburned shoulder. "But right now, Shelly Brom, we've got this trouble to deal with. Tell me where our brother—"

She jumped to her feet, quick as a fox, gazed all around the valley floor, up and across the sand dunes to her shack. Her gaze, intense as a clap of lightening, a dose of castor oil. I heard not the flicker of a moth's wings at a candle, yet the whistle of a bull elk filled the air. There was specialness in Shelly Brom, magic in her heart.

She turned full-face to Coot, her ruby-red disfigurement glowing like a volcano's flow in the morning sun. Her eyes soft, pleading. She pointed up the sandhill to the Reo, jabbing her finger. No doubt. She wanted us gone, *terrified*, as if she were afraid we'd be seen on her place.

We started back down the canal road.

"Coot, what's all that about Shelly Brom and IB being your sister and brother?"

"Known it forever. Too damn proud to admit being related to them. IB, a simpleton, Shelly, mute, hard to look at. I could hardly admit it to myself, much less claim them to the world. Those genealogical charts are old, the paper's yellowed. She's known all about it for years. Your papa and Uncle Doyl knew it. It's the reason why my daddy always told us to take care of IB, not let anybody pick on him."

"Coot, my friend, the closest thing I've ever had to a brother, you didn't learn a thing looking at the back of that door just now. So who told you they were your siblings?"

"No one. Figured it out myself. Do you remember when we were just little turds, reading Washington Irving's *The Legend of Sleepy Hollow*? Ichabod B. Crane was pursuing a lady-fair, Katrina, who was also being sparked by a man whose nickname was Brom Bones. Old Lady Crane named IB with the strange name of Ichabod, and then an even stranger name for a girl, Shelly Brom. Best I can figure is that their mother left a clue about who their daddy might be, a man who was *definitely* not Mr. Crane. Why'd she do that? Who knows. Maybe to get someone curious about it. Curiosity dern sure got me to ciphering on it. It's obvious Shelly Brom did a little ciphering of her own."

He banged on the steering wheel. "But now I'm more than a little curious about where IB might be. Shelly Brom may not have the capacity to speak, but she can read, which follows she can write. But she'll never write a word about their problem."

271

"Coot, I can appreciate how this is a sore subject, but has it crossed your mind that the Germans may be what have Shelly Brom and Josephina's mother so frightened, that maybe the Krauts are behind IB's disappearance?"

"I'm not certain about a damn thing anymore. We've known IB and Shelly Brom all of our fifty-seven years. Now we find out we didn't know her at all, only assumed she was just a disfigured mute, a know-nothing like her twin brother. I suspect she's protecting the man she spent nine months with in their mama's womb. Protecting IB's nothing new to her. She's been hard at it all their lives, and never, not *once*, giving us a clue as to who she really was. A mute woman with a bad birthmark, yeah, might say that—but also in possession of a superior intellect."

45

Back to the Saltlick One More Time. July 1, 1916

Coot hadn't stopped by the house since I couldn't remember when. Yeah, I saw him just last week when we went out to the Crane Place, but I'd declined to concern Zara with that worry. Rose was certain that Coot's absence centered on her losing the Curtiss at Carichic. I agreed that she was likely the cause of his absence, but nothing to do with a busted airplane.

"Have you checked on Coot lately?" Zara called out from the kitchen.

I'd answered that question fifty times in the past month. I heard her and Rose murmuring back and forth, the giggle of the ex-nun.

Zara came to the door between the kitchen and the living room, her hands on her hips, waiting *impatiently* for my reply. Stalling was *over*.

I went to her, snuggled her close. "No, my sweet, I haven't checked on cute-Coot buzzard-Boldt, but I'll go check on him. Any message for him?"

"Yes. Ask him to come for supper when Rose and I return from Dallas in ten short days. We want to visit with Mother Superior and the sisters at Sacred Heart. Now, get out of our hair. We must pack for an early train."

I hated checking on Coot. He'd never check on me, bite off his own fool tongue before that'd ever happen.

As I drove up to his place, I hit the horn. Maybe he'd come out. Better than me knocking on his screen door. I leaned on the horn again, this time for half a minute, just short of the time required for the horn to get stuck. I'd have to get out, open the bonnet, and yank the horn wire loose. That would set Coot to howling, rolling in the dirt.

I sat for a while, admired his crop. Lucky bastard. He could grow melons and squash in a double-decker-four-holer with a waiting line. Where was his Reo? Maybe he's gone. I stuck my thumb on the horn again.

Movement caught my eye over by his barn. He came out donning a blacksmithing leather apron and heavy gloves, picked up a leaf spring, stopped, squinted over at me. "Oh, it's you making all that racket." He turned and stepped back through the square black of the wide barn door.

The inside of his tin-topped adobe barn was cool, dark as inside a cow. I waited for my eyes to adjust so I wouldn't slip on the greasy floor, fall on a hay rake, devoured by a bailer.

"Glad you came by!" he yelled out between banging on the leaf spring under the Reo. "Runner out of Juarez paid me a visit two days ago. I'm installing leaf springs on the ass-end of the Reo. Model-T's broke down. Shelly Brom brought him. I took her some new clothes, but haven't heard a peep out of her."

"Shelly Brom brought who?"

"The runner."

"Shelly brought him, huh? Don't suppose she mentioned IB."

He scooted from under the Reo. "Naw, she brought the runner out here, turned around, ran off on those stubby legs of hers faster'n a jackrabbit."

"What about the runner she brought out here?"

"Oh, that. Gregorio Gonzalez's cousin. Brought word that Gregorio wants to meet us Sunday night in Juarez. Talk about getting the Curtiss out of Mexico."

"Today's Sunday, but if you think I'm going—"

"It is? It's *Sunday?* We best get poppin'."

"Damn it, Coot, I'm not going back to Mexico to fly that Curtiss—"

"Give me a hand with that crank. Hit it a lick."

He drove the Reo out in the yard, spun around, drove over a five-foot-high pile of fence posts like a rodeo clown. He smiled, stepped out, headed for the house, called over his shoulder, "You coming with me, or just stand out there gawking?"

"What exactly did Gregorio's cousin say? What's he got up his sleeve?"

Coot banged pots and metal plates around in the kitchen sink, poured water

273

in a bowl to wash-up. "Wants to plan how we're going to get back to *Circulo de Rocas*. Retrieve the Curtiss. Any more questions?"

"Nope, no questions, just a statement of final fact. I'll be pleased to see our fine Mexican friend. Share a loaf of *pan dulce*, a slab of goat cheese, a jug of mezcal, even be interested in hearing your plans. How *you* and that pencil-thin-mustachioed *little fart* will accomplish the task of getting the Curtiss out of Mexico without a pilot. *Without me*, 'cause this pilot ain't going! Promised Zara, remember? And damn it, Coot, we don't need that damn airplane! Buy another one if need be—which we don't!"

"I know, but we need to humor Gregorio."

◉◉◉

First time in recorded history, I prevailed! I'd finally ducked one of Coot's sucker-punch schemes. Didn't even fall for one of his favorite Spanish *dichos*: *Vida sin amigo, muerte testigo*. Life without a friend is death without a witness. I dodged that ditty, so he quoted Ecclesiastes, "Two are better than one; because they have a good reward for their labour. For if they fall, the one will lift up his fellow: but woe to him that is alone when he falleth; for he hath not another to help him up."

He had to yell out the last two sentences. Woe to *him*! His lifelong friend was trucking fast back to El Paso.

When I delivered Zara and Rose to Union Depot for their evening train, Zara asked, "Did you invite Coot to supper when we return from Dallas? Did he promise to come? How does he look? Is he taking care of himself?"

I kissed her on her forehead. "Yes." I kissed her on her cheek. "Yes." I kissed her on her nose. "He looks like a pile of crap." I kissed her on her lips. "Unfortunately, it appears he's going to live."

Rose batted her eyes. "Well, did he ask about me?"

"No, the subject of Rose Talamantes never *rose* to the surface. Just on me to go back and fetch the Curtiss. I told—"

Zara wheeled around, her finger at the end of my nose. "*Narlow Montgomery*, you are *not* going into Mexico until those people resolve their differences. Do we have *complete* agreement on that one issue? And you *promised* me."

"In other words, *never*."

"*Never*, my dear. You mean too much to me."

"And, you love me so much you couldn't go on without me."

"Don't press it."

◉◉◉

Zara left her long list of "to-dos" for me on the dining room table. Heading the list was a plea to wire her immediately should a letter come from Will. We had not heard from him in well over a month, a man who corresponded like clockwork. Zara was worried about him, worried me about it daily.

I took my cheroot and brandy out on the veranda, sat in the swing. It was hot, not a pinch of breeze. I gathered my necessities and went outback to the alley, sat on the kitchen stoop, a fresh breeze drifted up the hill from town and the river beyond. Sat wondering about Coot's visit with Gregorio in Juarez.

I set my brandy on the step, reached for a match. Headlamps flashed from up the alley, faint yellow, one lamp dangling in a death throw, the other cockeyed peering at the moon—the Reo.

"So how was *Senor* Gregorio Gonzalez? He and Mercedes ever get themselves married-up?"

Coot came over in the dark, put his boot on the step. "Gregorio's not too happy, but a lot happier than you're going to be when I tell you what he had to say."

"How's that?"

He put his hand on my shoulder. "They've got Will."

I bolted to my feet. "Who's got Will?"

"The *Rurales* have your boy. Gregorio says Will's all right. They sent Gregorio up here to deliver their demands."

"What do they want? *Money*? How much? How did the *Rurales* get their grimy mitts on Will in England?"

"Gregorio says that German undercover agents kidnapped him in London, took him south off the coast, put him on a skiff, and rowed him out about a mile offshore. Says the German Navy hauled him off in one of their U-Boats, what we call a submarine, *unterseeboot* in German, as Gregorio was forced to learn so he could repeat it to us. They steamed across the Atlantic, destroyed three American freighters along the way, ended up near Texas' Port Isabel near Brownsville, cross the Rio from Matamoros—"

"All that way in a goddamn submarine? How the hell—"

"Narlow, if you'll give me just one minute, I'll tell you all I know. Anyway, they off-loaded Will onto a skiff, again about a mile offshore, got him to Matamoros, where they boarded him on a train to Cuahtemoc, then by horseback to Carichic and *Circulo de Rocas*."

"Damn Latins and their drama! They couldn't just take him to Juarez or Mexico City to make their demands. What do they want? Money? How much? How long will they give us to get the cash for them?"

"No, my friend, they don't want money. They want us—you—me—Gregorio."

"When? How? Where?"

"Gregorio said that the *Rural* general, *Generalissimo* Hugo Garcia de Gomez, gave him specific instructions on the how, when, and where. He's the uncle of that bastard, *Rural Capitan* Manzana. We are to leave Juarez tonight, midnight train. We're to buy third-class fares to Chihuahua, then onto Cuahtemoc, third-class all the way. In other words, cattle car."

"*More* drama."

"When we get to Cuahtemoc, we look for a bright green *adobe* with an orange thatched roof, just south of the freight yard. Waiting by the side of that adobe will be two brown burros and a white, swayback mule. Gregorio and I are to ride the burros, the swayback's yours. An old man will be there. We are to pay him $500 for our mounts, and—"

"Five-hundred dollars for three-bits worth of—"

"The general makes the rules. Says we won't know the old man, but his name is Jorge Villarte, father of the big man you shot in the ear not so long ago. The general warns us to be careful with *Senor* Villarte. He has a Big Fifty musket, and anxious to use it on us."

I started to interrupt, but Coot waved me off.

"We are to ride those animals south, skirt around Carichic, riding directly to *Circulo de Rocas*, arrive after sunset tomorrow evening."

"Then what?"

"We wait. We do nothing. The general will show up with Will at noon the next day. One false move and Zara will have a long pine box delivered to her veranda, and it won't be you resting in that box. You, Gregorio, and I stay there—permanent-like. The occupant of that pine box will be—"

"Coot, I think I get it!" I sat on the kitchen stoop, stood, paced the alley. "Jees-amighty, Coot! What do I do? I can't just write Zara and tell her where we're heading, what's going on. Say goodbye. For chrissakes, I can't leave her a letter like that! What the hell would I say? I'm sorry. Love you very much. Go on with your life. See you on the other side."

I sat back down, slugged down the rest of the brandy, stood. "Well, my lifelong *amigo*, I suppose this is it. We're not coming back. Likely that Will won't be coming back either. Zara will never see us again."

I stood in the alley's gloom, slapping my leg with an open palm, squeezing my other fist as if milking a nanny. Thinking of Will, my Alley Boy, who said right across this very alley, "Traveler's a fine horse." Something I'd repeated in my head a thousand times, something I'd said to Papa twenty years before Will came along, at the Box, when Coot and I met Papa while living with the Apaches on their reservation.

I turned to Coot. "Well, partner, hell of a note. Let's go."

46

Circulo de Rocas

The sun set two hours before we had ridden the burros and mule to the edge of *Circulo de Rocas*. All quiet. Hand-groping black.

Coot struck a match to his bull's eye lantern, handed it to Gregorio. "Lead on, my friend. Find us a place to wait out the night."

We stepped through the boulders. Dark as the inside of the proverbial, it was.

The sun flashed on.

A voice spoke. "Perhaps these lights will assist you gentlemen in your search for your son and your *aeroplano*."

"*Aiii chingado!*" Gregorio screamed as he jumped back.

Coot and I reached for our weapons.

"Please, gentlemen! That would not be a wise thing to do. As you see, you are surrounded by officers of my *Rural* brigade."

Surrounded was an overstatement as I could only spot seven men, plus one young boy—sitting on a stump behind a machinegun with its cartridge-feeder belt in place, cocked and locked, an old Colt .45 slung at his hip.

"I know you were not expecting us until noon tomorrow, but my German friends made a gift of these lights. I had to put them to use in your honor. Aren't these brilliantly bright lamps wonderful? They shall assist me in the drama of this auspicious occasion."

The two large lamps were blinding white. Brighter than noon sun on snow, so intense they removed all color, leaving mottled shades of gray. The Curtiss appeared as a faint yellow goose in a gray block corral built of gray bamboo and gray salt cedar. Shadows were black as the bottom of a tar bucket. The red-and-green-on-white banner that had been displayed in Carichic, *Libertad O Muerte*, was hung between the wing of the Curtiss and Big George's massive drill press, the banner's message barely visible in the gray.

I looked around for Will, but the lights had me blinded.

The man strolled up, silhouetted by the blinding lights behind him, a mustachioed man in full *Rural* gray suit uniform, silver buttons, a silver-gray sash across his breast that flashed golden when shadowed, adorned with white feathers at the edges. The sash appeared to be more for hiding his ample double-bellied gut than a showy display of authority. A baton in one hand, a sheath of paper in the other.

"Welcome, gentlemen! Allow me to introduce myself. I am *Generalissimo* Hugo Garcia de Gomez, head of all of Mexico's glorious *Rural* forces. I will not, how would I say, play games with you. Possibly you do not recall, but you once heard my name. You see, gentlemen, I am *Rural Capitan* Ambrosio Manzana de Flores' uncle. His mother is my younger sister, rather *was* my younger sister. She poisoned herself when she heard the sad news about the brutal murder of her dear son, murdered at the base of a lowly sycamore tree. My source tells me that my nephew, *Capitan* Manzana, mentioned my name to you gentlemen when he first encountered you close by. He took great pride in our kinship."

He smiled, turned. "I will get to our other guests momentarily, but with your kind permission, I would like to introduce two—"

I shouted, "*Generalisimo* whatever your pompous name is, why don't you cut the theatrics and get on with the business at hand. You brought us down here to kill us, presumably not to stage a Broadway pony and dog show. For God's sake, man, don't harm my son. He's innocent of anything concerning you or Mexico. Let him go!"

"Mr. Narlow Montgomery, I assume. May I remind you that you are not in charge at this inquisition. I am in charge here, you are my guests, *now* I will consider you as my prisoners."

He strolled around, straightened his sash, then began swatting his leg with his baton. He tucked his baton under his arm, unsheathed his papers. His agenda, I supposed.

"Where was I? Oh, yes, I was about to introduce two of my staff members." He pointed his baton at the young boy sitting behind a very loaded machinegun. "Do you remember Juanito at Carichic? He was serving as *Comandante* Horacio Bienveniedes' orderly at his headquarters, only twenty-five kilometers north of this magnificent place, this place the villagers call, *Circulo de Rocas*. England has such a place as this, a place you may know—Stonehenge, I believe they call it. I know many, many, *many* interesting things such as that."

He stepped to the side of an officer, tapped him on the chest with his baton. "This man is *Rural Coronel* Joaquin Bienveniedes, younger *hermano de Comandante* Horacio Bienveniedes. I am certain you remember the *comandante*."

The barrel-chested young officer smiled, clicked his heels, licked his lips, touched his quirt to his billed cap.

"It is certainly understandable that you took such drastic action to protect yourself from the dire effects of standing before one of Mexico's *adobe* walls when you came here to rescue a certain lady by the name of Rose Talamantes. An ex-nun, I am told. You will soon learn that we share amorous desires for fair ladies. However, since I am so understanding of your circumstances, perhaps you gentlemen can understand my displeasure, and that of my dear sister, of your killing my nephew, her son. Correct me if I am wrong, but I believe that Gregorio Gonzalez is the one in your midst who killed *Rural Capitan* Manzano—in cold blood. Would that be a correct assessment, *Senor* Gonzalez?"

Gregorio's chin shot up. "*Si, Senor Generalissimo* Garcia. I kill the shit chicken, *pero*, it was nothing."

The general snapped, "Your insolence will have its rewards soon enough."

He studied his notes, looked up. "And you, *Senor* Montgomery. I've been informed that you are the taller of the two of you and *Senor* Boldt. Oh, I believe I've already established that. You confused me with your interruption, *Senor* Montgomery, but you are also responsible for the understandable displeasure of *Rural Coronel* Joaquin Bienveniedes for the brutal murder of *Comandante* Horacio Bienveniedes, his dear brother. Would that be a correct assessment, *Senor* Montgomery?"

"Well, General, may I first say that you have the advantage of us, and to put it mildly, to paraphrase a great Englishman, 'Soulwise, these are trying times.' But shuckens, *Generalissimo*, I suppose you could put it that way. But you gotta realize

279

that at the time, the *comandante* was going for his *pistola*. But I reckon I'm the guilty one in that instance."

I stepped forward. "But so what? I shot the bastard. Gregorio Gonzalez shot that son-of-a-bitch nephew of yours. They were both murderous cowards. We're ready to pay any price you choose to mete out. Get on with it, but allow my son to walk free. I assume he's here, but your Kraut-lights have us so blinded we can't find our asses with both hands."

Obviously, our little friend Juanito made it back to Mexican forces and tattled on us. After the shooting spree under Gregorio's sycamore tree and he took off running, we should have shot the little bastard. I thought about telling the general just that. So I did.

"And, *Generalissimo*, did this little snitch Juanito tell you that he ran off after all that shooting and killing? Tell you that we didn't raise a finger to stop him. Didn't fire off any wild shots at his backside, a young lad running away into the pitch dark of the wilderness. You have Mr. Boldt to thank for Juanito still being among the living, firmly ensconced behind that machinegun. Juanito's not to be faulted, don't get me wrong. Though I must say, sir, I find this sanguinary setting most inhospitable. Sir!"

"*Ha.* Mr. Montgomery, your linguistic abilities do you great justice. But you must refrain from any further interruptions. Oh! *Ha!* I failed to mention that your partner in the crime of running guns into Mexico, Mr. Fritz Hans-Smidt, made it far across the sea to his native Germany. But, sadly, the very moment that he stepped off his ship, he slipped and fell. I regret to inform you that Mr. Hans-Smidt died on that dock as a result of the injuries he suffered."

Again he consulted his notes. "Now, gentlemen, I have introduced two member of my staff, while failing to introduce one of your close friends. I apologize for my oversight. *Teniente* Dominguez! *Por favor*, bring forward our special guest."

The lieutenant stepped behind a bamboo curtain, a familiar voice yelled out, "*No!* I don' wanna see them fellers. They's Coot Boldt and Nar-low Montgomery. I dun 'em dirt. I dun 'em dirt."

The burly lieutenant appeared, manhandling IB by the arm, presenting him to his superior. *Generalissimo* Garcia stood silent, swatting his leg with his baton, smiling, giving us time to let this soak. IB was gaunt as a cattail.

"Does this man require an introduction to you gentlemen?" the general asked.

"No sir," Coot said. "IB Crane's a lifelong friend of ours. If this man 'dun us dirt,' as he phrased it, it was without malice. Doesn't have it in him. Obviously tricked. But he didn't go looking. *No, sir.* IB didn't go looking for a way to put us in any sort of harm. Give up his life first."

IB fell to the ground, began crying, murmuring our names over and over, begging for forgiveness, screaming, "My beautiful Josephina. Why? Why? Gen-e-ral, why'd you done it?"

The lieutenant tried to force him to his feet, but the general waved him off. "*Teniente* Dominguez, please ask these gentlemen to release any weapons they may have to your care."

For the second time in our lives, and within a half-mile of both instances, Coot and I reached under our coats, handed over our weapons.

The general launched on a ranting diatribe that would have embarrassed his dear nephew, putting his rather mellow ranting to shame. Rant and cruelty serve as the roots of many families. He saved the worst of his vast repertoire for his own people, Mexico's *pobres* especially, their "loose, whoring" women.

"You goddamn *gringos* think you know more about the conduct of Mexico's business than its own leaders. You are shit. You think we mistreat our *pobres*. You *cannot* fathom their stupidity, their ineptness to understand a damn thing about taking care of themselves, their own families, their own flesh and blood, blood that has far too much native Indian blood, insufficient amounts of pure Spanish blood such as myself. *Muy estupido!* We must furnish them water, *tortillas, frijoles.* They are lazy, *more* filthy than pigs. When I am elevated to *Presidente de Mexico,* I will stand every damn one of them against an *adobe* wall and direct Juanito to mow them down like so many cows in a pasture. *They are dirt.* They do not deserve to live with people such as myself. I spit in the ugly face of every *pobre's* mother! All whores!"

He stopped suddenly, began heaving, clawing for breath. My gaze went to Juanito, sitting on a stump behind his machinegun. Still a boy, but instead of the hard, mean look about him we had observed for so many days in Carichic, his eyes flew open in wide-eyed amazement as if he could not comprehend what his general was saying. Juanito's glance came to Coot, then darted back to his general.

The general gathered himself, took a deep breath, pointed at the boy behind the machinegun. "We—we will get to Juanito's place in this scenario soon enough. Give him an opportunity to display his skill with the killing machine that he sits behind, that he cleans and polishes meticulously so that it never fails him. The boy is special to me. I plan to keep him close. Close to me. *Generalissimo* Hugo Garcia de Gomez!"

The general had worked up a sweating froth. He removed his sash and gray coat, handed his dripping coat to his lieutenant, then draped the damp, feather-bedecked sash back across his chest, only partially hiding his ponderous gut, a bulky thing that was halved by his black belt, puffs of bulbous fat above and below his tightly pulled belt.

He sauntered around the clearing, gazing at his men as if inspecting them, tapped the barrel of Juanito's machinegun, feathered the drooping metallic cartridge belt with his baton that murmured like soft, lightly treaded gravel, a breeze through dry corn leaves.

Again, the general referred to his notes, rushed to *Coronel* Bienveniedes, slapped him, *hard*, then turned back to us. "That surprised you, did it not? I have read much of Napoleon Bonaparte's military tactics. He often slapped favorite officers, pulled the noses of his dearest soldiers. The ladies often tell me that I am somewhat of a Napoleon myself, don't you—"

"Bull shit!" Coot shouted. "You're no more man than that pimp Napoleon you idolize. You're not a loyal Mexican, but a Frenchman in disguise. Preferring Ferdinand Maximilian over Benito Juarez. And you no doubt have a crush on that bastard dictator, General Santa Ana. Bring along *Coronel* Bienveniedes back across the Rio Grande. He'd take you on and a dozen just like you with a bed slat. Put your slimy fat ass on the ground for slapping him."

"My officers are loyal to me! Loyal to *me*. They would gladly die in my defense. You must remain silent, Mr. Boldt, or I will have them demonstrate their loyalty to me to your complete satisfaction."

He straightened his blouse and sash, lifted his chin, consulted his notes. "Oh. *Oh, yes!* I must introduce a man who came all the way from England for this occasion. The son you have referred to: Will Montgomery. He's back there in the shadows. Step forward, please, Mr. Will Montgomery." A shadow came forward, and when the general told him that was far enough, the silhouette was sufficiently close to recognize Will's outline, the tilt of his hat.

Again the general consulted his papers. "You may exchange pleasantries if you wish."

"Hello, son. Forgive me for getting you involved in this mess."

"Dad, the only thing you ever got me involved in was life, the life you gave me when you and Mother took me in out of your back alley, and made me all I'll ever be." He waved. "Howdy, Uncle Coot."

"Howdy, yourself, Will Montgomery."

"Now, gentlemen, if you are finished with your idle chitchat, I should like to tell you a story, a story I believe you will enjoy as fellow virile men. You see, gentlemen, officers of my *Rural* troop are granted free and unlimited access to all women with whom we come in contact. Women, young girls, old women, in every village across Mexico that we conquer, my men push those sluts across a table, pull their skirts up, have their way. Those women are all dogs, incapable of keeping their knees together. Bitch dogs! We treat them as such."

His narrow-set eyes brightened. "Now, *another* surprise for you gentlemen. I adore surprises. I am most certain that you gentlemen are not aware that we kidnapped IB Crane's lady friend, *Senorita* Josephina Ortiz. Did you know that, *eh? Eh?* I thought not. Her kidnapping was accomplished almost a year ago. Is it not strange how fast time flies when one is enjoying one's self, as you would say, 'when you are having fun,' *eh?* For you see, my men have been having fun with Josephina *every* single night, *every* single day since her abduction. I, myself, have regularly participated in that enjoyment. Ha-ha! *Hijo!* Yes, indeed, many times. *Aiii caramba!* Many, many, *many* times over those many, many, *many* months. I even arranged for *Senor* Crane to observe as I performed on top of that beautiful naked plump lass' ass. I did so, not to embarrass either of them. *No no no no!* I did so that IB might learn the intricacies of my performance, to satisfy Josephina's every need and desire. If you will, the minutiae of my stroke."

IB jumped to his feet, screamed as he lunged at the general, "*Auuugggggggg!*" The general was down before his men could defend him. IB continued screaming, pummeling the general with his fists, kicking, biting, out of his mind with rage. Juanito took a step from his post, stepped back, glanced at Coot. The *Rurales* pulled at IB, but he hung tight, dragging the general, still hitting at him.

IB screamed, "And you *kilt* her! You kilt my Josephina!"

The lieutenant rapped IB a good one on the head with his pistol. He slumped, and was dragged aside. Coot made an involuntary move toward him. I grabbed his arm.

The general's men helped him to his feet, brushed him off. He threw them aside with much bravado, combed his mustachio with his fingers, straightened his shirt and sash, brushed his pants.

The general's gloved hand went to his mouth, glanced at the trace of blood on his white glove, took a hanky from his pocket and dabbed his mouth for a moment. He began stomping around, glaring at his officers, hustling across the area to gaze at Juanito, touched the boy's hair, then got in the face of another of his lieutenants, their noses a slim inch apart. The young lieutenant winced, as if expecting a blow. The general turned, stomped up and down with both feet, a constant scream of obscenities. His men glanced at each other, no suitable place for their gazes or hands.

He composed himself, sauntered back to the center of the circle, held his chin high, and resumed his braggadocio rant. "*Goddamn it to hell!* Not only did I enjoy Josephina Ortiz's company, I had my, shall we say, 'associates,' kidnap her younger sister. A girl of perhaps ten, maybe so eleven. No difference. Kidnapped from a Juarez barrio where no one cares when a young girl disappears. *Ah, yes,* Patricia Ortiz. A treasure. *My* treasure. Very fresh, new, untouched, without the displeasure of another man's hand between her golden thighs. I was the *first!* Do you hear me? The *first!* The very *first* was I! *Me! Generalissimo* Hugo Garcia de Gomez *en su servicio! En el servicio de cada mujer en México!* I am that man! The undeniable head of *Los Rurales.* The *only* man who can be at the service of *all* women in *all* of Mexico! *Me!*"

IB tried to stand, struggled but was held fast.

"Well, gentlemen, when I finished introducing Patricia to the ecstasies of my immeasurable manliness, her sister, Josephina, made a horrendous tactical error. *Oh yes!* It was all her doing. She ran at me with a butcher knife, stabbed me in my back. Only a flesh wound, for I am strong, muscular. I had all of my men seduce Patricia, *repeatedly.* I offered her to Juanito. Patricia could be his first. *His very first!* But he shook his head, ran away. Too bad. I forced Josephina to watch me mount her sister." He licked is lips, smiled. "I arranged that."

Time raced. We were dead men. I prayed that Zara would forgive me, to go on with her life. *Will, may a merciful God take you home to her.*

The general strolled across the area, swatted his leg with his baton. "After that evening, you can readily understand my position. I could not trust Josephina. It was Josephina's doing. *I, Generalissimo* Garcia, personally shot her in the head. I ordered *Senor* Crane and Patricia to clean up Josephina's bloody mess."

IB screamed, struggled, helpless.

And I looked, and behold a pale horse: and his name is Death, and Hell followed with him.

"Now, gentlemen, gaze upon *Senor* IB Crane. A pathetic wretch. *Most pathetic*. Not human. Merely a thing. A thing that—"

"That's my brother you're talking about, you bastard," Coot yelled. "You're the only *thing* present that's pathetic. My brother is more man that you'll ever be. Now, get on with your killing."

"Mr. Boldt, you must remain silent. If not I will first shoot Mr. Crane, then Will Montgomery, then you."

The general held the sheaf of papers up to the light behind him, studied them a moment, then slapped his baton on his leg. "As I was saying, Mr. Crane was bought for the princely sum of a one *peso* pencil sharpener. *A goddamn* pencil sharpener, you son-of-a-bitches! At first, he was cooperative with Germany's friendly agents, gentlemen that you would call spies. Told them everything about your travels. They gave him trinkets, a dollar or two on occasion. Then you gentlemen told him about the several attempts on your lives. He resisted the Germans, saying he would tell you of his deceit. That is when the Germans were forced to kidnap his lady fair, putting her in my capable care for safekeeping. I kept Patricia alive to force *Senor* Crane to keep us informed, but I soon learned he was not to be trusted. We took him into our custody only a few months ago. His sister, a twin sister, I believe, Shelly Brom was present when we took her brother. She was told that if she did not do our bidding, to keep us informed, that she would never see her brother *ever again*. Apparently she believed us, for she has served us admirably, reluctantly, yes, but most admirably. We learned she loved her brother, had cared for him, looked after him all their lives, even though she is a mute, without voice all of her life. I'm told she's also ugly as hell to look at."

I glanced at Coot. It was hell sorting all of this out, getting our understanding from such a bastard as the general. The general continued his prance, slapping his leg with his baton.

I said, "All right, general. You've got us dead to rights. Now, please, I'm begging you, please let my son go, and release Mr. Boldt's brother. Neither of them have harmed you, done nothing to harm Mexico. Please let these innocent men leave your country in peace. They are innocent. You know they're innocent—"

"*Silencio!* I know no such thing! Will Montgomery is *not* innocent. He is guilty of defrauding Mexico's ally, its friend across the sea. Mexico is a true friend to its friends and neighbors, unlike the *norte americanos* who have gone to war across that same sea. They tired of sticking their noses in Mexico's business, now they busy themselves in the Kaiser's affairs. Will Montgomery is a principal in

Everstart Industries. They had a manufacturing plant in Germany, producing munitions and bolts for the German Mauser. When it appeared that Germany was preparing for war to defend itself against the invading armies of France and England, Everstart, under Will Montgomery's direction, sold their German facility to well-connected German industrialists for a princely sum. After the transaction was completed, and their millions in London banks, the German industrialists took possession of what they assumed was a state-of-the-art factory to find that all of the required dies were gone. *Disappeared*, along with the blueprints and notations required to continue the manufacture of munitions and their improved Mauser rifle bolts. Your son is not only decidedly *not* innocent, he is guilty of espionage, fraud, treason, theft! Punishable in Germany by death in front of a firing squad. A sentence to be carried out in the land of the only true remaining friend they have—*Mexico*. I am profoundly pleased to be chosen to carry out that fair and honorable sentence. Let's not have any more claims of your son's innocent, for I—"

"A fair and honorable sentence, you say, General," I asked. "A sentence that was never handed down by a judge in Germany. That's what you call fair and honorable? Exact copy of Mexican justice under Porfirio Diaz. That brand of justice?"

"*Bah!* You *gringos* place far too much faith in technicalities of law. That's why you are a failing world power, one that will cease all together at the conclusion of this little skirmish in Europe. You will see. But, now, I must proceed with my agenda.

"Where was I?" He consulted his notes, his agenda. "Oh, yes! And, Mr. Montgomery, I must insist that you not interrupt these proceedings. I was about to tell you about Shelly Brom's part in this final, orchestrated curtain. Mr. Boldt will recall that she accompanied Gregorio Gonzalez's cousin to his farm requesting that the two of you meet Gregorio in Juarez the following Sunday. That despicable—that ugly, dumb, sexless woman had taken her brother's place and you didn't even know it! She couldn't speak, but she kept my German friends abreast of your activities."

He paused, glanced at his papers. "Goddamn *pobres* who follow their country's traitors! *Zapata! Villa!* I tell you—*I tell you,* if I had my way, I would kill every goddamn *pobre* across the great land of Mexico! Mexico is not the land of *pobres*. *Nuestro México. Mi México.* Never doubt that I would kill every one of them!" He stomped up and down with each word. "Every . . . goddamn . . . *pobre!* Women, children first. Their pathetic men would soon scurry after their tainted ghosts. *Generalissimo* Hugo Garcia de Gomez makes this promise! *Goddamn it!*"

286

I glanced at Juanito. Gone was the faraway, hateful waif on the *comandante's* porch. Instead, slumped against the barrel of gun in front of him, was the essence of a confused, beaten boy, who had witnessed much misery, much suffering at the hands of men, the suffering of thousands of women and their little ones at the hands of cruel men. Juanito's head rolled to the side, his gaze caught Coot's.

And they had breastplates, as it were breastplates of iron; and the sound of their wings was as the sound of chariots of many horses running in battle.

"Well, enough. *Bastante!* It is time to rid Mexico of the filth of you two *gringos*, time to rid Mexico of one of its traitors. We will save *Senores* Will Montgomery and IB Crane until the last. They will have the pleasure of watching their friends, their father, brother die. Deaths that IB Crane *alone* caused. A matter that is out of my control. I had nothing to do with it."

Mother. Papa's dying wish that we reconcile. I was never big enough.

The general strolled over to where his men were holding IB, tapped him hard on his head, turned, and began walking back.

"Gentlemen, you must forgive me for failing to bring cloth to bind your heads so that you cannot witness your own destruction. So that you may imagine the copper-plated bullets flying out of Juanito's machinegun, lead that will riddle you, cut you to pieces! Severe your head from your body. *To hell with you.* To Kingdom come! *My* will be done."

He bent over coughing. "In—in Mexico, we simply stand a man against an adobe wall. Shoot him, point-blank. But, I understand that in your country, you are much more civilized. Dead in either case, but you place a cloth, perhaps a gunny sack over the man's head, put a noose around his neck, and bolt his mount from under him. Most gruesome, you—"

Coot again stepped forward, pointing his friendly finger. "Let me tell you where to stuff your gunny sack, *Generalissimo Pinchi Pendejo!* You're a piss ant. A shit hook. No man at all. Humping a defenseless woman. In the presence of the man she loved. Humping her sister. A child. Shooting Josephina like a rabid dog. The way you eye Juanito, touch his hair, I say you like little boys, General Fat Ass. In possession of one sugar plum too many, you tub of pink shit. Get on with your killing, you maw dicker!"

I couldn't draw breath. What happened to my bravery, the courage that Coot claimed I possessed. *I'll never die!* My eyes fogged. I wanted to wipe them but my hand would not move to sweep away the mist. A cherub of a figure sitting on Juanito's shoulder with the smiling face of Na-Tu-Che-Puy. I shook my head trying to shake off the silly grin on my face.

The general pulled at his belt, adjusted his feathered sash. "Well, *Senor* Boldt. I, uh—I see that *Senor* Montgomery is not the only one in your midst with linguistic abilities. But your speech is just so much *pinche gringo* dribble. We will see how brave you are when you are peering down the black hole of Juanito's machinegun barrel. *We will see. I* will see! I have decided that *you* shall *not* see. To guarantee that you will not see, I have a request to make of you."

He stepped back to his men, then faced us. "I will ask you to turn around. *All of you.* I want to see your backs. You are cowards. You do not deserve to face me. Turn."

We stayed put, our feet in dry clay.

The general drew his pistol as he rushed forward, put the barrel at the end of Gregorio's nose. "*Turn around! All of you! Do not* tempt me, or I will put a bullet through this *pobre* traitor's thick skull."

We complied.

One woe is past; and behold, there come two woes hereafter.

I heard the general shuffling around, unable to determine what was going on.

My chest a vacuum. "*Because I could not stop for Death. He kindly stopped for me.*" *Please Lord, take care of my Zara. Make her understand.*

Coot bumped my arm. Gave me a tight fist sign. I returned it.

I yelled over my shoulder, "Will! You're a good man. I'm proud of you. Your mother and I love you, adore you."

Coot yelled, "That goes for me, Will Montgomery. You've proven yourself worthy of your father's name, the memory of Papa Abe Montgomery. *IB Crane!* Forgive me, my worthy brother."

"*Juanito! Prepare su arma!* Train your machinegun on the center of their backs. Be ready to receive my command."

Juanito pulled back the machinegun's activating lever, released it, and it clattered home.

And I saw the dead, small and great, stand before God; and the books were opened; and another book was opened; which is the book of life; and the dead were judged out of those things which were written in the books, according to their works.

Gregorio began praying in Spanish, broken English. Praying for the soul of

Father Estevan. For Mercedes, asking her forgiveness. Braced myself, wanted to scream at Gregorio to turn around, dare this son-of-a-bitch to do whatever he was going to do. *Please, Gregorio!*

Life and I were dancing a minuet, our glide frozen as a waterfall caught in a moment.

"*Listo*, Juanito!" the general commanded, then paused.

Zara's birthday. *Orion comes up at sunset. December 8. Never celebrate it again.*

Out of the corner of my eye, I saw the general turn, started walking away from the line of fire. He screamed, "Juanito! *Usted es un patriota verdadero de México!* Show these bastards how a true patriot of Mexico kills the traitors of his country, how he kills his country's enemies."

He paused. "Juanito! *Preparen! Apunten! Disparen! Fuego! Ya!*"

The blatting of the machinegun began. Repetive, rhythmic thump of a jackhammer. *Blatblatblatblatblat.*

I waited for the inevitable. Lead punching through my back. I steeled myself.

IB screamed his rage. Began running. Screamed again, this time in pain. Coot and I turned. The general was going down, cut almost in half from the blatting of the machinegun. Juanito turned his weapon on the colonel and his men. Will took cover on the ground. *Blatblatblat.* Falling like autumn leaves. *Blatblatblatblat.* Cut down like spring hay.

We had not moved a hair. Frozen in our tracks, pillars of anchor ice.

I reached for IB as he stumbled past, collapsing in Coot's arms, murmuring, "Sor-ree, brother. I'm sor . . ."

47

Chihuahua

Getting out of Mexico was harder than getting in, requiring tender care of our severely wounded man. A single bullet from Juanito's machinegun tore through IB's upper leg, shattering the bone. Juanito ran to his aid and got the bleeding under control. The lad knew of such matters. As we were leaving *Circulo de Rocas*, Coot warned Juanito that he would soon be a hunted man, that he should go with us, but he simply shook his head, and backed off. We left that place well-mounted on fine gray Arabians provided by the *Rurales*.

Five miles out of *Ciudad* Chihuahua, Coot swiveled in his saddle. "Look yonder." Juanito was coming up less than a hundred yards behind us. He said nothing, but I swear I spied the beginnings of a smile on his hard, dark features.

We hurried IB to a *medico* that Gregorio knew to be trustworthy in *Ciudad* Chihuahua, but found his small clinic scattered over much of the southern quarter of that city, destroyed by a rocket. We secreted IB on a train to Ojinaga, then got him across the Presidio bridge on a two-wheel hay cart pulled by a trembling, old burro.

Rodolfo answered our wire assuring us that he would have a physician waiting for us at his *hacienda*. We again said our goodbyes to Gregorio, then Coot, Will, IB, Juanito, and I caught the late night train for Tornillo. The doctor waiting for us was a man from New York who had been in Mexico since the outbreak of the revolution, a talented and skilled physician. He operated on IB's leg, repaired his splintered femur, and assured us that he would be good as new in a few months.

Juanito readily agreed to stay with Rodolfo in Tornillo. The lad was far from ready to venture further into "enemy territory" for now, besides he warmed to Rodolfo's easy manner and loving ways.

◉◉◉

My gunrunning days were a thing of the past. Again, I promised Zara that until Mexico's problems were resolved, I would neither set foot in, or fly over one square inch of our southerly neighbor's soil. Will wired Jonathon Everstart in England, assured him that all was well, and that he would stay with us until it was again safe to travel the seas for England.

Zara and Rose were in their element, entertaining Will with a dinner party most every night. Coot tried to convince Shelly to join in the festivities, but she was far too shy.

"She needs time, Coot," Rose advised.

Will announced that he was going to ask Elizabeth Everstart, Jonathon's younger sister, to marry him.

"Mother, she reminds me so much of you," he told Zara. "She's a head taller than you, but just as chipper, smart, pretty as a picture, just like you."

Immediately following the Armistice that officially concluded the War to End All Wars, Will caught a train bound for New York. From there, he'd sail for England, and hoped to be there by the middle of December, 1918.

Spring 1919

Coot insisted that Rose, Zara, and I accompany him out to the Crane Place. He had a surprise for Shelly Brom, something he had been working on for several months. Years ago, she signed us, asking that we not call her by full given name as her mother only did so when she was angry at her. She only wanted to be called Shelly Brom when someone loved her. We found that she was easy to love.

I'd heard that the old Casad home place had sold to an out-of-town trust.

Coot's only remark was, "A trust, huh? Probably easterners." What gives? An adjacent farm to his, and he's not even mildly curious?

We picked up Shelly and IB, then headed north along the main irrigation ditch, heading for the Casad homestead. While Mrs. Crane was alive, she regularly sent Shelly there for the *peso*-a-day cleaning-lady wages.

Coot showed us around the grounds and home place built of adobes in a horseshoe, Mexican *hacienda* fashion. The last time I was there, the roof showed signs of terminal neglect, the adobes bleeding chocolate brown down the walls onto the once-polished mesquite flooring. Now it was a shiny new dime, the hardwood floors glistened, the walls replastered, the decorative *vigas* refinished, even fuel wood waiting in the new wood-burning cook stove that sported two ovens.

Coot beamed. "Pretty nice place, huh? And it comes with 150-acres of prime irrigated farmland outback. What do you think, Shelly Brom? How do you like it, IB?"

He gawked around. "Reel-ly nice place here. Reel-ly nice."

Shelly shook her head, began backing away, signing that she didn't want to work here, that she had money of her own, liked cleaning the house her mother left her when she died.

Coot gathered her in his arms. "Shelly Brom, you don't have to clean this place *ever again* if you don't want to. But I bet you do. If you don't, IB will be tracking mud in here a foot deep."

He held her tight for a few more minutes, letting his words soak.

Shelly shook her kinky gray head, but it never came off Coot's chest.

He whispered, "You're the lady of this house, Shelly Brom, the owner, filed officially at the county courthouse. Four bedrooms, indoor plumbing, new kitchen stove, and the biggest library you've ever seen for your beautiful books. Maybe sometime you'll let me borrow one of your books—if I check it out, that is."

48

El Paso, Summer 1920

Coot came in my office, threw his hat at the hat rack, strolled over to my window that faced El Paso Street, shook his head. "Rose and I wouldn't have missed Will's and Elizabeth's wedding for anything, but you'll *never* get me back on a boat ever again! Heaving my guts all the way to England, and damned if the four of us didn't get back on that *same damn boat* for the three weeks of heaving on the ride back to New York City. Never again!"

I laughed. "That's strange. Zara's, Rose's, and my trip was right pleasant." I smiled. "Now, speaking of weddings, tell me, when are you and Rose going to get yourself hitched? I know you love her, be lost as a mangy hound dog without her. And she's told Zara that she loves you to death, but won't discuss it further than that. Think there's any chance?"

"Hell, I don't know. I've asked. Heaven knows I've asked, but when I do, she says, no. If I press her, she says, '*No!*' While we were in London, she mumbled something about not wanting the commitment of being a wife, taking on wifely duties that all married women are expected to do. I laughed and told her, 'Aw hell, Rose, you worry about the damndest things. At my age, I'm not going to crowd you too often about that kinda stuff. Hell's bells, woman, I've been diddling with a drooping prune so long, I can push a wheelbarrow with rope handles.'"

I chuckled. "Well, I hope it works out. You need a good woman. I usually don't warm to people with humility, but Rose wears hers with pride, and I like that. That, and her smile that hints she knows something about you, all combine to make her so special, such a delight to be around. Best not let her out of your sight. She's a prize. And, old partner, there may not be any wedding bells in your immediate future, but Zara's determined there will be in mine. She wants to throw a big shindig and repeat our wedding vows. Will and Elizabeth are on a three-month honeymoon, and after touring Canada beginning the first of the month, they'll swing down through the state of Washington to California, be here around the tenth of September. Zara wants to introduce the couple to El Paso and get our wedding vows restated, all at the same wingding on our twenty-seventh wedding anniversary."

49

El Paso, September 16, 1920

"Will, I must insist that you and Elizabeth sit at the head table. The Paso del Norte Hotel is a proper setting for the reception and ceremony, the table has been set, and your names appear on printed name placards. Please, my adorable son, do not disappoint your mother. Today is your father's and my twenty-seventh wedding anniversary. Won't you do this for us?"

Elizabeth spoke up. "Zara, my darling mother-in-law, a lady I shall forever refer to as Mother." She squeezed Zara, laughed. "Please, dear one, you shan't worry yourself on Will's account. I have the wherewithal to see that Will and I are property seated."

Zara and Rose had made certain that every detail of the ceremony was planned. The invitations went out, folks started gathering from near and far. The welcoming reception and dinner at the Paso del Norte behind us, the reason for all this "folderol," as Coot phrased it, was nigh.

On that bright shiny day, Rodolfo Bustamante enjoyed a special place of honor. He had just returned from Parral to visit Francisco Villa to renew old acquaintances. He reported that the general was the same egotist as ever, first blaming his men, then his one-time ally, America, anyone and everything except where the real fault lay.

Two other special guests from Sacred Heart School for Girls arrived: Mother Superior Pancretias, now retired, and Sister Juana Tsagaris, the nun who saved Rose in her childhood flight from Panama. Three of Zara's lady friends arrived who had fought by her side in their long battle for Women's Suffrage, all-abuzz about the ratification of 19th Amendment, just last month. Big George and Marina Smith, ever-broad smiles on their faces, Sly Fox and Broken Chain and their wives fetched another flavor to the occasion.

Darling Shelly Brom arrived in another gift from Coot, a brand-spanking-new metal-blue Stanley Steamer Touring Car with twin brother, IB. She, doing right-nice justice to a fine, veiled, silk gown. IB, all duded-up in a light blue, seersucker suit, green polka-dot bowtie, and a flat-top straw hat.

Good cheer filled the air. Hugs, kisses, *abrazos* all around. Life was grand on this singularly special day.

When the *padre* arrived, Zara and I stood at the makeshift alter in the hotel's ballroom, Rose stood to her right as maid of honor, Shelly as bridesmaid, Coot stood to my left as best man, IB as groomsman.

A somber affair that brought back a flood of memories, Zara, beautiful as ever. At the conclusion of the ceremony, and our "I do's" having been repeated, she and I stepped back, the lady to her right and the man to my left came together, and Zara and I occupied the space they vacated. The surprised crowd gasped, a rousing cheer filled the air.

Zara now stood between Shelly and Rose, IB on my left, the man to my right in a black, swallow-tail tuxedo and spats.

The *padre* asked, "Edwin 'Coot' Boldt, do you take this woman, Rose Marie Talamantes, as your lawful wedded wife?"

"Yes, sir, I do. I most assuredly do."

50

Coot yearned for adventure, convinced Rose that they needed excitement in their lives, excitement other than travel and entertaining.

"Like what?" she asked.

"Like teaching you about ranch life, that sort of thing."

Rose hugged his neck. "Tell me, Mr. Rancherman, what could you teach me about ranch life?"

"Well, for one thing, I know in my gut that you procrastinated about marrying me, fearful I'd soon have you with child. If you had been around animals instead of other couples' brats back at Sacred Heart, you'd know that female cows and horses and goats get in what is called 'season,' that dogs and cats and such get in 'heat.' They don't get pregnant unless they're ready. Same as the fair sex isn't equipped for childbearing after they're past ovulating. No little egg, no little chickies."

☺☺☺

The Mount Riley Ranch was, once again, repossessed by our old friend, Jon Hansen. Jon was a persistent man, pressed Coot and me to take it on, nothing down, pay him when we got the old ranch making money.

That big ol' place only had eighty acres of deeded land, the balance of the ninety sections was a combination of leased state and federal lands. Previous owners never invested in fencing, erecting windmills, the sort of necessities for a successful high-desert ranch. Why? Improvements made on leased land automatically became the property of the government. Those well-meaning cowboys were dead at the starting gate, couldn't make it pay, and Jon was tired of messing with ranchers who had neither pot or window.

That was of no concern to Coot Boldt.

"Who cares who owns the improvements?" he pointed out. "We'll make the improvements, run cattle on it for twenty years, recoup our investment, a bunch more on top of that, and get Jon Hansen finally shut of the place."

Cattle need water, and the Mount Riley Ranch was as dry as popcorn induced wind. We hired a witcher, Clydel Walker by name, who commenced to walk around in ever widening circles with a forked stick out in front of him, sorta pointing it out there ten feet or so, walking this way and that, for days-on-end.

At the end of the third week, Clydel arched his back, popped his galluses on his holey long handle shirt, stuck his boot on the drooping bumper of his Model-T pickup, reared back and said, "Fellers, I've witched every square foot of your grazing country, *every damn inch* of a million acres or so, without nary'a damn indication. Not nary'a damn one! Tomorree, I'm headed up in your high country. First thet peak over yonree, then thet'un over thet-a-way. If I don't come cross't an indicator, I'm draggin' my ass on home to my old lady. Cain't waste no more time on this dingleberry you call a ranch."

We watched Clydel all morning, climbing this hill then that. Suddenly, his "willer stick," as he termed it, commenced to begin to jump out of his hand, pointing straight down betwixt his size fourteens.

Clydel smiled. "This here's the place you should-oughta poke yor hole." He stuck his willer stick in the gravel. "Righ'*cher!* They's wa-tree down there for certain. Poke yor hole, put a big ol' twenty-foot mill on a windmill platform, and I gorantee you'll pump a thousand gallons an hour fer-*ever.*"

⊚⊚⊚

Things rocked along right smooth, then Coot determined that we needed a proper entrance to the ranch. We set out to erect an arched sign advertising the ranch so passerbys would know in whose high-presence they were traversing. We dug great holes in the ground and set large oak stumps in the ground, set them in four-feet of concrete to hold the heavy gate and overhead sign we planned. Forgot one thing: before setting the stumps in the ground, we should have used our weight on the brace and bit to drill holes for bolts to secure the massive gate. This would take some serious thought.

Rose drove her 1920 rainbow blue, Chandler Six touring automobile out the sandy road that parallel the railroad tracks, and she and Zara stayed with us for a week. Man, it was grand! Home cooked meals, clean sheets, feminine conversation, and polite company for a change.

One scorching-hot morning, Coot and I spent hours attempting to bore a one-inch hole in one of those tough oak logs with a brace and bit. The ground was sand and loose gravel, giving us no way of positioning ourselves in such a manner so as to put any meaningful force on our boring apparatus. The sun was past chest-high, yet we were not even halfway through the foot-thick, upright log. Adding injury to insult, our chore was doubled when we encountered a gnarly, rock-hard knot. Coot sat on the far side of the log, arms on either side, pulling on my arms and shirt in an effort to help me get a prize on the brace and get the hole dug. We were spent.

"Narlow, damn it, you should have drilled this damn hole while this log was horizontal so you could get some weight on it, *before* we set it in concrete."

I pushed back from the log, wiped the grime off my face with my dirty bandana, looked across at him, shook my head.

About that time, Zara and Rose drove up in a buckboard, both under pretty pink flowery parasols. They smiled down at us as we strained and sweated.

We were below ground level in our gravel and sand hole, me pushing on the brace, twisting the handle, Coot on the far side pulling on the brace and my arms in our fruitless effort. As hard as we huffed and puffed, pushed and pulled, grunted and groaned, pissed and moaned, that dull one-inch bit just would *not* bite into that damnable knot.

Zara smiled down at us. "Narlow dearest, why don't you just fire a bullet from your rifle through that tough knot? You're always bragging about how powerful that rifle is, so why don't you just shoot your way through it?"

We looked up at two sweet, smiling, bright, fresh-as-rain faces.

Coot glanced at me—I grimaced.

He whispered, "Do you think your rifle would blow a hole through this goddamn log?"

"My .45-70? *Hell yes!* It'd go clear through it. *Damn*."

"God, I hate this!"

He stood, took off his hat, dried the hatband with his shirtsleeve as he fought a grin, looked up at our ladies. I kept my seat in the dirt, wiping sweat and grit, trying not to smirk.

Coot asked, "Don't you gals have anything better to do than sit out here in the heat? Why don't you go back to the house and fix us something to eat? We'll be along dreckly."

Rose's dark, mischievous eyes flashed. "Oh no, Coot my love, don't you worry yourself about us. It's quite pleasant sitting up here in the breeze under our parasols. We'll just sit here until Narlow blows a hole through that knothole with his rifle. *Then* we'll go back to the house and fix you men a nice noonday meal."

51

El Paso, April 1, 1929, A Day After Our Seventieth Birthdays

For several years running, I'd flown alone to Oshkosh, Wisconsin to attend the annual Airshow held on the banks of Lake Winnebago, a setting as fair as a lass lounging on a carpet of fresh-mown hay.

Couldn't get either Coot or Rose to accompany me, but I was determined to convince Coot to go with me. The straw that got his camel in the front seat of my open-cockpit bi-wing was my relating the news item that Amelia Earhart flew as a passenger across the Atlantic. That ate on him until he relented.

We were in Oshkosh for eight days. True, Coot was not a pilot, but he sure as hell enjoyed hob-knobbing with the growing ranks of pilots. We spent seven glorious nights, swapping stories and lies of daring adventures, true and imagined. Young Great War veterans told their chilling, hair-curling stories. One veteran was shot down by the great German ace, Manfred von Vichthofen. He admitted he didn't go out of his way to challenge the Red Baron again, content to be only one of the Baron's eighty victories. Those young pilots were in their natural prime, as full of themselves as a Mexican *piñata*.

Everyone knew Coot and I had run guns to Pancho Villa, and begged us to tell about our many adventures and close calls. The story of my flying munitions into Mexico in a Curtiss got their attention. Some of the war pilots among us had flown the biwing in dogfights with the German Fokkers, and were amazed that a mere civilian had flown that beast and lived to tell the tale. When I made light of my flying experiences, one strapping young fellow slapped me on the back. "You may not have ever had a dogfight over France, but then none of us ever lit a cigar to a keg of dynamite tied on a shelf next to our ears, and doodled it off at a Mexican military post."

Coot thumped his chest. "Nothing to it, ladies. He had a world-class instructor."

We got folks to laughing, setting them at ease. Our "foreign" accent, our colloquialisms, manners, dress, and easy ways, melded together to make us the most sought after pair at the Airshow. Coot absolutely glowed with the attention. We were the rage, that's a certain—even won a cheap brass trophy recognizing us as the oldest "couple" to make the fly-in to the Airshow.

Sitting on my cot, listening to Coot expound, laughing uproariously about some escapade, a memory I hadn't thought of in more than half a century was a swirl of reminisces. His recollection of IB Crane's pet scorpion about brought the house down. Though he told that tale repeatedly, he'd hardly get started, get to belly-laughing before finishing the first sentence.

He'd wipe his eyes, and say, "Now, keep in mind, I'm not making fun of IB, 'cause he's my half-brother, been our best friend for all our seventy years. Anyway, to get on with IB— and— and his—" Again, he'd get the belly-laughs, and when he'd catch his breath, he'd say, "Aw, shit. Oh, forgive my loose tongue, ladies. Narlow, you tell that story. You tell it better than me anyway."

"Well, all right folks, I'll tell that tale again, just like this morning, three times yesterday, and the day before. Anyway, Coot's half-brother lived down the lane that separated Coot's farm from the Crane place. This lad's name is IB Crane. Believe it or not, his given name is Ichabod, as in Ichabod Crane. Bless his heart, IB is what you might say is the kind of feller that has both boots in the same stirrup.

"On this particular morning, the three of us were around fourteen or so, IB was a'skippin' along, heading our way, me and Coot hard at work, shoveling out an irrigation ditch on his mama's farm. We plopped ourselves down on the side of the ditch, cool, fresh-turned earth felt right pleasant on our backsides on that scorching day. IB sidled up, the morning sun behind him. Something dreadful was perched on his shoulder, but the sun was full in my face. Suddenly, *I see it.* I jumped to my feet. 'IB, do you know that's a full-grown gol-danged scorpion you have tied by that string on your shoulder?'

"That scorpion's stinger was standing at attention, waving around like a mule's ears in a stiff breeze. The sight of it made you flinch, made a man want to look the other way, but you *had* to see what that varmint was about to do to poor ol' IB.

"IB beamed. 'Yep, thet thar's a scor-peen aw-right, fellers. And, her name's One-Leg-ged Lilly.'

"Coot asked, 'IB could you tell us how you can be certain that One-Legged Lilly is a girl scorpion? Couldn't it just as easy be a boy scorpion?'

"IB flashed a toothy grin, boy had a gap between his buck teeth, you could stick your thumb clean through, with considerable more space between his buck teeth than his eyes.

"IB asked, 'Coot, you a'funnin' me?'

299

"'No, I'm not funnin' you, just sorta curious as to why you're so all-fired certain it's a girl scorpion, that's all.'

"IB smiled his all-knowing smile. 'Well, Coot, let me ax'd how you'd like to be a boy scor-peen with a name like One-Leg-ged Lilly—huh? Can ye jest answer me thet there?'

"Coot said, 'IB, I think you've bested me again. You have a scorpion named One-Legged Lilly, and it just follows that the scorpion's a girl. Where'd you get that thing and why—for heaven's sake—*why* do you have it tied on a thread around your neck? Aren't you afraid of that dern thing?'

"'Naw, Coot, I ain't sceered'a her. I stolt her from my twin-sister, Shelly Brom. She keeps her in a match box under her bed piller. What else did ye ax'd me—oh! You wanted to know'd why'd I have her tied on the end of this strang 'round my neck. If'n I didn't have her tied with thet strang, why she'd likely to run off'n a hole somewhar, 'n Shelly Brom'd get kind'er put out with me.'

"IB stopped, kicked at a clod, stuck his thumb in his ear. 'Lemme think now. What elst ye done ax'd me? Ye ax'd me so dern many thangs at onct, lemme think now . . .'

"With finality, Coot said, 'Nothing, IB! I don't want to know another blessed thing about that scorpion, so—'

"I said, 'Coot wanted to know why your sister would name a six-legged in-sect by the name of One-Legged Lilly.'

"'A six-leg-ged what?' He stood with his mouth agape, his yellow-green eyes glazed over in wonderment.

"I said, 'An insect—you know, a bug. Uh, let me start over, IB. Why would your sister name her One-Legged Lilly when she's got six legs'.

"'Well, Narlow, I'll just tell ye . . . .'

"As IB's explanation takes form behind his narrow eyes, I caught a glance of Coot's exasperated rage swell up in his dark eyes, and I took off a'runnin' down that lane, 'cause Coot was after me with a long-handled shovel."

Coot and I told stories about the Indian Wars, and the shoot-'em-ups of the old West. A young man sitting on the end of the cot asked, "Mr. Boldt, I know you gentlemen are from El Paso, but I read that the *real* old West was never in Texas or New Mexico, but over in Tombstone, Arizona. Isn't that true, Mr. Boldt?"

"Naw, son, that's just dime-novel-Hollywood crap. It wasn't until the turn of the century that the old West finally died out in El Paso. That dusty old border town is at the southern end of the Tularosa Basin that goes north nearly 250-miles into New Mexico. It was El Paso and the Tularosa Basin where the old West was alive and well until damn few years ago. We oughta know, 'cause we lived through the West's heyday."

⊚⊚⊚

At dawn the last morning, I lay on my cot wondering what's in store for us, for me and Zara, Coot and Rose, how IB and Shelly Brom would do. I always knew I'd live past my century mark, while Coot always expressed great surprise that he even made it past forty, mainly because his daddy died in his early forties. IB and Shelly Brom are our age, Rose will be sixty-five in August, Zara's the baby in our group, turning fifty-eight in December. As Coot would say, "We need to get poppin'."

Our sad good-byes having been said on that lazy, cloud-puff morning, we taxied out on the grass to go through my preflight checklist. Shouts of, "Say 'hi' to IB and One-Legged Lilly. See you next year," filled the early dawn air.

My open cockpit two-seater had controls in both the front and back seats, and could be flown from either position. As pilot, I preferred the back seat as it gave me a better view of the ground on landing. Six hours later, I slapped the canvas shell of the bi-wing between Coot and me. He turned back to see me with both hands clasped behind my head, off the controls. I yelled, "Hey, Coot! Take over for a spell. I need a snooze."

He grabbed the stick with one big fist, and for ten minutes he had us on a merry-go-round-roller-coaster ride that took us all over the wide panhandle of Texas. He over-corrected his dive to near stalls, flapping the wings this way then that, me all the time feigning sleep, my head bobbing on my chest when I knew he was set to turn to cuss me.

He turned his head away from the wind. "*You bastard!* Take over this damn thing before I get us both killed."

I fed him some navigational clues, and in due time, he had us hop scotched over two states and over El Paso, headed northwest around Mount Franklin for Wind Mesa.

When we crossed the Rio Grande, he held both arms over his head. "*That's it!* Take over this bitch."

As we banked over our airstrip on Wind Mesa, we saw scores of trucks and automobiles lining the strip, like half of El Paso had shown up for our return on that high sandhill mesa. I slowed the plane for landing.

301

Coot turned and asked, "What's this all about?"

"Beats me."

The mayors of El Paso and Juarez were on hand, as was every dignitary and every friend we ever had from the mayor and sheriff on down to some of El Paso's more noted bar-flies were there to welcome us home.

I cut the engine. "What's all the commotion about, boys?"

Mayor R. E. Thomason stepped up and began expounding something about Coot and me being named Chancellors Emeritus of the grand and glorious States of Texas and New Mexico.

"Chancellors and Emeritus, my ass," LeRoy Pearson yelled out. "That and a nickel will buy you a cup of coffee at Mike's Pretty Good Cup."

About that time, Jim Sleeper, a cub reporter for the *Times*, was trying to get our attention. I motioned him over.

"Mr. Montgomery, I was late getting out here this afternoon, and I was wondering if I could impose on you gentlemen to take off again in your airplane, and come back around. I'd like to get some action pictures for tomorrow's issue of the *Times*."

A chill raced up my spine. I was aware of a sound I'd not heard in years. The bugle of a bull elk, a purple mushroom blinded me. I pushed my way through the crowd, folks I'd known all my life, taking on the form of gargoyles, gruesome, purple. *Mama. Her horse quirk.*

"*Coot.* I need to talk to you. I—"

He grinned. "Well, what do you say, Narlow? Ready to see if we can stretch your hat size another couple of notches?"

"Coot—my mushroom—it's back. The bull elk whistle. I—"

"Aw hell, Narlow! You haven't mentioned those damn things in years. *Come on!* Let's give these folks a show!"

I shook it off. "Okay, get your ass up there and let's take her for a spin." Coot got in, fought with the seat harness, and buckled himself in. Mr. Zork was telling me about his Hollywood friends, but the crowd pushed me on, boosted me up to my seat behind Coot.

Smoke filled my nostrils. Smoke from an oak-fed fire, burning leather. A howling, bugling cry of a bull elk, a woman screaming in the wind. I glanced up—a double ring circled the sun.

Again, I shook it off, cranked her up, the crowd split, I poured the coal to her, and off we went. At last, *a real hot-dog.* Coot turned around to me, eyebrows arched, but said nothing. He didn't like something, but I was full of myself, couldn't care less.

We went streaking down the strip that overlooked the Rio and the long sandhill slope down to that slow moving brown stream. Twice in a single split-second, that damn mushroom fought for my attention, the bugle of the elk. Again I glanced up at the double ring, brushed them all aside. Streaking, *streaking* down the gravel strip. The bi-wing lifted off, the engine coughed, sputtered, the propeller fluttered to a halt. I nosed it over to maintain speed. Just as quickly, the engine leapt back to life. Before I could get her nose back up, we skimmed the end of the runway, clipped the edge of a small dune at the lip of the mesa. The bi-wing nosed in hard, flipped over tail-first, slid down the sandy slope of the mesa on her back, coming to rest with her tail submerged in the edge of the river, wheels clawing at the sky, spinning.

I was catapulted clear when we hit the dune as I had failed to buckle my seat harness, landed in the sand at an angle, slid all the way down the sandhill mesa to the edge of the river. I recalled getting up, dusting myself off, stumbling across the river, striping off as I sloshed along, washing the sand off my arms and face.

Big George and IB had gotten off to a late start for the welcoming, and were driving up the river road from El Paso. They crossed the shallow Rio within 100-feet of where the plane settled.

I heard Big George yell, "*Grab him, IB!* Grab Narlow. He doesn't know who he is or where he's going."

Big George turned back to the blazing bi-wing. Ignoring the flames, he cut Coot's seat harness and he tumbled into his arms, Coot's legs dangling in the water.

◉◉◉

Rose rushed down the hospital corridor, I embraced her, begged her forgiveness.

She pushed me back, smiled, took my hands in hers, Zara's arms hugging her from behind.

"Narlow, my darling, you know what this reminds me of? When you and Coot went to Carichic to rescue me from my own childish stupidity, I repeatedly begged for your forgiveness. Remember what you said? *Spilled milk, spilled milk!* There was nothing that could be done about the Curtiss' broken propeller any more than you can reverse what happened today."

"But I—Rose, I—"

303

"Yes, I know. You neglected to buckle your seat harness and forgot to go through your preflight list. The same procedure that you pounded into me when you taught me to fly your Curtiss Pusher. I suppose a magneto failed, or your fuel mixture was off."

"Yes, Rose, but damn me, I—"

"*Spilled milk*, Narlow!"

She hugged me for a long minute, me as limp as a wet rag.

"Now, what about my Coot? When Big George came out to the farm to get me, he told me all he knew when he checked Coot in at emergency. It wasn't good then, and I doubt it's improved."

"I'm afraid you're right. His burns cover a majority of his head, body and arms. His legs are the only things that escaped the fire. It doesn't look good for him."

"How long?" she asked, her dark eyes spilling over.

"Days. Three at the most. They won't be easy days for him. You either. Me? I don't know what to say. Coot's lifelong partner is already dead."

Zara and I sat with Rose for four days and nights, Rose biting her lip, Coot under a sheeted-framework, a clear plastic drapery curtained his bed. He regained consciousness the morning of the third day, attempted a smile, nodded, and drifted off.

52

Over the months, if I heard Rose say, "*Spilled milk!*" once, I heard it a thousand times.

Just last week, I was edging into blaming myself again, she said, "Narlow, dear man, you must always remember that when Coot died, he did so with his only lifelong friend by his side."

She smiled. "And oh how I would have loved to have been there when you took your hands off the control stick, and forced Coot to fly that bi-wing. That must have been *really special!*"

On Christmas Eve, Rose sat with Zara on our living room couch, squeezed Zara's hand.

"Zara, you have repeatedly begged me to come live with you and Narlow, but I so wanted to stay at Coot's old home place. But I still see him working out by the barn, hear the breathing of his forge, his hammer ping on his anvil, bringing wood for my cook stove, his handsome face winks at me from every nook and cranny, hear his boots scuffing down the hall, smell his sweaty old hat hanging on the hat rack, *everything*. When I go out to his barn to fetch a hammer or pliers, the tool is always warm. Warm, like he had been working with it and had just put it down. His essence is *everywhere!* I feel his hand on my waist while laying awake in bed, feel his caress, his breath in my hair, his lips on mine. And, then there's—"

"Rose," I said, "you know you're welcome—"

She raised her hand. "Narlow, you, *above all*, need to hear this. It's strange, but I think Coot had a premonition of his death. I *know* he did. The night before you left for Winnebago, we were sitting at the kitchen table. He bolted out of his chair, stood with his hand cupped to one ear. He said, '*Hear that?*' He ran to the back door, peering out into the moonlit night. He said, 'There it is again!' I went to him and asked what he had heard. He said, 'You don't hear that? A woman wailing. You don't hear it?' All I heard were crickets and a clucking hen.

"After a moment, he turned to me and smiled. 'My god, Rose, that's not a woman wailing, that's Narlow's bull elk call, like the bugling they do during rut. He's always heard that high-pitched bugle when danger is near. Nothing I can explain to you, but I witnessed it countless times over the years, all the way back to when we were boys living with the Apaches. The last time I recall that he heard it was when it warned him that four Mexicans wearing *sombreros* were waiting to ambush us on the Rio up at the San Pedro crossing. I didn't hear it then, never heard it all those many years—until just now."

Rose stood, strolled to the fireplace, and turned.

"Coot was always so stable, stoic, so matter-of-fact, so different from all other men. Again that night, he put his finger to his lips to shush me. 'There it is again—*louder!*' He gazed through the back door at the shadows caste by the moon. He said, 'Rose, *look!* There's Na-Tu-Che-Puy sitting on that old cottonwood stump by the barn, and there's Many Fast Feet Two Sticks standing behind him. And, by God Almighty and all that's holy! *Rose!* There's Narlow's papa, my Uncle Abe! There all beckoning for me to join them in the dark. See them waving me to them?'

"Coot pushed through the screen door and walked out in the yard. I asked him not to go, but he kept going. I watched him walk over by the barn, heard him call those old Apache's by name, Papa's name, several times, then after a while he came back in the house.

"He said, 'Did you see that, Rose? See those men? See that ring around the moon? God, I wish Narlow was here to see that! But he'd just laugh, call me a fool, remind me that a pale moon can sport a double halo, but never a ring like the sun.'

"Hours after we went to bed, he awakened me, told me that if anything happened to him, he'd rest easier knowing that I'd gone to you, moved in with the two of you. Around three in the morning, I heard him rummaging around in the kitchen. Said he was looking for a nib for his pen. I found one for him and went back to bed. Just before he left the house the next morning to meet you at Wind Mesa for your flight to the Airshow, he gathered me in his arms like he always did, folded me close for the longest time, like he was breathing me inside him."

Rose sat back down by Zara, took her hand.

"Then Coot said, 'Rose, you know that, next to you, Zara's the finest woman in the world, and I can vouch for Narlow. He'll take care of you, he senses things we don't. Has Power. He'd eat the head off a diamond back, chew it up and spit it in the eye of any man who would harm you. There's another thing about my friend. He'll outlive both you and Zara by several years—always said he'd live to be 107. I don't doubt him. Advise you not to doubt him about that—or *anything!* I want your solemn word that when something happens to me, you'll leave this place, move in with them in town. Promise. *Promise me!*'

"Of course I promised him, then watched him get in the Reo and drive down the lane. And that's when it dawned on me, his words crashed down on me, their force like a mountain of granite. When he awakened me during the night, he used the phrase, '*if* anything happened to him,' but just before he left, he used the word, *when*. That good and true man sensed his own fate.'"

I said, "You know, Rose, I always wondered how you could have been so calm at the hospital when you first arrived after my stunt at Wind Mesa. But you had steeled yourself, knowing far in advance that something was about to happen to your Coot. You knew he'd had his own vision."

"Yes. Yes, when I walked into the hospital, I was my own slab of granite, could have told you everything that happened at the airstrip, how you were thrown clear of the wreckage, how Coot was caught in the flames. Yes, I was in a fog, and yes, I was grieving, but I knew it was coming. Nothing anyone could do about it, not even you. As you said, I had steeled myself."

She walked over to the Christmas tree, picked an envelope off a back branch, then sat back down.

"I know we'll exchange gifts in the morning, but here's a present that just will not wait. I found this letter in Coot's things."

She handed the envelope to me. "Open it, please."

"But, Rose, this is in Coot's hand. A letter to you."

"Yes, it is. Please read it aloud for Zara."

Wee hours, April 1, 1929

My dearest Rose,
Life has been a wonderful windmill, a whirlwind-duster of a ride. With you by my side, that duster was my ticket to heaven. I've just about done it all, at least all I ever wanted to do.
Zara will recall last Christmas Eve, I told her off to the side that I had been keeping a journal of our lives, mine and Narlow's over all our years. I made mention of it to her in response to her earlier admonition to Narlow that night. You'll recall that we were all standing in their living room, sipping a brandy, laughing, talking about old times, then Zara stood before him, thumped him on the chest, and said, 'Narlow Montgomery, there's a story in there and you're going to tell it. You are going to write a book!'
You see, dear Rose, I began keeping those journals about the time Zara

and Narlow were married in 1893, went back to our childhood, scratched out everything I could recall to that time, and continued my scratch to this very day.

You'll find those thirty-some-odd journals in an old travel chest in Big George's storage shed out behind his shop. He knows about them. When you give that big old box to Narlow, tell him that all he has to do is write in the necessary spit and polish, do some T-crossing and I-dotting, and he'll have himself a finished book. Take it to Hollywood. And for goodness sake, tell him to make me look pleasing to the ladies.

I love you, my dear Lady Rose, and like that old gospel song goes, I'll love you ten thousand years from today,

Coot

Epilogue

Zara called from the kitchen. "Shelly Brom dear, Rose is helping me get the turkey out of the oven. Would you please see who's at the front door?"

Zara and Rose heard a refined lady's voice. "Good day, madam, I am Lela James with the *El Paso Times.* I was going to ask if I may impose upon you for a few moments this morning, but I see you are dressed to leave your home. Perhaps another time."

Rose rushed to the aid of both women at the door. "Hello, I'm Rose Boldt. I heard you say that you are with the *Times*. May I help you?"

"I do apologize for this intrusion, but I wish to speak to you and Mrs. Zara Montgomery for the briefest time. I fully realize you have refused other interviews with reporters, but I thought perhaps that my being the daughter of Joseph and Pricilla James might persuade you to grant me an interview. You see, my mother and Mrs. Montgomery worked side by side during the struggle for the passage of the 19th Amendment. Additionally, my father is the publisher of the *Boston Globe*, so I suppose that it follows that I have a natural bent to journalism, the only female on the *Times* staff.

"I'll come back another day and—"

Zara wiped her hands on a cup towel as she went to the door. "Did I hear the name Pricilla James just now? You're her daughter?"

"Yes, ma'am. But please forgive me. You ladies were just leaving and I—"

Rose and Zara laughed, realizing the three of them did indeed appear to be dressed to leave the house.

Zara hugged Shelly. "Oh, these full-length mink coats! This old house is so drafty and cold that we wear them to stay warm. We never have occasion to wear them since we lost our men, so we wear them to stay warm. They're nice and toasty, but they definitely make us look like three little old crazy biddies, don't they?"

She turned to Rose and Shelly. "Ladies, this beautiful young lady's mother and I served together on countless Women's Suffrage committees. We must have marched through all of Massachusetts, Missouri, and half of Texas during those years. If we are ever to grant an interview, I believe it should be given to Miss James."

Shelly took the young reporter by the hand and seated her in the parlor.

Rose smiled. "This will be a delightful day. I'll heat water for tea."

Lela James sat at the end of the settee, prim and proper as a shiny twenty-dollar gold piece, her stenographer tablet and pen and ink in her lap.

Zara sat next to her, put her hand on hers. "You are as stately and beautiful as your dear mother, same slate-gray eyes, just like my Narlow's papa's eyes. Please call me Zara. The three of us are all friends of well over a half-century, and hold formality to a minimum."

Rose served tea, then sat by Shelly across the long coffee table on the facing couch.

Zara asked, "Well, Lela, how can three little old gray-haired ladies help you? You've read about all that can be said in the newspapers, and no doubt heard accounts of our men on the radio. Some true, others greatly exaggerated."

"Yes, everyone knows of Mr. Boldt's death and Mr. IB Crane's passing, and of course the recent tragedy suffered by Mr. Montgomery. But what interests me, and hopefully my readers, is the spine, the flesh, as my publisher-father would say, the 'back story' of your lives with your extraordinary men. That's what I want to hear, and with your kind permission, what my readers will feel and experience on the printed pages of the *Times*."

Zara said, "Well, I don't know exactly where to begin."

Lela looked up from her writing pad. "Tell me about Narlow and Coot as men, their hopes, dreams, friends. What were they like to be around on a Sunday morning? What was it about them that set them so far apart in the eyes of so many who knew them?"

"Well, I believe Rose will agree that Coot was the more realistic of the two, Narlow the more idealistic, the dreamer of the two. Narlow lost his first wife to diphtheria, and Coot had an equally tragic previous marriage to the lady who used to live just across the street. She moved back to Connecticut soon after Coot's death. Coot became, shall I say, aloof, toward most women." She paused, smiled across the coffee table. "That is until Rose came along. But Narlow was always a bit of a romantic, though a bit off the beaten path."

Zara laughed, squeezed her arms tight. "Narlow's idea of romantic was like the time just last July when he was set to go to Sacred Mountain, he gathered me in his arms, said, 'Zara, you've always given me the crazies, make me want to drink the rheum from your eyes and nose.' He was in such a rush to get on the road, that I let it pass. Later, I looked it up." She giggled. "Narlow drinking the watery fluid from my eyes and nose is not the most endearing thing I've ever heard, but coming from him, and for *whatever reason*, to this very day it makes me squeeze my arms and smile. It was—it was just *him*."

Lela smiled. "The love you shared shines so plainly in your eyes."

Zara said, "Rose, you must tell Lela what you did almost immediately after your Coot's passing. It's so special the way you honored your husband."

Rose smiled, put her hands on her knees, squeezed her shoulders up. "Coot was such a dear. It was a shame he didn't have a son, and though he never had one, I did what I knew he would want me to do. I contacted Sacred Heart Orphanage in Dallas, and arranged for the adoption of a splendid sixteen-year-old boy. He came here to El Paso; brilliant, mannerly, eager to please, big, raw-boned, just like Coot. His only fault was his considerable vocabulary that Papa Abe would have termed, 'muleskinner' adjectives. His name was Mansfield Weatherly Smith, and he didn't like it. Not one bit. After a couple of weeks working out on the farm, he came in for lunch, sat down, threw his hat across the kitchen at Coot's old hat rack, and said, 'Mother, I believe I could eat the ass out of a skunk.'" Rose laughed. "It was as if Coot had been reincarnated. The lad's mannerism, his speech, *everything* was just like my Coot. When he finished his noon meal, I asked him to stay, to talk about his life with me on Coot's farm, what he saw for his future. He loved it, said his long visits with Narlow, his telling of the old days with Coot, that he had learned about a man who would have been his stepfather, and he was already proud of the man he would never know. We talked on, then I asked him, that since he didn't care for the name he was given by a mother he never knew, if he would like to be named, Edwin 'Coot' Boldt, Jr. He grabbed me up, swung me around the kitchen and jumped for joy! I am so proud of him, a man who's been my son for fifteen-years, a man who's married to a darling woman, and they have a baby on the way. If it's a boy, he'll be named after his father, after my Coot."

Lela said, "You have been such a blessing to that young man. I admire you *so* much."

She turned back to Zara. "Now, may I ask you tell me about the recent past at the Fort Bliss airstrip? How did that horrific day have its beginning? How could all of that have been arranged with the army?"

"You mean Narlow's ride in the P-38 dive-bomber as a civilian? Well, it's such a long story, but first, you must know that my husband was a pilot whose flying began back in 1913." Zara smiled across the coffee table. "I would wager that you didn't know that Rose was also a pilot, one of the very first lady pilots. A woman, a nun straight out of Sacred Heart! Can you even imagine? But anyway, my husband 'hung up his goggles,' as he referred to it, immediately after Coot met his tragic end. To move the story forward, you must know something else about my husband. As a sixteen-year-old boy, he studied to be a medicineman when he and Coot lived with the Apache. The medicineman under whom Narlow studied was convinced that he had what they called Power: he could see through boulders; an elk's bugle and a purple mushroom warned him of danger. You've seen the phenomenon of ice crystals forming a ring around the sun on a clear day. That ring foretold eminent danger that invariably showed itself to Narlow. I realize those words sound so—"

Zara hesitated, turned in her seat to face her guest, took her hands in hers. "Lela child, I cannot prove any of this, but you must accept it at face value to move forward with what I have to say."

"Yes, Zara, of course. Mother assured me that I could believe anything you have to say."

Rose laughed. "And my Coot said just before he died, that if I ever doubted Narlow, that he'd spank my backside."

Zara went on. "Well, just last June, Narlow began pestering me about his wish to climb the Apache's Sacred Mountain, what the New Mexico map shows as Salinas Peak. He wanted to view what his vision had spoken of for many months, a vision that demanded the presence of Sly Fox and Broken Chain, two now-ancient Apache men who Narlow and Coot knew from their days with the Apaches. The particulars of their days on top of that pile of rocks, as I referred to Sacred Mountain, were reported rather willy-nilly by the *Times*, but we all now know that they witnessed the world's first atomic bomb blast from the crest of that mountain, precisely as described in Narlow's vision.

"The army thought they had taken all necessary precautions so that the outside world would never learn what had occurred only eighty-five miles north of El Paso just last July in the middle of the Tularosa Basin. The army even arrested and forcibly evicted ranchers from their homes so no one would know what the army was about.

"But those two old Apaches and Narlow knew! When Narlow returned from the mountain, he told his coffee group down at JJ Newberry's all about it. Bill Paul

Schultz, your fellow reporter, overheard the story and printed it." Zara laughed. "Not precisely, but he printed it.

"Well, wouldn't you know, that afternoon, Fort Bliss' General Morsely visited us here in our home, told us it was a matter of national security that Narlow sign an affidavit retracting his story, that it was all pure fabrication, the dreaming of an old man.

"Narlow knew that he'd face much humiliation, but my eighty-six-year old darling husband faced all comers."

Shelly began signing Rose. She laughed. "Shelly Brom wants you to tell Lela about Narlow's night in jail."

Zara chuckled. "Oh, *that!* I must admit that episode was not one of Narlow's high points, but I could not blame him. The day after his retraction appeared in an extra edition of the paper, he was driving Coot's old six-wheel Reo down Texas Street, stopped at an intersection, and one of El Paso's elites, Mr. Richard Spency, pulled up beside him in a little yellow sports car, and began shouting, warning motorists to be careful. 'Look out! Here comes Narlow Montgomery and he's throwing bombs!' Narlow crammed the Reo in six-wheel-low, and raced down the street where the little sports car was stopped for a traffic light. Narlow said he could see Mr. Spency's face framed in his rearview mirror as the big Reo dropkicked him across the intersection, the rear wheels and axle sprawling everywhere. The sheriff arrested Narlow and put him in a holding tank with one of the town's 'soiled doves,' Miss Sugar Teat Tissy. I made both of their bails. Miss Tissy was most thankful, and later reimbursed me for her bail."

Zara stood. "Whew! Forgive me, but I must get out of this mink coat. I swear I'm getting the vapors, getting hot-blooded in my old age." She turned the coat inside-out, folded it and placed it on an easy chair. "Where was I? Oh, yes. After the horror of Hiroshima and Nagasaki was revealed to the world, Narlow's part in keeping the government's secret was revealed. General Morsely was dead-set on getting the newly established Presidential Medal of Freedom for Narlow, but he refused it, telling the general that he had only one thing he wanted, something that the general could easily arrange—a one hour ride in one of his dive bombers—the Lightning P-38. A twin-engine airplane, crafted by Lockheed.

"General Morseley arranged the flight of the war machine. Word of the flight spread like wildfire, and on Narlow's big day, half of El Paso and Juarez lined the fences of El Paso's airport, waving the red, white, and blue, and an equal number of the red, white, and green. Narlow was dressed in his old beat-up leather flight jacket, his flop-eared leather aviator's cap, and bulging flight goggles. He was a sight!

"The military band was playing, the bright, colorful flags were waving, and the crowd was cheering on one of their favorite heroes. The P-38 pilot took his place in the cockpit, Narlow waved to the crowd, kissed me, then said, 'Have I told you lately how blessed I am? God granted me an immense favor when He gave me your company over these many years. I owe Him.' Rose will recall that he hugged her, scolded her, telling her to take care of me and Shelly Brom. Then he sauntered over to the ladder that led up to the cockpit. When he touched the ladder, he jerked as if a lightening bolt had struck him, stepped back, a stunned look on his face. I asked, 'What is it, Narlow?' He smiled and said, 'Oh, that damned old purple mushroom of mine just buzzed overhead. You didn't hear my bull elk bugling at me? It's nothing my darling wife. You've read about it in my book.'

"He stepped back to the airplane, glanced up toward the sun, then to Rose and me, pointed up at the sky and the large crystal ring around the sun. He grinned, then boarded the P-38.

"The pilot took the P-38 streaking down the runway and seemed to go straight up long before it reached the end of the airstrip. We watched the airplane circling the thunderheads over the Sierra Juarez mountains, then dive-bombing downtown El Paso. I know Narlow had a mile-wide smile as the pilot whirled that beautiful bird through its paces. We watched the airplane disappear into the western sky as they streaked toward Coot's and Narlow's Mount Riley Ranch.

"A cameraman from *World News* was frantically setting up his equipment at the base of the stands. He asked an on-looking friend a question, who turned and pointed me out in the grandstand. He rushed over and explained that he had arrived too late to witness the takeoff and asked if I might persuade the pilot and Narlow to take off again so he could get footage of the event.

"I started to respond, but Rose grasped my arm, shook her head. *It struck me!* I turned back to the man. "*No!* No, I won't ask and I will not allow them to do so even if they agree to do it." The man looked at me as if in the presence of an insane person, and stalked off.

"Please forgive me," I called out after him. How could I find the words to explain? The memory of Narlow and Coot complying with the cub reporter's request to take off and land their aircraft at Wind Mesa, and Coot's death in that fiery crash swept over me. I pulled my scarf close around me, hugged Rose, to relive the chill I felt on that sunny day.

"After what seemed an eternity, we caught a glimpse of the craft coming around the Organ Mountains from the north. The pilot circled high above the airport, seemingly tracing the circle of ice around the crisp sun. Narlow always pointed out that bit of Nature to me, saying it was a warning of evil or foreboding or some such nonsense. Nonsense, by the way, that never failed to show its veracity to him. Suddenly, the pilot swooped the craft straight down at us, and at the last possible moment, he brought the plane around and came in fast for a beautiful landing. The two larger wheels touched down, barely throwing off puffs of gray-white smoke, and as the nose wheel touched the tarmac, the right engine sputtered and died. The plane careened down the runway, jerking this way and that. For an instance the pilot seemed to regain control, then the craft went up on one wheel, flipped over on its back, skidded to a fiery stop, exploding in a tremendous ball of flames. The tragedy of two lifelong friends, Coot and Narlow, both of those dear men, perishing in separate airplane crashes, is beyond my ability to fathom: one, upon takeoff, the other upon landing, both fiery, brutal."

Lela sat, her mouth almost agape. "That's the most incredible story I have ever witnessed. Thank you for sharing your insight with me and my readers. Now, dear lady, perhaps you could tell me about their childhood, possibly their days with the Apache."

Zara smiled. "Oh my, where to begin? Narlow's papa always said that Coot and Narlow were joined at the hip, and if there were ever two boys that were closer to brothers, well, that wonderful man didn't know about it. But oh my, they were such men, such gentle, strong men. I know that Shelly Brom and Rose will recall the time when we all . . . ."

Readers Guide

Narlow Montgomery tells this story from the vantage of 1945 in his eighty-sixth year. Imagine the changes in this world that old gent witnessed. From the horse and buggy, the horseless carriage, man's flight, to the horrors of the atomic age. The ring around the sun phenomenon was visible as a warning from the crest of Sacred Mountain as it was repeatedly throughout the book.

Rodolfo Bustamante asked Narlow and Coot Boldt to help him run guns to Pancho Villa during the Mexican Revolutionary War. He trusted them, knew their character. He needed men he knew to be reliable without a moment's doubt. He knew them to be Henry David Thoreau's men, "striking at the root" of evil. Mr. Thoreau was speaking more of philanthropy than the evils of a vile dictator, but the phrase fits. It is not difficult to distinguish a dictator's boot against the back of your neck from a philanthropist's brag about his giving. Narlow and Coot were no match for Rodolfo's university training in Europe, but Narlow dug his heels in over those months before the revolution picked up steam.

Narlow's papa, Abe Montgomery, just waved his son off with a smile when he asked his advice as to what to do, saying, "Son, I gave up on trying to persuade you to do anything since you refused to attend the new university over in Austin. Before that, I couldn't even get you to wrap a tonsil around a single drop of horehound candy. Why would you think I'd suggest what to do in this instance?"

Q. Most fathers would do anything to keep their son from such a dangerous mission. Was he wise, or just resigned?

Throughout *Ring Around The Sun,* Narlow's mama called him a son-of-a-bitch, replacing a mother's love with her vile contempt, a daily treatment of the cold shoulder.

Q. Why would a learned man like Papa Abe allow anyone to abuse his only son? Why didn't he divorce his wife, or simply leave with their son? It wasn't for lack of money. While only a goat herder, he had pouches of gold stashed at the Brazito cave. Why? If nothing else, why didn't he slap some sense in that copper-lined woman's head?

Narlow fought the idea of sticking his nose in Mexico's mess, a bloody muddle not of his making, but the memory of Rodolfo saving them as sixteen-year-old boys at the peril of his three-year-old daughter nagged him. There was no escape, but he fought it. Big George's story of his father saving the life of a plantation overseer by the name of Zeke after he refused to lay the leather to him; a count of 200 lashes would have killed him. Big George told Coot and Narlow that he wasn't at all certain whether two men "as snow-white as a set of powdered cupcakes" could understand exactly what his father did to repay the debt owed Zeke.

Q. Can any white man fully understand Big George's father's commitment to right?

Narlow and Coot crossed the bridge to Juarez, stepped into the cool of a *cantina* for a shot of *mezcal* and a *befstek*, and as they returned to the dirt street, a legless lad on a board with skate wheels in the gritty dust of Juarez Avenue tugged at Narlow's trousers. His galluses must have been tied to his heartstrings. He bent to drop a dollar in the boy's cup. The boy's death-glaze-black eyes gleamed up, demanded more for Mexico than a coin from Papa Abe's son. Coot said later that it was that legless boy, a youngster who never new childhood that pushed Narlow into running guns.

Q. How could a one-minute encounter tug so violently at a man's heartstrings, forcing him into the dangerous business of gunrunning?

Q. What tugs of conscience can drag two fifty-one-year-old men into a dangerous enterprise like running guns in a foreign country when the likely outcome is a firing squad against an adobe wall, or forty-years in Leavenworth with no possibility of parole? Was it the money after all?

Narlow's and Coot's years with the Apache at the Arizona Territory Indian Reservation tugged at him; the medicineman, Na-Tu-Che-Puy advice about not dwelling on Narlow's mama and her evil ways. She'd made him guilty, guilt that was not his.

Q. How does a man walk away from his own mother, a woman who called him a son-of-a-bitch every day of his life?

Over those months before the first shot in Mexico's revolution, the death-glaze eyes of the boy on a skate wheel board nagged at Narlow.

318

Q. In spite of all Rodolfo, Coot, and Big George could do or say, would Narlow have ever gotten mixed up with that insanity?

Finally, the hopeless gaze of the boy on the board turned the trick in favor of Rodolfo Bustamante. Narlow's conscience could bear it no longer.

Narlow and Coot found a source of Mausers and ammunition in Socorro, New Mexico. They didn't like the owner of the establishment, a weasel of a man, Fritz Hans Smidt, by name. Didn't trust him. Didn't trust his German heritage during a time of that country's continuing effort to embroil the US in Mexico's problems, and out of The Fatherland's plans for Europe. Coot tried to find other munitions sources, but US embargo of guns to Mexico dried up all other avenues.

The pair began experiencing repeated threats on their lives.

Q. Why did it not dawn on them at the outset that Fritz was behind their troubles? Fritz was a "pudg" of a man, a habit of pressing his trousers with his white-gloved hands. But is that enough for them to overlook that important possibility?

Q. Did Rodolfo's promise of a million dollars cloud their vision, blinding them to that possibility? Was Fritz the only one of the three who would kill for money?

Some historians now claim that Mexicans were no better off after Madero and Villa ridded the country of Porfirio Diaz.

Q. Do you concur?

Coot chastised Narlow for shooting the four Mexicans in the foot when they attempted to ambush them as they crossed the Rio Grande at San Pablo. After he thought on it for a minute, Coot agreed that Narlow had done *exactly* what had should have been done.

Q. Can you think of a better method of handling their problem, considering their isolation at the time?

Rose flew 5,000, 45-70 cartridges aboard the Curtiss Pusher into the village of Carichic.

Q. Was there even a remote possibility that she would be successful pulling off that scheme, or was she so headstrong that it did not matter to her, thinking only that she could do a man's job?

Q. When did Coot first become smitten with the ex-nun? Did her story of her youth add to his growing adoration?

Narlow and Coot were well-to-do men, and Rodolfo was a millionaire many times over.

Q. Why didn't they just hire trained mercenaries to strike at the heart of Chihuahua and whisk Rose away from the *Federales* and harm's way? Is it plausible for them to leave the Curtis biwing at the *Circulo de Rocas* without making an effort to retrieve it?

While captives of the *Federal Comandante Horacio Bienvenides* and *Capitan Ambrosio Manzano de Flores*, Chico's uncle, Jeronimo Chavez, becomes distraught over the killing of his nephew. He approaches the *capitan* and shoots him, but only wounding him. The *capitan* makes great sport of brutalizing Jeromino until finally Narlow is forced to grab the heavy rifle from the tormentor's hands and kills Jeromino.

Q. Can you think of other ways Narlow and Coot could have handled that situation other than standing by witnessing such carnage? What made Narlow relatively certain that *Comandante* Bienvenides would not allow the *capitan's* retribution for spoiling his fun?

Gregorio Gonzalez and Father Estevan were minor players in the story, yet key to the solution and outcome to both ridding Carichic of their unwanted guests and getting Narlow and Coot safely out of Mexico. Both men had led lives that had been astray of the right path, yet strong-willed, honest, committed to the *pobres* of their country.

Q. Have you known men such as these? Would our country be better served by men and women of their ilk? If they knocked on your kitchen door this evening, dirty, disheveled, would you invite them in for a bath, a cognac, a sit-down supper? Why not? The Good Book tells us that angels appear to us if we would just look.

After Narlow and Coot are safely on the Texas side of the border, they head for Rodolfo's *hacienda*. After loading gold in the Reo for more munitions, they leave for El Paso to head-off Rose's and JJ Umbenhauer's rescue attempt. Shelly Brom was with Rodolfo for her own safety, playing with a little girl in the dust, refused to go with them to El Paso, ran and hid from them.

Q. Is it plausible that they ignored her warning when she pointed down the dark, muddy road, muffling the indecipherable, motioning for them not to go, then running off into the dark? In their rush to keep their friends from flying back to Carichic, was there anything else Narlow and Coot could have done?

Zara heard repeated rumors of the danger her husband faced while running guns, couldn't understand why he just didn't, or wouldn't, quit, or why he felt obligated to both Coot and Rodolfo. Neither could she understand the men's commitment to one another, their love, respect and dedication they held for each other, nor why they would lay their lives down in defense of the other. The stark differences between men and women intrigued her as she could not think of a living soul she would die for other than her husband, their son, Will, and perhaps her parents and Papa Abe. She wrote it off as just the chivalrous nature of men, or maybe it had something to do with a woman's first priority to see to the safety and nurturing of her offspring.

Q. If you disagree with Zara, list and explain your thoughts.

Narlow came up with the diabolical notion of post-holing Fritz Hans Smidt. Leaving him in the lonesome desert for days at a time was a cruel thing to do.

Q. Can you think of an alternative to get the truth out of him? If you were standing in that upright grave with Fritz, would you have broken down immediately, or never? Remember, if he had broken down at the outset, Coot would surely have killed him. Would you have Fritz's strange brand of courage and refuse Narlow's pleading almost to the very end?

Narlow accepted Fritz's confession, but was unable to get him to say who was in on this with him, swore there was no one else involved in keeping the Germans informed of their every move. Fritz knew some of their travels, but not all of them.

Q. Who could have been feeding the German operatives information that kept them in constant peril?

Gregorio shows up in Juarez with the demand from *Generalissimo* Hugo Garcia de Gomez, head of all of Mexico's glorious *Rural* forces that Narlow, Coot, and Gregorio return to *Circulo de Rocas* to retrieve Narlow's son, Will. All three of them do as demanded though they know in their guts that the *generalissimo* would kill Will whether they go or not.

Q. What makes a man go to such extremes for the sake of another? Will is Narlow's son, not that of either Coot or Gregorio. Why would they comply with a demand that will surely lead to their deaths? Do women generally make such outlandish decisions? Are they wired the same as men in that regard? Compare your answer to Zara's thoughts on the matter. Men take extreme measures in war at the flip of a coin, but do women? If you believe they do, can you provide examples of such action?

CPSIA information can be obtained at www.ICGtesting.com
Printed in the USA
LVOW08s0639220813

349029LV00004B/17/P